P9-DND-539

"My Colonial Minx," Kells Murmured, and Bent to Plant a Kiss . . .

upon his love. Carolina stretched luxuriously, deliberately tempting him. "Go to sleep," he laughed, rumpling her hair. And more softly, "And dream of me."

Carolina drifted into slumber, knowing that he loved her. He had proved that with the delicacy and ardor of his lovemaking. She nestled down into the bed, a woman secure.

Her dreams were lovely ones—but she awakened to the scraping of boots and the light clank of a scabbard that surged against the door as it was opened.

She sat up, startled. The door was open a bit and a man's tall figure was discernible against the dimness of the hall.

"Is that you?" she said, confused.

"Yes," came Kells's voice. "I am sorry I woke you."

"But—why rise so early?"

"I sail with the tide at dawn," he said. . . .

WINDSONG

by *New York Times* Bestselling Author

VALERIE SHERWOOD

"ONE OF THE TOP FIVE MOST WIDELY READ
AUTHORS IN THE UNITED STATES TODAY."
—*Winston Salem Sentinel*

Books by Valerie Sherwood

Lovesong
Windsong

Available from POCKET BOOKS

Coming Soon

Nightsong (September 1986)

Most Pocket Books are available at special quantity discounts for bulk purchases for sales promotions, premiums or fund raising. Special books or book excerpts can also be created to fit specific needs.

For details write the office of the Vice President of Special Markets, Pocket Books, 1230 Avenue of the Americas, New York, New York 10020.

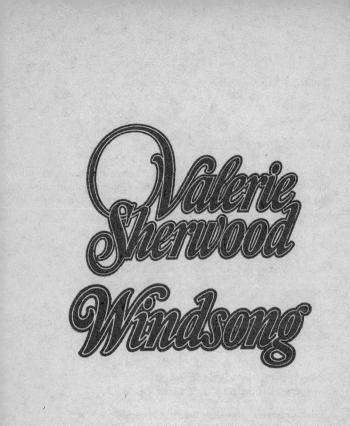

Valerie Sherwood

Windsong

PUBLISHED BY POCKET BOOKS NEW YORK

This novel is a work of fiction. Names, characters, places and incidents are either the product of the author's imagination or are used fictitiously. Any resemblance to actual events or locales or persons, living or dead, is entirely coincidental.

Another *Original* publication of POCKET BOOKS

POCKET BOOKS, a division of Simon & Schuster, Inc.
1230 Avenue of the Americas, New York, N.Y. 10020

Copyright © 1986 by Valerie Sherwood
Cover artwork copyright © 1986 Elaine Duillo

All rights reserved, including the right to reproduce
this book or portions thereof in any form whatsoever.
For information address Pocket Books, 1230 Avenue
of the Americas, New York, N.Y. 10020

ISBN: 0-671-49838-X

First Pocket Books printing March, 1986

10 9 8 7 6 5 4 3 2 1

POCKET and colophon are registered trademarks
of Simon & Schuster, Inc.

Printed in the U.S.A.

WARNING

Readers are hereby warned not to use any of the cosmetics, unusual foods, medications (particularly such items as "High Spirited Pills"!) referred to herein without first consulting and securing the approval of a medical doctor. These items are included only to enhance the authentic seventeenth-century atmosphere and are in no way recommended for use by anyone.

DEDICATION

To the never to be forgotten memory of beautiful Princess, my very first cat, who strolled into my life on soft white paws in those faraway childhood days when I lived in the fabled South Branch Valley; Princess, whose soft gray and white fur and dainty ways suited so admirably her Colonial setting among the great homes that lined that lovely river; Princess, who slept like a soft and fluffy furpiece around my neck on cold winter nights and played with me in the boxwoods and irises and lilies so dear to my mother's heart; Princess, who bore four lovely kittens and taught me so much about joy and tenderness—to Princess, the first cat ever to win my heart, this book is affectionately dedicated.

AUTHOR'S NOTE

In this turbulent tale of love and treachery, of passion and heartfelt revenge set in the stirring 1600's, I have brought forward the adventurous love story of aristocratic Carolina Lightfoot of Virginia's Eastern Shore, who became the celebrated Silver Wench of the Caribbean, and her dangerous buccaneer lover, Captain Kells. Their path was indeed thorny but I believe it to be not uncharacteristic of the exuberant times in which they lived, when notable impersonations sometimes took place (and men were hanged for far less than the incident involving Aunt Pet which took place off the Virginia coast).

Although all the characters and events depicted herein are entirely of my own imagination, the surroundings and many traditions are often quite real:

The "river pirates" of the Thames were certainly real enough and "Swan Upping," presided over by the royal Keeper of the Swans, is a pleasant custom that has existed on the river for centuries.

The "no questions asked" marriage ceremonies held without crying of the banns in certain "privileg'd Churches" did indeed take place—in fact, during the time of my story the register of one of these churches— St. James's, Duke's Place—revealed that some *fifteen hundred* such marriages a year took place!

And indeed London's "Fleet Street brides" were in

Carolina's day a problem—even though the marriage registers of these illegal weddings were often produced as court evidence in bigamy cases.

I have always striven for authenticity in my novels and gone to great lengths to achieve it. This has been a source of great delight to me, for both my husband and I are born-and-bred genealogy buffs; we used to vacation round the country in county courthouses, researching our various family lines, reading the original documents, some of them—especially in Virginia's "lower counties"—in quaint old English handwriting. We ran all our family lines on all sides for both of us and made the happy discovery that every single line had been in this country well before the American Revolution—some in the earliest 1600's. Long a member of the Daughters of the American Revolution (when in residence at Dragon's Lair, for some thirty years our Washington residence, we frequently did our research at the D.A.R. Library in Constitution Hall) and of the Daughters of the American Colonists, it was a great treat for me to once again research the Tidewater and the Eastern Shore for this novel.

Since one of the most entertaining ancestresses on my husband's side of the family was an accused witch (she was charged with having "flown" through a window), I took delight in basing the charge of witchcraft in my novel on the famous case of Grace Sherwood, perhaps the best known "witch" of the southern Colonies, although her witchcraft trial came several years later. She lived in Princess Anne County, Virginia, was the wife of James Sherwood and brought suit against those who claimed she was a witch, had bewitched their cotton, had arrived in the night and departed through the keyhole or a crack of the door as a black cat, etc.—poor Grace, she has my complete sympathy! A reading of her case suggests to me that Grace Sherwood was a wealthy woman and the complaints brought against her were for considerable sums of money, i.e., 100 pounds sterling, a very large sum in those days. She had the misfortune to have as the forewoman of her jury in 1705–06 the same Elizabeth Barnes whom she herself had sued for slanderously claiming Grace had bewitched their cotton and from whom she had sought 100 pounds sterling in reparations. She was ordered into the ordeal by water ("ducking"). Though bound, Grace swam determinedly, to everyone's horror, proving *ipso facto* that she was indeed a witch, but somehow the charges against her seemed to peter out, thereby proving that the people of early Virginia had some sense at least, for Grace died in 1733, apparently unincarcerated!

Most of the houses included in my novel actually exist today—or did exist; many early Colonial houses were destroyed by fire or other disasters. All are authentic as to type. Level Green, the home of my heroine's family on the York, is of course storied Rosewell, and nearby Shelly, which I mention in the book, is the home of the Pages. Although of slightly later vintage, I could not resist including Shelly because the Pages of Shelly gave birth to the noted author Thomas Nelson Page, whose "The Burial of the Guns" I consider one of the finest short stories of all time—and I was delighted some years ago to find one of my own short stories included in a handsome anthology right next to one by Thomas Nelson Page! I felt I was in good company!

As to historic Fairfield, family seat of the Burwell family, the mansion burned long ago and I have been unable to obtain a description of the actual interior, save for the arches of the basement and the fact that one wing contained the ballroom. I have therefore decorated Fairfield and its mirrored ballroom in a manner suitable to the times.

I should like to add that wherever possible, the furnishings described—even the chamber pots!—are completely authentic, and many of the pieces can be found in Williamsburg and Yorktown today.

While I am on the subject of chamber pots, let me regale the reader with a few simple facts. Chamber pots are among the most common items to be found in Colonial America's archaeological sites; from apple-green glazed to tortoise-shell leadglaze—our ancestors were well supplied. But the potters and pewterers are said to have copied the designs of the silversmiths, who set the style in chamber pots—and Aunt Pet, in my story, could rightly consider the heavy silver chamber pot that traveled with her a mark of distinction.

I must add that although reliable sources indicate that Yorktown was not actually founded as a "town" until 1691, of course many homes in the area existed prior to that date, so for clarity I have referred to "Yorktown" throughout. Similarly, it was hard to actually "date" the Raleigh and its Apollo Room, but I thought that for Letitia's legendary vanquishing of her rival, Amanda Bramway, readers would enjoy a background of "dinner at the Raleigh."

Because I have found my readers, from the many letters they write me, to be both well read and knowledgeable—indeed in every way a cut above the pack—I have, for their sakes, sought to be meticulously authentic even in small details.

For example, on sword-canes (and I was especially interested in sword-canes because my father owned one and thrilled me with it in my childhood) the interesting sword-cane used by Sandy Randolph in my story is based on one presently in the Wallace Collection in London—that sword-cane too contains a small wheel-lock pistol but its head is cast bronze rather than silver, its shaft of ebony, mahogany and ivory. This seemed rather a lot for my heroine to observe from the head of the stairs, so I simply categorized it as "bronze-headed ebony," while Rye's more standard sword-cane is "silver-headed Malacca," Malacca being the material of which most of the finest sword-canes of the time were made.

For the geographically minded, I would point out that Salamanca, while presently the capital of the province of Salamanca in western Spain, was at the time of my story a city in the ancient province of Leon, Salamanca not having been established as a province until 1833.

I would note also that the sea rovers of the Caribbean, when ready to attack, customarily ran up the personal flag of their captain. These were of many types, some red, some black, some with skull and crossbones, etc. For a man to fly a woman's petticoat as a battle flag would be perfectly consistent with the times—thus the "Petticoat Buccaneer" of my story.

And let me carry you along with me as:

I sing of loves forgotten, of dreams that did not last.
Of hopes that went a winging,
Of lovers' voices ringing,
Oh, join me now in singing—a lovesong to the past!

Valerie Sherwood

CONTENTS

CONTENTS

Early Winter 1689

Lover, come close, lie down by my side,
Though I may never be your legal bride. . . .
Words spoken over us, can they mean more
Than what we have now on love's golden shore?

I

The Wedding Night

Moonlight whitened the beach and silvered the palms that rustled through Tortuga in the soft Caribbean night. A shimmer of stars, brilliant against the black velvet night, cast their cold light on the gray forbidding walls of the Mountain Fort that guarded the entrance of this mighty buccaneer stronghold. But the sleepy red and green parrots perched among the fronds were to know no sleep this night, for the sounds of a raucous buccaneer wedding still rang along the island's waterfront and echoed across Cayona Bay.

The revelry, the dancing, the drinking, had been

1

going on all day on the Island of Tortuga, and had not slackened even during the ceremony when shouted good wishes from shore had nearly drowned out the vows being taken by the handsome young couple on the *Sea Wolf*'s deck. Now, well past midnight, the buccaneers and their bawds on shore were still drinking deep to Captain Kells, their departing leader, and to his beautiful bride, Christabel Willing, the glorious Silver Wench over whom half Tortuga had fought a bloody battle. From the quay, from the beach, they waved tankards and cutlasses in a last salute to the lean gray *Sea Wolf* as she spread her canvas and fled down the moonpath, and their clamorous farewell echoed as her great sails billowed and she drove across the silver blackness of the bay, seeking the open ocean.

On her clean swabbed decks there was laughter too, and drinking, and singing rising above the wail of the stringed instruments of a knot of lounging buccaneers. Amid it all the father of the bride, an aristocratic Virginian named Lysander Randolph—but whom the world called "Sandy"—leaned his green satin-clad arms upon the taffrail and stared moodily at the departing winking lights of the Mountain Fort that guarded this great stronghold of the Brethren of the Coast—and remembered his own buccaneering past with Morgan, nearly forgotten now.

He remembered other things as well, things that seared his memory. A vision of the bride's mother, a blazing beauty with whom he had shared a Christmastide of passion, rose up before him, then faded. His beloved Letty . . . But he had not taken her home to Tower Oaks, his plantation on the broad banks of the James. For Letty was another man's wife and she had gone her way. So long ago . . . and yet tonight the scars were fresh again and the pain cut deep.

There was an ache in Sandy Randolph's throat as he thought how "Christabel"—the wondrous daughter he could never claim back in Virginia—had glittered tonight in her ice-blue satin gown, its wide drifting skirts all set with brilliants. Her coloring was the mirror image of his own, for her eyes were a flashing silver and her ice-blonde hair a moonlit halo. It had been a surprising wrench to "give her away" on the deck of this rakish buccaneer vessel! It had come to him, as he watched her standing straight and proud and confident, taking her vows beside her tall dark-haired buccaneer, that it should all have been different, so different. . . . That she should have trailed decorously down the wide curving stairway of Tower Oaks, with all the Tidewater gentry admiring her descent. That Letty's dark blue eyes should have brimmed with tears as he, Lysander Randolph, gave the bride away. That the bridegroom should have been some easygoing Virginia planter, set to live a life of ease with saddle horses and whisky, instead of this dangerous buccaneer Kells, off to seek a chancy pardon. Faced with the imminent likelihood of war, England's king had offered a general amnesty to the buccaneers, but a king's word was the wind's word and easily blown away, and Sandy knew too that there were uneasy rumors about the recent activities of Captain Kells, such rumors as could bring a man down. . . .

Leaning upon the taffrail, still cold sober after enough wine to sprawl an average man full length across the deck, Sandy Randolph thought his bitter thoughts and envisioned a world that might have been—and was not.

But in the moonlit great cabin of the *Sea Wolf,* the din ashore and afloat were both forgotten as a tall man and a slender woman faced each other, smiling.

3

The radiance of the bride's countenance softened the hard gray eyes that looked down upon her so penetratingly. This was not the grim and purposeful visage that, on so many slippery decks, men had viewed down the shining length of a cutlass. His lean sun-darkened face had lost its saturnine cast, and it was a boyish smile the buccaneer bridegroom flashed upon his lady.

"Christabel," he murmured—and her name was a sigh upon his lips.

"Kells," she whispered on the wisp of a breath, and swayed toward him in her billowing satin skirts. She arched her neck, throwing back her lovely head, lifting her lips for his kiss. Her gesture had a delicate feminine grace not lost upon the captain, and her unusual silver eyes, shadowed by that fringe of dark lashes so at odds with the frosty blonde sheen of her hair, were luminous with love of him.

The tall buccaneer caught his entrancing lady in his arms and she rested against his broad chest, feeling his quickening heartbeat race against her own.

"'Tis not legal, you know," he murmured against the lemon-scented cloud of her hair.

Christabel nuzzled against him. She savored deliciously the slight tangy scent of his fine white cambric shirt against her cheek, aromatic with the faint but identifiable scent of leather and sea spray and fine Virginia tobacco. "What isn't legal?" she murmured.

"This marriage of ours. It has no force of law." His lips moved lightly across the moonlit shimmer of her hair, found her ear, the white column of her neck, moved downward to the pulsing hollow of her throat.

The tingling thrill of his touch went through her, made her knees feel weak.

"I care not," she said. "And anyway, we can remedy that when we reach Virginia."

And at that moment she did not care. At that moment neither gods nor devils could have kept them apart—nor any laws made by man. All the clouds of their stormy past were swept away, vanished. Their future seemed to them as clear and as pure as the moonlight pouring through the slanted bank of stern windows that bathed them both in pale gold.

He chuckled. "I had thought you *would* care," he murmured.

"Then you were wrong, Kells. I care only for you." *And to be the one woman, the only woman in your life.* It was not spoken, but it was understood, this pact between them.

"And that you shall ever be, Christabel," he said in a deep-timbred voice. "Forever."

Together, ignoring the table piled with food by a buccaneer cook who had sought to keep the bride-groom's strength up, they swayed toward the bunk.

Christabel could feel the ripple of Kells's muscles as his hard body responded to her womanly softness. She could feel the sudden urgency in his kisses—and felt that same urgency communicated to herself. And then —as if to some unspoken command—they were tearing off their clothes with eager fingers. Too eager—a hook gave here, a seam was rent there. No match for this impetuous assault, the elegant ice-blue satin bodice was slipping down from Christabel's white shoulders; the wide drifting skirts, all set with sparkling brilliants that caught the moonlight cold as ice crystals, were sliding over her smooth, curving hips and down her trembling limbs. There was naught but her sheer white lacy chemise between her and the lean hard body of this man who had married her such a short time before— married her under a name not his own—there on the *Sea Wolf*'s swaying deck.

For the arms that held her so triumphantly were indeed the strong arms of the celebrated Captain Kells, the Irish buccaneer who, it was admiringly said, could hold all Tortuga at bay—but Kells was not his name and neither was he Irish. He was in reality Rye Evistock, gentleman of Essex, and his daunting gray eyes were smiling down at the wench he had just married as "Christabel Willing." But that was not her real name either, this "Silver Wench" the buccaneers held in such esteem. The girl, whose shining ice-blonde tresses were just now loosened by trembling fingers to spill down over her bare shoulders, whose lacy chemise slipped lower, lower, hesitating at the outthrusting pink tips of her breasts and then falling suddenly away to cascade down her pale naked body to the floor, was in reality Carolina Lightfoot of Yorktown—and every billow of those great sails that flew above them and cast their shadows across the *Sea Wolf*'s moon-washed deck was carrying her closer to home.

Tomorrow she would wonder what her mother would say when she appeared at the front door of Level Green—Carolina the runaway, coming home at last with a lover. For she and Kells and Sandy had agreed among them that once they reached the Tidewater, this "buccaneer wedding" performed on the *Sea Wolf*'s deck would be their own secret, and that under their real names of Rye Evistock and Carolina Lightfoot they would be wed again—and more decorously—in the new Bruton Parish Church. Unless, of course, Letitia Lightfoot preferred to see her daughter trail down the wide stairway at Level Green, a blushing bride.

But that was tomorrow. . . .

For tonight Carolina's unhappy childhood in Fielding Lightfoot's house on the Eastern Shore was all forgot; her beautiful rebellious mother, Letitia Lightfoot, was forgot; and her mother's cousin Sandy Randolph, whom she'd learnt just before she ran away was her real father—though they both knew he could never claim her save in some godforsaken spot like Tortuga—was forgot as well.

Tonight, in this magical unreal world, even her real identity as Carolina Lightfoot was forgot. Tonight she was Christabel Willing and he was Kells and there was no world out there waiting for them—there was only the moonlight and love's bright passion driving them on.

On the wings of that magic she felt herself lifted to the bunk, deposited there, feather-light, to lie with parted lips, her breasts rising and falling as her anticipation mounted. Through the dark fringe of her lashes she watched as Kells undressed with astonishing speed. She flung back an arm that somehow had become entangled in her long hair and with the gesture tossed that fair skein shawllike across the pillow. She stretched and breathed a deep luxurious sigh.

Kells's clothes, she noted dreamily, seemed to be disappearing from his sinewy body almost as if a strong wind was blowing them away. She had earlier heard the clang of his basket-hilted sword as it struck the floor, and then his boots, thump, thump, flung away from him. His trousers came down with a single sweeping gesture—and his fine cambric shirt would never be the same for she heard it rip as it went. And then, aware of his tall muscular frame looking more formidable than ever in dark silhouette against the moonlight, she felt the smooth heavy satin of his throbbing flesh as he lowered his big body down upon hers, felt the light probing pressure of his knee between her willing thighs.

She yielded meltingly, remembering when she had fought him. . . .

But that wild time when she had defied him was over. Forever. She would always be his woman, she knew that now. All the misunderstandings, all the torment, lay behind them. Ahead stretched the future—blindingly sweet.

His lips were on her own, questing, moving. His body was claiming hers with that sure touch that was ever his. Every moment had a tingling urgency, every whisper, every touch a deeper meaning.

"Kells," she whispered vibrantly, and then on a drifting sigh as their bodies joined, "Kells . . ." that name she had come to love.

And lost in the demands of the moment, the lean buccaneer did not remind his lustrous lady that when they reached Yorktown she would have to start calling him Rye again. For he must be careful not to court arrest before he could claim the king's pardon that was being extended to all buccaneers now that war was looming and England would soon need privateers for the king's service. And anyway, the name "Rye Evistock" would be more palatable to the aristocratic Colonial planters he would face in Yorktown than "Captain Kells"—a buccaneer name with all the glamour and menace of the Spanish Main about it. For he was all too aware that it might be hard for this plantation aristocracy to accept even a pardoned buccaneer into their charmed circle—and pardoned buccaneer he soon would be. Her family would be taken into their confidence, of course, but to spare Carolina and her mother, to the rest of the world he would be Rye Evistock and she Carolina Lightfoot once again.

But here on the *Sea Wolf* they were still Kells and Christabel—for that was the name she had used on Tortuga, where the buccaneers had christened her the

"Silver Wench" for her hair like spun white metal and her luminous silver eyes.

But in these ecstatic moments of silken joining, both Tortuga and Virginia's shores were but a distant shimmer, eons away. For now they were like other lovers, lost in a dream of love. . . .

Entranced by love are they tonight,
The stars have never seemed so bright,
The moon has ne'er had such a glow—
Ah, that it could be ever so!

II

The Honeymoon Voyage

Their voyage to Virginia seemed a charmed one. No storms beset them in this blue water world of wind and wave. The weather continued fair with a stiff breeze blowing. Onward toward the mainland sped the long gray ship—sometimes with an escort of playful dolphins cavorting off her bow—leaving behind her a creamy wake. Her white sails billowed full against a clear ultramarine sky where cormorants and gulls soared and dipped against the sun. In this enchanted world, flying fish leaped from the water to bank and glide over the waves, and by night the air was cool and a silver phosphorescent sea lapped against the *Sea Wolf*'s wooden hull.

Carolina wished it would last forever.

The mood on board was boisterously cheerful, for the men who had elected to come with them were still jubilant at the thought of returning to home and hearth with gold jingling in their pockets—and with full pardon for their buccaneering. The talk was of farms in Surrey and in Hampshire, of cottages in Kent and Essex, of planting, of country frolics—and of the wenches they'd left behind.

Sandy Randolph was his customary urbane self, brooding often by the rail, drinking too much, but gallantly toasting Carolina's eyebrows in captured Madeira or Canary. And Kells had turned away from the dark side of his life. He was boyishly happy, full of plans for their future in Essex—and he reveled in her company.

Only once during that delightful journey did Kells's mood of buoyancy change. That was on a day when they sighted two fat merchant ships ploughing through the water; as the ships drew near both promptly piled on more canvas than was safe and fought mightily to pull away from Kells's ship.

"That's strange," Kells muttered. From the *Sea Wolf*'s taffrail, he was regarding their antics through a glass. "They fly the English flag and so do I. Why this haste to be gone?"

Carolina, wearing a gown of linen pale as sea foam, had been standing beside him watching a blue-green dolphin pace the ship. She answered him absently, "Perhaps they've heard of the *Sea Wolf*."

"But that's even less reason to avoid us." The man

beside her frowned. "'Tis well known I've never attacked any ship that did not fly the flag of Spain." His lips tightened. "I've a notion to catch up with them and ask them why!"

And that would mean having their captains on board for supper and endless talk of navigation and weather and the state of things in various ports.

Carolina sighed. She was already weary of ship's talk, for she got too much of it when they dined with Kells's officers. Even Sandy seemed full of ship's lore for all that he was by trade a planter. "Come away," she said restlessly. "What do you care why they ran? Perhaps they're timid men and fear all buccaneers!"

Kells shrugged and lowered his glass. "I'm marveling that they would risk capsizing to avoid me."

But her warm little hand in his was pulling him away from the rail. Toward their cabin. Toward their wide bunk that promised such delights.

The lean buccaneer caught her thought and his gray eyes kindled. He went with her very willingly.

The soft scented winds of the Caribbean were gone now and cold sharp winds with the promise of snow had taken their place, for it was winter and the rakish prow of the *Sea Wolf* was driving through leaden greenish seas off the Virginia coast. From the slanting deck of the lean gray ship Carolina felt a hint of snow on the sea wind—and imagined what it would be like on shore.

There would be snow in Williamsburg now and perhaps her family would be there, visiting at Aunt Pet's checkerboard-brick, green-shuttered house on Duke of Gloucester Street. A bright fire would be burning on the hearth and a world of glistening white would be beckoning through the frosty windowpanes.

From the kitchen would come the tangy scent of frying bacon and the little hot cakes of which Aunt Pet was so fond. Aunt Pet loved to breakfast late and she would be trying to keep them all at table, but Carolina's slim beautiful mother, Letitia Lightfoot, restless as always, would be tapping her foot, eager to be up and away. Her dark blue eyes would meet her husband's across the table as he finished his morning coffee. Tall dark Fielding would be staring back at her—vengefully perhaps, if she had danced once too often with another man at some ball or other, for Fielding had never been able to control his jealousy of his enchanting Letty.

Indeed, they might well be quarreling—they so often did. In which case Aunt Pet would be making helpless little fluttering gestures of alarm and inserting quick placating little remarks designed to keep the peace. If they were *really* quarreling, this handsome couple, sitting there garbed in the latest fashions, then the two younger children, Della and Flo, would be summarily dismissed from the table, and Carolina's older sister Virginia would have her head down, her attention fixed with almost painful concentration on her plate, as she tried to stay out of it—for the stylish combatants were apt to lash out at anyone nearby when they were at their worst, and if Virginia chanced to say the wrong thing she might find herself denied a seat in the family carriage to the next party!

Carolina sighed, remembering. Life on the Eastern Shore when she had been growing up had been hectic at best, and at its worst awash with tears, but as she approached that familiar shore, she realized that, strangely enough, she had missed it. Missed the familiar brick and frame houses of Williamsburg and Yorktown with their little gardens, their fruit trees, their neatly clipped boxwood. Missed the warm hospitality of the Virginia planters. Missed all that she had ever known of home.

Now she tried to tuck a stray lock of fair hair back beneath the hood of her scarlet velvet cloak. Grateful for the green wool that lined the cloak, she pulled the garment a little closer about her, for the wind had an icy bite to it. She had had time to think during those long days when the sparkling aquamarine waters of the islands had turned to this duller winter-green off the mainland, and although she had at first intended to take her family into her confidence, it had come to her that she could not go home quite as she had planned. She could not just stroll up to the doors of Level Green with her buccaneer beside her and announce that this was the famous Captain Kells, who planned to marry her under his real name of Rye Evistock.

For she had abruptly remembered what in her excitement at going home again she had forgotten: Fielding hated the buccaneers. *"Damned pirates,"* he called them. Carolina had never before understood the reason for his hatred. But now, having learned from her real father, Sandy Randolph, that he had once been a buccaneer, indeed had sailed with Morgan on the sack of Panama, she felt she had discovered the reason. There had always been wild rumors about Sandy—rumors she had discounted, for her mother had sniffed disdainfully whenever they were mentioned. One of those rumors was that Sandy Randolph had been in his youth a buccaneer. Plainly Fielding believed it—thus his openly expressed hatred of all buccaneers.

No, she could not walk blandly through the front door of Level Green and tell them she was about to marry the fabled Captain Kells, whose name echoed throughout the Caribbean. Worse, that she had already married him in a buccaneer ceremony! Fielding might deny him the house!

And *that* would certainly not make her mother happy!

She decided she must speak to Sandy about this.

She found him standing by the taffrail. He was wearing a maroon woolen cloak against the weather, but he was not wearing his hat. The wind whipped back his hair, which seemed to glow on this gray day like white metal—so like her own. Held to his eyes was a glass, and he was studying a passing ship with such intensity that he did not at first hear her greeting.

"What are you watching?" she asked as he turned to her.

"The action of that ship," he said, frowning. "I know her. She is the *Tandy Cole* out of Philadelphia and she came close enough to see that we fly the English flag—I know because I could see her captain studying us with his glass from the deck. But when she came close enough to read our name she sheared off and as you can see, she has piled on near enough canvas to capsize. And it is not the first time that has happened on this voyage."

"But the *Tandy Cole* has no reason to fear the *Sea Wolf!*" Carolina exclaimed indignantly.

"Aye, one would think not," he murmured.

"Kells has never attacked an English ship!" That was a matter of pride with her. Her buccaneer's personal war was with Spain and he knew his enemy.

Sandy's ice-gray eyes were thoughtful as he turned to her. "So Kells *says.*" It was a blunt statement, clear in its inference. And for the first time since the journey began Sandy had called his half-legal son-in-law "Kells"—not "Rye," as had been his wont. Instantly Carolina caught his meaning.

"And I believe him!" she cried defensively.

Sandy shrugged. "There are rumors, Carolina," he murmured.

"What rumors?"

He shrugged again. "Idle talk that the *Sea Wolf* of late has gobbled up other shipping than that of Spain."

"Ridiculous!" she scoffed. "Rye hardly left harbor in Tortuga after he brought me there."

"I don't doubt it." Sandy's pale gray gaze passed appreciatively over his beautiful daughter. "Still . . ."

She brushed aside his doubts. "I came to ask if you think it wise to keep *everyone* from knowing that Rye is also Kells the buccaneer? Even"—she sounded troubled—"even those at Level Green."

"Very wise," agreed Sandy in such a cynical tone that Carolina glared at him, planting both feet on the deck.

"Gossip is always rife about men such as Kells," she said sharply. "Why, in Yorktown and Williamsburg there are rumors about *you!*"

He laughed. "And some of those rumors are undoubtedly true! But you are right, of course, there's probably nothing in it."

"I'll settle it—I'll go ask him!" The words came out in a flash.

"I wouldn't do that," Sandy said thoughtfully. "A man prefers his bride to believe him. In all things."

"What I was hoping," she admitted tentatively, "is that the suggestion would come from you. I mean, I would not want Rye to think that I did not trust my family. . . ."

He gave her a shrewd look. *Because you don't,* that look said.

"Well," sighed Carolina, "you know how Fielding raves against buccaneers. . . ."

Sandy Randolph turned away suddenly. His gaze was speculative, and for a moment it trailed the English ship, careening away from them in terror under a mountain of canvas. "I think it will be snowing along the James," he said abruptly, veering from the subject.

Carolina pulled her scarlet cloak about her tighter. "Then you will suggest it to Rye?" she asked in a small voice, staring in sudden confusion down at the deck.

"Of course."

She looked up at him and smiled. Sandy was her real father—as anyone looking at them now could plainly see, for she shared not only his coloring but his aristocratic features, although hers were softened in a feminine way. "I shall tell Mother that you came for me," she said softly.

He gave her an uneasy look, a look that spoke volumes. He loved her mother so much—but he had been married when he had fallen in love with Letitia and his wife was mad; he could never divorce her. He had let Letitia go to Fielding Lightfoot's arms, hoping she would find happiness there. But then—all too briefly—the winds of fate had driven her back to him. And Carolina had been the result. The scandal had been hushed up, of course. As far as the world went, Carolina was Fielding Lightfoot's third daughter by the glamorous Letitia, but at home relations between Fielding and the child who was not his own had always been strained. It had been a long time before Carolina had learned the truth, and it was a truth that even now she must cloak. For her mother's sake. For all their sakes.

"Explain to Letty when you get home that I thought it best not to accompany you to Level Green," he said in a somber voice.

Carolina nodded soberly. His futile love for her

17

mother was a personal tragedy and she would not add to it. "I will tell her—in private. I expect she will be at Aunt Pet's and not at Level Green for she hates being out in the country this time of year."

He laughed. "Perhaps the magnificence of the new house Fielding has built at Level Green has seduced her into staying home!"

"I doubt it." Carolina regarded her real father whimsically. "You know how much Mother loves parties. She would rather be in town when the snow flies!"

Father and daughter smiled at each other in perfect understanding.

"We will sight the coast soon," he remarked restlessly.

"Yes, I know." She sensed that he was on the verge of telling her something, and her gaze on him was questioning.

"Carolina, I would not have you take amiss what I am about to say," he began slowly, weighing his words.

Her slender gloved hand fluttered down on his, rested there lightly. "I would never take amiss *anything* that you might say," she said with that impulsive warmth that had so endeared her mother to him.

The ice-gray eyes that she looked into—so like her own—were cynical. But his voice was gentle.

"'Twas only a 'buccaneer wedding'—you know that."

She gave him a puzzled look.

"I mean 'twas not legal. There was no license, no parish register, no banns were cried, the 'minister' who performed the ceremony was long ago cast out from his church—the man told me so."

Carolina drew a deep breath. Her gaze upon the father who could never claim her back home in Virginia was a level one. "It was a marriage to me," she said steadily. "And I am wed to Rye forever!"

His expressive shrug spoke volumes of hard living and blasted hopes. "I but wanted you to know the truth of the matter," he said with a sigh. "Until the knot is tied in Yorktown, you are still a free woman. Free to leave him, free to seek your fortune elsewhere."

"Why? Why do you tell me this?" she challenged him, perversely refusing to admit that she had already known her marriage had no force of law. "Do you not like Rye?"

"I do," he replied moodily. "But"—a troubled frown crossed his countenance—"but you are my daughter and to me you must come first. I could not let you arrive in Yorktown thinking that you were well and truly wed."

Her expression softened. He was very winning, this newfound father of hers. "I thank you, sir," she said, dimpling. "But in my heart I am already well and truly wed—no matter what I must pretend in Yorktown."

"That is where I will be leaving you," he told her. "I will be going directly to Tower Oaks when we disembark."

"Of course." She nodded, repressing a shudder that he must return to a house devoid of children, whose mistress was a madwoman, for Sandy's young wife, always unstable, had never recovered from a terrible childbirth that had nearly taken her life. She was seldom lucid, and when she was, she blamed him for that disaster as well. She had attacked him once with a carving knife and he bore the scars of it. Wild, wicked Sandy Randolph, so in love with her mother, who must return upriver to his private hell. "I will understand if matters upriver prevent your attendance at my wed-

ding," she said, choosing her words carefully. "But"—
she flashed him a misty smile that turned her luminous
gray eyes to shimmering silver—"I will be honored, sir,
if you do attend."

He gave her a hunted look. *If he attended, he would
see her mother again, his wild lost love of yesterday—
and that was dangerous.* "I would see you safe and
settled," he muttered. "Not sailing the seas in some
buccaneer vessel."

"And soon I will be," she told him with a confident
lift to her chin. "Rye plans to take me back to England
with him and we will settle down there—perhaps at his
family seat in Essex."

"Pray God you will be happy there," he murmured
fervently and for a moment pressed her hand. "And if
you ever need me . . ."

"I will sail up the James and seek you out at Tower
Oaks!" she laughed. "Oh, Sandy—dear Sandy, for I
can never call you 'father'—be happy for me!"

He gazed down at her with pride. "We are alike," he
muttered. "Both of us eager to set out on some wild
venture, to best the world."

"And we will have the best of all possible worlds!"
she declared, laughing. "We will have it yet!"

His own pale silver eyes kindled. "Perhaps," he
sighed. "Well, I had best find this 'husband' of yours.
We have matters to discuss."

He left her then, strolling away down the clean-
scoured deck.

Carolina, leaning upon the taffrail, smiled after him.
The brisk sea wind whipped back her scarlet velvet
hood, took her hair, pale as the ocean foam, and sent it
in disarray around her slender shoulders. For a moment
it blew around her head in a bright tempestuous whirl

and two sailors, climbing the rigging, looked down and nearly fell from their perch at the beauty of the sight.

The *Sea Wolf* cut the water cleanly, flying the English flag, driving straight and true toward the mouth of the Chesapeake Bay. Above Carolina, standing on the deck, the canvas crackled noisily as she fought to pull her hood back over her flying hair. And the crack of the sails and the lazy creaking of the gray ship's timbers were musical sounds to her, blithely calling out that it was all going to happen at last—that she, Carolina the runaway, was coming home in triumph, coming home with her true love beside her, to a wedding as befit a Colonial belle of Yorktown.

She wrapped her arms around her against the cold and shivered in her cloak—but there was not a cloud on her horizon. And the song the cold wind sang aloft in the topsails was more than a windsong to her—it was a lovesong born of the wind and the sea.

BOOK I

The Hush-Hush Bride!

Dearest love, lie down with me beneath the summer sky,
Whisper that you love me—even though you lie!
Cover me with kisses, promise me a ring
So I'll know what bliss is—make my heart sing!

PART ONE

The Change in Plans

Sing to me a lover's song,
Tell me where our love went wrong,
Lie to me, beneath the moon,
Swear you will return—and soon!

THE YORK RIVER, VIRGINIA

Winter 1689

Chapter 1

A light snow was falling when they cast anchor below the familiar bluffs of Yorktown. It drifted down through the blue dusk, melting as it fell—but causing the air to be damp as any cellar. The soft flakes wafted down upon Carolina's blonde hair as she and Rye bade Sandy Randolph good-by and transferred themselves to a longboat for the ride upriver, for Carolina was so eager to gaze upon this Tidewater world she had thought lost to her that she forgot to put up her soft French velvet hood.

As the town fled by to the steady sweep of the oars, it seemed to her that all their plans had changed since they had left Tortuga. The lean gray vessel which they had left anchored behind them had had her name changed during the voyage from *Sea Wolf* to *Sea Waif*, and the buccaneer crew they left behind them in Yorktown looked almost boringly respectable. The *Sea Waif*'s new "captain," chosen to hold authority while Kells was gone (and chosen partly because of his ability to hold his tongue as well) had about him no hint of the buccaneer. And in the longboat beside Carolina, Kells was once again the sober gray-clad country gentleman he had seemed when first she met him.

Kells and Sandy Randolph had worked it all out together.

"'Twould be a mistake for you to come swinging in with a cutlass, proclaiming yourself to be the notorious Captain Kells—even to your new in-laws," Sandy had counseled the younger man over captured Spanish wine in the great cabin during their last dinner on board ship. Sandy was elegantly turned out in a stiff brocade coat that gave the effect of etched buff, heavily encrusted with gold braid. The froth of lace at his throat and cuffs was impeccably white, his trousers of the latest cut. Carolina thought he would have looked perfectly at home at the Court of St. James and was proud of him.

Seated across from him, toying with his glass of Madeira, Kells cut a more sinister figure. His deep-cuffed coat of claret velvet had somewhat tarnished braid, but it fitted his broad shoulders arrogantly. His thick dark hair was not meticulously tied back and caught with a black grosgrain riband as was Sandy's; it hung carelessly to rest, gleaming, upon his shoulders. The lamp above them highlighted the strong planes of his face, the square set of his jaw. In deference to the heat of the cabin (kept warm for Carolina in her low-cut crimson velvet gown) he had tugged open his collar and presented a carelessly casual appearance somewhat at odds with that of the other two.

He made no immediate comment on Sandy's suggestion, and Carolina, watching the two men in silence, wondered suddenly how much of Sandy's present argument had to do with her request of him earlier and how much had to do with her shrugging off his suggestion that she was not *really* married to the lean buccaneer who now regarded them both with such a steady look.

"Better to appear to be a passenger on a merchant ship, arrived to pick up cargo in Yorktown," pursued Sandy. *"Then* if there's any trouble with your pardon . . ."

Then you can make your escape before the authorities learn you're Captain Kells, Carolina thought with a pang. *By sea* . . . It brought home to her how precarious was their life together, she the Tidewater aristocrat who had passed herself off in Tortuga as one Mistress Christabel Willing—and Kells, the counterfeit Irishman whose buccaneer façade hid an English country gentleman yearning to go home. . . .

"D'ye anticipate trouble with my pardon?" Kells wondered abruptly, and for a moment his gray eyes were bleak as if he had seen a longed-for world snatched away from him.

"No, of course not." Sandy Randolph's handsomely brocaded shoulders moved in the slightest of shrugs— but the gesture was nonetheless eloquent. Gold usually changed hands to secure a king's pardon, and who could trust this general amnesty that had been declared to include such a famous buccaneer as Captain Kells, on whose head there was a price of forty thousand pieces of eight in Spain? "I will promptly intercede with my friend the governor on your behalf—without telling him your real identity, of course," Sandy assured the younger man earnestly. "But since you are giving the world your real name—Rye Evistock—I think it would be best to give that name only to the Lightfoot clan as well. That way there can be no chance slips of the tongue to endanger you. And in the meantime I will check into this matter of the pardon for you."

Kells swung around to face Carolina. "Is that what you desire?" He was regarding her keenly.

Carolina flushed, and the color that flooded her cheeks spread down her throat and prettily pinked her bosom and the pearly white tops of her young breasts so attractively displayed in the elegant low-cut gown.

"Y–yes," she said, stumbling over the word. "I think it best too, Rye."

"So be it," he said, but he looked thoughtful, and Carolina for a moment felt hot shame that she really could not trust all those at Level Green not to betray him. Perhaps Fielding Lightfoot in his hatred of Sandy and his dislike of her—no, no, she would not face that possibility, and she would not *have* to face it if no one knew Rye was a buccaneer.

And so the officers and crew of the newly rechristened *Sea Waif* had been warned to use extra caution and to pass themselves off as having signed on a merchantman out of Bristol, here in Yorktown to load on tobacco to fill the long clay pipes of England. And now the *Sea Waif*'s longboat, with wary taciturn seamen at the oars—men who, once they received their pardons, could return as wealthy men to their native country—was making its way up the tide-swollen York.

Carolina's heart was racing when they reached the landing at Level Green and she saw the great red brick turreted house of Flemish bond—largest in all Virginia —rise up before her. Candles winked from the downstairs windows. Perhaps they had guests? Oh, it would be awkward if they did! For all the Tidewater knew that Carolina Lightfoot had run away from home! And now she was back, still unchaperoned, flaunting a new scarlet cloak and with a commanding gentleman in gray at her side.

And then they were tying up at the pier and hurrying

over the wide snow-covered lawns and banging the big knocker. And being let in by a startled servant and stepping over the threshold, shaking the snow from their cloaks and setting down their luggage in the majestic hall with its tall pilasters and its massive carved stairway that could comfortably accommodate eight abreast.

Suddenly it all seemed like a dream to Carolina. She had come back to this house from England still a schoolgirl and left it a runaway to avoid being forced into some safe respectable loveless marriage. And now she had returned—she who had been for a space the daunting Silver Wench of the Caribbean! Fate worked in mysterious ways. . . .

Her reverie was interrupted by an elegant woman in violet velvet who appeared in the great hall. A woman with a great mass of fair hair whose slender figure froze to stillness at sight of them.

Carolina tossed back her head of wet blonde hair on which snowflakes still sparkled and prepared to stand her ground.

"Mother." She nervously addressed the small-waisted woman in the wide skirts who now swept toward them. "May I present my betrothed, Rye Evistock?"

If any words had been calculated to silence the greeting that sprang to Letitia Lightfoot's lips, those were the ones. She came to a halt. She did not embrace Carolina. Instead her handsomely coiffed head lifted alertly as if she might be facing an adversary, and her dark blue eyes glinted as they raked the smiling countenance of the tall man before her.

"Welcome to Level Green, sir," she said on a note of irony. The barest inclination of her aristocratic head acknowledged Rye's sweeping bow. "I am grateful that you have brought Carolina home to us. And I see you have brought your luggage as well." She glanced down at the two bags Rye had carried over the lawn and set down upon the floor of the hall. "I will have it taken upstairs, 'and rooms prepared. And the men from your barge, what of them? They will need to be cared for in the servants' quarters—"

"They have already departed," Rye told her easily.

"What, at this hour?"

"It was a longboat, Mother," Carolina put in quickly. "And the men were eager to get back to Yorktown and the wenches there."

At this mention of wenches, her mother's high-arched brows lifted a trifle but she made no comment; she merely looked pointedly at Carolina's scarlet velvet cloak which she had not seen before. Carolina moved uneasily under that look. *Unmarried daughters of the gentry do not accept valuable gifts from men— particularly clothing,* it seemed to say.

Carolina opened her mouth to answer that unspoken criticism—and closed it again. Her mother was as usual in complete command of the situation and she felt awkward, gauche.

"Delcy." Imperiously Letitia signaled the servant girl who had let them in, and who had been standing there goggle-eyed, to help them off with their wraps.

"I am still cold—I think I will keep my cloak on until I thaw out," murmured Carolina, declining Delcy's offer of assistance.

And indeed she felt cold. Not merely because her elegant emerald-green satin gown was too thin for a night like this—she had recklessly worn it because of its great sweeping skirt and the abundance of gold embroidery on its emerald-green velvet petticoat, now water-stained from the snowy lawn—but because she felt that perhaps they would not be staying, perhaps she would be sent away. . . .

Her mother must have caught that thought for she gave Carolina a sardonic look. "Have you supped?"

"On board," said Carolina hastily for she wanted to get her mother's questions over with—she might well choke on them at supper.

"Well, perhaps you will join us then in a glass of wine?" Letitia might have said more but from the head of the stairs Carolina's older sister Virginia had just then glimpsed the newcomers. Now Virginia picked up her heavy black skirts and fled down those stairs with a glad cry and embraced Carolina.

"Oh, Carol, you're back!" she cried joyfully. "We were all sure you were dead!"

That fact was immediately evidenced when Fielding Lightfoot entered the hallway and missed a step. His face had gone as pale as his fawn satin coat but he kept a good grip on himself as introductions were made and Carolina said merrily, in answer to Virginia, "Don't listen to gossip! As you can see I am returned in good health and soon to be"—her figure in her enveloping scarlet cloak was taut but her reckless silver gaze challenged her mother's penetrating dark blue one—"wed."

"Wed . . ." repeated Letitia woodenly. Suddenly she seemed to gather her forces. *"Soon* to be wed, you say?" Then, briskly, "Perhaps we should talk about that?" Her voice had a slight edge to it. "In the library. There is a good fire burning there. You can warm yourselves." As she turned to lead the way to the library she cast another frowning look at Carolina's scarlet cloak.

She is thinking that I might be pregnant! thought Carolina indignantly. *And that is why I do not take off*

my cloak! She had a sudden desire to tear off her cloak
and throw it aside—but to do that would reveal the
barbaric splendor of the emerald necklace she had
chosen to wear to match her gown. It felt cold against
her neck and it would require explanation because she
had not left home with jewels like that! Virginia would
exclaim over the necklace, and Carolina's nerves were
by now so jangled that she wanted to get whatever
tongue-lashing was coming over with before Virginia
began to "oh-h-h" and "ah-h-h" over her jewels.

Following her mother's straight-backed elegant
figure—Fielding Lightfoot trailed gloomily behind
them—Carolina thought whimsically how like her auto-
cratic mother it was to call them both like children into
another room so that she might point out the error of
their ways. But surprisingly, such seemed not to be the
case.

"I would be glad to see Carolina suitably married, of
course," Letitia told Rye frankly when the four of them
were at last alone—Virginia having been shooed away
like a child from this family conference. "But"—her
calculating gaze scanned Rye's sober gray broadcloth
clothing—"we must first know more about you. Before
we can give our consent."

The fire crackled in the hearth of the big pleasant
paneled room. Standing before it, Carolina was nervously conscious of Fielding's glowering stance as he
crossed to a table, poured a glass of wine and silently
handed it to Rye.

But the man who had dominated the wildest port of
the Caribbean these years past proved equal to the
occasion. "I am the third son of Byron Evistock, Lord
Gayle," Rye told his future mother-in-law gravely.
"My family seat is in Essex and has been since before
the Norman Conquest."

"Indeed?" The faint edge in Letitia's voice suggested that she might or might not be impressed by such an illustrious line. She signaled irritably to Fielding to offer Carolina a glass of wine as well—which Carolina promptly refused, feeling that even if the wine did not choke her she might well drop the glass. "And can you support my daughter in the style to which she is accustomed?" She shot the words at Rye. Her negligent gesture included the handsome room with its rich paneling, its crimson damask chairs and silver sconces—and all the rich rooms and corridors that lay beyond their vision.

Carolina thought of the gold candlesticks and jewel-encrusted goblets that reposed in the great cabin of the *Sea Waif* and was tempted to speak. But she caught Rye's eye and was silent.

"I will do my best," said her beloved cheerfully.

Letitia's fine high-riding brows shot up and she seemed to grow a shade taller. "But you are the *third* son," she pointed out frostily, "and as such not likely to inherit the title or the family seat, I take it?"

The erstwhile Captain Kells inclined his dark head in agreement. "I have endeavored to make my own way," he said modestly.

Carolina, choking back sudden mirth, hoped he would not be goaded into explaining just *how* he had made his own way but he seemed imperturbable. She caught his gaze just then and saw that there was a hint of laughter gleaming in his gray eyes.

"And you think you can support my daughter in *this* manner?" Letitia's tone was one of disbelief.

"With luck I might just be able to," was the laconic reply.

"With *luck?*" she echoed. She stared at him scathingly. "Are you aware, sir, that this is accounted the finest house in the Colonies?" Her haughty tone asked him to consider that spread about her were thirty-five rooms, nine corridors and three oversize hallways.

"Mother," broke in Carolina desperately. "Let me show you my betrothal ring."

She tore off her left glove and held up her hand to show the ring. It spoke for itself. It was an enormous square-cut emerald from the mines of Peru, set handsomely in gold. She had a brief satisfying glimpse of Fielding's shocked face. "And there was another betrothal gift as well," she added recklessly, throwing open the cloak she had not yet removed so that a necklace of enormous chunky emeralds set in gold flashed green in the firelight.

Her mother drew in a deep breath. "Such emeralds are seldom to be found outside of Spain," she observed, shallow-voiced.

"Just so." Rye Evistock favored her with a sunny smile that lit his saturnine countenance. "But sometimes the dons are persuaded to part with them."

If she guessed then what he was, Letitia did not say so. And nearby a glowering Fielding had his gaze bent not on the jewels but on this bad penny of a girl who kept turning up, this child who was not his own, but whom he must appear to have sired—and even to love.

"It would appear that you can support my daughter, sir," Letitia said in an altered voice.

"Oh, indeed, Mother, he can," cried Carolina, almost weak with relief for she had been afraid that the elder Lightfoots might press too hard to learn the source of such obvious wealth.

Standing there thoughtfully, her mother suddenly made up her mind. She turned her head regally. "Virginia," she called. "You may stop listening at the door and join us."

The door was opened with alacrity and Virginia, her face stained red with embarrassment that her mother had guessed her to be eavesdropping, came into the room in time to hear Carolina say merrily that she had been all this time in England visiting school friends. Beside her Rye said nothing—nothing about her having been captured by the Spanish, nothing about his having saved her and taken her to Tortuga. It was the story they had agreed upon on the voyage, but as Virginia exclaimed over the flashing emeralds Carolina thought she saw a knowing light in her mother's cynical dark blue eyes, and she flushed. "I brought Rye back to the Tidewater," she finished frankly—and this at least was the truth, "because I thought you would like me to be married at home."

"And so I would." The Inquisition over, Letitia now bestowed on her runaway daughter a brilliant smile. "It would be wonderful to have a wedding here at Level Green." She embraced Carolina.

"I had intended for us to be married in Essex," put in Rye. "But Carolina—"

"Nonsense," interrupted Letitia, turning to him. "I won't hear of your leaving before you are married! Carolina's will be the first wedding ever to be held at Level Green and"—she gave an expressive little shrug —"considering the way my daughters run away to be wed, 'tis likely to be the last for some time to come!"

There was a little growl from Fielding at that, as if to say that his two older daughters might have dashed off to the fabled "Marriage Trees" to be wed by strange ministers who lay in wait across the border in Maryland, but his two younger ones, still too young to be thinking about such things, certainly would not! And as for this one—well!

His wife gave him a quelling look.

"We would be pleased to have the wedding here," he said in a strangled voice.

Letitia smiled at him. "And now, Carolina." She turned briskly to her daughter. "You look tired."

Carolina blinked. She was not at all tired—and she was sure that as excited as she felt, she certainly couldn't *look* tired!

"You have just finished a long sea journey," her mother reminded her. "Virginia, take Carolina up to bed. The girls will want to see her if they are still awake."

Carolina knew she was speaking of her younger sisters, little Della and Flo. "Oh, yes, I do want to see them," she began. "But they're probably asleep by now and tomorrow will be time enough to—"

"Now. At once," said Letitia imperiously, cutting off her daughter's protests. "Fielding and I will want to have a private conversation with your betrothed," she explained as Carolina shot a wild look at Rye.

Bewildered by this turn of events, Carolina let Virginia sweep her away in triumph upstairs, talking all the way. She wondered suddenly if her mother was actually going to broach the subject of a dowry!

LEVEL GREEN
THE YORK RIVER, VIRGINIA

Winter 1689

Chapter 2

"Father *says* he will be pleased to have a big wedding here, but I doubt he will enjoy it," laughed Virginia, as they reached the top of the wide carved staircase. "But mother will be more than pleased—she will be in her element!"

Carolina paused on the landing. "You don't really think Mother's going to offer Rye a dowry, do you?" she asked, frowning.

"Not likely!" said Virginia blithely. "Father couldn't scrape one together! Indeed, if everyone hereabouts weren't so in awe of this great pile of a house—which *does* make it look as if we have money, you will admit—Father's creditors would be closing in on him right now!"

"But, Virgie—"

"More likely she's saving face for Father," observed Virginia candidly. "She'll make some graceful suggestion of a dowry and wait for it to be turned down!"

Which of course it would be. Carolina had little doubt of that, for she had already made Rye aware of Fielding

Lightfoot's straitened circumstances now that he had built his "folly."

"Unless, of course, she hopes to borrow money from Rye!" giggled Virginia as they turned down the familiar corridor to Carolina's old room. "She wouldn't want us to hear *that*. There's been a lot of discussion about debts lately." She sighed and abruptly changed the subject. "How does it feel to be back?"

"It feels—wonderful, of course." Carolina paused in the doorway of her old room for a moment, and a feeling of homesickness swept over her—which was ridiculous for she *was* home. But somehow the sight of those misty blue walls and those dainty blue and white curtains and that white quilt with the large blue fleur-de-lis design worked into it had awakened memories.

"I see mother has added a new double valance to my bed—and it's lined with blue silk!" she exclaimed.

"Yes, and she'd have done more if she'd known you were coming back, I don't doubt!" Virginia had run lightly up the stairs with her black skirts raised, but now she seemed to waver as she approached the bed. She paused and smiled. "Oh, Carolina, I've missed you so! Christmas was the worst—without either you or Penny."

"You've still heard nothing from Penny?" asked Carolina sharply, for she had hoped to find news of her older sister on her return.

"Nothing at all. Not since she left Emmett in Philadelphia," declared Virginia. "And Christmas was very gloomy—for me at least. Mother, of course, takes everything in stride, and who knows what she's thinking? And Father just shouts—as if *that's* going to help anything! But *I* moped about—I was sure you and Penny were both dead. How was your Christmas, Carol?"

"Why, why it was—" Carolina thought how she had really spent Christmas—gliding over the clear aquamarine waters of the islands, basking in the sun. Amid a round of merry-making she had rechristened the *Sea Wolf* the *Sea Waif*—that had been on Christmas Day. And afterward they had all drunk toasts. And after that, with the white fire of tropical stars flashing like distant jewels in the black velvet night, Rye had pulled her to him and murmured, "We'll spend next Christmas before our own hearth. In Essex." *And we'll have a great Yule log that will burn the whole twelve days of Christmas!* Carolina had thought, leaning against him. *And friends will come to call . . . but will it be better than this, here in your arms?*

"It was late in our voyage coming over from England, of course," she told Virginia hastily. "It was a very dull Christmas. Those on board—made the best of it, of course."

"How awful for you," said Virginia with sympathy. "I had forgot. Of course you were aboard ship. How awful to spend Christmas Day at sea in a cold damp vessel!"

Carolina recollected that the weather had been hazily sunny. They had been becalmed and Rye had hastily taken her to the prow of the ship because the buccaneers had elected to swim naked off the stern in the clear warm waters. They had returned aboard hastily, shouting, when a shark had appeared, lazily circling the ship. "Oh, yes," she agreed guiltily. "Awful."

"But how wonderful that you chose to come back and be married here! Mother's wanted a big wedding at Level Green ever since the house was built. After all, Penny escaped her net by running off to the Marriage Trees—and I've been such a terrible disappointment to her." A bleak look came over Virginia's too-thin face.

41

She sighed and sank down on the big feather bed as if she had suddenly run out of strength.

Carolina frowned at her. Virginia was certainly very scrawny and she had been overly plump when Carolina had left. Her thick red-gold hair seemed dirty copper now; it had lost its springiness and its luster—and it was pinned back unattractively as if Virginia didn't care how she looked.

"Are you all right, Virgie?" she asked doubtfully.

"Of course." Virginia's voice, which had once had an earnest ring to it, was flippant, almost hard. "Don't you think I look better this way? *I* do!"

Carolina certainly didn't think so. Looking at Virginia's skeletal features made her feel alarmed. She wondered if her mother realized how fragile Virginia was now, she who had always been so sturdy. "You can't be eating enough, Virgie," she told her sister bluntly.

"Oh, I don't seem to want food," said Virginia indifferently.

Carolina's "Whyever not?" was cut off as the door opened and a child's pretty face peeped into the room, immediately to be withdrawn with a glad, "Come along, Flo. It's Carol—she's back!"

There was a patter of slippered feet and their two younger sisters—those children born to Letitia and Fielding in later years—scampered into the room in their voluminous white nightclothes to hug Carolina and join their two older sisters on the edge of the big bed, their legs dangling over the white and blue quilt.

They were big-eyed when they learned that Carolina was going to be married and clamored to learn where she'd been and what she'd done since she left. Carolina hated having to lie to those eager upturned faces but she could hardly tell them it was the notorious Silver Wench of buccaneer Tortuga they were talking to!

"Will I be one of your bridesmaids?" piped up little Flo, interrupting Della's rapt questioning about recent doings in London.

"Yes, of course you will," laughed Carolina, glad to be on a safe subject. "You both will. And Virginia will be my maid of honor. Although I doubt it will be a very big wedding with all the bad weather this time of year."

"Ha! Don't you believe it!" cut in Virginia. "Remember, Mother was a runaway bride herself and—"

"Yes," laughed Carolina. "*She* dashed off to the Marriage Trees herself, just like Penny did and like—" She stopped, flustered, remembering that Virginia too had made a dash to the Marriage Trees. With Hugh. Only for her it hadn't worked out.

Virginia gave her a sardonic look as though for her the Marriage Trees were long forgotten. "So Mother will make up for *her* lack of a big wedding with *yours*, Carol, depend upon it!"

Carolina, who was trying to regain possession of her hand as little Flo, bubbling over with talk, fought to get a closer look at the big emerald betrothal ring which Della was studying with such interest, grimaced. "Let's hope it doesn't turn out like the wedding held at Oakcrest four years ago," she said. For the wedding at Oakcrest had been a total disaster. A sudden ice storm had glazed the roads and snow had fallen on top of the ice. Three carriages had lost wheels, one group had been seriously injured and on arrival at Oakcrest had had to be put to bed and a doctor called. The fires had been built too hot and sparks had set fire to the roof; the bride and groom had had to leap from their nuptial bed and run outside in their scanty nightclothes to save their lives—and the entire wedding party had spent the night fighting the fire and getting frostbite to boot!

"Oh, *your* wedding won't turn out like the one at

Oakcrest," said Virginia moodily. "Things always turn out well for you, Carol."

But not for me, was the implication. And Carolina, eager to avoid that touch of envy that Virginia must feel to see her arrive so full of health and strength and happiness, with a big emerald betrothal ring on her finger, spoke quickly. "I was surprised to find all of you here at Level Green at this time of year. I half thought to arrive and find that Mother had packed all of you off to Aunt Pet's in Williamsburg!"

"Oh, she might have." Virginia reached a thin hand over to tousle little Flo's abundant curls affectionately. "But she couldn't, you see, because Aunt Pet has gone visiting to Philadelphia."

Of all the Randolph relatives—excluding Sandy, of course—Aunt Pet was Carolina's favorite. At Virginia's words her brow furrowed. "Did she take her silver chamber pot with her?" she asked instantly.

"She took it," affirmed Virginia.

"Oh, then she'll be gone a long time, I suppose," said Carolina, disappointed. For Aunt Pet took such pride in her silver chamber pot, that if she intended to be away from home for any length of time, it always accompanied her. Silver chamber pots were rare—most were of lead-glazed earthenware, and even those at lavish Level Green were only of pewter. That silver chamber pot was a mark of distinction—it had come along with Aunt Pet from England. Aunt Pet had smuggled it in actually, for there had been a ban on the export of silver from England at the time. Determined not to leave behind such a precious possession, Aunt Pet's mother had suspended not only the silver chamber pot but a pair of fine silver candlesticks and a dozen of the fashionable new silver forks beneath the wide

cage of a huge wheel farthingale and lumbered aboard
with a fortune in silver beneath her voluminous skirts!

The smuggling episode had been kindly forgotten,
the candlesticks had long since been given to Letitia
and the fashionable silver forks were in constant use in
the dining room of Aunt Pet's high-chimneyed two-
story Williamsburg house, but the silver chamber pot
was rather conspicuously displayed in her bedchamber,
not—as those who had earthenware pots were prone to
remark enviously—hidden away behind a screen or a
hanging as chamber pots were supposed to be. Indeed
Aunt Pet was forever promising generously to will it to
this one or that when she died—whoever she was
pleased with at the moment. Letitia had always chuckled that Petula would refuse entrance at the gates of
heaven if she couldn't take that chamber pot with her,
and Carolina was inclined to agree. And now Aunt Pet
had taken it to Philadelphia with her. . . .

"When will she be back?" she wondered.

"Oh, not for months," said Virginia. "She's making
a round of visits to old friends."

Carolina sighed. Outside of her mother and Virgie—
and Sandy, who could not be counted on to attend—
Aunt Pet was the one person she had most hoped to
have with her at the ceremony. Somehow she didn't
think she'd feel quite married unless Aunt Pet was
there to witness it and cluck over her gown and tell her
she was marrying quite the handsomest man in all the
Colonies—for Aunt Pet was partial to bridegrooms and
always viewed them through rose-colored glasses.

"Perhaps if Mother writes to her, she'll come back
for the wedding," Virginia suggested sympathetically.

"Oh, I'm sure there won't be time for that," objected
Carolina, who meant to get herself wed and be gone.

Virginia's quirked eyebrow said their mother would have something to say about that. She'd require time to marshal her forces and stage a big wedding.

"What about the local war?" Carolina asked whimsically. "The one right here at Level Green?" For the battles between the warring Lightfoots were legendary.

Virginia shrugged. "Oh, things have been relatively quiet since you left."

Carolina winced. *Her* absence was the reason they had been getting along so well, she supposed, for jealous Fielding Lightfoot could not forgive his wife Letitia for that long-ago Christmastide desertion that had resulted later in a daughter—Carolina. And the sight of her when she was growing up had always reminded him. She wondered if Virginia knew they were really only half sisters, and decided she did not.

"Indeed the Chattertons now dominate the local gossip," Virginia told Carolina. "Millie Chatterton left Wilbur, and Wilbur posted a public notice saying she was a slovenly housekeeper and used vile language! And then Millie posted a reply for all to see that she'd learned the vile language from him, and that he had kept two mistresses all the time they lived together and when he came up with a third, she left!" Virginia laughed. "I doubt any of it's true, but it's kept the gossips buzzing!"

And had given the Lightfoots of Level Green a welcome respite, thought Carolina.

"And what of Sally Montrose?" she asked, expecting to hear of some new madcap adventure of her old friend who lived up the James and had lent her so many exciting novels with names like *The Innocent Adulteress*.

"You won't know Sally at all," said Virginia promptly.

"Whyever not?" demanded Carolina instantly, for carefree, impetuous Sally was her best friend in Virginia.

"Well, you know what a tomboy she used to be? She isn't anymore. She's very elegant—minces around spouting French and acting very toplofty."

Carolina's laughter pealed. She couldn't imagine easygoing, good-natured Sally acting toplofty. But her laughter broke off at Virginia's sober expression. "What happened to change her?"

"You remember Sally was always in love with Brent Chase but he married her older sister?"

Carolina nodded raptly.

"Her sister—Brent's wife—died in childbirth. It happened right after you left, Carolina. And Sally thought to marry him then—I think that was why she hadn't married even with so many offering for her; she knew her sister was frail and something might happen. But—"

"But it's posted in the parish church that a woman may not marry her sister's husband," finished Carolina for her. "Poor Sally!"

"Yes, I think she was planning to live with him in sin," said Virginia thoughtfully. "But he wouldn't have it. He married one of the Crawford girls in October and Sally claimed she was too 'indisposed' to attend the wedding even though the Crawfords were neighbors, but someone saw her out riding, jumping fences as if she was trying to break her neck! The first time we saw her after the wedding, we all stared. She was wearing a black face mask and she had hennaed her hair and she was wearing so much powder that it was whitening her cloak!"

Sally, who had always scorned pomades and powders!

"I'm sorry for Sally," said Carolina slowly.

It came to her eerily that of all her friends, of all those close to her even, she seemed to be the only one destined to be happy. Her London school friend, Reba, had fallen in love with a married marquess—and lost him. Her older sister Penny had run away to the Marriage Trees—and disappeared after the breakup of her marriage. Virginia's life was the saddest of all: After being pushed into marriage she had been as suddenly widowed. And now Sally's hopes were crushed. . . .

"Perhaps we'll see her soon," she said soberly.

"Oh, we're sure to." Talking about Sally's troubles seemed to give Virginia more animation. "She goes everywhere, flirts with everyone, dances her slippers off! But you'll find her changed—she's very bitter."

And with reason! thought Carolina, feeling an ache in her heart for her old friend.

By now the two younger girls were looking sleepy and Carolina was suddenly aware of something that in the excitement of her homecoming she had overlooked —that Rye had been put in a room somewhere, she was not sure where. He had no idea where she was and he could hardly be expected to prowl a strange house, knocking on doors in the night to find his hush-hush bride. And besides, she realized that all three of her sisters, sleepy or not, seemed prepared to spend the night in her room, talking and giggling.

"I'll want Sally for a bridesmaid," she meditated, wondering how to get them all out of her bedchamber so she could go looking for Rye. "Perhaps that will cheer her up."

"She needs cheering now—not in the future," Virginia said gloomily.

48

"Well, I'm not talking about the future," protested Carolina. "I expect to be married right away!" *Pardon or no pardon!*

"Ha! Not a chance!" scoffed Virginia. "You know as well as I do that mother will insist upon a *huge* wedding with all of Virginia and half of Maryland and the Carolinas invited! Wait and see if I'm not right. Just planning it will take at least a month. And then there's your wedding gown, remember—everything for it will have to be specially ordered from England—or at least Philadelphia."

"But that's ridiculous!" Carolina cried in dismay. For the first time she realized what a prodigious undertaking she had stumbled into—and after all her blithe romantic notions of a quick marriage at home and then away to England! "I've a perfectly beautiful gown that will serve admirably!"

"No matter how beautiful, it will have to be something brand new," insisted Virginia. "In fact it will probably have to be the dress mother always wished she had worn herself at *her* wedding if she hadn't run away to the Marriage Trees!"

"Whatever *that* is," grumbled Carolina.

"We'll know when she picks it out," laughed Virginia.

"Well, do use your influence with her, Virgie," sighed Carolina.

"I don't have any influence with her," supplied her sister promptly. "And I never did—as well you know!" She propped up a pillow and leaned back against it as if exhausted.

"What's 'influence'?" piped up little Flo, who had been staring at her newly returned sister in silence.

"Something you'll never have unless you get your

sleep," said Carolina instantly, taking this opportunity to get rid of the small fry. "Get them to bed, won't you, Virgie? Mother was right—I *am* terribly tired."

Virginia blinked. Those sparkling silver eyes looked anything but tired. "I'll pack them off to bed," she said, giving little Flo's bottom a playful spank as the child slid off the high bed to land squarely on both bare feet on the wide planked floor. "Remember to bank the fire a bit before you go to sleep, Carol," she called back over her shoulder as she held open the door and shooed the two children from the room.

Carolina cast an indignant glance at the hearth where orange flames still licked the hickory logs. "Where do you think I've been living, Virgie," she demanded tartly, "that I'd forget to bank the fire?" For she had carefully stuck to the story that she'd been living in England since she'd left.

Virginia's tone was sardonic. "Someplace warmer," she said. "Where emeralds are easy come by. And if you *should* forget to bank the fire"—there was an undertone of mirth in her voice—"I'll stop by after I've seen the children off to bed."

Softly she closed the door.

Carolina stared at that closed door. Virginia was not so easily hoodwinked as she had expected. She had guessed Carolina's secret. And why not, when Carolina had showed up in the dead of winter with the remnants of a toasty tan still burnishing her fair complexion and flaunting a fortune in emeralds, gift of a tall man with the lean grace of a swordsman and too deeply bronzed to have got that tan last summer. . . .

Carolina frowned at the door. Virginia would say nothing of course. Nor would her mother. But they knew, *they knew*. . . .

She waited no longer. Hastily she donned a robe and

went out into the cold corridor. There was only a hint of light out there—just enough to keep her from banging into the walls as she went—but she hesitated to take along a candle. Because her mother was a light sleeper and she had very sharp eyes and if she should happen to come out into the corridor for any reason, she could not fail to see a lighted candle sending dark shadows wavering up the walls but she *might* miss a dark figure tiptoeing along shivering. . . .

Ah, there it was—a gleam of light under one of the bedroom doors. Rye had kept his candle burning!

The hinges were well oiled. Silently she slipped inside. She was in what her mother had named "the bronze room" because she had chosen for it bronze draperies and bedspread. It was comfortable but not very large—indeed it was a room in which her mother frequently put less-favored guests.

In the big walnut bed Rye was just about to pinch out the candle flame. His long muscular arm was extended over the table and he looked up alertly as she entered and smiled at her.

"I had just about given you up," he said.

"My sisters converged on me and I couldn't get away," Carolina explained, her teeth almost chattering, for the hall had been freezing.

"Shall I stir up the fire?" he asked, sitting up as he noted her shiver.

"No, no, stay where you are—I'll join you."

As she hurried across the room, Rye threw back the bronze bedspread and the quilt and she plunged into bed beside him. He reached out a long arm and scooped her to him. She lay shivering with cold, warming herself against the naked length of him. He seemed to generate more heat than did the fire on the hearth, she thought lazily.

"You shouldn't be running about these cold corridors barefoot," he reproved, taking her bare feet in his warm hands and massaging them.

"All I brought with me were satin mules," she said ruefully. "And they have heels that would clatter along these uncarpeted halls loud enough to wake the dead!"

"Well, we wouldn't want that," he said, chuckling.

Carolina relaxed against him, feeling warmth flow through her body as he caressed her. "Virgie wanted to talk," she explained. "And my two little sisters came in. And then there was the fire to bank—" She sat up. She *had* forgotten to bank the fire after all!

"What's the matter?" he asked alertly.

"Nothing." She sank back beside him. Virgie would bank the fire. Virgie had been trying to tell her, in an oblique way, that *she knew* where Carolina was going to spend the night: in her lover's arms! "What did you talk about—downstairs after I was gone?" she asked Rye.

"Your mother tried to persuade me to purchase land along the York and settle here. She thought you might be too enamored of foreign lands."

"She what?" Carolina's head lifted in astonishment.

He was chuckling again. "She's very alert, your mother, and I think perhaps the necklace made her guess how matters really stand with me."

Carolina sighed and snuggled back against him. Rye had warned her not to wear the necklace, that it might make trouble, but she had been adamant. "But Mother didn't actually *accuse* you of anything, did she?"

"No," he said thoughtfully. "But I think she was telling me in a roundabout way that she didn't want me taking you to sea again. . . ."

"What did Fielding have to say?"

52

"Very little. He just sat and drank and watched us."

"I was sure *he* wouldn't suggest you settle here," she murmured.

"Does it matter to you?"

"No, I suppose not." It might have been too much to expect Fielding to feel toward her as a father might, but it would have been nice if they could at least have been friends. . . .

She sighed, and he settled his long body more comfortably against her womanly softness and cradled her in his arms. "Warm now?"

"Yes." She nuzzled against him, feeling happy and tender and sleepy and yet so very alive. Tomorrow . . . they would solve all their problems tomorrow. Tonight they would forget this was a forbidden tryst, that she wasn't supposed to be here, that there would be great consternation if she were to be discovered here in this room, in this bed! Tonight in their shared hideaway they would forget the world and surrender to passion and dreams.

His hands on her body were warm, his lips tender. Her blood sang a lovesong as she pressed close against him and let the fervor of her own passion match the fervor of his.

The fire on the hearth might be banked and growing cold but the fire that burned in their blood became a raging cauldron that consumed them yet renewed them, and left in its afterglow smouldering embers that could be relighted and flame up again at a touch, a smile, a murmured word.

Dawn was breaking when Carolina rose to steal back to her own room.

Rye wakened as she got up. In the chill morning light she could see he had one eye open. Did he never sleep?

she wondered. Had all those nights when to fall asleep was to die so conditioned him that he would always wake at the slightest touch?

"Go back to sleep," she murmured. "Mother must not find me here."

He reached a strong hand out for her, smiling, then thought better of it. "I suppose you are right," he agreed reluctantly, and rolled over with a sigh.

Carolina treasured the sound of that sigh all the way down the dim empty corridor.

Chapter 3

After breakfast the next morning Carolina sought out her mother, who was supervising the sorting of linens in the big chests just as though nothing so momentous as the arrival of a runaway daughter with her betrothed had happened. Her mother, thought Carolina whimsically, could never really look the settled housewife—not even in her indigo fustian gown. She would always look like an adventuress—which was exactly what the Tidewater gossips considered her to be.

Carolina came right to the point. "I'm worried about Virgie," she said bluntly. "I've never seen her thin like this. I couldn't ask you with her sitting there at breakfast, but what exactly is wrong with her?"

Letitia frowned. "There is nothing wrong with her," she said curtly. Her quick deep blue glance flicked over the two serving girls in their neat white aprons, busy fetching and sorting. "Virginia caught a deep cold in early fall and she has never really shaken it off. I keep hoping she will put on some weight."

"How can she?" protested Carolina. "She eats like a bird! You could see that she hardly touched her breakfast." She saw one of the serving maids nudge the other.

"I know." Letitia sounded indifferent. "She insists on taking tiny portions."

"And she doesn't seem—as interested in things as she should be," added Carolina meditatively. "She just seems to glide about, not caring about anything really." The two serving girls exchanged meaningful glances and her mother's lips tightened. Carolina felt bewildered. "What does the doctor say?"

"Doctor?" said her mother carelessly. "I have not felt that Virginia needs a doctor. She will doubtless eat more presently. When she decides to."

Her daughter gave her a baffled look.

"Let us hope," added Letitia, her dark blue eyes of a sudden flashing grimly at Carolina, "that the excitement of your homecoming will raise Virginia's spirits and cause her to take more interest in life."

And suppose I had not come home? Carolina wondered silently. *What then? Would Virgie just have been allowed to waste away?* It was very strange because both Fielding and Letitia were very fond of Virginia. Red-haired, laughing Penny had been their favorite of course, but now she was gone, and Virginia was still here.

Carolina might have said more but, typically, Letitia seemed to have dismissed the subject. Once again the linens absorbed her attention as she corrected one of the serving girls, "No, Ida, the tablecloths go in this chest, the napkins over here." With things going smoothly again, she turned her keen blue gaze onto Carolina, who, unlike Virginia, was bursting with health. "I expect to give a small dinner party at the Raleigh in Williamsburg for you and your betrothed when the governor returns," she said.

"When he returns? Where is he?"

"In Barbados visiting his mother."

Which meant that Sandy Randolph would have no chance to use his influence with the governor until he returned. And Rye would have to wait to receive his pardon, for who knew about lieutenant governors? They might have their open palms out for gold and with a general amnesty declared, Carolina doubted that Rye would stand for that.

"How long will the governor be gone?" Carolina asked cautiously.

Letitia shrugged. "He should be returning any day now."

But travel this time of year was uncertain. Carolina wished fervently that Sandy had not gone away up the James. Perhaps *he* would know how to proceed with the governor gone!

As if she had read her daughter's thoughts, Letitia said, "Carolina, come with me." She left the serving girls still sorting the snowy linens and led Carolina down the corridor to a handsome bedchamber next to that occupied by herself and Fielding. "Did you happen to see Sandy Randolph in your travels?" she asked in an offhand way.

Carolina started. She had not expected to be asked that.

"We returned to Virginia on the same ship," she admitted cautiously. *From England,* she meant to add, for that was what she and Rye and Sandy had all agreed upon. But she did not say it, for suddenly the lie stuck in her throat.

A wistful smile passed over her mother's face. "So Sandy found you," she murmured. "He said he would." She paused, waiting, but Carolina did not choose to elaborate. Letitia's dark blue eyes glinted. "Sandy will find more than he bargained for when he returns home," she muttered. And in answer to Carolina's puzzled look, she added, "His wife, Estelle, threw a gravy boat at one of the servants and followed up by attacking him with the gravy ladle. She near put out his eye—to say nothing of ruining the best French wallpaper at Tower Oaks!" She shook her head. "That woman will be the death of him."

"Poor Sandy," murmured Carolina, heartily sorry for this new trouble to beset the master of Tower Oaks. "I suppose she has no relatives to whom he could send her for a while to—to have a rest from her?"

"Estelle has no living relatives. No, I am afraid Sandy must bear the burden alone." Letitia gave her daughter a jaded look and threw open the door. "I had not yet gotten around to this bedchamber before you— left us. How do you like the way I have decorated it?"

Carolina took in the rusty rose "Vase carpet" from Persia, the mellow old gold coverlet and window hangings that turned to shades of lemon where the sun struck them, the soft muted tones of the fine English needlework upholstery on the mahogany chairs.

"It's beautiful," she said, thinking as she so often had that her mother had the best taste in all the Tidewater.

"Good," said Letitia briskly. "I am glad you like it, Carolina, for I have decided to move your betrothed to this room. It is nicer and has a better view of the river."

"Oh, but I am sure Rye is perfectly well satisfied where he is," protested Carolina in distress. For if Rye were moved to this room next door to the room where

Letitia and Fielding slept, her mother could hear any creak of the door, any creak of the bed, any murmured voices—she would be afraid to visit Rye in the night!

"I am sure he is well satisfied where he is," said her mother smoothly, but with finality. Letitia Lightfoot was nobody's fool. She had noted her daughter's sleepy-eyed pleased demeanor at breakfast this morning and had instantly decided that Rye Evistock's sleeping quarters were too conveniently close to Carolina's. "Nevertheless we must do our best by him now that he is about to marry into the family. I will have his things moved this morning."

Carolina gave her a mutinous look which was serenely returned.

"You might go and tell Rye he is to be moved," suggested her mother gently. And watched thoughtfully as Carolina's slate-blue skirts moved away from her.

Carolina found Rye in one of the turret rooms where a wan-looking but smiling Virginia was showing him around. He was turning about, studying with interest the windows which were on all sides of the small room. "An excellent lookout spot, Mistress Virginia," he approved.

"And we have two of them," said Carolina, who had come up silently behind him.

"I heard you coming up the stairs." Rye turned to smile at her and Carolina was reminded once again how keen was his hearing—indeed all his senses. Sharpened by the dangerous life he'd led, no doubt.

Virginia was staring out the window at the wide expanse of river below. "Oh, you must excuse me," she said. "For I think I see the Rosegill barge approaching and I must make sure it stops so that I can return the books Mr. Wormeley so kindly lent me from his library." With a swish, she brushed her black silk skirts by Carolina's slate-blue broadcloth ones and made her almost weightless descent down the turret stairs, leaving the lovers these moments alone together.

Carolina gave her sister's departing form a grateful look, then turned to tell Rye first about the governor's absence, which provoked no comment, and then about the relocation of his sleeping quarters.

"It's terrible," she said in a worried voice. "I don't know if I'll dare to come to your room!"

"Then perhaps I'll visit yours," he said with a shrug.

"Oh, that's dangerous," fretted Carolina. "For Virgie is nearby—*she* wouldn't say anything, but Flo and Della are always running in and out of her room. And in and out of mine as well. If they find the door locked, they'll pound until they're let in!" She began to pace about. "Oh, why couldn't Mother let well enough alone?"

Rye quirked an eyebrow at her. "Your mother is determined to avoid scandal. She prefers not to have a pregnant bride." And at Carolina's disdainful sniff he turned to study the advancing barge on the river below. The snow had stopped falling last night but the sky was still leaden. It looked as if it might snow again.

"It's ridiculous!" Carolina was fuming as she joined him at the window. "Why should she put stones in our path? After all, I came home to be married just to please her!"

"'Twill not be for long," Rye told her restlessly. He was watching the panorama as the barge pulled up at the wooden wharf and Virginia, waving and without a cloak, burst from the house carrying an armful of leather-bound volumes and ran down the snowy lawn toward the barge. "We'll get this wedding over with and then we can respectably move into the same bedchamber while we wait for the governor to return so I can secure my pardon."

"Oh, you don't know my mother!" warned Carolina. "Virgie says she'll want a lot of time to plan this—and she's probably right. The guest list alone will take forever!"

Rye shot her an uneasy look—and then an exclamation passed his lips.

Below them on the slippery lawn with its dusting of snow, Virginia's running, black-clad figure wavered for a moment, then plunged to the snowy grass with her wide skirts spread out. Books flew in every direction.

"Oh, dear, Virgie's slipped and fallen!" cried Carolina in dismay. She and Rye turned as one to race downstairs and out of the house to pick up the fallen girl.

But Virginia had not just fallen. She had fainted, collapsed onto the thin shimmer of snow that whitened the ground from last night's light fall.

It was Rye who carried her inside.

"She weighs nothing," he remarked as Letitia appeared and took over, her indigo skirts leading the way to Virginia's green and white bedroom, her brisk voice ordering up brandy and smelling salts and hot soup and a bed warmer.

"She will eat or else!" Letitia told Carolina grimly. "I cannot have her collapsing like this—why, she could fall down the stairs at the wedding!" And then she shooed them all away to "go down and entertain Ralph Wormeley."

But Carolina, seeing the thinness of Virginia's gaunt features against her pillow, the blue shadows beneath her eyes, thought it might not much matter if Virginia ate that particular bowl of soup, for she seemed bent on starving herself. Virginia—so changed—was slipping away from them.

"Ralph Wormeley is already being entertained," objected Carolina, for she had seen Fielding heading for the barge from another direction as they carried Virginia into the house.

"Then show Rye about the house." Her mother's voice was crisp. "For you are not needed here. Virginia is already stirring."

The door closed firmly in their faces.

"I am glad you brought me home," Carolina whispered to Rye. "It may be the last time I ever see her." Tears trembled on her lashes and Rye led her away in sympathetic silence. "Everything is—is breaking up," she told him when they made their way downstairs and into the unoccupied library. "Penny's gone and Virgie soon will be."

"Not everything," he said firmly. He took her slender hand in his big warm one and stroked it. "For you and me life is just beginning."

She smiled at him blurrily and then dashed away her tears and showed him the finely engraved Sheffield brass box which held writing implements. "Virgie's favorite spot," she said wistfully, indicating the little slanted writing desk that reposed upon the heavy oaken table.

But Rye was more interested in the fine twenty-inch pistol made by R. Silke in London. "I have one very like this," he told her, turning the handsome pistol around with practiced ease, balancing it and sighting down the long barrel.

God grant he would never have to use another one of those, Carolina thought, brushing a hand across her still-damp cheeks.

It was there in the warm library before a roaring fire

that Ralph Wormeley and Fielding Lightfoot found them. Ralph Wormeley's cheeks and nose were red with cold. He was wearing a suit of spice-colored taffeta with gold-worked buttonholes and a profusion of gold buttons beneath a warm brown woolen cloak which he doffed with a sigh at sight of the fire. Beside him a frowning Fielding (frowning at sight of *her*, thought Carolina, glad that it no longer hurt so much to have him despise her) was splendid in a rich tan damask coat with wide velvet cuffs.

By contrast Rye was very simply dressed in his plain gray broadcloth, but Carolina thought him a commanding figure nonetheless. She stood beside him proudly as Fielding made the introductions and curtsied with a dimpling smile to Wormeley, whom she had always liked.

After inquiring whether Mistress Virginia had been injured in her fall on the lawn, which he had observed from his barge, and being told she had not, Ralph Wormeley promptly informed them that he had only stopped by to deliver a message from Lewis Burwell. Lewis Burwell was giving a ball at Fairfield a fortnight hence and he hoped all the Lightfoots would attend. "And especially Mistress Carolina and Mistress Virginia," Ralph Wormeley added gallantly—ignoring the fact that Lewis Burwell could hardly have been expected to know that Carolina was back—for both girls had always been great favorites of his.

Fielding Lightfoot, at that moment occupied in pouring glasses of port wine, responded warmly that they would be there. Carolina did not demur. Yesterday she would have felt obliged to say that she and Rye would probably be gone by then, on their way back to England—but it had come to her since with some force that such would probably not be the case.

Carolina left the men talking by the hearth and drinking port and went up to see how Virginia was getting along. She found her sister tucked into the linen sheets, lying back exhausted against the long bolster, with a hot brick wrapped in a piece of blanket at her feet, and almost smothered by a wealth of coverlets despite the roaring fire on the hearth. Letitia had gone but her orders to build up the fire had been obeyed. The pleasant room with its soft green walls, dominated by a great bed with a green and white petticoat valance lined with green silk, was almost *too* warm.

"You should not have run over the lawn when it had a skiff of snow on it," scolded Carolina. "It's slick as glass—no wonder you fell."

Virginia nodded meekly. "I agree I should not have run," she acknowledged. "But I feared the barge might not stop unless I flagged it down, and I had *promised* to return those books to Mr. Wormeley when last we were at Rosegill. He is so nice to let me use his wonderful library. And now"—she looked about to cry—"I am afraid I have ruined his books, letting them fall into the snow like that!"

"Ralph Wormeley said you were not to worry about the books. They have all been gathered up and dried off and no serious harm was done to them. He was more worried that you might have been hurt when he saw you fall to the lawn and lie still." She nodded toward the bowl of soup that lay scarcely touched on the table beside her. "Virgie," she said abruptly, "why won't you eat?"

Virginia realized that the question had to do with more than this particular meal and returned a frank answer. "At first I didn't eat because I thought I was too fat and that was why nobody loved me. And then I just somehow lost the taste for food, and then I caught a deep cold, and now food chokes me."

"Oh, Virgie," said Carolina. "Don't you know we *all* love you?"

Virginia's sigh came from deep in her soul. "I don't mean you. I mean—a man. Hugh didn't really love me. I ran away with him, but when we were caught he turned to someone else and forgot all about me." *And stole your gold to boot!* thought Carolina, hot with anger for her sister. "And then Mother pushed me into marriage with Algernon," went on Virginia, "and he didn't love me either. And then he died and I had a miscarriage. And—and while you were gone I met someone I thought really *did* love me." Her voice trembled and Carolina saw that her fingers were clenched white in the lace of the top coverlet. "He gave me a posy ring, Carolina."

Posy rings were not valuable; they were usually of silver and were often given for friendship. But a posy ring *could* be the start of some richer, deeper relationship with a man.

"I don't see you wearing it," said Carolina, studying her sister's thin ringless fingers.

"I—I'm wearing it around my neck," admitted Virginia. She touched a thin golden chain that disappeared down into her bodice. "I don't want Mother to know I'm still wearing it. Not after what happened."

"What happened?" Carolina was almost afraid to ask.

"Mother didn't approve of Damien. She said he was a rake and a wastrel but"—Virginia's voice grew muffled, almost disappeared—"I loved him."

"What happened to him?" asked Carolina in alarm.

"He offered for me," said Virginia sadly and Carolina held her breath. *Surely her forceful mother hadn't deliberately frightened the fellow away, surely even Letitia—wrapped up in other things—must have seen how much Virginia needed someone!*

"She made you refuse him?" ventured Carolina.

"Oh, no. She said since I wanted Damien so much she would not stand in my way."

"Then—" Carolina was bewildered because Fielding would never have disputed the match had Letitia been for it. "Are you saying *you* didn't accept Damien?"

"Of course I accepted him!" Virginia's voice that had been so weak now took on power and with it a quivering sense of pain. *"I loved him!"*

"Then—then what went wrong?" Carolina said, alarmed at the terrible intensity of her sister's blue eyes, darkening with remembered grief.

"It was only my dowry he was after," Virginia told her with a terrible simplicity. "When Damien learned there wasn't going to be any dowry, when he learned how deep in debt Father was, he went away without saying good-by. He just disappeared, Carol. And he's never even written to me."

Carolina felt her eyes smarting. "Take that posy ring from around your neck, Virgie," she choked. "And throw it in the fire!" Her gray eyes were stormy. "Don't wear it another minute!"

"It isn't the ring that's at fault." Virginia wasn't looking at her now. Her gaze was on some distant remembered hell. "It is me." Her voice took on a kind of sing-song litany. "I wasn't pretty enough for him, you see. Damien liked pretty women." She gave a soft discordant laugh with no mirth at all in it. "He'd have loved *you*," she said bitterly. "He wouldn't even have asked for a dowry for *you*. But plump little me—!"

"You're *not* plump!"

"I was then," said Virginia sadly. "And so I thought —I thought if only I were *thinner,* more like you and Mother and Penny, that maybe someone *would* fall in love with me. For myself, I mean." Her voice had fallen to a whisper. "But it didn't happen," she added wistfully, and her head bent like a fallen flower. "And now I know it's never going to happen. Ever."

Carolina couldn't speak. Her throat had closed up.

So Virginia was starving herself to death because some fortune hunter had betrayed her!

Now Carolina understood why her mother had acted so strangely this morning when Carolina had questioned her about Virginia. Letitia wouldn't face the fact that she had a daughter starving herself to death because if she'd been thin she might have been able to hold onto the fellow! The man wasn't good enough for Virginia and Letitia knew that, but Virginia loved him and so she had reluctantly given her consent—and *then* he had abandoned Virginia because of Fielding Lightfoot's inability to provide a dowry! It had been too much for a proud woman like Letitia. She would not admit even to herself that her daughter's health was failing, indeed that she might never see another winter.

"You see," explained Virginia gently, as if she were speaking to a child, "it wasn't just *one* man who didn't love me—it was all three of them: Hugh, who ran away with me to the Marriage Trees but when we were caught, turned to someone else. Algernon, who married me because his mother wanted him to. And now Damien, who was only after the money I didn't have. . . ."

She sounded so forlorn it caught at Carolina's heart. "If it will make you feel any better," she said steadily, "you're not the only one who was jilted. You remember Lord Thomas?"

"Oh, yes. I was afraid to ask you about him when you arrived with a new man in tow."

"Lord Thomas jilted me," said Carolina calmly. "Perhaps it will comfort you to know that."

Virginia was looking at her round-eyed; her large dark blue eyes seemed like black spots in her pallid face. "I can't *believe* it, Carol!" she gasped.

"Well, it's true," asserted Carolina. "I loved him so much I thought I would die of it but"—she shrugged—"as you can see, I got over it. And found a better man." She waited while that sank in on Virginia. "And it's obvious that Emmett really didn't care for Penny or he'd make some effort to find her. And Mother—" She hesitated.

Virginia looked up alertly. "What about Mother?"

Carolina took a deep breath. She would never tell Virginia this except in the hope of saving Virginia's life. "We're only half sisters, Virgie," she said quietly. "I am Sandy Randolph's daughter."

Virginia took a deep breath and expelled it slowly. "So *that's* why . . ."

"That's why Fielding hates me and Sandy usually avoids me. And why people look at me as they do—and mutter behind their fans. But you mustn't let on that you know. Mother doesn't even know that I know. I only told you so you'd see that Mother—as beautiful and as devastating as she is—has trouble where men are concerned. You don't have a corner on that kind of trouble, Virgie!"

With the words she silently proffered Virginia the bowl of soup. Virginia ignored it. She was looking almost in disbelief at her beautiful sister.

"But—but you and Mother have had trouble with only *one* man," she pointed out at last. "And there was another right there to take his place. But with me"—she gave a helpless shrug—"I used to dream at night that I'd end up like the heroines of the books I read: married—and happy. To someone who would love me madly. And now I know that no one is ever going to love me." Her face looked pinched and sad.

Carolina ached for her. She fought back the feeling. "Virgie," she said sensibly, "there are *hundreds* of men in this world who could love you. All you have to do is meet them. Meantime, if you don't eat this soup I'm going to overpower you and pour it down your throat!"

To her astonishment, Virginia bent meekly to Carolina's stronger will. She began feebly spooning up the soup. Carolina sat and watched her.

It seemed to her as she watched that life was like a ride in a jolting coach. Virginia's coach had lost a wheel and she wanted to get off—she wanted death to rescue her from life. . . . Carolina shivered, thinking of Tortuga and the buccaneers, of men she had seen die. Death reached you soon enough without whipping the horses to make the coach go faster!

"I really think you should have another bowl of soup," mused Carolina when Virginia had finished.

From the bed Virginia shuddered. "I'd throw up!"

Confronted by a situation she'd never met before and where no one seemed able to guide her, Carolina hesitated. "All right," she agreed at last. "But I want you to forget all this mooning about. I'll be back in an hour with more nourishment. I'm determined to take you to England with me and you can't go unless you build up your strength! Did I tell you," she added soberly, "that Essex is just *bursting* with eligible men?" It might not be quite true but it was important for Virginia to think so. She had to have something to hold on to, to look forward to! "You're *sure* to find someone you like," she added firmly.

"Oh, I've had no trouble finding those *I* like," said Virginia bitterly. "It's just that *they* didn't care for *me!*"

"You'll find someone who likes you in Essex," Carolina promised solemnly. "Remember, I've seen them for myself!"

Virginia gave her a derisive look but there was a little color in her cheeks now, Carolina noted.

"Besides, we're all invited to a ball at Fairfield a fortnight from now," Carolina told Virginia, hoping it sounded enticing. "You must get up your strength if you're going dancing!"

"Mother will think I shouldn't go," Virginia said with a sigh. "Too tiring. She said that the last time we were invited to a ball. And so of course I didn't go."

Too tiring? Or did proud Letitia want to keep the world from seeing what her jilted daughter looked like? Was she putting off Virginia's re-entry into the world until she looked more able to face it? But that might never be!

"Nonsense, of course you'll go!" Carolina felt her indignation rising. How could her family let Virginia slip away from them like this? How could she herself have been so fatalistic a short time before, with Rye? Virginia had had several tragic experiences but this was not the end for her—she, Carolina, *wouldn't let it be!*

"All right, I'll go." Virginia sighed, as if she wasn't up to arguing. "If I'm up to it."

And when Carolina, true to her promise, came back upstairs an hour later wearing a grim expression and carrying a silver porringer containing hot gruel and a glass of milk, Virginia sat up and ate almost half of it and drank all the milk.

"You'll have your hands full keeping the girls at the ball from flirting with Rye!" she told Carolina with a flash of her old self.

"They can flirt all they choose." Carolina laughed, happy that Virginia had not had to be coaxed to drink the milk.

"Yes, but suppose he flirts back?"

That was a possibility Carolina had not considered. On Tortuga she had had no cause to be jealous of the flaunting bawds who swarmed the waterfront—women whom Rye had largely ignored. And he had, she remembered, shown no interest other than friendship in Katje, his handsome young housekeeper, although she had never been sure how Katje felt about him.

"He won't flirt with them," she said confidently.

"Want to make a small wager?" Virginia said with a chuckle from the bed.

"Food has given you a wicked tongue!" chided Carolina, delighted to find a spark of life left in her sister. "Get some sleep and digest that gruel—I'll be back with more for dinner and then a late snack—*and you are going to eat it, Virgie, make up your mind to it!*"

"You sound like Mother," murmured Virginia. She executed a mock salute. "Yes, Colonel! Your troops will obey!"

Carolina smiled at her but she thought she had best not stay lest she wear Virginia out. For leaning back against the pillows, Virginia had begun to look tired and pale again.

She closed Virginia's door softly behind her and met Rye as she started downstairs.

"Where were you?" he asked. "I've been looking for you."

"I have decided to bring Virgie back from the dead," announced Carolina in a vigorous voice. "She's been starving herself because some fortune hunter jilted her. Pining away because she thinks no one loves her! And everybody's been letting her go downhill! *Well, I won't!*

I'm going to move a cot into her room and make sure she eats almost hourly!"

Rye gave her a fond look. "Ever intemperate!" he murmured. "But I love my headlong wench." He pulled her to him for a long kiss, savoring the sweet touch of her lips, the flutter of her breast as his hands roved down her back.

"Rye—we're on the stairs," she protested breathlessly. "Anybody who comes into the hall below can see us!"

"Let them!" he said hoarsely. "I must take what crumbs I can from your table, now that I've been moved next door to your mother."

Laughing, Carolina tried to pull away. "Oh, there's another advantage to moving in with Virgie that I haven't told you. Her room is closer to yours and her door never squeaks like mine does! And Virgie's very discreet—she knows I spent last night with you but she'll never tell!"

"Minx!" He laughed, but he let her pull away from him and followed her down the stairs.

Chapter 4

Carolina went down the wide stairway to discover that Ralph Wormeley had been persuaded to stay to luncheon. Ralph was good company and the conversation was spirited as they all sat down to a hearty meal of steaming pumpkin soup, fat Chesapeake Bay oysters, sturgeon and wild rice and Sally Lunn bread and hominy pudding.

"Had we known you were coming, sir, we would have prepared a great tart," said Letitia, who got on famously with broadminded Ralph Wormeley. She had changed into an amethyst taffeta gown for lunch, and the ruffles at her elbows rustled faintly as she talked. "As it is, you have got an impromptu meal set before you!"

"Ah, but who could fault this Damson trifle?" he cried merrily as a smiling serving girl in a white apron brought in a handsome dessert of spongecake soaked in brandy and loaded with Damson plum jam topped with custard and swirls of vanilla-flavored whipped cream. "Or this wondrous dark fruitcake? Impromptu indeed!

Mistress Lightfoot, I marvel at your culinary wizardry!"

"Rye cannot hope for food like this in Essex—when we are established there," sighed Carolina.

"Perhaps Carolina's mother can be persuaded to visit us there and impart her culinary skill," said Rye gallantly.

Letitia laughed but Carolina, watching her, knew she was pleased for in the Tidewater her mother had never been considered much of a housewife—a mirror of fashion, yes, a sparkling wit, yes, and a good manager —perhaps a better manager than the agent Fielding employed. But a housewife—no.

"My mother is a woman of many talents," Carolina said, leaning toward Ralph Wormeley. "Just now she is showing me how a big wedding should be managed."

"And a beautiful bride you will be," he told her warmly, his approving gaze encompassing her slate-blue broadcloth gown so heavily trimmed in black braid.

When lunch was over Carolina promptly excused herself to see if she could not get at least some pumpkin soup and nourishing oysters into Virginia. But she found her asleep. Lying there in the big bed, Virginia looked so tired, with blue circles from sleeplessness under her eyes, that Carolina could not bear to wake her. Instead she set the food down. Virginia would find it when she waked—and perhaps eat a few bites.

Carolina stood silently contemplating her sister. In the warm room with its roaring fire Virginia had thrown back the green and white coverlet. Curled up childishly, her too-thin form looked young and very vulnerable.

Virginia never quite grew up, divined Carolina, looking down at her sister tenderly. *She fell in love, she ran away, she married, she conceived a child, she lost her husband and then her lover—and yet her viewpoint is still that of a child. I used to think she was shallow but it isn't that. She has never really accepted responsibility for her own life. And now, childishly, she is going to strike back at life for disappointing her—by leaving it.*

Lest Virginia grow cold when the fire burned lower, Carolina gently pulled up the coverlet.

Virginia needed help. But how to help her? Virginia was a romantic. She yearned to have some gallant swooning at her feet for love of her.

Carolina had known someone else who had yearned for something—and had tried to achieve it. Auburn-haired Reba Tarbell, her roommate at Mistress Chesterton's School for Young Ladies in London, had yearned to be a marchioness—and lost her virginity in a wild attempt to reach her goal. And Reba too had been left by the wayside.

Carolina's head went up. She didn't know exactly how she was going to accomplish it but Virginia wasn't going to be left by the wayside! Not if *she* had anything to say about it!

Quietly Carolina stole out, closing the door behind her.

As she was returning downstairs, through a window she glimpsed a yellow barge coming upriver. Yellow . . . Sandy Randolph had a yellow barge. Guessing that he might have come to discuss Rye's pardon for buccaneering, she hurried downstairs and made a dimpling entrance into the drawing room where they all sat on comfortably overstuffed furniture and sipped after-dinner wine.

"I have come to borrow this gentleman from your company," she told them, smiling as she indicated Rye. "For he has not yet seen the rose garden Mother planted and I would have him see how nicely it is laid out before the snow comes in earnest." She cast a significant look out at the grayness of the sky above trees still dusted with yesterday's fall.

"We must hurry," she told Rye when they reached the hall. "I thought I saw Sandy Randolph's barge coming upriver and we'll want a private word with him before he reaches the house—we might not get a good chance later."

"Perhaps he won't be stopping," suggested Rye as he helped her on with her tall pattens and adjusted her red velvet cloak about her shoulders. "Perhaps he's going on."

"Oh, of course he'll stop! I know what you're thinking but there's never been any open break. And remember, Sandy's a cousin."

Rye shrugged and took her out the front door, apparently to tread the winter-bleak paths of the rose garden her mother had so meticulously laid out. Their walk took them past the windows where her parents sat entertaining Ralph Wormeley. As the yellow barge tied up at the wharf below, they left the fashionable geometrical pattern of mounded roses and boxwood to hurry down the slippery lawn half glazed with ice. Carolina had her slate-blue skirts tucked up, and her white chemise ruffles fluttered around her flying legs. With her scarlet cloak blowing, she made an attractive vision of red, white and blue that the men from the barge noted appreciatively.

Twice she slipped but both times Rye's strong arm beneath her elbow held her footing for her as, taking long strides, he dug his booted heels into the slippery surface. *I wonder if he has ever fought on an icy deck in the sleet,* she thought suddenly, and decided that he had not. *His* battles had been fought beneath the blazing tropical sun of the Caribbean or in the soft dangerous darkness of the Spanish Main with the trade winds blowing death toward him.

"I marvel that you can keep your footing on this stuff!" she gasped.

"One learns—in Essex," he told her laconically, and she flashed him a smile for his words had reminded her that when he was growing up he might have tramped through a bit more snow than she!

They had not reached the pier before Sandy Randolph, a handsome figure in orange tawny and a gold-trimmed cloak, and sporting a silver-headed cane, was hurrying across the pier toward them.

"What news?" asked Rye curtly for he detected a certain tension in their visitor that even the brilliant smile Sandy gave his daughter could not hide.

"The governor is gone to Barbados and will not be returning to Williamsburg for some time," Sandy told them. He was not wearing a hat against the weather and his hair, even on that gray day, seemed to have a glow—a perfect match for Carolina's own misty blonde locks.

"We already knew that," said Rye.

"But Mother says he is expected any day!" protested Carolina.

Sandy shook his head. "Word arrived this morning that the governor's mother has been taken ill. No one knows the seriousness of her condition but it is plain that he will be detained on Barbados for some time. And that," he added bluntly, "holds up everything, for I do not trust the lieutenant governor."

Rye looked thoughtful, but Carolina cried, "Why not?"

"He is deep in debt," explained Sandy with a frown. "Hard pressed by his creditors."

The full meaning of that crashed in on her and her face whitened. *He was telling her that Rye—pounced on in the night and spirited away—could be sold to Spain for forty thousand pieces of eight!*

"But—but surely he would not—?" she gasped.

"No, I do not think he would," said Sandy, seeing how his words had upset her. "But when a man's back is to the wall, it is best not to dangle salvation before his nose and expect him to ignore it!"

"Well, no one here knows Rye is a buccaneer," said Carolina quickly. "I think Mother and Virginia have guessed but they would never tell."

"No," said Sandy quietly. "Letitia would never tell."

Somehow his confidence in her mother buoyed her up. "It must not appear that you came here to see Rye," she cautioned Sandy as they strolled back to the house over the crisp slippery ground. "I mean"—she blushed—"I had to tell Mother that we all returned from England on the same ship but it must not seem that we are—conspiring," she finished unhappily. She was worrying about the effect on Fielding, and Sandy guessed her thoughts.

"Oh, I have a good reason for stopping here," he told her grimly, looking up at the massive expanse of Level Green stretching out before him—a baronial expanse. Fielding Lightfoot's American barony. He turned to Rye. "'Tis indeed a good thing you did not come prancing in announcing yourself to be Captain Kells, here to claim the king's pardon—for Fielding Lightfoot is a close friend of the lieutenant governor and might have seen nothing amiss in mentioning your true identity to him!"

Rye shot him a look. Fielding Lightfoot was also deep in debt and desperate for money.

Carolina did not catch the inference. Telling herself there could be no danger so long as Rye's true identity was not known, she had recovered her aplomb. "But since no one knows Rye is also Kells, we can all go where we like," she said lightly. "Including the ball at Fairfield to which you will doubtless be invited!"

The two men exchanged glances above her head.

"You might be asking too much, Carolina," said Sandy bluntly. "Many a trader comes to these shores who has also visited Tortuga."

"I will take Carolina to the ball," said Rye, "since she desires to go."

"Let us hope your men anchored outside Yorktown do not drink too much or wench too much and as a result talk too much," muttered Sandy.

"They will not," Rye assured him grimly. "They have as much to lose as I have."

Their lives, thought Carolina with a sinking feeling. "Perhaps we should make some excuse and not attend the ball," she said in a troubled voice.

"No, I am taking you to the ball," Rye said flatly.

She skidded along between the two men, telling herself that anyone could surely seek a pardon for past deeds now that there was a general amnesty declared to all who sought it. Or could they? Must one give one's self up in order to be pardoned? She did not know.

Before she could voice further doubts they were going into the great hall and a servant hurried forward to take their cloaks. Then Carolina was ushering their guest into the drawing room where Fielding Lightfoot rose and drawled a cold welcome to his wife's "favorite" cousin.

"Good day to you, Fielding." Having bowed to his hostess, Sandy hardly glanced at Letitia, who was regarding him with a smiling stillness in her dark blue gaze. "I am afraid I have stopped by to speak to this gentleman"—he nodded toward Ralph Wormeley—"and thus save myself a journey to his house. I wanted to thank you, Ralph, for coming to Estelle's defense in my absence."

Letitia stopped the motion of her fashionable ivory fan in midair and regarded Sandy intently. Estelle was Sandy Randolph's wife—the madwoman of Tower Oaks, the woman he could not divorce.

"Well, I could not have the Bramways calling her a witch," retorted Ralph Wormeley mildly. "To say that she had cast a spell upon their tobacco—and to say it at the Raleigh!" His eloquent shrug spoke volumes.

"Essie too would thank you if she could," Sandy said moodily. "But she is presently confined to her bed with one of her migraines. As it is, I thank you on her behalf."

Carolina knew that Estelle's bouts of madness were always passed off as "migraines"—which seemed appropriate for she was said to be prone to clutch her head and moan and scream about the pain.

Ralph Wormeley acknowledged this tribute gracefully. "I was about to take my leave," he said diplomatically, noting the growing tension of his host. "Would you care to accompany me home to Rosegill, Sandy? You have recently been in London and I need some advice concerning my London agent. I have heard ugly rumors about him and you might have a suggestion for me as to a new one."

"Perhaps I do," said Sandy. "So, ladies, if Ralph is

leaving I will take my leave as well. Fielding, by your leave?"

"Oh, don't let me detain you, Randolph," said his host with a slight edge to his voice. At his wife's sudden frown, he added, "I realize how delicate a matter it is to secure the proper agent."

"Who was it who accused Estelle of witchcraft?" Letitia's clear voice rose above their farewells.

The elegant figure in orange tawny turned toward her and Sandy Randolph drank in the sight of the tall commanding woman who stood before him. His silver eyes softened as always at sight of her. Letty . . . *his* Letty. Even though she had shared a roof these years past with Fielding Lightfoot, he would always think of her as his.

"Duncan Bramway's wife Amanda," he said tersely.

Letitia caught her breath. Amanda Bramway was the beautiful brunette Fielding Lightfoot had once been expected to marry—before she had stolen him away from her. This September past Amanda Bramway had married her cousin Duncan Bramway and gone to live in Bramble Folly, his small estate on the James that adjoined Tower Oaks. "Amanda Bramway!" She muttered the name like a curse.

"Just so," said Sandy Randolph. His handsome face—scarred long ago by his mad wife's knife-wielding hand—betrayed no expression at all.

Letitia's did. Her dark blue eyes had gone stormy. "Fielding, you have kept this story from me," she murmured. And then to Sandy, "Tell me more of what Amanda Bramway said," she commanded.

"I am told she regaled the entire Apollo Room with an account of how last summer poor Essie had come to her in a dream and announced that she was running through their tobacco fields by night, cursing every stem! And that she had leaped up and peered out of her bedroom window and seen Essie there in the moonlight running through the tobacco plants in her nightdress!"

"At that point I felt I must intervene," said Ralph Wormeley. "Amanda may have seen someone running about, but certainly not Estelle. I pointed out with some heat that Estelle was doubtless locked safely away the whole time, for Randolph here would have left strict orders that the house be kept locked by night for her protection."

"As of course you did!" cried Letitia. "And what did Amanda say to that?"

"She replied," Sandy told her through his teeth, "that Essie, being a witch, could have gone through a locked door quite easily!"

Letitia swung around to Ralph Wormeley. "And what did *you* say to that?"

"I said that she must have dreamt it all, that the whole tale was ridiculous on its face—Duncan Bramway's tobacco fields are hidden from his house behind a grove of trees and lie in the wrong direction to be seen from their bedchamber—which I know for a fact, having been a guest at Bramble Folly no longer than a fortnight ago!"

"But she had an answer for that, didn't she?" guessed Letitia, turning her narrow gaze upon Sandy.

"Yes, she did," he told her stonily. "She said that on the night in question she had been indisposed, and so as not to disturb Duncan by her turning and tossing, she had sought another bedroom on the side of the house toward the tobacco fields. She said that the trees had been swept bare of leaves and that she had seen Estelle in the moonlight wandering through the fields just as in her dream."

"And I am sure that even if all that is disproved,

Amanda will invent fresh lies to shore up her accusation," murmured Letitia. "She will say that it happened on some other night, or that she has seen Estelle do this more than once, that she slipped out of the house and went stealthily over the dark lawn and observed her from behind a tree!" She shot Fielding a glance. "Why have I not heard of this before?"

Fielding looked uncomfortable.

"Probably because I managed to silence her," sighed Ralph Wormeley, taking a pinch of snuff. "At least I hope I did. I told Duncan that no gentleman would accuse a neighbor's wife of such a thing in his neighbor's absence. And at that he had the grace to quiet Amanda." He closed his enameled snuffbox with a snap.

"Well, Randolph is now back, Letitia, and he can deal with his own problems," said Fielding, eager to see the door close behind his rival.

"Indeed I am, and indeed I will," said Sandy. His light gray eyes glittered and he fingered the hilt of his sword lovingly.

He is going to call Duncan Bramway out! thought Carolina with a little thrill of unease. Her mother's next words told her that Letitia was of the same opinion.

"Have you spoken to Duncan Bramway and told him that Amanda should be restrained from spreading such unfounded tales?" she demanded.

Sandy Randolph gave her a steady look. His expression was a daunting one. "I tried to. I hailed his barge and he waved me off, called out that he had nothing to say to me."

"How infamous!" Letitia's slim figure stiffened at this further affront. "And what did you do then?"

"I rammed his barge," said Sandy calmly, and Rye Evistock hid a grin. An experienced buccaneer—which

83

Sandy Randolph was—should have no trouble in downing a wallowing river barge!

"Good God!" cried Fielding Lightfoot.

And Ralph Wormeley exclaimed, "Did he drown?"

"No." There was a note of regret in Sandy's voice. "I saw him swim to shore and crawl out—shaking his fist. I was some way downriver by then. All aboard made it," he added, and Ralph Wormeley's expression lightened.

"Amanda Bramway, I take it, was not on board?" There was a glint in Letitia's eyes.

"No. I'd not have rammed the barge had there been women aboard."

"Too bad," murmured Letitia with a shake of her head. "*I* would have had no such qualms!"

"Being a woman," he said, and smiled at her.

But she was not to be seduced into regarding the situation with humor. "You had best start carrying a pistol, Sandy," she advised. "And give Bramble Folly a wide berth."

"Oh, come now!" expostulated Fielding. "Duncan Bramway's no savage! He won't lie in wait for Randolph here and ambush him!"

"Who knows what anyone will do?" Letitia said lightly. "Be on your guard, Sandy!"

He nodded gravely, and his gaze as he took his leave was wistful when it rested upon her. She should have been his, this gallant lady, *would* have been his save for a cruel twist of fate. . . .

"Letitia, you are not to meddle in this!" cried her husband, vexed, when their guests had cleared the door and were seen to be sauntering down the lawn. His dark brows met in exasperation. "This quarrel is between Duncan Bramway and Sandy Randolph."

Letitia shrugged her taffeta-clad shoulders. "'Tis not my quarrel," she declared cheerfully, her gaze following Sandy as he swung away from the house. "I but counseled Sandy as I would have counseled you—to have a care. Amanda Bramway is a dangerous woman and her husband is too big a fool to realize it!"

Fielding snorted. "I doubt she will shoot Randolph!"

His wife ignored that. "Did we not hear that Amanda Bramway has gone to Williamsburg for the birth of her niece's first child, Fielding?"

He nodded.

"To that tiny house on Botetort Street?" exclaimed Carolina, startled. "I wonder that they could squeeze her in!"

"Yes, and now with cousins visiting from England, there must be at least sixteen people crowded inside," agreed her mother.

"Oh, Amanda will no doubt be staying round the corner at the Raleigh," said Fielding indifferently. "Amanda couldn't stand to be crowded in like that, with her—"

"Delicate sensibilities?" suggested his wife with a dangerous smile.

"With her dislike of feeling confined!" exploded Fielding. "You have heard her say yourself that she feels trapped like an animal in that small house at Bramble Folly."

"Oh, I'm sure Amanda would be *far* happier in a large house," said Letitia with an edge to her voice. "This one, for instance."

Carolina, hearing that note in her mother's voice, thought suddenly, *She is jealous! Jealous of what Fielding might still feel for Amanda Bramway!* And suddenly she appreciated, as never before, her mother's predicament.

It was Letitia's misfortune to love them both: elegant Sandy with his easy smile and tarnished reputation, and unpredictable, spendthrift Fielding who would have fought the world for her.

Carolina's gaze rested on her beautiful mother for a moment with heartfelt sympathy. Life had trapped her!

Fielding's lowering gaze was also upon his wife. "Damme, Letty, can't we talk about something else?" he burst out, running his fingers angrily through his dark hair. "And not go on about Amanda Bramway all day?"

"I am entirely through discussing Amanda Bramway," Letitia said calmly.

But it was no surprise to Carolina when the next morning her mother announced at breakfast that she must go to Williamsburg to take a look at Aunt Pet's property in her absence. And—since Rye had not seen Williamsburg and Carolina had been gone for such a long time that it would be a treat for her too—she was going to take them all with her. "Including Virginia," she added firmly, with a glance at Virginia, who, feeling stronger, had trailed down to breakfast.

Carolina shot a worried look at Rye but his saturnine face was imperturbable.

Fielding, however, looked up from his eggs and corncakes which had been fried in an iron frying pan with legs called a "spider" since it crouched spiderlike over the hot coals. His expression was one of surprise. "But Petula's property is being well looked after," he protested. "You had a report on it not four days ago!"

From across the table Letitia favored him with a vague smile. "Yes, but I've had a premonition about it since. Last night I dreamt of falling chimneys and you'll remember we *did* have high winds just before the snow fell. Suppose some roof slates have blown loose? Rain could come in and ruin her furnishings! No, I must go."

Briskly. "Petula would not forgive me if I let anything happen to her house. And besides," she added dismissively, "there is the material for Carolina's wedding gown to be searched for in Williamsburg—or had you forgotten about that?"

Her husband groaned.

"We're going to Williamsburg!" Della cried rapturously from down the table.

"No, you and Flo are going to stay here—with nurse. Just Carolina and Rye—and Virginia, of course, who is looking much better today—are going with us."

Above the clamor of the younger children's protests, Carolina, just spooning Damson preserves onto her hot corncakes, asked, "Where will we stay?"

"At the Raleigh," said her mother distantly. "I wouldn't want to open up Petula's house just for an overnight stay."

"It looks like snow," observed Fielding gloomily, glancing out the window at a milky sky. "There may not be a room to be had at the Raleigh, for if it snows, those who are already in town will remain there."

"Nonsense," was the airy response. "I've already sent a servant riding to Williamsburg to tell them to expect us, that we will be there in time for supper."

"Letitia," Fielding grumbled to the world in general, "seems to expect everything to fall into place for her. *What if there are no rooms to be had at the Raleigh?*"

Letitia gave him a scathing look. "There will be," she said confidently.

Virginia and Carolina exchanged mirthful glances. They knew—if Fielding did not—why their mother was always so confident of securing a room. In a day of rigid price controls with the cost of accommodations set by law, she would have sent a servant ahead with a healthy tip—enough gold to make it feasible for an innkeeper to reshuffle his guests' accommodations or even to boot out some slow payer to make room for the Lightfoots.

Carolina's silver-gray eyes sparkled as she looked at Virginia. With Amanda Bramway already in residence and Letitia and her brood about to arrive, she felt there well might be a bit of excitement at the Raleigh!

PART TWO

Sparks Fly at the Raleigh!

You want my husband, do you?
Each hour your love grows stronger?
You'd last with him five minutes—
And not a moment longer!

THE RALEIGH TAVERN
WILLIAMSBURG, VIRGINIA

WINTER 1689

Chapter 5

True to Fielding Lightfoot's gloomy prediction, the snow began falling from a fleecy sky before they were halfway to Williamsburg. By the time they had reached the outskirts of the town it was descending at such a rate as almost to blind the coachman.

"Flakes like snowballs," was Fielding's disgruntled comment as he lifted the leathern flap that covered the window beside him to peer out as the first houses appeared, their gambrel roofs and tall brick chimneys dimly seen through a curtain of white.

"Large flakes mean the snow will soon stop falling," scoffed Letitia, clutching her seat as the carriage rocked violently from side to side over a road whose ruts were becoming obscured by snow. She was wearing her best plum velvet cloak trimmed in beaver and beneath it her best gown—of supple violet velvet over a rustling lavender silk petticoat.

Virginia had protested at the sight. "I can't believe it—you're wearing your best gown for a long ride in a coach?"

"If the weather's as bad as your father predicts, we'll

arrive late and there'll be no time to dress for dinner," said her mother dismissively. "We should all be dressed to dine."

And dressed to dine they were.

Carolina, who had brought little ashore with her for she had expected her stay in the Tidewater to be short, was wearing one of the gowns she had left behind her at Level Green—a crystal-encrusted pale ice-green velvet with an elegant figure-hugging bodice that wondrously outlined her firm young breasts. The wide velvet skirts, split down the front, had been drawn over her knees in the cold coach but before dinner they would be artfully swept back into puffed panniers over each hip, the better to display her rippling ice-green satin petticoat. And over all was a French gray velvet cloak trimmed with fluffy black fox.

Virginia too was a marvel. She had pleaded to be allowed to wear her warmest brown woolen for the cold drive but her mother had been adamant. Virginia could wear all the warm woolen petticoats she owned, but above them would be one of gleaming amber silk, and above that a striking gown of bronze cut velvet trimmed in acres of copper lace, and above that a bronze velvet cloak, fur lined. Topping all that off, in her effort to keep warm, Virginia had borrowed a red fox hood and muff from Carolina.

"I'm always cold now," she had explained as she snatched up a woolen blanket to wrap around her feet in the coach.

And Carolina had urged on her the hood and muff, and had cannily taken along a box of sweetmeats to be taken out by their kid-gloved hands and nibbled in the coach.

The men kept warm in another way: They closed gauntlet-gloved hands around leathern flasks and sipped brandy against the numbing cold. They were more soberly garbed. Both were wearing fashionable dark tricorne hats, each with a feather—but there the similarity ended. For Fielding's bronze-feathered tricorne sat atop a huge black periwig which rested on the shoulders of a voluminous dark brown cloak which occasionally parted to reveal a bronze velvet suit, the coat loaded with gold braid and gold buttons. And brown leather boots.

Rye Evistock's gray-feathered tricorne sat atop his own dark hair, pulled back into a decent queue at the rear and tied with a bit of black grosgrain riband. His clothing was notably somber—indeed the same in which he had arrived: a suit of fine gray broadcloth, the coat of which was of the new narrow-waisted wide-skirted variety, with a slit down the back for riding and slits down both sides for better convenience in grasping a sword hilt; it was modestly trimmed in black braid and sported silver buttons. Black jackboots shone polished against his dark gray trousers. Only the spill of frosty white lace at his cuffs and throat—the latter enlivened by the flash of a single emerald—identified him for the gentleman he was. And Carolina knew he wanted it that way. He wanted to melt inconspicuously into the crowd, an unnoticed stranger visiting the hospitable Lightfoots of Level Green.

Looking at him now, she felt proud. He would far have preferred to ride—as would Fielding—but Letitia had said she would not hear of it, she wanted their company in the coach. His lean face with its saturnine features had maintained a suitable gravity even when Fielding and Letitia had started wrangling in the coach about—of all things—her feather fan, which dangled from her violet leather-gloved wrist.

"Ridiculous!" Fielding had snorted, eyeing it in the

gloom of the coach. "Should be fur-trimmed in weather like this! Why women insist on fanning themselves in dead of winter is beyond me!"

"Nonsense!" retorted his wife. "Fans are as fashionable in winter as they are in summer. I carry a fan with me against—against hot rooms!"

"Hot rooms? Cold rooms, more likely, with frost webbing the windowpanes! And you have one too!" He glared at Virginia.

"Father." Virginia felt called upon to explain, although her mother had actually forced the fan on her. "If you were dancing or sitting too near a roaring fire, and were wearing the tight stays most women wear, which hardly let them breathe at all—"

"Virginia," said her mother sternly, mindful of their guest, whose eyes had brightened, "that will be enough. Ladies do not mention their undergarments in mixed company!"

Virginia had subsided but Carolina, bounced about by the coach, had been convulsed with laughter. Her merry eye had caught Rye's and she had seen a twinkle there but he had maintained an impassive countenance, even though she guessed he had been thinking—as she had—of the lacy undergarments which they had not only discussed at some length but which he had ripped from her back one moonlit night in Tortuga!

Now, as the coach lurched into Williamsburg, she had the flap beside her open and was pointing out the local landmarks to Rye as they lumbered by.

"And there is the mill!" she cried—and stopped, because Virginia's first love had been Hugh, the miller's son at this very mill. "Are we going to drive by Aunt Pet's house to see if it's all right?" she asked hastily.

"No," said her mother shortly. "Whatever is there

today will be there tomorrow. We don't want to be so late as to miss supper."

"Good, I'm starved," said Virginia with a toss of her head. Not that she was, but she wanted Carolina to know that she no longer cared about Hugh!

"I am happy to hear it," said her mother grimly. "I will remind you of those words at supper!"

They were driving along Duke of Gloucester Street now, with the horses pulling hard through deepening snow and the carriage wheels moving soundlessly across a field of white. Thankful to have made it, the coachman pulled up before the white bulk of the many-dormered, green-shuttered Raleigh Tavern. The men alighted and helped the ladies down to scuttle through the snow on their tall platformlike pattens.

They came through the Raleigh's painted front door —before which, in better weather, slaves, goods, and even whole plantations were auctioned off—bringing with them such a swirl of snow that everyone turned to look. In the candlelit interior Carolina saw instantly that the Bramways were among those present, indeed just descending the stairs, on their way to a late supper, no doubt.

Standing beside her stocky ginger-bearded husband, who was wincing as he made it downstairs on a cane, Amanda Bramway was not quite the brunette beauty who had once confidently expected to marry Fielding Lightfoot. But she was still a handsome woman. She eschewed the taller hairdos that were coming into popularity as a reflection of the French mode, believing that with her narrow face and large black eyes she looked better with her hair flatter on top and set into bangs with large "spaniel's ear" masses of curls held out by wires to enhance and widen her narrow face. Nevertheless, she was a mirror of fashion in her own

mind. Her sulphur-yellow damask gown, of so heavy a
fabric that it crunched when she walked, cascaded over
what was still a handsome figure—not willowy like
Letitia's but robustly female with ample curves. Her
panniers were pulled back at either side by large ecru
lace rosettes and revealed a deep chrome-green petticoat. Ecru lace sparkling with brilliants wandered
across her deep bosom and her thick black curls were
striped with bands of saffron ribands.

"She looks like a bee alighting on a dandelion,"
whispered Virginia, eyeing Amanda's saffron gown and
green petticoat.

"A yellow jacket," retorted Carolina, remembering
how viciously she had once been stung by one.

Letitia did not appear to see the Bramways, even
though Fielding had gone over to greet them—she was
busy brushing the snow from her velvet cloak. When
she had finished, the Bramways had already disappeared into the Apollo Room.

The landlord hurried over, rubbing his hands together, and Fielding looked relieved to find that the rooms
they had "bespoke" were waiting for them "with fires
already lit." Rye was to share quarters with "a Mr.
Huddleston, a most delightful gentleman from Maryland" but there were two private rooms waiting for the
Lightfoots and their daughters. Carolina cast a distressed look at Rye. She had hoped that he too would
be given a private room so she could slip out and join
him, but it was the custom of the day when inns were
crowded to put two or even three people into a bed
(many of them slept fully clothed anyway, particularly
in this inclement weather) and she knew she could do
nothing about it.

"Come along, girls. Fielding." Letitia marshaled her

brood. "We will join you in the Apollo Room, Mr. Evistock," she told Rye.

"I doubt there'll be room for us in the Apollo Room," demurred Fielding.

But the landlord, still hovering near the entrancing Mistress Lightfoot and her beautiful daughter, heard that. "A table has already been bespoke for you," he beamed, rubbing his fat hands together again. "And will be waiting when you come down."

"Which will not be long," announced Letitia, gathering up her violet velvet skirts and leading the march upstairs after the little serving girl who pattered up ahead of them to show them to their rooms. "You'll have only time to powder your noses."

They barely had time to do that. But Carolina did manage to pin up her velvet panniers into great puffs at each side and to add a burst of ice-green ribands to her high-piled blonde hair—ribands that exactly matched the shining satin of her ice-green petticoat. And Virginia, who spent most of her time combing out the back of Carolina's handsome coiffure and patting stray curls back into place, did find time—at Carolina's insistence —to apply a bit of rouge to her pale cheeks and to touch her lips with Spanish paper.

"Now," said Carolina, as she prepared to open the door and let her sister glide through it, "we will see what Mother has in mind!"

What Letitia had in mind was not immediately apparent. That she intended to dine in the Apollo Room was patently obvious for she bore a straight course for the Apollo with Fielding and her daughters in her wake. Rye greeted them there, in a room aswirl with smoke from the long clay pipes the gentlemen affected. Strong wooden tables scarred by dice boxes had been laid for supper and more than one was still empty—although the Bramways and several friends were already seated at theirs.

The Lightfoots and their guest were led to a table before the hearth where a roaring fire blazed.

"Now do you see why I might need my fan, Fielding?" murmured Letitia, arranging her wide velvet skirts about her. "That fire"—she glanced toward the hearth—"may well blister your back before the night is over."

"'Tis a welcome blaze," he said grimly, eyeing the Bramway party, who were talking and laughing across the room. Carolina guessed that he would prefer to endure the heat rather than to see his wife move any nearer to Amanda Bramway!

Seated beside Rye, she looked up at the motto above the mantel. HILARITAS SAPIENTIAE ET BONNE VITAE PROLES. Merriment and good living there might be here at this table, she thought ironically, but *prudence?* That was sorely lacking!

They dined on scalloped oysters and Welsh "rabbit" and blue crabs and white perch—in all, no less than nine courses. And Carolina told Rye that the enormous "great tart" as well as the Sally Lunn had been baked in the two dome-shaped red brick ovens at the back, behind the Raleigh. Everyone was very merry as they sat in the comfortable candlelit room, watching the snow come down ever more heavily outside—for Letitia's comment had not proved true; the large flakes had turned to little ones and from the windows of the Raleigh one could not see across the street.

Although Carolina's eyes sparkled when some new arrivals at the table next to them gleefully discussed the ramming of the Bramway barge—adding that Duncan

Bramway had turned his ankle on the way home, which accounted for his limp—Letitia did not appear to notice. Fielding Lightfoot relaxed when he saw that his wife seemed to be planning no attack upon her arch rival across the room. Even Virginia was persuaded to eat, although she kept insisting she was already "stuffed." As they ate, the room filled up again, the early diners having gone, and there was the tinkle of ladies' laughter as well as the deeper guffaws of the gentlemen as they quaffed their Madeira and brandy. And then the board was being cleared and the gentlemen settled down to toasting their ladies' eyelashes.

"To the most dazzling lady anywhere—Mistress Carolina Lightfoot!" Rye said recklessly, lifting his glass with a smile at Carolina. "I toast her"—he was looking rather fixedly at the well-displayed tops of her white breasts, and Carolina felt her face pinken and gave him a reproving look—"her eyebrows," he said at last.

"And to that other lovely lady, to whom I am married!" cried Fielding, his good humor reflecting his relief that his lovely lady and that other lovely lady across the room had not come to blows.

They were still drinking that toast when across the smoky room the Bramway party rose to leave. Instantly Letitia, who had been waiting for the right moment—when the room was full of important gentry and the brunette in saffron yellow would be conspicuous by standing—spoke:

"Why, 'tis Amanda Bramway!" she cried in a voice of surprise. "I had not thought to see you here!"

Amanda Bramway's dark head swung about warily and there was a sudden slackening of conversation roundabout, for Letitia's sharply raised voice had cut clearly across the room.

"And why should you be surprised, Letitia," demanded Amanda Bramway, a trace of resentment coloring her voice, "that I should be found dining at the Raleigh?"

"Oh, 'tis not your dining at the Raleigh that surprises me," Letitia said contemptuously. "In times like these, they are forced to accept anyone. What surprises me, Amanda Bramway, is *that you would dare to face me!* And after having *bewitched our tobacco* so that we have hardly had a leaf for shipment! I little wonder that your own tobacco shriveled this summer—your curse has no doubt turned back upon you!"

Beside her, as the first words of his wife's barb were delivered, Fielding Lightfoot had choked on his wine. Now purple of face, he was being thumped on the back by a frightened Virginia.

His wife ignored him. Her attention was centered entirely on her longtime adversary across the room.

The reply was not long in coming. Amanda Bramway's narrow face was thrust forward on her long neck, giving her the appearance of a striking cobra. The big dark clusters of "spaniel's ear" curls swayed as she cried, "*I* bewitched your tobacco? Oh, how dare you? How *dare* you accuse me?"

Letitia had now risen to her feet. She stood there, a regal beauty, swaying in long-stemmed slenderness in her violet velvet gown. Behind her the firelight haloed her fair hair and cast rippling red lights along the soft folds of her gown.

"I accuse you because *you* are the witch who did it!" she cried in a ringing voice. "You came into our house at Level Green in the form of a bat!"

Beside her Fielding found enough voice to choke out the words, "Sit down, Letitia!" then went off into another paroxysm of coughing.

Carolina gave Virginia's foot a slight kick under the table.

Virginia, reacting to that kick, which meant "Come to Mother's aid," stopped beating her father on the back and instead threw herself into the violent exchange between the two older women. "And you left our house in the form of a weasel, Amanda Bramway! I was there and *I* saw you too!"

"And in between, Mother and Virginia *both* told me," cried Carolina, not to be left out, "that once you had flown in through the window as a bat you promptly turned into your real self again and it was *in human form* that you cast a curse upon our tobacco! They said you were standing in our dining room when you did it!"

Rye watched this interchange among the women in fascination. He was reminded of nothing so much as a mother cat, fluffed up and spitting defiance, and her kittens rallying to the mutual defense against danger.

"Oh-h-h-h!" screeched Amanda Bramway, snapping her ivory fan in half in her anger. "To hear such words from a wanton!" She would have broken free from her husband's restraining arm to run across and rain blows upon Letitia, but Duncan—white-faced—held her fast.

"And *you* are not a wanton only because you do not have the opportunity!" Letitia would have come to meet Amanda but Fielding kept a grip on her, despite a spasm of coughing. "But a witch you certainly are—and you will mind your tongue or I will have you up at the next court session not only for witchcraft but for slander as well!"

Half the gentry were on their feet now, staring. Some were shouldering each other to get a better view. The nearest seemed poised to pounce upon these warring women and wrest them apart should their husbands chance to lose their hold on their respective wives (although several would be heard to remark later that they were sorely vexed that Letitia and Amanda had been restrained from bodily combat for they would dearly have loved to see those two spitting cats fight it out!).

But Letitia's last sally was too much for Amanda. Physically held back from lunging at the glamorous woman in violet velvet who was taunting her safely from a distance, Amanda Bramway crouched lower, trying to free herself, and her sulphur-yellow skirts seemed to spread out and stiffen. ("It was as if a purple and white iris had attacked a dandelion," Virginia would report to her little sisters later. "And the dandelion was shaking itself out to do battle!" "Who won?" they would ask in fascination. "Mother won, of course," Virginia would tell them, adding airily, "Doesn't she always?")

But at the moment there seemed to be some doubt as to who would "win." All eyes were focused in fascination on the two women. Save for their piercing voices and Fielding Lightfoot's incessant coughing, there was not a sound in the room. Footsteps could be heard fast approaching as word of the combat spread and servants and guests alike converged to see whatever was going on in the Apollo Room.

"You—dare to insult me so?" Amanda Bramway panted. She was struggling so desperately to free herself from her husband's arms that some of her ecru lace came loose. ("A slightly tattered dandelion," Virginia would later report.)

"Witches must not have such tender feelings," taunted Letitia. ("A swaying long-stemmed purple and white iris. Absolutely *regal*," Virginia would tell them with admiration glowing in her voice.)

Something in the thunderstruck glances of those around her must have communicated itself to Amanda. She realized her danger then, for witchcraft was a serious charge—indeed the unease about witches in general was pervasive throughout the Colonies. Witches had been tried before in Virginia—and would be again. Scenting this danger, Amanda abruptly changed her tune.

"*I* am not the witch," she flung out haughtily. "'Tis our neighbor, Estelle Randolph, who is the witch! Oh, I have forborne to bring charges because the woman *is* a neighbor, but she bewitched *our* tobacco—and no doubt yours as well."

Letitia had been expecting that.

"The witch who changed from a bat into a woman in our dining room wore only a petticoat—nothing else— but she had *your* appearance," she declared in a ringing voice. "Furthermore she had a large brown mole just below her left breast." (Letitia had learnt that from one of her serving women who had years ago worked for Amanda Bramway's parents when Amanda was growing up.) She leaned forward. "Would you care to select three ladies of this company and disrobe in private that they might see that you *do not* have such a mole?"

Amanda fell back, no longer trying to fight free of her husband's grasp. Her face paled.

"Ah, I see that you do have such a mole," purred Letitia. "And since I have never seen you naked, how could I know *that* if you had not appeared in only a petticoat in my dining room?"

"Before leaving as a weasel!" cried Virginia.

All the charges were ridiculous—but nobody laughed. Women had been burned at the stake for less—and all present knew it.

Overcome by rage and frustration, Amanda collapsed sobbing, and her white-faced husband thrust her aside. His ginger wig had been knocked askew as he tussled with his wife, and every hair of his ginger beard seemed to be quivering as he advanced upon Fielding, shaking his large fist. His charge was somewhat marred by a wobbly gait and the fact that he was forced to lean heavily upon his cane with his other hand.

"Come out from behind that table, Lightfoot!" he barked. "'Tis bad enough that ye married Randolph's castoff doxy without ye must come to her aid against honest folk!"

His wavering steps had not brought him halfway across the space that separated them before Fielding, who had got his breath back in him at last, vaulted the table. In his wild charge toward Duncan Bramway, he caught his foot on the leg of a chair that was being hastily pushed back and lunged into Duncan, managing to keep his footing only by seizing Duncan Bramway by the cravat with its thick swatch of lace around his throat. Duncan Bramway's stockier form staggered beneath this assault and he fell back against a table. He lost his grip on his cane as Fielding plummeted into him and would have gone down, taking tablecloth and dishes with him, had not Fielding's death-grip on his cravat and his own clawing fingers on Fielding's coat kept him just barely on his feet.

"I'll not have you insult my wife!" roared Fielding. "Apologize to her at once, or by God, I'll call you out, cripple or no!" He had such a grasp on Duncan Bramway's cravat as he spoke that he was throttling the man. Gasping and unable to speak, Bramway's face was steadily turning purple as he was shaken as a terrier shakes a rat.

By now the whole place was in an uproar. Chairs were overturned in the Apollo Room as gentlemen abandoned their pipes and tankards and wineglasses and laid hands upon the antagonists, dragging them apart.

Bramway, hauled off backwards, had both hands to his throat. He could not speak but wheezed and gasped. Nearby Fielding Lightfoot was being restrained by three or four well-meaning souls whose soothing words were lost in his own roars.

Through this uproar, Letitia Lightfoot made her sinuous way unnoticed in so much commotion. When she reached Duncan Bramway, who was still stroking his throat and gasping for air, she leaned forward.

"I am nobody's castoff!" she cried, and her hand lashed out against his cheek.

With a screech worthy of a banshee, Amanda Bramway lunged at Letitia—and was jerked back summarily by her friends.

In a flash Rye Evistock was beside Letitia.

"Mistress Lightfoot, unless you wish to see murder done this night, I think you'd best desist," he muttered.

Letitia, who had made her point and had got her lick in, flashed him a winning smile.

"Come, girls," she caroled to her daughters. "We must all to bed. You too, Fielding—these Bramways are not worth your attention!"

And she was off on Rye's arm while Carolina and Virginia trailed along after and Fielding Lightfoot's friends urged him forward until they had all reached the stairs, leaving the Apollo Room to the furious Bramways and their friends and observers.

"And that was checkmate," murmured Carolina, watching her elegant mother ascend the stairs with her head high. But her own eyes were misty and she almost missed a step. For Letitia had demonstrated her loyalty to Sandy Randolph once again. Characteristically she had come forward—and saved for him the woman who had, all these years, stood between them.

Chapter 6

But by the time they had reached the head of the stairs, Carolina was seeing the funny side of it all. Letitia had worked out her strategy very cleverly—and had triumphed over her rival. Publicly. And Amanda Bramway would probably be frightened enough that she would beg her husband to forget all about the incident—indeed, Letitia had probably prevented a duel between Sandy Randolph and Duncan Bramway that could have left one of them dead upon the snow. Her spirits soared.

"The gossips will have a field day tomorrow," she whispered behind her hand to Virginia. "They will say the Lightfoots have done it again!

A little wan now from the excitement downstairs, Virginia nodded.

Rye saw Letitia to her door and then walked on with the two girls as a fuming Fielding Lightfoot caught up with his wife and fairly propelled her into their bed-chamber.

"I see that life in the Tidewater has not been dull for you," Rye said conversationally.

Carolina shot him a brilliant smile. "My parents were in their usual form," she declared as they reached their door.

He opened it and Virginia went in. His hand upon her velvet arm detained Carolina.

"I will get rid of Huddleston if I have to fetch him a blow and render him unconscious," he muttered, for Carolina had not been able to pass her mother's door last night since it had been kept ajar.

She gave him a witching look.

"I will knock softly," he promised. "Wait up for me and do not undress for you would be too conspicuous if you were seen in the corridor in your night clothes."

She nodded and went in to watch Virginia make ready for bed.

"Are you going to sit up all night fully dressed?" yawned Virginia as she crawled into bed, for she had not heard Carolina's whispered conversation with Rye at the door.

"I hope not," said Carolina, giving her a bright-eyed look.

"Oh," said Virginia, catching on. "Oh, I see." She sat up. "Would you rather I went back down to the common room? I could dress and go down."

Carolina shook her head. "I thank you, Virgie, for the thought but that would cause comment. People would wonder about it—and Mother would hear. Rye is going to get rid of that man from Maryland who is sharing his room—that Huddleston fellow—somehow."

It took about an hour.

Carolina was on her feet at the first sound of Rye's discreet knock. A moment later she had the door open and had slipped into the hall. There was no one about. On almost soundless slippers she followed him down the hall to his room.

"What did you do with Huddleston?" she demanded as he shut the door behind them and they were alone in a dormered low-ceilinged room.

Rye had gone over to stir up the fire on the hearth. It crackled and sent off sparks. The pattern of its flames cast a glow over the white plastered walls and the bright multicolored quilt of the bed, which was the small room's main furnishing. Through the dormered panes Carolina looked out into the blue-black night and saw the snow still coming down, piling up on the window-sill.

"I got him drunk in the common room," Rye reported over his shoulder. "And it took longer than I thought it would." He stood the poker against the brick fireplace. "*And* I crossed the landlord's palm with gold to keep Huddleston down there snoring till morning."

She dimpled. "What did you tell the landlord?"

"That I was tired and needed sleep—alone in bed."

"Did he believe you?"

Rye laughed. "Hardly. He winked at me."

"Sir," she told him as she moved seductively toward him and twined her slim arms around his neck, "you are compromising my reputation. Indeed I see nothing for it but that you should marry me! Pray latch that door for I do not intend to let you out of here until dawn."

With a laugh he pulled her down on top of him onto the bed. It did not have the enveloping softness of the goose-down feather beds at Level Green—indeed the mattress must have been stuffed with wool, and long use had made it lumpy. But the lovers did not care. Under the rafters or in a summer meadow, it was all the same to them. Carolina, seeing the glowing colors the flickering firelight imparted to that worn old patchwork quilt, thought it gorgeous.

"I've already latched the door, wench! Did ye not see me reach behind me as we came in?"

No, she had been aware only of his dark smiling face bent over hers, the flash of his white teeth, the slight masculine scent of whisky and tobacco and leather that emanated from him as she had pressed close against him coming through that door. . . .

He had lifted his head to nuzzle against her throat, her bosom, and now his eager lips were wandering downward, straining against the top of her bodice—already near its limits in restraining her round young breasts.

"You'll ruin my dress, Rye," she cried breathlessly. "And I've no other to wear!"

"Ah, then we must be very careful, must we not?" With a lithe gesture he rose, sweeping her up with him. Holding her carefully against him as if she might break, he set her on her feet. "Tonight I shall be your lady's maid," he announced. "And I shall begin—so." He pressed a kiss upon the cleavage between her breasts at the base of her low-cut neckline. The flesh below her crystal-encrusted velvet bodice shivered in anticipation. "Perhaps twice," he said thoughtfully—and did it again.

Carolina caught her breath. She could see he was in a playful mood. "You can begin by untying my sleeves," she suggested, trying to keep calm.

"Very well," he said. "First, the sleeves." Skillfully he untied them—for although they matched the bodice, they were separate from it—and as he removed each sleeve, his fingers sought the underside of her upper arm, toyed with her shoulder, advanced upon the white column of her neck.

Carolina gave a gasping laugh and pushed him away. "And now the bodice," she said breathlessly.

"Ah, yes, the bodice." He turned her about and began working the hooks on the back of her bodice, his lean fingers tingling along her spine as he did so.

The bodice came free, falling away at the front, and he whisked it down. Carolina stepped out of it and he tossed the entire gown lightly to a chair before he whirled her about again to face him. His eyes gleamed in the firelight.

"You had best remove those ribands," he said in a rich voice, smiling down at her. "For I intend to run my fingers through your hair."

Carolina's fingers trembled as she hastily removed the burst of ice-green satin ribands from her white-gold hair. She did not know how pretty she looked in the firelight with her soft breasts moving rapidly up and down with her quickened breathing and the firelight glistening up and down the satin of her petticoat, turning pale green to gold. The sight of her delicate breasts winking at him through the sheer fabric of her chemise was almost too much for Rye. He moved toward her and she knew that gesture—he was about to take her.

"My petticoat first," she said quickly, for she had felt a pulse begin to beat responsively in her own throat and she must act quickly if she did not want that petticoat to look in the morning as if it had been slept in! "'Tis—'tis satin, you see. And satin crumples."

"I see," he said gravely. "We must be careful of satin."

"Yes," she said nervously. "It is very delicate."

"So is the skin beneath," he observed as he deftly unfastened her satin petticoat and she stepped out of it. As she did so his open palm grazed her buttocks in her light chemise.

"In such weather, you wear so little," he marveled, surveying the luscious piece of womanhood who stood challengingly before him attired only in stockings, slippers and a sheer chemise afroth with lace.

"Well, some wear flannel petticoats and stays and all manner of things," she admitted shakily. "But not I. I like the feel of sheer cambric against my skin."

"So do I," he said in a husky voice. "And even better do I like the silky feel of your bare skin against my own." He was pulling down her chemise, trying gently to tug it down over her breasts as he spoke.

"It has a riband drawstring," she told him breathlessly. "All good lady's maids know that!"

"And where do we find this drawstring?" he wondered, feeling about her chemise top, pretending to look for it everywhere—although it was tied in a bow in front. As if he could not see that bow, he kept searching, exploring down her back, under her arms, across the soft tingling mounds of her breasts. His gentle fingers moved caressingly around her narrow waist, and the soft skin of her stomach quivered convulsively at his touch.

"It is hidden!" he declared in mock dismay. "What, shall I look for it under here?"

And of a sudden he had lifted her skirts and impudently peeked upward.

Carolina jumped and stepped backward as his dark hair brushed her thigh. She tossed her light chemise skirt away from his head in a frothy billow.

"Stop, you fool, you'll tear my chemise!" she said in

a shaky voice, but her gaze on his dark head, which he lifted to smile at her, was tender.

"Ah, there it is—the lock that unlocks all!" he cried, as if he had just found the satin bow. With a swoop he had untied it and stood back to watch the entire chemise glide down her slim body and collapse in a dainty heap around her trim ankles. "'Tis too cold for you to be standing there clad only in stockings and slippers," he chided her. "We must get the slippers off at once."

He knelt and lifted her left foot and with a quick gesture removed her satin slipper, tossed it to the floor at the corner of the bed. "And now the other." He removed the slipper from her right foot and tossed it to join its mate.

He looked up smiling, seeing her face between the twin peaks of her breasts—and lingered over detaching her garters, his warm hands roving over her thighs, his lips kissing her knees.

"Rye!" she said in a choked voice.

"Ah, there we are!" Expertly he detached the last garter, flung it to join its mate atop the slippers. "And now the stockings, my lady, and we will be ready for bed! On second thought, you're growing cold out here"—for he had felt her slight shiver—"and the stockings may as well be removed in bed with your feet upon me as a bedwarmer!" He picked her up in a single swoop and delivered her to the bed, where he tossed back the multicolored quilt and deposited her on the lumpy mattress.

Carolina leaned back luxuriously and made no effort to draw the quilt or blankets or top sheet over her. The sheets were of raw unbleached muslin—not the fine smooth linen sheets she was used to at Level Green—

but who cared about that? They made a fine back-ground for her pale body and she was well aware of the tempting display she made with her bright hair cascad-ing down over one breast, the other breast revealed and moving rapidly with her breathing. Her bottom had settled down in one of the hollows of the lumpy mattress so that the sides of her hips were almost hidden by the rise of the sheet around her but the silky hair between her legs caught the firelight and seemed to glitter beckoningly. "You have not completed your duties until both garters *and* stockings are removed," she complained seductively.

"Aye, and 'tis all I can do not to remove them at once," he told her. "But to have you entirely naked in my bed might be a sight that would prove too much for me, and I'd fall into bed with my boots on!" He was tugging at one of his jackboots as he spoke. "Damme, they're tight tonight!" he muttered as the boot resisted him.

"Here, I'll help you." Flirtatiously she rose from the bed and presented her naked back to him. "Hold out your leg!" She bestrode the boot, leaning over with her buttocks toward him. "Now push me as I pull!"

"Faith, but it goes against the grain to push these away!" he murmured as, big warm hands against her buttocks, he pushed her body away to help her remove his boot.

She broke free, panting with the jackboot in her hands. "And now the other," she said with a winsome smile.

This time he pulled her to him instead, slid her naked bottom up his thigh until she was seated on his lap and he was toying idly with her breasts, cupping them in his strong hands and tweaking the nipples into hardness as he nibbled her ear.

"It's too cold for this sort of thing out here," she said breathlessly, trying halfheartedly to squirm away from him, for she could feel herself losing control. "Come to bed!"

"That's what I've been trying to do ever since you arrived," he said perversely. "Now I think I'll remove your stockings here on my lap instead." While she squirmed he toyed with the tops of her stockings, tickling her knees and thighs as he did so. And then slowly, slowly he eased her stockings down, bending down to rain kisses on her bare tingling breasts as they descended.

She could feel his hardening manhood against her buttocks, could hear his very real sigh as he put her from him once again to continue disrobing. Once again he deposited her tenderly in the bed and this time she was pulling the covers over her with trembling fingers as she heard his last boot drop.

Moments later he had joined her beneath the sheets and his warm naked body took the chill off a bed that had been left to the cold dampness all day in a room only heated up this evening.

Carolina too was in an impish mood. The confrontation below in the Apollo Room had excited her and when Rye sought to grasp her, she slipped away from him, diving under the coverlet. Rye promptly dived in after her and they found themselves headfirst in a dark tangle of blankets and quilt—and Carolina was gigglingly aware that Rye was nipping at her drawn-up knees. She jumped as his warm lips collided with her inner thighs, and darted away from him in mock alarm.

"We'll suffocate down here!" she gasped, her voice muffled by the stifling bedclothes.

He did not heed her. Instead he took his time, deliberately catching her by a flailing ankle and drawing her back to him like a spider to his innermost web. She found that web a most exhilarating place to be. His lips, his hands were everywhere, caressing, teasing—she could not keep still.

"Rye!" She moved convulsively and gasped as delicious shudders went through her at this sweet assault.

"You want to play?" She heard his muffled laugh. And of a sudden he had turned her over and nipped her bottom smartly, then whirled her about so that—seemingly from nowhere—his manly hardness was between her pulsing breasts.

"Rye!" Carolina fought her laughing way up out of the covers to circle his sinewy neck lovingly with her arms. The bedclothes fell in all directions to the floor. But when he would have made love to her she slipped away again, laughing, to the other side of the mattress.

"My playful lady!" He flipped over on his back, reached out and drew her loved form down on top of him. Panting from her mad exertions, and with her whole body tense and tingling, she rested against the deep throb of his chest and felt the light furring of dark hair graze her nipples as her soft breasts crushed against him. He ruffled her hair. "You like a fight, do you?"

"Sometimes." She moved her head lazily and gave him a gamine smile in the firelight, then nestled closer in his arms, seizing one of his legs in both of hers.

He looked upon her tenderly—and then before she could more than gasp, she was flipped over again and pinned beneath him and his manliness had penetrated her feminine softness with a single deft stroke that brought alive every nerve of her young body.

Now the playfulness was over and his hard body was demanding, searching, strumming her innermost female being to a savage exultation and a deep awareness of senses hidden—hidden deep but overwhelmingly powerful now—senses of which she was hardly aware except during these wild moments in his arms. Their passion seemed as always bright and new. Heady and sweet, it was a river of wine on which they drifted this winter's night in the radiance of summer, and every motion, every half-spoken murmur, was a promise of further delight. On and on they drove each other down that wild river, sweeping through rapids and over falls, ever touching, ever thrilling until their straining bodies seemed melded as one and the river of wine had turned into a river of brandy and intoxicated them, each with the other. Their hair was tangled together, their arms and legs entwined. Outside the snow was falling heavier now; inside the fire on the hearth had burned low—but they were oblivious to all.

And so they were swept on in a last deep surge of desire, then flung at last onto distant shores, only to realize that they were still here in a dormered room at the Raleigh, sharing a lumpy bed before a dying fire—and that their covers had all fallen off.

"I'll stir up the fire." Rye pressed a quick kiss on the crest of Carolina's breast, and got up.

Lazily she watched him from the bed. His lean naked body glowed in the firelight as he prodded the spent logs to life. The fire blazed up suddenly, turning his broad shoulders and narrow hips and powerful thighs to flame. He looked formidable, larger than life, this lover of hers—a man to dream of.

"Come to bed," she murmured, still tingling in the afterglow of passion.

He did so—but not before, gray eyes gleaming, he took a last look at the lovely sight of her, tumbled into the mattress.

"And reach me the quilt," she added languidly, stretching. "I don't seem to have any covers at all!"

But his inspection of her feminine nakedness as she stretched out in the firelight, her pink-tipped breasts glowing rosy, her body gilded, had heated him up again.

"I've a better way to warm you than by quilt," he declared huskily and spread his broad-shouldered form over her again, teasing her deliciously, making the afterglow turn into sighs of desire, and desire flame into passion—causing her every nerve to quiver with delight as he stroked and caressed and teased her slim responsive body. Until once again they were melded as one, tingling and aglow.

Once, in between bouts of lovemaking, they lay there peacefully with the quilt half over them and he stroked her breasts as they talked.

"I have learned tonight that you are your mother's daughter," he said meditatively, stroking the smooth satin with gentle appreciative fingers.

She snuggled up to him, enjoying the quivering delight his roving fingers brought her. "Yes. I was always that."

"And the Bramway woman was standing in *your* dining room when she cursed the tobacco. . . ." he murmured in amusement.

"I was afraid Mother and Virginia were forgetting that if a bat or a weasel cursed our tobacco, they could hardly charge Amanda Bramway with it," declared Carolina, leaning down to nip at his fingers which were just then worrying her right nipple.

"What will happen to her? Amanda Bramway?"

"Nothing will happen to her," Carolina said with a shrug. "Or to Estelle either." She shivered as her shrug caused the fingers of his left hand, which was just then roving over her stomach, to drop lower. "It will be a stand-off—you'll see. Amanda Bramway won't dare to bring witchcraft charges against Sandy Randolph's wife now—she'll be too afraid she'll be charged with witchcraft herself! Mother was just getting Sandy Randolph out of a bad mess. She guessed that he had found me and had brought me back, and she wanted to repay him."

"He might have preferred repayment in other coin," Rye murmured thoughtfully, remembering the open hunger that had flashed in Sandy Randolph's silver eyes when he looked at Letitia.

"Yes. He might." Carolina's voice was suddenly sad. "It is too bad about Sandy and Mother. Sandy is what I guess you would call her 'natural mate.' They think alike, feel alike about things, rise to the same challenges. But I think she truly loves Fielding, too—in a different way. A different way altogether."

"Women," pronounced Rye—as had many a man before him, "are difficult little monsters to understand."

Carolina's laugh gurgled, as much from what he had said as from the sudden tickling in intimate parts that was making her bounce about the bed. "Rye, we mustn't make so much noise!" she gasped. "It's late and the inn's quiet—people will hear us and there'll be talk that you had a woman in your room tonight!"

"And I wonder who they'll think it was?" he said, his lips suddenly pressing down on hers to silence her admonitions, while his lean body swept her away to wonderland.

Later, when they had returned to earth and were mere mortals again, almost drifting off to sleep, when the fire had been banked and the whole world seemed still, she said, "I'm sure you didn't understand but the quarrel really isn't between Sandy Randolph and the Bramways. It's between Mother and Amanda Bramway. You see, Mother was in love with Sandy but she couldn't marry him because he was already married and his wife was mad and he couldn't divorce her. And Amanda Bramway had expected Father to marry *her* but Mother took him away from her. It was a runaway marriage, very sudden—they just dashed off to the Marriage Trees and tied the knot. But Amanda Bramway has never forgiven Mother and she's been a vicious enemy to us all these years. She knows if she hurt Sandy that Mother would feel the pain, so she was just striking back at Mother and using Sandy's mad wife to do it."

"Ah, that makes a difference," he said softly. "It must have cost your mother a deal to come to the defense of the woman who stood between her and her lover."

"Yes," said Carolina. "It must have." She sighed. "But Mother is like that. She wasn't going to let Sandy be hurt by the Bramways—because if his wife really were *accused* of witchcraft—put on trial, I mean, Sandy would storm the jail and take her out, I know he would."

"Yes," said Rye. "I believe he would."

"And then Sandy would be a fugitive and he could never come back here and Mother would never see him again and, don't you see, that's what Amanda Bramway wants? Mother made her unhappy years and years ago and she's never forgotten or forgiven—she's determined that since *she* couldn't have Fielding that Mother shall not have them both—she wants to cost Mother even those little glimpses she still gets of Sandy. Oh, Rye—" Suddenly she clutched him. "Mother and Sandy's story is so *sad*. Think how unhappy they've been all these years! Oh, Rye—" Her voice held a note of panic. "Tell me that nothing like that can ever happen to us!"

His hands, his lips were soothing, his long body curved as if to protect her, and his voice in her ear murmured quite convincingly that nothing so dreadful could ever happen to them.

Somewhere, far off, the gods were laughing. . . .

PART THREE

Candlelight and Wine

Shadows of madness, dusting the hills,
Danger and witchcraft, combing the rills,
Hearts ever breaking, love without frills,
Soul to soul, heart to heart, clashing of wills!

Winter 1689

Chapter 7

Carolina crept back to her room just before dawn and crawled in beside a sleeping Virginia. She woke to find Virginia up and dressed and peering out the window.

"We're snowed in," commented Virginia without turning from the frosted windowpanes. "I went downstairs and heard someone say that the road to Yorktown cannot be negotiated by a coach. I also saw"—she turned to smile at Carolina—"the landlord helping a gentleman upstairs who kept clutching his head and groaning. The landlord called him 'Mr. Huddleston.'"

"Poor Mr. Huddleston," sighed Carolina, stretching luxuriously. "I fear he will have a vast headache this morning from so much overindulgence in wine. Rye drank him under the table last night and left him downstairs in the common room."

"Yes. Well, Mother knows about it," sighed Virginia.

"She what?" Carolina sat bolt upright in bed.

"She was just coming out of her room as the landlord was urging this groaning gentleman down the hall, saying, 'Now, Mr. Huddleston, spending the night downstairs should be enough for ye—'tis not much farther and ye'll be in your own bed.'"

"Oh, dear," cried Carolina, scrambling up. "Now there'll be the devil to pay!"

But there wasn't.

She was just fastening her ice-green satin petticoat about her slender waist when her mother came through the door, fully dressed and pulling on her gloves.

"What, so late abed, Carolina?" she said carelessly. "And yet we were not so late to bed last night!"

Carolina gave her an uneasy look.

"Well, hurry and dress," urged Letitia, "so that you will not keep us waiting."

"Waiting? Where are we going?"

"To Petula's. We're far too crowded here at the Raleigh, and it's too bad to have one of our party put into a room with a total stranger." Her gaze on Carolina was bland. "I've already told the innkeeper we'll be leaving this morning and Fielding is rousing Mr. Evistock now." She insisted on being formal and calling Rye "Mr. Evistock," Carolina noted. "So throw on your clothes and come down."

Carolina already had her dress on and Virginia was working the hooks. "But what about breakfast?" she asked with a look at Virginia, still so painfully thin.

"Virginia shall run down and pick up some hot crumpets and Sally Lunn and a keg of hot cider and we shall all picnic in Petula's kitchen. Along with you, Virginia. I'll finish these hooks."

It was on the tip of Carolina's tongue, once they were alone, to tell her mother about that other not-quite-legal wedding, but her mother kept up a light conversation that brooked no interruption, ending with, "There you are—oh, let your hair alone, your hood will cover it." She tossed Carolina her cloak and started for the door.

"But what of our coach?" cried Carolina.

"Already ordered."

Carolina grabbed up her pattens and followed her mother. Downstairs in the common room, already bustling at this hour, the rest of their party was waiting, Virginia with a large linen square full of some of the hot breads and pastries for which the Raleigh's kitchens were famous. Tall and smiling and looking not the least bit the worse for wear—indeed he might have gotten a full night's sleep instead of a couple of hours—Rye Evistock stood watching them descend the stairs. He set down the keg of hot cider he was holding and helped Carolina on with her pattens.

Fielding had been frowning about him as if looking for Duncan Bramway, and when Letitia told Carolina impatiently they must get started, he warned her, "The horses may get stuck in this snow."

"Nonsense, 'tis but a short way and then they'll be bedding down in Petula's stable!" Imperiously Letitia would have led the way out, ignoring the depth of the snow which had not yet been swept and was deep where it had drifted against the inn, but Rye stopped her.

"Mistress Lightfoot, allow me to carry you to your coach."

"*I'll* carry Letty—you take charge of the girls." With a resigned look at them all, Fielding hoisted his velvet-clad burden, while Rye turned to the girls, who stood waiting in their pattens and cloaks, with, "I'll take Mistress Virginia first."

Virginia looked pleased to be thus carried ceremoniously to the coach but Carolina, alone for the moment with Rye as he returned to carry her through the snow, said, "Mother isn't fooling me. She knows the Bramways sleep late and she's anxious to avoid a confrontation between Fielding and Duncan Bramway—that's why we're leaving so early. And by the way, she knows. About us. I mean, about last night."

He sighed. "Am I to be hauled onto the carpet for bedding my own wife?"

"Well, she doesn't *know* I'm your wife," corrected Carolina. "And she hasn't actually *said* anything, but Virginia said she saw the landlord escorting Huddleston up to his room this morning." She cut off as they reached the coach and Rye handed her in, but she cast a questioning look back at him.

His whimsical shrug said, *what would be would be.*

Over snow not yet cut up by cart wheels and wagon wheels, the horses floundered through the rutted streets to Aunt Pet's green-shuttered pink brick house where snow crested the tapering brick chimneys and mounded over the boxwood and the clipped live oak hedge. Snow fell from the dormers and roof as they drew up before the house, and Aunt Pet's well-cared-for garden with its fruit trees and its sunken turf panel—whose sculpted corner seats, shaded by tall locusts, were so lovely in summer—was well-nigh unrecognizable beneath a thick blanket of white.

"Well, Petula's property seems to have survived the wind and snow," observed Letitia, peering out the coach window to view the neat dormers and the handsome iron knocker on the familiar green-painted front door.

"I told you it would be, but you must needs come and see for yourself," declared her husband morosely as he lifted her down from the coach. "Premonitions!" He snorted, stomping on snowy boots through the deep snow to Aunt Pet's front door.

When Carolina was carried in, it came to her almost with a thrust of homesickness how many happy hours she had spent in this house, for at Aunt Pet's she had felt more welcome than even in her own home. It was a forlorn feeling to arrive shivering in these cold rooms and know that Aunt Pet was far away in Philadelphia.

"We always spent our holidays here," she told Rye wistfully as he set her down. And looking about, it seemed to her that she could almost see the house alight with the candles that had sparkled on the decorations of so many Christmases past, bright with the waxy green of the holly and its vivid scarlet berries, the bayberry and mistletoe and boxwood—she could almost hear the carolers and bell ringers outside and almost smell the fruitcake and plum pudding above the scent of the fragrant hickory logs that had burned so brightly on the hearth those holidays past.

While the men busied themselves making fires—for Petula's house had prudently been left with logs in the fireplaces ready for immediate lighting—the women busied themselves spreading a tablecloth in the dining room and setting out plates and cutlery, crumpets and Sally Lunn and tankards of hot cider from the keg they had brought along with them from the Raleigh.

"I must find me a horse that is rested and strong and get me back to Level Green today," Fielding told his wife as he downed his still-warm cider.

"Fielding, the plantation can get along without you!"

He frowned at her. "I'll not leave the children alone like this!"

"But the servants—"

"Are only that," he corrected her. "Who knows, they may build the fires too high in this bitter weather and burn the place down about their heads."

She was silent, studying him—and there was a smile in her eyes. Carolina in that moment felt very close to her mother.

"And *you* can't stay here, Letty," he worried. "Even though I've no doubt Evistock here will see no harm comes to you"—at this point, across the table, Rye nodded gravely—"there are no proper provisions in the house. It will be impossible to procure them in this snow, and you know as well as I do that Petula's servants are working elsewhere while she is gone."

"Oh, I know you are right, Fielding," sighed Letitia, who was being very conciliatory now that she had gotten her way about everything. "I realize you must go back today, but of course the rest of us must stay. For how else will I be able to obtain the materials for Carolina's wedding dress?"

So, swiftly, she had arranged it. Fielding was packed off to Level Green—and to safety, thought Carolina, from another brush with Duncan Bramwell. And as it turned out, her mother had no intention of doing any cooking. They would eat their meals at various inns—indeed, the Raleigh would do well enough tonight.

With some alarm on the girls' part, they all trooped back to the Raleigh for supper, over streets where the snow was now cut to ribbons by sleighs and carts and carriages. But if they had expected another confrontation between Letitia and Amanda Bramway, it was not to be. Letitia passed the Bramways as if she did not see them, and Amanda only sniffed as they went by. But Rye was quick to note the sullen glances that followed them.

Obviously, Duncan Bramway had had a talk with his wife about the danger of charging Sandy Randolph's mad wife with witchcraft—the danger to herself.

Carolina had a feeling it had all blown over—and said so lightheartedly to Rye, when the next morning the four of them were scouring those shops whose proprietors had managed to clear pathways in the snow.

"I hope so—for your sake." His gaze was tender on this girl he loved so much.

They had gone through a blue-painted shop door with a clanging bell to announce their entrance and had fallen behind to talk to each other as Letitia critically inspected some blue and white Delftware plates "on which to serve the bride's cake."

"But you have not enough of them," she told the shopkeeper with a sigh.

"I expect a new shipment from England any day now," he assured her. "Coming in on the *Bristol Maid.*"

Hearing this, Letitia ordered such a number of plates that her daughters were quite dazzled—and followed by recklessly ordering a vast amount of new cutlery which would be arriving on the *Bristol Maid* as well. And then turned her mind to bridal finery.

Still lingering behind her mother and Virginia on their trek down Duke of Gloucester Street, Carolina turned from the inspection of a passing sleigh, jingling with sleigh bells, to shoot a glance upward at Rye. "What would *you* like me to wear for the wedding?" she asked curiously.

"Anything," he said promptly. "Just so we can get us wed and—the other matter taken care of."

The "other matter," she knew, was his pardon. But there was still no word from the governor and he had not returned.

Letitia found at last the material she wanted for

Carolina's wedding gown. "I think you would be most striking in white," she said critically, holding up a length of rippling white velvet.

"It's beautiful," agreed Carolina dutifully. For herself she would have preferred some pale shade—delicate blue perhaps or a pastel green. But bridal white was coming into vogue and her mother had always an eye to the latest, the smartest thing.

"With a long-trained skirt," mused her mother. "And a *Cul-de-Paris* at the rear."

Virginia looked impressed but Carolina gave her mother a doubtful look. She had seen them, of course, but she was not sure she *liked* bustles!

"It's the latest thing," Letitia assured her. (Carolina sometimes thought the French dressmakers must send her mother letters describing what they were planning for future fashion dolls, so accurate were her assessments of the trends of style.) "The sleeves should be slashed to reveal a satin lining. White satin, I think, with edgings of silver. And I have some very good mechlin to edge the sleeves."

"But won't the lace of my chemise cuffs do?" protested Carolina, for practically everyone let their lace-trimmed chemise cuffs spill from the elbows of their gowns.

"No, that's going out," said her mother. "And I have just the petticoat for you at home—I have not worn it. It is of white silk crisscrossed with a lattice of silver thread."

"Oh, it's beautiful, Carol," cried Virginia. "Wait till you see it—*it* has a train too!"

"And a circlet of holly, I think—silver gilt—for your hair. After all, this is a country wedding and we do not have to be so fashionable." Letitia looked complacent.

Carolina almost choked with amusement. Even here

in the Colonies, across the seas from Paris and London, her mother seemed to have an unerring instinct for the latest thing. Besides which, she had natural style. The shopkeeper regarded her with respect.

And so it was all accomplished, and after a week spent in Williamsburg during which Rye and Carolina had very little chance to be alone together—indeed there had been a round of teas and morning calls and sleigh rides and dinners at several private houses, besides their usual meals at the Raleigh—the roads were moderately clear again, though muddy, and they returned by coach to Level Green. They arrived laden down with laces and garters and ribands and fabrics, full of plans not only for the wedding but for the upcoming ball at Fairfield.

They found Fielding grouchy, annoyed by their long absence, and the children fretful and bickering. Even the servants seemed not to be speaking to each other.

"A typical homecoming at Level Green," Virginia said ironically when Carolina remarked how things seemed to have gone downhill in their absence. "Father insists he doesn't need Mother but things always fall apart when she's gone."

Carolina laughed. "I seem to remember that at Farview, when we were children, things seemed to fall apart when they were *both* at home!"

"Will there be time to get this elaborate gown made up for you?" wondered Rye as he accompanied Carolina up the wide staircase with its handsomely carved balustrade.

"Mother says so. And anyway, the governor's not back yet."

"But when he does come back," muttered Rye, "I'll be eager to get us gone."

Carolina shrugged. Who knew to what lengths her

remarkable mother would go? Indeed she might change her mind and insist that the entire gown be embroidered by hand—and the wedding postponed until it was ready! She leaned over the banisters to call down to Virginia in the lower hall and did not notice Rye's sudden frown.

To her own surprise, now that they were back at Level Green, Carolina found that she was enjoying being home with her betrothed, having much made of her—with fittings, dozens of decisions, and all the trappings of a great wedding being underway. Rye might be marking time, chafing at the delays, but she felt he was quite safe here on the banks of the York. The governor would soon return and they would be married with great fanfare, and then they could journey to Essex and a new life!

Meantime there was the world she knew—the plantation world of Colonial Virginia—and there was not only the wedding to be held at some unspecified date but there was the ball at Fairfield coming up right away!

She had a marvelous time getting ready for the ball.

"Virgie, we will make you a *femme fatale!*" she cried, pirouetting across the floor of Virginia's green and white bedroom. "We will *both* powder our hair! It will look *ravishing!*"

"Yours doesn't need powdering, it's almost white now—well, not *white* exactly, it has that shimmering silver-blonde sheen. Powder would only hurt *your* looks," said Virginia sensibly. "And as for me, my strawberry-blonde hair is my best feature! Why should I change it?"

"You're right," agreed Carolina promptly, glad that Virginia was at last taking an interest in her appearance. "We'll pomade it, we'll brush it, we'll give it more sheen, we'll pile it up, we'll curl it with an iron, we'll—"

"We'll wear it out," sighed Virginia. "Couldn't we just sweep it up and let it fall down in a couple of curls?"

"Yes, *that* might be dramatic," agreed Carolina instantly, eager to go along with any suggestion of her sister's. "And we must do something about your gown. Did you know that all your gowns are too high-necked? They don't show your bosom at all and your skin is *very* fair."

"That's because I've kept it covered up," muttered Virginia.

"Just so! And if we drop the neckline of your best bronze velvet lower—quite a bit lower—the effect will be devastating!"

"I'll catch cold," objected Virginia. "Ballrooms are notoriously drafty."

"They're notoriously *hot!* Ladies often faint in the crush!"

"But there's the trip going there on the barge—"

"Nonsense, you'll arrive bundled up in a cloak. Indeed you won't be wearing your ball gown on the river at all, but a traveling dress. For Mother says we're to arrive early and stay the night!"

Virginia gave her younger sister an uneasy look. "I don't think, Carol, that you're going to make me into a bird of plumage that easily," she said doubtfully.

"Nonsense, of course we will!" Carolina said, laughing. And promptly set about it.

Rye helped.

"Ah, I see I am to squire the *two* most beautiful young ladies in the Tidewater!" he said when Carolina and Virginia came downstairs to join the senior Lightfoots on their way to the Fairfield ball. He was gazing in open admiration at the picture the two girls made in their ostrich feather hats and handsome dresses. Carolina had decided that riding clothes would look quite dashing for their arrival at Fairfield and she was wearing a sky-blue and silver riding habit, and a broadbrimmed hat with a sky-blue plume. Virginia was even more elegant in amber velvet trimmed in gold braid and wearing a hat that sported a gold buckle and orange plumes.

The weather had moderated but Virginia still shivered when they went down to the landing. "I'm going to abandon this hat and put on a hood and cloak," she said, turning and running back to the house.

"I doubt I will ever make Virginia into a butterfly." Carolina sighed, watching her sister scurry over the lawn with her skirts lifted over her smart little boots.

"Do you need to?" asked Rye gently. "Perhaps she needs to find someone who appreciates her as she is, someone who doesn't seek a butterfly, doesn't really want one."

Carolina gave him a jaded look. "All men want butterflies," she said firmly. Hearing that, her mother hid a smile. "Anyway," she added confidently, "wait till you see Virginia's ball gown. It's a marvel!"

Virginia returned, hooded and cloaked, and their barge was river borne toward Fairfield. After waving good-by to Della and Flo, who had been promised they could come along "next time," Carolina turned all her attention to Rye. Excitedly she pointed out landmarks along the way, and Rye bent over her, careless that her dancing blue ostrich feather plumes were tickling his chin, just to smell the lemony fragrance of her hair. He had seen many a riverbank and many a handsome home that bordered one, but never a sight that pleased him so much as Carolina, waving her gloved hand at this house or that great oak or the meadow yonder. He thought of how it would be for them in Essex, when all this secrecy was far behind them and they could stride forth proudly as man and wife, and thinking of it softened his hard features.

Suddenly Carolina tilted back her head and looked up at Rye, laughter brimming in her eyes. "Are you really going to do it?" she asked under her breath.

Rye didn't have to ask her what she meant. He had told her this afternoon that he meant to bribe one of the Burwell servants into finding some other place to sleep for the night, and they would both slip away and tryst there in the room vacated by the servant.

"Only if one of them can be corrupted," he murmured.

Carolina's laughter bubbled and she leaned closer to him, feeling already that the evening would be full of joy.

Another barge pulled up beside them as they neared Fairfield. It was painted red and crowded with people, including a tall chestnut-haired girl in a green cloak who stood up and waved madly.

"Why, 'tis Sally Montrose!" Carolina was on her feet, waving to her old friend.

Rye reached out to steady her and they arrived at Fairfield's landing waving and calling out to each other—and embraced enthusiastically upon the wharf.

Sally Montrose had indeed changed, Carolina thought, even as she introduced Rye to the various Montroses—there were no less than eight of them piling out of the red-painted barge, eager to exchange pleasantries with the Lightfoot clan. The old madcap Sally was gone, and in her place was a cynical young woman whom Carolina felt she hardly knew—even though she had embraced Carolina with all her old fervor. Sally's green cloak sat on her shoulders jauntily and blew open to reveal a tangerine wool gown that brought out the best in her figure. There were brave tangerine and yellow feathers blowing on her hat. She carried her head higher than ever but wore her mouth in a straight line, and when she laughed, it was a sharp staccato sound with no mirth in it.

Virginia was right, Carolina realized. Sally had been hurt. Deeply. And she still bore the scars. She decided to ask Sally about it as soon as they were alone.

Meanwhile, separated by the swirling crowd from Sally Montrose, Carolina was trudging across the wintry lawn beside Rye—the weather had moderated, and the snow was gone except in patches—along with other guests streaming toward a house that was considered architecturally unique. The two wings of the main house extended back at right angles—and one of those wings, she knew, contained a ballroom. She was eager to see it for it had not yet been completed when she had left the Tidewater. She remembered her mother talking about the new house being built by their neighbors and how the basement, with its brick arches supporting the ceiling, was to have a vault in the center. It seemed less a Colonial planter's home than a bit of old England, she thought critically, viewing it. Somehow the steep roofs and relatively small windows made it seem all the more massive. And the handsome chimneys were like those at Bacon's Castle—reminding everyone that Lewis Burwell's wife Abigail, who had died in 1672, had been not only the rebellious Nathaniel Bacon's niece, but his heiress as well.

"I've been dying to see this house," she told Rye breathlessly. "Everyone says it's *wonderful!*"

He smiled down fondly upon her head, and resisted an urge to kiss that excited face beneath the hat with the bouncing blue plumes.

Once inside, they found that the ladies were to be given rooms to rest in before the ball started.

"Although I've certainly no need to nap!" declared Carolina, whose feet were already dancing as she tripped up the stairs. "Have you, Sally?" She turned to Sally Montrose, who had joined her again.

"I don't care if I never sleep again," said Sally in that new harder voice that Carolina couldn't get accustomed to.

Virginia went over and threw herself down on the bed in exhaustion once they reached the bedroom assigned to them, and since the rest of the ladies had chosen to stay downstairs for a time, Carolina found the chance to draw Sally aside to a window that looked out over the silvery expanse of the York.

"Virgie told me about Brent—marrying someone else," she said awkwardly. "Oh, Sally, I'm so sorry!"

"I'm not," said Sally crisply. "I'm glad I found him out. Imagine his caring more about what was posted in the parish church than he did for me!" She gave a hard little laugh.

"But—but there are penalties, I'm sure, and they could well have been invoked if you had married your sister's husband, Sally."

Sally defiantly shrugged a tangerine-clad shoulder. "I'd have run away with him," she said flatly. "I'd have gone anywhere. I told him that. I told him I didn't care if we got married somewhere else under some other names and never came home—or if we never got married at all, just so long as we were together. But Brent was worried"—her lip curled—"about what people might *think!* Imagine! You spend all your life loving a man and you find out he cares more about what people might *think* than he does about you!"

Carolina could well imagine it. Brent had always been by far the most conventional of all Sally's beaux. Indeed she had always thought Brent had married Sally's older sister—who had strongly resembled Sally —because Sally's devil-may-care view of life had unnerved him. While attracted, like so many others, by Sally's verve and charm, he had preferred to bestow his name on a more predictable woman, a woman who could be counted on never to cause the slightest ripple of gossip in the community.

"And the worst of it was that all the time my sister was alive, Brent kept telling me how he wished he had married *me* instead of my sister. He harped on what a big mistake he'd made because we 'belonged' together. He said he should have married me because my 'wild ways' suited him so well!" Her lip twisted bitterly. "And he kept right on saying that *until he had the chance to marry me*—and then he backed off. So that's what men are, Carolina! Don't trust any of them."

Carolina looked at her friend, appalled. "You mean" —she faltered—"Brent actually—"

"He actually told me after he'd married my sister what a mistake he'd made and how he regretted it and how much he wanted to marry me."

"And you believed him?"

"Of course I did! I suppose I believed it because I wanted to, but I should have known he was only luring me to bed! Oh, I slept with him, yes. I wouldn't admit that to anybody else but I did. I knew it was unfair to my sister but I told myself she'd taken him away from me in the first place. Anyway, I was so crazy in love with him I didn't care." Her tortured gaze met Carolina's. "In fact, we'd been together that very night—the night she went into labor and . . . and died. I'll go to hell for that, won't I?" Sally's smile was twisted. "I'm sure that shocks you but—oh, Carolina, all I'd ever cared about was Brent. I never wanted anyone else! And he cared for me too—at least at first. I know he did." Her voice went wistful. "But then after the funeral his mother got at him and told him it would be a mortal sin to marry me—not to mention being against the law! Oh, God, Carolina!" Her voice was suddenly grief-stricken and her gamine face seemed to break up before Carolina's worried gaze. "I would have gone away with him—he'd only have had to say the word and I'd have gone with him like a shot! But no, he must have the 'approval of the community'—I think that was the way he put it. And then when he decided to get married again he said that we shouldn't see each other anymore, *at least not for a while.* Honestly, that was the way he broke it to me! He looked so hangdog—oh, Carolina, I can't tell you how that made me feel. Like a—a common prostitute!"

"Oh, Sally!" Carolina flung her arms around her friend. "All men aren't like that! Forget Brent, find someone else. You always were the most popular girl on the James!"

But Sally Montrose stiffened and flung away from her. "Oh, yes, they are all like that," she said on a vicious note. "All of them—and don't you forget it, Carolina, or it will happen to you too. Maybe not quite like it happened to me, maybe Rye won't find someone else right away, *but he'll find someone,* you can count on it! They all do!"

Carolina gave her friend a helpless look. She wanted so desperately to comfort Sally, but there seemed to be no way. Headstrong Sally, blinded by grief, was headed for hell in her own way, and it seemed that nobody could stop her.

"And do you know I find I *like* luring men on, making them fall in love with me—and then casting them aside!" Sally's green eyes had a menacing gleam. Her whole stance as she stood there by the window was arrogant and predatory. "I *enjoy* making them suffer!"

"But it was Brent who hurt you," protested Carolina. "How can it help to make someone else pay for what Brent has done?"

"I don't know," Sally said with a short laugh, "but I'm going to find out!" She glared out the window at the silver river.

"Will Brent be here tonight, do you think?"

"Undoubtedly—and with his bride, that little pinch-faced Agnes!" Again that short hard laugh. "And he will see me romancing half the gentlemen present—I'll make sure of that!"

"Sally, you've got to get over him," urged Carolina. "Don't let him do this to you!"

"Oh, he hasn't 'done' anything to me," said Sally. "It's what he *didn't* do that counts! But he *has* shown me one thing—what men really are! I can't wait to break someone's heart!"

"You'll end up breaking your own," sighed Carolina.

"No chance of that! *That's* already been done." Sally whirled on Carolina. "Can you imagine what it's like to *die* of jealousy? To imagine him night after night in someone else's arms, to know that he's making love to her, holding her—" Her voice broke. "Oh, God, the days are bad enough but the nights! They're terrible. . . ."

Carolina's heart ached for her. She patted Sally's arm awkwardly, not knowing what to say to ease her pain.

Sally jerked away from that commiserating touch. Carolina's obvious sympathy had wounded her pride. "Suppose it were Rye?" she shot at Carolina. *"Suppose it were Rye, Carolina?* Oh, he loves you now—or *says* he does, you can never trust men—but suppose he *stopped* loving you?"

"He'd never do that!"

"Oh, no?" Sally gave her a derisive look. "Suppose he turned to somebody else?"

Suppose he did, came a sudden shivery thought. *Suppose he did. . . .* It was almost possible to imagine it happening under Sally's hard penetrating gaze. She shook her head to clear it. Rye loved her, she was certain of that.

"It shook you, didn't it, just thinking about it?" Sally's voice had that new hard edge to it.

"Yes, it did," said Carolina soberly. "And I'm very sorry for you, Sally, because I think you're going to ruin your life!"

"And then people will say how clever Brent was to escape me," said Sally flippantly. "Since I was so obviously 'after' him! And they'll sigh and say 'Poor Sally, she never was much good!' But before that day comes, I'm going to cause so much trouble that the men in the Tidewater will never forget *me!* And the best way to do that *is to make them fall in love with me!* Then I'll have the power to hurt them!"

Carolina sighed. There was no use talking to this new Sally. She was going to have to work out her own problems. Maybe she'd meet some new man and everything would change for her. Carolina hoped so.

Meantime—her gaze flew to the bed where an exhausted Virginia was already asleep—there was her sister to be thought about, to be launched.

"I'm going back downstairs," said Sally restlessly.

She turned at the door. "I'll take care of Rye for you," she said in a taunting voice.

Carolina shook her head as the door closed. Sally had certainly changed. But temptress or not, she would get nowhere with Rye, Carolina was certain of that. And then there were others coming into the room where several beds had been set up, and she was surrounded with light conversation.

She decided to follow Virginia's example and take a nap herself. After all, she needed sleep as much as anyone—Rye had kept her up half the night before!

She would have lain sleepless if she had known what lay in store. . . .

Winter 1689

Chapter 8

However Rye had spent his afternoon, at the ball he was giving Sally Montrose a rather wide berth. Looking over the banisters into the crowd below, Carolina was quick to notice that. Guests were still arriving, she saw, as she and Virginia reached the head of the stairs. The Pages of nearby Shelly were just coming in, and there was Ralph Wormeley of Rosegill and some of the Shirleys from upriver—they swept in on a cloud of laughter in a medley of blue and green and lavender satins, lit by the sparkle of gold buttons and silver braid and sparkling brilliants.

They came down the wide stairway together, Virginia and Carolina, for while Letitia was already downstairs mingling among the guests, her daughters had lingered, taking time in arranging their coiffures—for Carolina was determined that tonight Virginia should sweep all before her.

For her first ball since her return to the Tidewater, Carolina had chosen the gown she had worn the night she first met Rye in Essex. She had taken it lovingly out of the big clothes press in her bedchamber at Level

Green and held it against her face and sighed, for it brought back precious memories of a snowy Christmastide in England. She had had one of the maids press it carefully with one of the heavy irons before she had stowed it in a large box to be carried to Fairfield on the family barge. She was even wearing the same delicate stockings she had worn that night—of gray silk with embroidered clocks that seemed to flash silver, like her gray satin dancing slippers with their high red heels! Her daringly cut gown was of rippling dove-gray velvet, so thin it was almost sheer. It shimmered over her beautifully molded young breasts, caressed her tiny waist and formed a perfect setting for the burst of brilliants at each shoulder. Its tight, pointed bodice swept out smoothly into a dramatically wide skirt with an impressive train. And now that skirt was swept into wide panniers at each hip, the better to display her gleaming gunmetal satin petticoat latticed with rich silver embroidery. She was even carrying in one slim gloved hand the same sculptured ivory fan trimmed in silver lace and set with brilliants—for she meant to wake memories this night in Rye as well.

Teardrop pearl earrings dangled from her ears, but now—as it had not been in Essex—the white column of her neck was circled with Rye's magnificent emerald necklace, and Rye's big square-cut emerald betrothal ring gleamed atop the glove on her finger. It had taken some urging to get it there but the gloves were of such delicate gray kidskin and so tight that she had finally managed it!

Beside her, trailing down the long staircase, was Virginia. A completely new Virginia. She was wearing her best bronze cut-velvet gown and it still supported above its gleaming amber silk petticoat acres of copper lace—but now the neckline had been daringly lowered, so daringly that the pale creamy tops of Virginia's young breasts were displayed for the first time in mixed company.

Everyone had seen the gown before but it looked different tonight in other ways too. The onlookers would not realize it, but the bodice had been taken in so that it now gave Virginia a wasp-waisted willowy slenderness. Her too-pale face had been artfully rouged, her soft mouth touched with Spanish paper, and a tiny diamond of black court plaster—placed just like Carolina's—set off her fair complexion near her mouth. Her abundant red-gold hair had been brushed and pomaded and swept up, save for several fat curls which lay along her shoulder—the same coiffure her sister was wearing. And she was wearing her mother's glowing topaz necklace and brooch as well as gold and topaz eardrops.

"I feel strange," muttered Virginia, clutching her skirts with one creamy gloved hand and hoping she wouldn't trip on her train and disgrace herself—she had never been any hand with trains although Carolina seemed to kick her own train aside with arrogant delight. "And I feel undressed," she added reproachfully.

"You look better than you ever have in your life, Virgie," murmured Carolina, smiling down on the company below. "Remember that and don't act *grateful* if someone asks you to dance. Just lift your head and smile full into his face and then glance quickly over his shoulder and bat your eyes—make him think you're arranging a rendezvous with someone else or shrugging off a dancing partner who arrived just a shade too late."

"I realize that I am studying at the feet of a master—excuse me, *mistress* of flirtation, but how am I to do all this, pray tell, if nobody asks me to dance?" asked Virginia ironically, remembering what usually happened.

"They *will*. Oh, Virgie, hush, we're almost downstairs. Turn to me and laugh and say something and I'll laugh as if you've just said something extremely witty and people will look up and see how beautiful you look!"

"I expect to break my neck with this train," said Virginia—with a wild laugh that shook her red-gold curls.

"How *wonderful!*" exclaimed Carolina in a carrying voice and joined Virginia in a cascade of laughter that caused heads to turn. "And here we are!"

And here they were. From the colorful crowd, Rye stepped forward to receive them and they strolled to the ballroom, one on each side, each clasping one of his arms. Across the hall, heading for the ballroom on the arm of a flushed-faced young buck, Sally Montrose regarded Carolina cynically.

"Rye, would you mind leading off with Virginia for the first dance?" murmured Carolina when they reached the big mirrored ballroom where the dancers were already whirling.

Virginia's sharp ears heard that. "Oh, *no!*" she protested in an agony of embarrassment. "It will look *strange* if your betrothed doesn't lead you out on the floor first. And besides, there are so few people dancing just now, I'd feel conspicuous!" She shivered.

"All right," Carolina said resignedly, for she had hoped to show Virginia off to one and all right away— and what better way to display one's new self than on the dance floor? "The next dance, then, unless you're already claimed. Lead me out, Rye!"

Tall and commanding—and smiling down on her with a glint in his gray eyes—her lover led her out upon the polished floor and they swirled lightheartedly among the dancers.

Embarrassed by her changed appearance—and indeed feeling quite naked in her low-cut dress—Virginia shrank back against the wall.

Carolina loved dancing. And she loved her surroundings tonight. About her the row of tall pier glasses set into marble and gilt on either side of the room reflected a glittering assembly and amplified many-fold the candle power of the chandeliers and mirrored wall sconces. Sally Montrose danced by with one of the Carnaby boys. Her color was high, her hair so alight with orange brilliants that for a moment Carolina thought she was afire, and the pumpkin satin gown she wore over a gold embroidered velvet petticoat was trimmed in wide swaths of heavy black lace. Carolina privately thought that Sally had overdone it, with four patches of black court plaster on her face, but she was laughing as she swept by—indeed, she seemed to be almost hysterically enjoying herself—and half the young bucks in the room were pursuing her.

"Did you do it, Rye? Arrange to bribe someone?" Carolina asked pertly as Rye whirled her about, giving her gleaming skirts a chance to billow out.

"I did." He was smiling down at her, a confident lover. "A little gold did the trick neatly."

So tonight would bring the added excitement of trying to find her way through the dark corridors of a strange house to keep a clandestine tryst with her lover! She gave him a shadowed look through lashes gilded by candlelight. "What if I can't get away?" It was fun to tease him.

"You will," he predicted, his grin growing even more wicked.

She knew she would too! Nothing could stop her. . . .

"Have you—been talking to Sally Montrose?" she asked him suddenly, for she could not help wondering if he had spent the afternoon with Sally—this new predatory Sally, out after every man in sight.

"She showed me the gardens," he said, and Carolina felt a twinge of jealousy. She cast a swift look at Sally, sparkling and vivacious, just then whirling by among the dancers.

Suddenly Sally's laughter took on a higher pitch, her smile flashed brilliantly, her glittering eyes were almost fever bright. Carolina turned her head swiftly to survey the room.

Ah, that was it: Brent Chase and his bride Agnes had just entered the ballroom. Brent, handsomely got up in buff and orange, was trying desperately not to look at Sally, whose dancing partner had now whirled her quite near him—indeed, Brent's hazel eyes were looking almost everywhere else. Beside him little Agnes rustled in her peach and plum gown almost smothered with a profusion of ecru lace. Carolina looked at that small pointy face with its black birdlike eyes with some distaste. Sally was right to say Agnes had a pinched face, she thought—and she simpered too much.

She caught Sally's eye at that moment and repressed a shiver. Sally looked wild enough to do anything—even to attack the bride. Carolina remembered suddenly a phrase about hell having no fury like a woman scorned—that certainly described Sally tonight.

The dance ended, someone else claimed Carolina, and Rye danced once with Virginia, then drifted away into the crowd. And then there was another dancing partner and another. All her old beaux seemed to be here tonight, Carolina noted with satisfaction. After all, it was pleasant to have Rye see for himself how popular she had been back home. Watching her with speculative eyes were Ned Shackleford and Dick Smithfield, both of whom had once ridden, wearing her colors, in an impromptu "tourney" on the wide lawns of Rosegill. And Ned, who had styled himself "Knight of Gloucester" for the tourney, had crowned her Queen of Love and Beauty beneath one of the big branching trees on Rosegill's lawn. That was the day she had learnt that Sandy Randolph was her real father. The day that Opened Her Eyes, she thought wryly. The day she had borrowed passage money from Sandy Randolph and run away, lest her mother and Fielding force her into marriage with one of their "good catches."

And thinking of Sandy made her look about to see if the Bramways were in evidence. They were not. But there was Sandy across the room. Clad in a deep-cuffed pale amethyst brocade coat and supple plum velvet trousers, he was just then lifting a glass to someone. She caught the ruby gleam of port, followed his gaze and saw her mother's slender figure, slim as a girl's in amethyst satin over a rustling purple silk petticoat laced with silver. Letitia had a glass in her hand too. Almost imperceptibly she lifted that glass to Sandy—and then turned quickly, talking with great animation to the group she was with. Tonight, thought Carolina with a pang, Sandy was deliberately wearing her mother's colors. Old loves died hard. . . .

Carolina glimpsed Virginia once again on the sidelines but she could not reach her before Ned Shackleford claimed her for the next dance. Ned's brown eyes were glowing. He seemed to have grown bulkier since she had seen him last, to have lost his wiriness.

"I heard you were back, Mistress Carolina," he said, and there was a glow in his voice too. "And I said ''Tis good news!' when I heard it, for all of us here in the Tidewater missed you sorely when you left."

"I came back to be married, Ned."

"Aye, so they told me." He sighed. "Do I see him here?"

"Yes." Carolina's silver-gray gaze scanned the crowd, spotted Rye dancing with Virginia again. Virginia looked quite flustered but her excitement had served to heighten her color—Carolina thought proudly that Virginia looked awfully well. "Over there, dancing with my sister, the tall man in gray." That description hardly did Rye justice, she thought. His broad shoulders imparted style to his charcoal velvet coat, his wide cuffs edged with silver braid supported a burst of white mechlin that drifted over fine hands, and his long lean legs were encased in gunmetal satin breeches. He moved as lightly as a dancing master—or a fencer—as he guided a blushing Virginia across the floor. "That's Rye," she said, and could not keep the pride out of her voice.

"I see he is wearing a long sword," observed Ned.

Carolina sighed. That was one thing Rye had been adamant about. She had not been able to persuade him to wear one of the short dress swords most of the other men were sporting—for the terrible Indian massacres of 1622 and 1644 were still remembered in the Tidewater, as well as the slaughter of settlers which had brought on Bacon's Rebellion and thus had led to the burning of Jamestown. It behooved a prudent gentleman of the Tidewater to wear a sword. But Rye's sword was long, as a fighting man's should be, and it had a very serviceable basket hilt which Ned had glimpsed through the side slash of Rye's skirted charcoal coat as it swung out when he guided Virginia through a difficult measure.

"Yes," Carolina told him ruefully, "Rye is very fond of that sword."

"And has used it a deal, I'll wager," said Ned, studying the man narrowly.

There was something formidable about Rye, Carolina thought unhappily, something that even Ned had noticed. You felt it, even when he was dancing. Something about the square set of his jaw, something cold and challenging in his gray eyes, in the hawklike set of his saturnine features.

"I suppose so," she agreed, for she considered that a dangerous subject. She sought for another one. "I half expected to return and find you married, Ned. Have you not found yourself a lady?"

"I found one," he said, and his young voice was suddenly unhappy as he looked deep into Carolina's eyes, willing her to love him. "But I lost her somehow. . . ."

This too was dangerous ground. Carolina did not wish to incite Rye to jealousy. She remembered too well how he had "defended" her on Tortuga. "And Dick Smithfield?" she asked hastily, glancing in Dick's direction.

"Dick?" Ned snorted. "Aye, Dick married not three months after you left."

"Anyone I know?"

"A girl from upriver, near the Falls, very pretty. She's home now, finds it inconvenient to travel."

Which meant in all likelihood that she was pregnant with her first child—"pregnant" was what they usually meant when they said a woman "found it inconvenient to travel."

Her eyebrows shot up. "And Dick's here? Leaving the poor girl at home alone?"

"Oh, she isn't alone. They've moved in with her family until Dick can get his house built."

"Nevertheless!" Carolina arched her slim neck haughtily. "*I* shall snub him for treating her so!"

Ned chuckled. Those were words that would have done his heart good in the days when he had hung on her lightest breath. "Is it true you're to be married very soon?" he asked abruptly.

"That's right. Here at Level Green."

"Your parents will like that," he said hollowly. "And what then?"

"And then to England, Ned." He looked so forlorn at hearing that she was leaving that she felt called upon to point out that there were other girls in the room. "I always thought you liked Sally Montrose, Ned."

He shook his head. "Not the way she is now."

"And how is she now?" demanded Carolina with asperity.

"Mean," averred Ned. "She accepted a betrothal ring from Keith Avery a fortnight ago—let him propose on bended knee, ask her father for her, all that—and then strolled into the dining room and before company tossed it back to him and said she'd changed her mind. I wonder that her parents let her back out of it!"

Sally was headed for grief, all right. Word was getting around. . . .

"Doesn't Virginia look lovely tonight?" she said,

hoping to channel his interest toward this newer, more stylish Virgie.

"Virginia?" said Ned blankly. "Where?"

Annoyance sharpened Carolina's voice as she answered, "Dancing with Rye," for surely Ned could hardly have escaped noticing Rye's dancing partner, especially after his attention had been called to her!

"Oh—Mistress Virginia? Oh, yes, she does indeed look fine," was Ned's tepid response. "Lost some weight, hasn't she?" he added vaguely.

"Too much," sighed Carolina. "I would like to see her gain some of it back. But being so slender does make her look very striking, doesn't it?"

"I suppose," agreed Ned without enthusiasm, as the dance ended.

Before Carolina could suitably chastise Ned for his lack of interest in her sister, Dick Smithfield had almost sprinted across the room to claim her for the next dance, and she made him talk the whole time about his young wife to punish him for leaving her at home.

And then the Willis boys, and Mortimer Wade, and what seemed like countless others were clamoring to dance with her. Breathless, Carolina felt she might never have been gone at all as one by one they whirled her past the tall pier glasses whose mirrors reflected the candlelight, and made bright eyes brighter, and gleamed off satin, and gilded fair complexions to delicate gold.

The evening whirled by with laughter sparkling like the wine. Carolina, dancing with this one and that one—and always again with Rye—hardly knew where the time had gone. He smiled down at her happy face as he spun her about the floor.

"You're enjoying this, aren't you?"

"Oh, yes! But I think I'm starving. Shall I go and collect Virginia and whoever she's with? Then the four of us can attack some of that food that's piled up like a castle in the dining room!"

He laughed. "Yes. I'll have a word with Sandy while you're gone."

Much to her chagrin, Carolina found Virginia in the drawing room, which was now mainly deserted as the guests were drawn toward the large dining room. She was crouched on a chair, mouselike and silent, apparently listening to the conversation of two elderly gentlemen, one of whom was resting his arm near the central finial of the mantel. Her gaze was fixed on that finial—an urn, its bowl carved in bas-relief. Both men were ranting about the price of tobacco—"which will break us all, mark my words!"—and Virginia, looking wan despite her finery, seemed to be hanging onto their words.

Carolina approached them, vexed to find her sister without an escort. She pulled Virginia away and neither of the old gentlemen noticed her going, so heated was their discussion. "What happened, Virgie, after I got swept away from you?" Carolina demanded.

"I danced with Rye. And with Ned Shackleford. And Dick Smithfield."

So Ned had taken the bait! "Ned and Dick," Carolina murmured. "Did they show interest?"

"Only in you," Virginia said truthfully. "Ned wanted to know if I couldn't persuade you to stay in the Tidewater, and Dick wanted to know what you had against him that you kept badgering him about his wife all the while you were dancing. He sounded quite aggrieved."

At the moment Carolina *felt* aggrieved. It hurt her to

see Virginia so gorgeously gotten up yet looking so downcast.

"Virgie," she said vigorously, "I've made a mistake. I had forgotten that everybody here knows us and has long ago formed an opinion about us. Just changing a hairdo or a gown won't change their attitude. They'll keep on thinking of us the way we *were*, not the way we *are!*"

Virginia gave her an unhappy look. "They've certainly made up their minds about *me!*" she murmured.

"What we need," insisted Carolina, "is to bring you out in Essex. There you'll be a dashing wench from the Colonies and everything will change, you'll see!"

"I doubt I'll ever see Essex." Virginia sighed. She seemed so pessimistic that Carolina was alarmed.

"Nonsense." Reassuringly Carolina linked arms with her sister. "Rye is waiting for us. We're going to attack all that food out there!"

At the mention of food Virginia grimaced, but when they reached the dining room, under Carolina's urging, she submitted to having food piled upon her plate. Lewis Burwell was known for setting a good table and Fairfield was famous for its hospitality—but tonight even Fairfield was outdoing itself. The long walnut table fairly groaned with platters of big plump oysters from the Chesapeake, dainty golden omelettes covered in rich sauces, steaming pink shrimps and scallops and crabs, fricassees and sallades, rock-hard hams cut into parchment-thin slices, tiny succulent sausages still sizzling, little buttery pancakes, Sally Lunn and tender yellow spoonbread, rich Damson plum tarts, peaches spiced in brandy, tangy persimmon pudding—indeed, such a variety of sweetmeats and nuts and pastries that one could not keep count.

"Virgie," said Carolina sternly, setting her white teeth into a thin slice of dark fruitcake. "Clean your plate! Remember what Mother used to say—there are countless children starving in Boston who would love every bite!"

Virginia restrained herself from retorting, "They are welcome to my portion!" and managed a few more nibbles. She was only gradually getting used to eating more normal portions and really did feel "stuffed" from very little food.

At that point the young Pages from Shelly turned up and Virginia was able to dispose of her plate while Carolina told Rye that Shelly, the Pages' dormered frame house where she had enjoyed so many parties, was actually named for the quantities of shells that had been found all about. It had been a feasting place for the Indians, she told him. They had piled their shells there.

Rye smiled and quickly charmed the young Pages by taking an interest in their plantation—and showing surprising knowledge for an English gentleman. But his gaze often strayed to Carolina. She read in it a longing to get her alone, and she felt a breathless catch in her throat. Now that he had been successful in bribing one of Fairfield's servants to provide them with a private cubbyhole, she found herself looking forward—for the first time ever—to the last dance of the ball and a tryst in the servants' quarters! It would be a "first" for her!

The roguish Carnaby boys joined them, making Virginia blush with their sallies, the conversation became general, and Carolina drifted off with her group to the drawing room where the two elderly gentlemen, empty plates now in hand, were still snarling over taxation and the price of tobacco, as if eating their supper had not even broken their stride. Ned Shackleford came up to hover near Carolina, and Dick Smithfield brought the showy Ashby girl from Accomack as if to flaunt her before Carolina. People drifted in and out, and suddenly Carolina heard someone say, "I just noticed that the Bramways aren't here tonight."

And someone else laughed and said, "I'm not surprised. I'm told that when Lewis Burwell delivered the invitation to Bramble Folly, he told Amanda Bramway he hoped she and Duncan could arrange to come in Sandy Randolph's barge since he'd heard theirs had been unfortunately sunk and he'd just invited everyone from Tower Oaks!"

There was a ripple of laughter and Carolina was reminded that Lewis Burwell and Sandy Randolph were close friends.

She turned to see if Rye had heard that but he was gone from her side, and a quick glance around the room showed that he was not in evidence. The spot where he had been standing gave a good view of the moonlit river just below the landing. She wondered suddenly if a longboat from the *Sea Wolf*—she could not get used to the ship being called the *Sea Waif*—could have glided up to Fairfield's pier, and if Rye had recognized it in the moonlight and gone down to speak to the occupants. She was well aware that sometimes in the dark a longboat had silently pulled up to the landing at Level Green. Once or twice she had looked out of one of the windows late at night or just before dawn and seen Rye slip from the house and go striding down the lawn to the river, there to have a brief hurried conference with the boatmen before returning. The longboat had vanished into the shadows as if by magic.

No one had ever commented on it—or even seen the longboat arrive, she supposed. Rye himself had never mentioned it, and she had been reluctant to bring up the subject—it seemed like spying on him.

"I must say I'm impressed by your English lover." An amused voice at her elbow interrupted her thoughts —and Carolina turned to find Sally Montrose at her side.

"Say 'betrothed,'" Carolina chided. "It sounds better!"

Sally laughed. "I prefer 'lover'—and it's probably more accurate! Oh, do come away from that fire, Carolina—it's stifling in here." She was fanning herself vigorously with an ivory fan as she spoke, and she drew Carolina away from the group and out into the hall. "And I can tell you, your 'betrothed' has a stone heart! Not even a brisk walk through the boxwoods this afternoon warmed him up! By the way, where *is* Rye?" She looked about her.

Carolina stopped dead and frowned at her friend. So *that* was what Sally had been up to this afternoon and why Rye had seemed to be avoiding her! "I don't know where Rye is," she said. "But Sally, you have too many patches of court plaster on your face. People will think you're hiding blemishes!"

Sally shrugged. "Let them think what they will. Black patches are fashionable! And the very next ball I go to, I'm going to powder my hair. That will make me stand out in the crowd—and I hear it's the latest thing in Paris."

In Paris maybe, but not along the James. Looking about her tonight, Carolina had seen wigs aplenty— full-bottomed wigs, campaign wigs, high-piled ladies' wigs—but they were all natural colors. It had come to her that maybe Virginia had been right. It would have been a mistake to be the only women present with powdered hair.

Sally, annoyed at having her black patches criticized, struck back. "Well, *I* may not have made much impression on Rye," she drawled with a sidewise look at Carolina. "But did you see him dancing with that Ashby girl from Accomack?"

"Yes," admitted Carolina, who had indeed noticed Rye dancing by with the dazzling brunette beauty. "I thought she looked very nice. And she's certainly a better dancer than she was when I left," she found herself adding.

"Nice?" said Sally. "Indeed Glynis Ashby does look nice! She looks *wonderful,* more's the pity, and she's considered the best dancer in the Tidewater!"

No doubt Rye had discovered that! Carolina felt a pricking of jealousy.

"I wonder where she is—Glynis Ashby, I mean." Sally's light drawl bore a trace of malice. *"She* seems to have disappeared too. . . ."

"Oh, come now!" said Carolina, nettled. "You surely aren't implying that Rye and Glynis Ashby have gone off somewhere together?"

"Oh, of course not, Carolina!" Sally's denial was a shade too hasty. "I just"—she turned about to scan the dancers as they reached the ballroom—"wondered where they'd both got to."

Carolina sighed. Sally was upset; Sally wanted everybody else to be upset too. So much for friendship!

Both girls were promptly claimed by eager dancing partners, and Glynis Ashby turned up dancing with Ned Shackleford, but that did not keep Carolina from asking in her first breath "Where were you?" when Rye appeared to claim her for a dance.

"Outside," he said briskly.

"The longboat . . . ?"

"Yes." His face was grave. "Carolina, come outside with me. Where we can talk without being overheard."

She was almost afraid then of what he was going to tell her.

She was silent as he drew her fur-trimmed velvet cloak over her shoulders. "I won't need a hat," she told him. "Not for a short stroll. And I won't bother with my pattens either."

"As you wish," he said restlessly, and she noted with some alarm that he was wearing his cloak.

It was dark on the lawn when they cleared the front door for the moon had dipped behind a patch of clouds and the trees were blurred shapes, the river only a silver glimmer, half seen. Rye took her arm to steady her, but she was sure-footed in her dancing slippers.

"Carolina, I've just had news. One of my men was drinking tonight in a Yorktown tavern. He talked too much. No one is sure how much he said but—" He frowned.

"You want me to leave with you?" she asked breathlessly, divining what he was going to ask her.

"No," he said. "I want you to understand."

She stared at him fearfully. "Understand what?"

"That I must leave here. Now. Tonight."

A terrible stillness seemed to steal over Carolina. "But you aren't sure," she protested. "You don't know what he said!"

"No, I don't." Rye's tall figure seemed to hover over her, dark against the night sky and the old trees as he spoke. "But whatever he said alarmed my crew. Carolina," he told her bluntly, "I can't wait around here forever. Somebody will recognize me. There's a price on my head, remember?"

"But that's in Spain!" she protested unhappily.

"And that price is high enough that there are those who would deliver me to Spain for such a rich reward," he pointed out in a grim voice.

She subsided, realizing the truth of what he had just said. "What will you do, Rye? Go to Barbados and see the governor there?"

"No, I'll sail to Bermuda and seek my pardon. The governor there is a friend of mine."

"Oh, Rye, why couldn't you wait just a little longer? You're safe here."

His voice held an edge of bitterness. "No buccaneer is ever really 'safe.' There are always those who will try him." He sighed. "My men are restless. They feel like targets, sitting here anchored in the York! If I don't leave soon, they'll upanchor one day and sail without me. And need I remind you that I've a fortune stowed aboard that ship?"

"I thought you'd already sent most of your gold to London," she said falteringly. "To your London agent."

"Not all," he said grimly.

"All right." She sighed, capitulating. "But not tonight—I can't leave tonight. I'll go with you tomorrow if you like."

"Carolina," he said gently, taking her face in his hands and looking down deep into her eyes. "You aren't going. I've seen what a wonderful time you're having here among all your old friends. Can't you see it would excite attention here if the bride and groom suddenly sailed away together *before* the nuptials?"

"But I don't want you to leave me here!" she protested.

He sighed. "You came here to please your mother,

and God knows she's planning the wedding of the century! Do you want to run away now and cause a scandal and break her heart?"

"No, of course not." Carolina realized that she was trapped. And naturally Rye was restless—for her mother had taken to leaving her bedchamber door open and reading by candlelight, making it very hard for Carolina to slip down the hall to Rye's room. She had protested to her mother on the two occasions that she had tried to slip by and been caught, that she had seen her mother's light and had thought to quietly close her door against the cold draughts of the hallway, but her mother had given her a cynical look and pointed out that she was wearing a thick woolen wrapper and "hardly felt the cold." Carolina had felt her cheeks redden beneath that knowing glance. It had been on the tip of her tongue then to say, "Mother, we're married!" but she had not. After all, she had gone this far on a half-truth; she could go on a little longer, especially since knowing the truth could only make her mother unhappy. "I suppose you must go," she agreed reluctantly.

"Yes. I must." The determination in his tone allowed no room for compromise. Silently he bent to kiss her and she clung to him. Her arms wound around his neck, willing him to return to her.

And then he was gone, melting into the shadows beneath the trees. Carolina stood and watched the shadowy shape of the longboat pull away, and then there was only the empty stretch of silver river shining in the moonlight.

How long she stood there she did not know, but there were tears on her cheeks, and the cold breeze that had come up made those tears feel like rivulets of ice sliding down her face.

"Carolina, come away," said a sympathetic voice behind her, and she turned to see a blurry vision of Sandy Randolph, elegant in his amethyst brocade coat with its stiff skirt and wide cuffs.

"He's gone," she said, and there was grief in her voice. "Rye is gone."

"I know," he said. "He told me he was going. I came out to talk to you so we would all tell the same story. He suggested we use the excuse that he had received word of a friend's death and was needed to help settle the estate—and that, rather than disrupt the party, he had departed quietly, leaving you to make his apologies to his host."

"A friend where?"

"Barbados."

"But he's going to Bermuda!" she protested. "To seek his pardon."

"Best to say he went to Barbados," Sandy advised. "Then if there's any problem, the authorities won't be looking for him in the right place."

"But why should they be looking for him?" she cried. "They didn't know he was here!" She studied Sandy fearfully for there had been an undertone of warning in what he had just said, an implied threat to Rye. As if Sandy knew something she didn't. Sandy kept silent and she sighed. "All right, I'll say he went to Barbados."

"If you're worried about what your mother will say, I'll tell her," he offered.

Carolina nodded. That would be best. Her mother was bound to be upset and Sandy had a way with Letitia.

She glanced back toward the big bulk of Fairfield with its gaily candlelit windows spilling light upon the lawn. Even from here she could hear the tinkle of the music drifting out toward the trees and the river. It sounded so festive when she felt so sad . . . for who knew when her lover would come back to her?

She reached down to pick up her skirts for the walk back to the house. Her gray satin dancing slippers, she thought in a detached way, would be ruined by the damp grass.

"His men would have been growing restless," said Sandy, beside her.

"Yes. He said so." Mechanically.

"And he couldn't risk the uncertainty of the governor's return."

"No, I suppose not." As they neared the house the light from one of the windows revealed Sandy's face. He was studying her keenly, with sympathy in his eyes. And suddenly she guessed what he was thinking: *He may never come back.*

"Carolina—suppose he goes back to buccaneering?"

"He won't!" she cried, stung.

Sandy's gaze grew meditative. "Men who live by the sword usually go back to it."

And men who live by the sword die by the sword—and go back to no one. . . . The inference was clear.

"Rye will be back in time for the wedding," she mumbled.

"And when will that be? As I understand it, Letty won't allow a date to be set yet."

"She's waiting to hear from Aunt Pet," sighed Carolina. "And for the governor to return," she added resignedly.

Sandy laughed, his morose mood mercurially changed. He knew as well as Carolina did how Letty loved spectacles—great dramatic events, carefully staged. As she was planning to stage this one.

"One other thing," he cautioned as they reached the

front door. "I wouldn't say anything about his leaving just yet. Why not wait till morning? Make excuses for him, say he's talking to someone, he spilled Madeira on his cuffs and has gone to change his shirt—anything you can think of. Don't let anyone know he's gone until morning. Then you can say at breakfast that he woke you up at dawn and told you he'd been called away."

"Why?" she asked steadily.

He hesitated. "Just in case . . ." He let the words drift off.

Again that hint of something terribly wrong. . . .

"In case of pursuit?" she demanded, as they reached the door.

"Possibly . . ." He frowned. "And don't stand in the door talking. We could be overheard."

He threw open the heavy front door and Carolina went in, chilled not so much by the river damp as by Sandy's words. He drifted away from her toward the ballroom and she wanted to run after him, crying, "Tell me what you know!" But she knew it would do no good. When Sandy was ready to tell her, he'd tell her. And not before.

Rye had promised to take her to the Fairfield ball. He had kept that promise.

He just hadn't told her that he would leave before it was over!

LEVEL GREEN
THE YORK RIVER, VIRGINIA

Spring 1689

Chapter 9

Now that Rye had sailed for Bermuda and they were all back at Level Green, Carolina had plenty of time to think. To think about what it would be like to lose a husband—as Virginia had. Or to be abandoned by the only man you ever loved—as Sally Montrose had. Or to go running back to the man you loved so desperately, only to have to leave him again because you were both married to other people—as her mother had.

What would be would be, she had told herself fatalistically when their barge took them back from Fairfield to Level Green. She had fended off Sally's curious questions and Virginia's anxious ones, but she had been uneasily conscious of her mother's thoughtful gaze upon her on that return trip and guessed that her mother was puzzled by it all. But she had tried to look calm as she stared out over the wide expanse of the York, shining silver beneath a gray winter sky—as silver as her eyes. Or Sandy Randolph's.

True to his word, Sandy had backed up her story. He had told everybody he had been up early and run across Rye leaving. Told everybody so smoothly that he had been believed. Or at least not challenged.

So life had slipped back into its usual pattern at Level Green—save that the wedding plans had gathered momentum as winter in the Tidewater slipped into spring.

Now the weeks had sped by and Carolina was standing on the damp spongy earth, with early spring bulbs just peeking out of the ground, and watching—as she so often did—for any sign of a sail.

But there was no sail.

Carolina sighed and her thoughts drifted to Virginia.

For Virginia the ball at Fairfield had been a disaster. She had gained five pounds since Carolina's return, but after the ball she had become listless and had begun to lose weight again.

She's lost hope, Carolina realized. *Virgie looked better at the Fairfield ball than she'd ever looked in her life—and it still didn't help. And that was because people decided early on what they thought about you and it took something really major to change their opinion,* thought Carolina. But watching Virginia turn away from food all that first week after the ball had made Carolina desperate. Obviously her mother, wrapped up in plans for a wedding that might never come off, wasn't going to do anything about Virginia. It was up to *her.*

The night Virginia hardly touched her supper and then retired to bed, saying she felt "a little light-headed," brought things to a head. Carolina had watched Virginia's wavering, almost weightless progress up the stairs with real alarm and had come to an abrupt conclusion. Quickly, before she could change her mind, she snatched up some hot chocolate in one of the new fashionable "chocolate cups" and followed her up. What she was planning might not be the right thing to do, but she felt she had to take the chance—it could mean saving Virginia's life.

She walked briskly down the hall, took a deep breath, and flung open the door to Virginia's pleasant green and white bedchamber. Virginia had not lit a candle and the bed with its green and white petticoat valance was only a large square shape in the dimness. It was a misty night and only the palest of early moonlight filtered into the room, but that was enough to reveal that Virginia had thrown herself across the bed in exhaustion.

Carolina latched the door and advanced upon the bed. She did not need candlelight for what she was going to say.

"Virgie." Carolina sat down upon the bed.

Virginia stirred. "Oh, is that you, Carolina?" she murmured without opening her eyes.

"Yes. I have something important to talk to you about."

"Oh?" Virginia sounded far away; she still did not open her eyes. Carolina felt that Virginia was drifting away from her—perhaps into an unconscious state in which she'd be unable to eat.

"Oh, Virgie!" She was almost in a panic. "Please buck up! Open your eyes and look at me. Can't you see I need you?"

Virginia opened her dark blue eyes and stared upward. There was Carolina's anxious face, swimming before her in the wavery light. "What—what did you say, Carolina?" she demanded weakly.

"I said I *need* you. Oh, Virgie, I've got to tell someone. Rye is playing a dangerous game—he could die of it! And if he dies, I think I'd die too. I need you, Virgie, to help me through it."

Something lost and forgotten in Virginia stirred. She had been absorbed in her own personal failures and tragedies for so long. And around her all her life there had been nothing but blazing success—or so it seemed to her: proud passionate Penny, going her own way; beautiful sought-after Carolina; indomitable Letitia— all three of them sweeping all before them. And in the background there was Fielding, absorbed in his fantastic new house, and forgetful of his less attractive daughter and her lighthearted self-sufficient younger sisters. And now, out of the darkness had come this strange new thought—voiced by, of all people, the great beauty of the family—Carolina. She was *needed*. Something she had never been before. *Needed*. The film seemed to leave her eyes and she saw Carolina's beautiful pleading face clearly at last.

"Oh, Virgie," sighed Carolina. "You're too weak to take it all in. Sit up and drink this chocolate and I'll tell you about it."

Obediently Virginia sat up and sipped the chocolate as Carolina told her. About Rye. About Tortuga. About her brief violent life there as the Silver Wench.

When Carolina was finished, the chocolate was too and the story had left Virginia gasping. "I only thought Rye was mixed up with the buccaneers in some sort of clandestine trading," she cried. "I never dreamed he was their *leader!*" She grew even more distraught. "But suppose for some reason Rye can't get his pardon? Suppose there's some hitch?"

"Exactly what I've been thinking," said Carolina in a worried voice. "Because he's been gone so long, and there's been no word. Maybe the governor wasn't there, maybe—oh, so many things could have gone wrong!"

"And you never told me!" cried Virginia accusingly. "You bore all this by yourself?"

"Virgie, you were so weak and fragile, I was afraid it would be too much for you to know. But now—oh, suppose Rye comes back and needs help, Virgie? I can't ask Mother or Fielding—Fielding would promptly turn him over to the law and say 'Good riddance!' And I don't know what Mother would do! And Sandy might not be readily available, he's always going away somewhere. Oh, Virgie, I need someone to—to back me up in case there's trouble. Someone I don't have to explain to, someone who already knows all about everything and who'll keep my secret for me."

"*I'll* keep your secret and *I'll* back you up!" cried Virginia, filled with hot chocolate and excitement.

"Oh, you say that now, Virgie, but when the time comes you'll be so weak you won't be able to," sighed Carolina. "You'll have starved yourself so you'll simply faint and be no help at all. If only you had some strength!"

"I won't faint," insisted Virginia, her voice infused with newfound energy. "And I *will* help—I'll *find* the strength!"

"Then begin by coming back downstairs and eating at least a few bites of dinner—we can find something in one of the pantries. Everything won't have been cleared away yet."

"Well . . ." Virginia hesitated. She did not really want dinner, but Carolina was already urging her to her feet.

"Suppose Rye's ship ran into trouble? Suppose he's shipwrecked somewhere? It could take him a long time to get back to me—and you know Mother; she's hot to have a big wedding this spring, and a big wedding she will have—even if she has to substitute a new bride-groom!"

That last goaded Virginia into action. She padded across the floor and accompanied Carolina back down-stairs to whisper and scheme.

And as she nibbled the assortment of cold meat and Sally Lunn and corn fritters that Carolina was able to find, Virginia became so interested in Carolina's prob-lems that when Carolina sighed, "So you can see, Virgie, if you waste away and die on me—" she almost laughed. For of a sudden she had no intention of dying, or of wasting away either. She intended to eat. All her abused stomach could tolerate. For she had a purpose in living now—she was needed! It had just come to her, what her mission in life was to be. She might not be able to find happiness for herself, but she could help someone she loved find happiness. She made up her mind right then: She was going to Get Carolina Through It!

Since then Virginia had gained ten pounds. It wasn't enough—she was still thin as a rail—but it was enough to please their mother, who had smiled at Virginia only last week and had told her graciously that she was "looking much better" and it was "certainly high time she forgot that miserable fellow!" This reminder of the reason for Virginia's decline had frightened Carolina—she had given Virginia a pleading look. But Virginia had smiled bravely back, even if her smile was a little crooked. It was hard to be reminded, but in spite of that she had managed to eat most of her dessert.

Carolina had been proud of her.

And all this time there had been no word from Rye.

"I cannot understand it," Letitia had said irritably at supper last night. "Plans for the wedding are nearly complete. And Rye Evistock seemed so—responsible. Why does he not at least write?"

Virginia, who was at that moment spooning up pumpkin soup with some determination, looked up. "Maybe he can't," she volunteered. "Maybe he—"

Carolina gave Virginia's ankle a light nudge under the table. Looking down at her plate she found her food suddenly tasteless. "I am sure Rye must be terribly busy," she muttered, "settling his friend's estate."

Her mother had only sniffed.

"Maybe his ship ran into pirates!" cried Della, who had a flair for the dramatic, and little Flo said, "Oh-h-h-h!" and her eyes shone.

Carolina had given them both an unhappy look. Had he run into trouble getting his pardon in Bermuda, she wondered, as he had here in Virginia? Or had something happened to him?

Speculation on that had kept her awake far into the night. . . .

Now on the tender springtime grass, she stood by the riverside, as she so often had of late, longing for Rye to come back. Overhead a flight of geese winged noisily by, on their way north. A single bald eagle soared gracefully above, seeming almost stationary, a lonely sentinel in an empty blue sky. Robins were pecking for earthworms among the new grass blades and bluebirds scolded from the branches of the flowering redbud and the creamy white dogwood nestled among the giant oaks.

Before her the river was a shining expanse of blue, reflecting the azure sky, sharing no secrets, telling her nothing. . . .

After a while she gave up watching the empty river

and went back inside the massive brick house that Fielding Lightfoot might never be able to pay for, but that suited him and his Letty so superbly well. She found Virginia settled into a big chair by a window in the paneled library. As usual Virginia had her head in a leather-bound volume—probably Latin, thought Carolina—which she closed as Carolina entered.

"You were watching for Rye, weren't you?" Virginia said in a commiserating voice. "I saw you standing out there by the river."

"Yes," admitted Carolina with a sigh. "I was."

"Like Iseult the Fair," Virginia declared mournfully —for she had just been reading the medieval legend of Tristan and Iseult and was steeped in tragedy. "Falling in love at the wrong time and the wrong place—"

Carolina interrupted her before she could add "and with the wrong man—like me." She was familiar with the legend and she didn't like the inference that Rye was not coming back, that perhaps he had found— as Tristan of the legend had—another woman. "I'm not as well read as you are, Virgie," she interrupted crisply. "But I am very certain that I am not like Iseult."

"Your wedding dress is all done," mourned Virginia. "And where is the bridegroom?"

"Safe and well, I hope!" Vexed, Carolina looked past Virginia, down the broad lawns toward the river.

"It may be I've brought you bad luck!" Virginia hugged the leather volume to her flat chest. "I've managed to ruin my own life and now maybe my bad luck is spreading to you as well! Maybe Rye will never come back and you'll fall into disuse like me!"

"Stop that!" said Carolina sharply. "You're working yourself up for nothing, Virgie. And—" As she spoke she was looking out the window at something outside, and her voice changed, grew excited. "There's a long-boat coming up the river—oh, Virgie, it's Rye, I know it is! He's come back!"

BOOK II

The Lightfoot Lass

Of all the lads on bended knee
Who ever sought to wed you,
Ask yourself, do you think that he
Will wed you now he's bed you?

PART ONE

The Wedding
Nobody Ever Forgot!

The wit and wisdom of the world
Have changed her not a whit.
She flies at fate, all flags unfurled,
With eyes like beacons lit!

LEVEL GREEN
THE YORK RIVER, VIRGINIA

Spring 1689

Chapter 10

No expense had been spared to make this wedding of aristocratic Carolina Lightfoot to Rye Evistock, gentleman of Essex, the event of the season in the Tidewater. Certainly it was the most lavish wedding in human memory along the banks of the York. All morning barges and boats had been plying up and down the York and the James, bringing satin-clad ladies and gentlemen to alight at the river landing and make their way across the smooth oak-dotted lawns of Level Green where—in what was easily the largest house in all of Colonial Virginia—a great wedding was soon to take place.

A whole smokehouse of rock-hard hams were even now being sliced thin as paper for the repast after the ceremony. Two dozen wild turkeys were being turned on spits set up outside. A whole army of servants, many of them newly hired and some of them borrowed from other plantations, were scurrying about the endless corridors with pressing irons and wine bottles and billowing dresses and pewter chamber pots.

As with most great occasions, there had been a few hitches.

The blue and white plates had arrived, smashed to smithereens by improper packing, and the extra cutlery Letitia had ordered had never been shipped at all. But neighbors and friends had rallied to their aid. Chargers and trenchers and cutlery—all cleaned with a mixture of ashes of wheat straw and whiting and burned alum rubbed vigorously with a woolen cloth—had been contributed by Ralph Wormeley of Rosegill and others, along with grooms and serving wenches to "help out" in the expected crush. Great cheeses from Cheddar and Cheshire had been brought to Level Green fresh from English ships and a hunt was organized for wild turkeys, which were becoming scarce. Perspiring serving girls were even now pounding coffee "berries" with a pestle. The servants whispered that they had never seen so much of that expensive drink—tea, poured from conical-topped pots, or chocolate which was to be served in special chocolate cups set, Spanish fashion, in silver frames. For themselves the servants preferred brandy or the new "geneva" which was brandy mixed with juniper berry juice and would eventually come to be known as "gin." There were dozens of greenish glass wine bottles with glass seals being brought up from the big cellars—and it was rumored that Fielding Lightfoot had imported several large "pipes" of wine which might well be consumed before the marriage festivities were over. An extravagant affair it would be for a man deep in debt—as most of the planters were—but then, had not the Lightfoots always lived beyond their income? And did not the vast bulk of Level Green itself cause tradesmen to murmur to each other that while payment was slow because tobacco prices were down, tobacco prices might soon be up? And then they would be glad they had not pressed Fielding Lightfoot too far and driven him to take his custom elsewhere!

The bride's gifts were lavish: fine blackwork embroidery, silver sugar boxes, cruses for vinegar, a handsome brass cistern to set flagons of beer, a coverlet of "stump-work" embroidery, a marquetry striking clock, an almost endless collection of silver mugs and goblets, several silver teapots with hinged dunce-cap tops, a set of red Turkey cushions, and from the bride's family a pair of handsome branched silver candlesticks (although Virginia, who had had a rather frightened look in her eyes ever since Carolina had told her the truth about Rye, had muttered to her sister that the bride of a former buccaneer captain would have no need of more plate—Spain had already provided that!).

The house too had been decorated for the wedding. All the spring flowers that could be found had been strategically placed, and a long garland of gilded holly now decorated the handsome carved banisters of the broad stairway.

Carolina had planned to wear a garland of gilt holly on her gleaming hair as well—for bridal veils had not yet come into fashion and the only veil worn currently at weddings was a bride's own hair, loosed and combed down to float around her shoulders and her slim waist. "Wedding circlets" were customarily worn around the head. But Rye had decreed that Carolina had no need of prickly holly, gilt or otherwise, and had presented her only this morning with a long rope of pearls from an island off South America, a rope which she and an astonished Virginia had fashioned into a gleaming circlet.

Aside from that, poor Virginia had been no help at all in getting Carolina ready for the ceremony. Spirited Letitia had decreed that her remaining marriageable daughter—for little Della and Flo were still too young for suitors—should not be "sober-sided" for this great occasion and had dosed her with "High Spirited Pills" which contained among other things "salt of steel," castor, assafoetida, camphire and amber. Virginia had weakly protested that she was by nature quiet and that to be in noticeably high spirits might be considered unseemly—as if she wanted to be rid of Carolina. But her mother had scoffed at that and had said that half the time Virginia went around looking frightened (it was true enough but of course Letitia could have no inkling of the reason). So under Letitia's stern gaze, Virginia had bravely gulped down the High Spirited Pills—and ever since she had been walking slightly aslant with a glazed look in her dark blue eyes. For a bridal gift Virginia had given Carolina a beautiful red velvet–bound volume which contained not one but two racy novels, *Wives' Excuse, or Cuckolds Make Themselves* and *The Clandestine Marriage,* bound together but upside down to each other as was the fashion, so that the book had to be reversed to read the second novel. The name of that second novel, *The Clandestine Marriage,* had given Carolina a momentary twinge— she had shot a quick glance at her mother, but her mother hadn't remarked on either title so Carolina had relaxed.

"Can we not get this accursed ceremony over with?" Rye had muttered when on arrival he had discovered that the wedding would be several days away, there being so many days considered "unlucky" for weddings.

Carolina had laughed. "Whatever Mother takes up, she does it with a vengeance! We're lucky not to have an *autumn* wedding!"

Rye had snorted.

But her wedding day had come at last. She had found to her surprise that she was too excited to eat breakfast. She excused herself, and Rye found her standing on the lawn and looking about her as if she were viewing it all for the last time—as of course she might be, for once she had embarked on her new life far away in England, who knew if she would ever come back to the Tidewater?

"Do you think I will ever see it again?" she asked wistfully, looking down the wide river.

"Of course," he said in a restless voice, for these past days of marking time waiting for the ceremony—now that he was back with his pardon—had irked him. "You'll come back for visits."

Studying the old trees, the familiar landscape, Carolina wondered silently if Sandy Randolph would come to see her wed or whether he would remain at Tower Oaks listening to the endless screams of his mad wife who, it was reported, could scream for an hour at a time for no reason whatsoever. Thinking of what life must be like for him there, she shivered.

"You cannot be cold," frowned Rye. "Indeed 'tis unseasonably warm." His restless fingers eased the lace at his throat.

"Oh, I'm not cold," said Carolina instantly. "I was just thinking. . . ." She did not want to discuss her real father's unhappy situation, not on her wedding day. "I wish Aunt Pet were here," she said plaintively. "She's my favorite relative, outside of close family, and I do think she might have chosen some other time to journey to Philadelphia."

"She had already departed before you arrived," he pointed out reasonably.

"Yes, but we *wrote* to her and she should have come back."

"Perhaps she never got the letter."

That was always possible but it upset Carolina that Aunt Pet with her twinkling eyes and her kindly affection should not be here to see her wed. Of all her mother's relatives, Aunt Pet was far and away her favorite. She had always good-naturedly taken the Lightfoots into her Williamsburg house, no matter how they warred among themselves.

"Perhaps she'll get here before we leave," she said, sighing.

"'Tis my intention to cut short the festivities as much as possible," he said quickly. "Now that I've my king's pardon at last, I'm eager to be off to England and get on with our lives."

"Couldn't you perhaps consider settling in the Colonies?"

Rye stared down at her, his dark face impenetrable. "I didn't know you wanted to stay in the Colonies," he said slowly.

"Well, I didn't really think I did, but now—" Carolina looked around her at the familiar surroundings she would soon be losing, and sighed.

"I thought you preferred Essex."

"Well . . ." She *had* loved Essex. It was to Essex that her school friend Reba had taken her for the Christmas holidays, and it was in Essex, during those same Christmas holidays, that she had fallen in love with Rye. Essex was—romantic. But . . . Virginia was *home*. It would be hard to leave here.

"We'll talk about it later," he said with finality. "I see your mother advancing upon us."

Letitia Lightfoot was an imposing figure as she came up the garden walk toward them. She was already gowned in the lustrous lilac silk she would be wearing this afternoon for the ceremony and a broad-brimmed

hat afloat with lilac plumes rode her imperious head.
She glanced at her prospective son-in-law. "A pity you
did not take my advice and wear white satin trimmed in
gold braid," she murmured. "We could have postponed
the wedding whilst it was made up by a tailor in
Williamsburg."

"I am not the bride," pointed out Rye evenly, "but
only the bridegroom."

His irony was lost on Letitia, wrapped up as she was
in making this wedding a memorable spectacle. "It
would have been better." She frowned. "With Carolina
in white, you would have *matched*."

Carolina looked up at her tall bridegroom proudly.
He was dressed handsomely in dove-gray satin trimmed
richly in silver, and a ruby of price flashed in the burst
of mechlin at his throat. He had such an affinity for gray
that she had several times heard him called "the man in
gray" but she had never mentioned that to him because
she thought it might make him stop wearing gray and it
was a color that well became his cold gray eyes and
thick gleaming dark hair. "I like Rye in gray," she told
her mother defensively.

Rye's prospective mother-in-law sniffed. "Come
along, Carolina," she said briskly. "You have barely
time to bathe and dress now if you're to look present-
able for your wedding!"

With a wicked smile at Rye, who frowned after them,
Carolina let herself be pulled along, to soak endlessly in
a hot tub sudsy with scented French soap, and then to
be pomaded and powdered and brushed and combed
and dressed at last in the silver-latticed petticoat and
the white satin wedding gown. The fashionable *Cul-de-
Paris* bustle of the long trained skirt was held up by a
large brooch of brilliants. (There was some doubt
whether she could sit down in it but then, as Letitia had

said sweepingly when she had approved it, whyever would Carolina wish to sit down in her wedding gown? A woman should have strength enough to stand upon her feet until she reached the bridal bed!)

Dressed at last, and surrounded by bridesmaids and her mother, Carolina gave the long train an experimental kick with her white satin slipper and studied the effect in the mirror in her bedroom. It glided dutifully just where it was supposed to, and her two little sisters, dressed in identical petal-pink silk dresses, applauded from their seat on her big square bed.

"The train makes the gown heavy," commented Carolina.

Virginia, in her sky-blue gown, staggered forward to adjust one of Carolina's panniers. "At least you don't have to have someone in there with you," she said, giving Carolina a somewhat owlish look. "Like that poor French Princess Henrietta Maria, when she was married to King Charles I by proxy at Notre Dame. *She* had such a heavy train that not only did it take three ladies of the court to hold it up but a *man* had to crawl underneath and hold it up with his head and hands so she could walk!"

The two young girls seated on the blue and white coverlet in their matching pink dresses burst into such giggles that their mother gave them a reproving look and they subsided. The bridesmaids tittered and one of them—Sally Montrose—said pertly, "Maybe we should make *your* train heavier, Carolina!"

Suddenly Rye appeared at the open door. With a nod to the company he strode inside and held out his hand to Carolina.

"I forgot to give you these earbobs," he said. "I thought you might want to wear them."

Carolina turned and for a moment the tall buccaneer was dazzled by the winsome beauty of the girl before him. Carolina's long fair hair hung like a glittering shawl of moonlight as it cascaded over her white satin shoulders. He caught his breath at the sight.

Letitia stepped forward. She lifted her head and fixed her prospective son-in-law with a look meant to quell him. "Carolina is wearing quite enough jewelry. Well"—she was taken aback at the size of the great fiery green stones that glittered in a hand that reached out from a spill of mechlin at the wrist—"perhaps she *should* wear them after all." She snatched up the emeralds and gave them to Carolina, then turned back to Rye. "But *you* should not be talking to Carolina before the ceremony nor see her in her wedding gown—it's bad luck."

Rye shrugged. "I've had indifferent luck all my life. Why should it turn now for the worse?"

Letitia moved forward, shooing him out of the room, and accompanied him along the corridor, discussing exactly how it would all be done, for they had not rehearsed the actual ceremony—someone had suggested that too might be "bad luck."

"In any event you should remain downstairs," she told Rye firmly. "Do not try to see Carolina again before the ceremony. And"—she looked down at his sword which had clattered against one of the balusters for they had now reached the head of the stairs—"you must not wear that. All the gentlemen will have removed their swords so they will not make an unseemly clatter during the ceremony!"

Rye hesitated. That sword had never left his side, save in bed, for so long that it had almost become a part of him. For a moment he was tempted to retort that he would be married sword at his side or not at all but—it was a small thing. And for a short time only. After the ceremony he would buckle it back on!

Silently he handed his basket-hilted sword in its scabbard to Letitia and went down the stairs to join the gentlemen below, where the eldest Whitley brother was making sure everyone knew he had been to London by loudly telling Sandy Randolph, who had got there after all and was leaning upon a handsome bronze-headed ebony walking stick and trying to hide his boredom, how he had been forced to pay "spur money" to the choir boys when he had forgotten he was wearing spurred boots and ventured into the cathedral wearing spurs. Sandy's silver eyes were glazing as the Whitley lad trumpeted that at places of the "lower sort" in London, ale was so cheap one could get drunk for tuppence.

"*I* could get drunk just looking at a lady," Sandy murmured—and his gaze was on Letitia, a lavender vision at the top of the stairs.

Nearby the Layton girls had begun laughing almost hysterically—not so much because they were amused at Whitley's remarks but because their mother had thought them too dull and had fed them so many "High Spirited Pills" that the least thing reduced them to helpless mirth. They continued giggling as Rye brushed by to speak to Sandy.

At the head of the stairs, Letitia hefted the heavy sword Rye had silently handed her and cast about for somewhere to put it. Her bedroom perhaps. . . . But at that moment a voice called to her urgently from down the hall. Little Flo had hidden a plum tart in the pocket of her lace-trimmed apron and the plums had dribbled upon her pink dress—with the ceremony about to begin, what was to be done?

Confronted by this new emergency, Letitia hastily set Rye's sword down at the top of the stairs, left it leaning against the banisters and hurried back to determine that the dress was ruined and that the wailing child must be dressed again—in yellow, there was nothing else for her; she had not another pink dress to her name!

The sword remained at the head of the stairs—forgotten.

Now at last, amid excited little cries from her bridesmaids—and a final emotional hug from Virginia, who was weeping and dabbing at her eyes—Carolina stepped forth from the bedchamber into the corridor and let the girls arrange her long train for the showy walk down the stairs. Letitia hurried downstairs and the wedding party began to make their slow progress toward the company below. Carolina walked carefully down the corridor, practicing her mincing steps, for the circlet of pearls sat rather uneasily upon her long fair hair that fell in a shining veil about her shoulders, and she was well aware of how shamed her mother would be if that circlet chose to fall off as she descended the stairs.

"You must carry your head regally," had been Letitia's final admonition to her daughter, and now Letitia waited downstairs with the crowd of wedding guests for Carolina to make her descent. *(Your mother would have preferred a coronet,* Sally Montrose had whispered as she adjusted the circlet on Carolina's long fair hair.) *And it was undoubtedly true,* thought Carolina as she made her stately way to the head of the stairs.

Out of that sea of upturned faces in the great hall below she caught sight of Sandy Randolph in ice-green satin and carrying a walking stick. Her heart rejoiced. Her real father would see her properly wed at last even though it was Fielding Lightfoot who would give the bride away!

Fielding himself looked impressive in a new suit of cloudy-blue, laden with gold braid and gold buttons. Like his shiny boots the suit had been bought especially for the occasion (his tailor and his bootmaker would soon be dunning him). And beside him Letitia was a tall swaying flower in her enormously wide-skirted lilac silk embroidered here and there with silver violets. (Had it been winter, Virginia had muttered earlier, their mother would have been wearing purple velvet and it would have been hard to dissuade her from marking this triumph by trimming her gown in ermine!) *As became,* thought Carolina whimsically, *the new queen of Tidewater society staging her first big wedding in her new Tidewater "palace"!*

She herself, in gleaming white satin, was a princess of that society—a princess about to be wed to the prince of her choice.

Now, standing there at the head of the stairs, not yet married in the sight of the world, she looked down at Rye Evistock waiting below, tall and grave in elegant gray satin richly trimmed in silver—and saw him suddenly as he had been on the deck of the *Sea Wolf,* lithe and muscular and carrying himself with the effortless grace of the strong and all the confidence of the successful buccaneer captain he was. And through her memory at that moment, with the sun shining down upon the York, came the glitter of the moonlight on Cayona Bay. . . . Through her mind drifted the sights and sounds of their own "buccaneer wedding" held on board the *Sea Wolf's* swaying deck with all Tortuga cheering from shore and waving tankards and cutlasses. . . . Here in a great plantation house far from the wild world of the Indies, she was about to make her mother's dream come true—and her own dream as well, for now she would be legally his—forever! She took a graceful swaying step to descend that wide stairway that could accommodate eight abreast and smiled down into his eyes—those hard gray eyes that grew so soft at sight of her—and above the music of the harpsichord being dutifully pounded by Mistress Bottomley, she seemed to hear all the churchbells of Tortuga ringing. . . .

She had been afraid for so long—afraid something would go wrong, something would happen to mar their happiness. Now a sense of lightness and joy filled her. Rye was back, tanned and purposeful, he had won his pardon in Bermuda—though not without some delays —the old buccaneering life was behind them and nothing, *nothing* could go wrong now! And as if to prove that, she saw nearby Rye's long sword in its scabbard leaning carelessly against the banisters—that sword that, God willing, he would never have to wield again!

There above that intent sea of faces she wondered, suddenly, what her mother would say if she were to learn that Carolina had already been wed to Rye in a buccaneer ceremony on a ship in Cayona Bay—and decided that at this point her elegant headlong mother would only shrug and cry, "On with the wedding!"

And now she must live up to her mother's expectations.

The first bride of Level Green took a deep breath and prepared to descend the stairs.

Chapter 11

But as Carolina lifted her satin-covered foot to take that first step down the wide stairway, there was a commotion outside, the front door burst open and a disheveled Aunt Pet, clad in rumpled gray traveling clothes and with her wig askew, burst into the room. She gave the assembled company a wild look, then her gaze found Carolina, resplendent in white satin, about to descend the stairs.

"Oh, I am not too late!" she cried almost tearfully.

Letitia stepped forward, lavender skirts rustling. "Petula, we are delighted to see you," she chided. "But you are disrupting the ceremony!"

But Aunt Pet was too worked up to worry about the proprieties. "I have been attacked by pirates!" she cried, aggrieved. "Coming back from Philadelphia our ship was set upon and sunk and we were all cast adrift in small boats. It was that terrible Captain Kells who did it!"

There were exclamations of dismay but they were overridden by the deep voice of the bridegroom.

"You were not set upon by Kells," he said with flat finality. "*I* am Kells."

In the stunned silence that followed that revelation, Aunt Pet fell back a step. Then she peered forward, staring at the tall man who stood—from her direction—with his back to the light, almost in silhouette.

"If this man is Kells," she gasped, "what is he doing here, Letty?"

"He is the bridegroom, Petula." So far Letitia had managed to keep her composure save for a tightening around her mouth and an ominous gleam in her dark blue eyes. "And you must be mistaken in saying that he—"

"The bridegroom!" bleated Aunt Pet, her voice rising upscale in incredulity with every word. Her stained traveling skirts fairly quivered. "You would allow your daughter to marry this—this corsair who attacks English ships?"

Rye's voice rang out, cutting into her tirade.

"I have never attacked an English ship, madam. Buccaneer I have been, but I have attacked no ships save those of Spain."

"You attacked the *Ophelia,* that poor little coastwise vessel that was carrying me here—and you sank her!" cried Aunt Pet scornfully. "Indeed, 'tis your fault"—she pointed an accusing finger at Rye, who was regarding her in amazement—"that I have nearly missed Carolina's wedding!" In her overwrought state, the incongruity of being aggrieved at that last did not occur to her. She spread out her plump hands and turned dramatically to the assemblage who, like the bride standing frozen at the head of the stairs, were hanging onto her words. "I tell you this man's ship attacked us at dusk, his men swarmed aboard and herded our crew and passengers into open boats! They tossed us some ship's biscuits and water casks and laughed and said that these were compliments of Captain Kells!"

There was a growl from Rye at that point and Aunt Pet threw him a burning look. "We looked back as we rowed away and we saw the *Ophelia* burning and the gray shape of the *Sea Wolf* pulling away from her! Four days I have been in an open boat gnawing stale biscuits and drinking foul water! Had the weather been worse we would never have made the coast at all— we would all have been killed!" There was a rising mutter among the crowd and dark glances were cast at the bridegroom. "Ask him—ask him where he has been! For I can tell you he can't have been *here!*"

"He has been on Barbados, Petula!" cried Letitia. "Oh, can't you be silent? You are ruining the wedding!"

"I have been in Bermuda seeking a king's pardon from the governor there," Rye corrected her, stepping forward—which brought him a little nearer to the door as he confronted his accuser. "Which I have now secured." His face was dark with anger.

"Ha!" cried Aunt Pet, no whit convinced. "And anyway, Letty"—she swung upon Letitia—"this man cannot marry Carolina. He already has a wife—I heard them say so!"

"I *had* a wife!" roared Rye, and from the top of the stairs Carolina felt her world blow apart. "But she is dead in Spain."

Midway down the stairs Virginia crumpled into a dead faint. And Carolina felt as if a cold wind had passed over her breast, for Rye had told her there had been a woman once—he had never said she had been his wife.

"What?" screamed Letitia, losing her calm at last. "You had a wife, you say? How do we know she is dead? *How did she die?*" For it was well known in the Colonies that many a man who landed upon these shores chose to forget that he had left a legal wife back in England.

"She died of the hatred of her kinsmen," grated Rye. "Their hatred of me!"

"He lies! There was a blonde woman on the ship with him!" cried Aunt Pet. "And one of his men said she was his wife. Oh, arrest him! Arrest him, I say!"

"This 'pardon' Evistock speaks of will not hold good if what Petula says is true!" roared someone. "For this attack on Petula's ship would have taken place after the pardon was issued. Seize the blackguard, I say, and let the law deal with him!"

From the head of the stairs, with one white satin slipper sticking out stiffly before her as she prepared to take her first step down the wide stairway, Carolina was goaded into action. She had been stunned by Aunt Pet's words but now she put former wives far away into the back of her mind, for in a flashing vision she saw what would happen next: The wedding guests would seize the bridegroom, he would be dragged off to jail, his men aboard the newly rechristened *Sea Waif*—short-handed and without a leader—would hear of it and promptly upanchor and sail away, heading, leaderless, for Tortuga or God knew where else. But they would leave Rye here, his story would not be believed, and he would be forthwith hanged, amid general rejoicing, as the notorious Captain Kells!

At that moment her gaze fell upon the sword standing so near her hand. She swooped upon it and dragged it from its scabbard.

"Kells!" she called upon a sharp carrying note.

The wedding guests looked up in time to see a blade flash against white satin. Then the sword Carolina tossed described a wide arc over their heads—to be caught deftly by its hilt by the bridegroom.

Rye's smile flashed upward in gratitude to his lady.

"Thank you, Christabel," he murmured, using the name she had called herself on Tortuga.

And then, as he felt the familiar grip of that serviceable basket hilt, as his strong fingers closed about the weapon that had made him master of so many slippery decks, the crowd milling about saw him transformed: From Rye Evistock, indolent country gentleman of Essex, he became of a sudden the legendary Captain Kells, whose name resounded throughout the Caribbean.

"Ye'll give me room, gentlemen," his cold voice rang out. And a practiced gesture snaked the gleaming blade in a swishing arc around him that drove everyone back. "Carolina!" he called peremptorily and waved her to join him.

Carolina's foot was on the top step but the heavy train of her cumbersome bustled gown was dragging her backward. She knew in panic that she would never make it, that she would hold him back in her high-heeled slippers if she tried to run across the lawn encumbered by that long train.

"Go without me!" she cried desperately. *"Oh, don't wait!"*

"To the door!" cried someone from the crush. "We can block the way out with our bodies and others will lay hands upon him and seize him from the rear!" There were screams from the women as several men pushed forward. One or two ladies fainted.

"Back, gentlemen!" A new voice joined the din and this one held such a note of menace that the commotion was suddenly stilled. In surprise, heads swung about to see that Sandy Randolph's ice-green form now commanded the door and that his bronze-headed ebony cane had suddenly been transformed by a flick of a lace-frothed wrist into a sword, for a long "damascened" blade inlaid with silver had snaked out of it. And the bronze-headed top had become of a sudden a small wheel-lock pistol which he waved in his left hand. "Back, I say! The bridegroom is leaving!"

Carolina felt weak with gratitude as Rye spun through the now-confused crowd and bounded past Sandy with a nod of thanks. Then he was through the front door and running down the lawn toward the river.

"Steady!" warned Sandy grimly, waving his pistol. "I'll shoot the first man who follows!"

His face convulsed with rage, Fielding Lightfoot leaped forward.

Even as he moved, his wife threw herself upon him, seizing his arm to hold him back. Aunt Pet shrieked.

"Sandy, *don't shoot him!*" cried Letitia in an agonized voice. She was trying desperately to keep the two men she loved from killing each other.

From the top of the stairs where she was now leaning over, gripping the banister the better to see, Carolina was vaguely aware of all that. Aware that Aunt Pet had sagged against Ned Shackleford, who had bounded forward and was now sharing his burden with Dick Smithfield, who was calling out for smelling salts. Aware that on the stairs below her Virginia—ignored in the general excitement—was now sitting up dazedly. Aware that servants were rushing in from other parts of the house. But her heart was with the absent bridegroom, running down the lawn beyond her vision with his blade flashing bright in the sun.

"How dare ye help the fellow get away, Randolph?"

Fielding's voice, almost a bellow but choked with fury, rose above the clamor. "And *in my house,* to boot!"

He lunged forward, dragging Letitia with him, and Sandy's pistol swung toward him. And Sandy's cold face was above it. There were more screams, people fell back, fell silent, sure they were about to see murder done.

But it was not to be.

With a quick look at Letitia, whose dark blue eyes held a wild appeal as she sought to hold her husband back—and indeed he had now come to a stop, faced with a pistol pointed at his heart—Sandy Randolph waved the gun languidly at his host.

"Faith, you should thank me!" he retorted coolly. "For I have rid you of a problem, Lightfoot. Did you want to see your daughter weeping outside the jail, demanding to be wed to a man about to be hanged? Screaming to him from below the gibbet?"

"No, of course not," growled Fielding, mindful of the pistol. "Nor would she have!"

"Then you don't know women," said Sandy bluntly. "Look at her." He gestured toward Carolina on the stairs. "Had she been able to divest herself of that train, I dare say she'd have run away with him!"

"That is true!" cried Carolina—and caught her pearl circlet just as it slid off her head.

"And where do you think she would have gone with him?" mocked Sandy. "Letitia, did you want to lose your daughter to the hellholes of the Caribbean?"

"No, of course I didn't!" Letitia had been clinging to her husband's arm but now he shook free of her. But his expression had changed for he had realized the good sense of his rival's argument.

"I take your meaning, Randolph," he said in an altered voice. "But there is another course you have not thought of. We will seize the fellow before he reaches his ship and have him transported elsewhere to be tried! Carolina"—even now he could not bring himself to call her "my daughter," Carolina noted—"will not be involved."

"And have you lose a wedding guest or perhaps your own life to a man who's known to be the best blade in the Caribbean?" was Sandy's grim retort. He waved the pistol at the eager crowd who fell back once more. "Not a man of you here can match the fellow with either sword or cutlass! You'd be signing your death warrant! Indeed, I'll not stir from this spot until I'm sure he's got away."

"Sandy speaks the truth," said Ralph Wormeley soberly. "To catch up with this buccaneer is to die, most like."

Sheepish looks were exchanged among the well-dressed planters. They were brave enough in defense of home and hearth, and many of them had fought marauding Indians, but this mad pursuit of a desperate and fleeing buccaneer would be sheerest folly—it would be throwing one's life away!

From high on the stairs with her wedding circlet clutched in one tense hand, Carolina closed her eyes and silently prayed that the longboat on which Rye had told her they would slip away during the festivities, despite what anyone might think, had arrived early and was waiting for him. Fervently she thanked God for Sandy—and made desperate silent promises to God of all the ways in which she would improve if only He would let Rye make a safe escape.

She opened her eyes to see that Virginia, somewhat revived now, was being borne away from the stairway on the arm of Lewis Burwell, who had managed to keep his head though others had not. Several fainting ladies were having smelling salts waved beneath their noses, others were being carried away to couches. One or two crying children were being comforted by excited mothers. Outside a dog was furiously barking. Sandy Randolph still commanded the door—only turning his head slightly when one of the servants who had been "borrowed" from Lewis Burwell for the wedding festivities, burst in from outside. His weathered face was pale and he was out of breath and indignant.

"A man went runnin' by me just now waving his sword. And when I'd have had a word with him, he knocked me aside!" he reported, aggrieved, looking around for his employer to complain to. "I came in to see what's about?"

"That was our late bridegroom," Sandy told him ironically. "Gone now, alas."

The servant stopped stock still and stared in disbelief. "Lor'!" he burst out, forgetful of all the imposing company about him. "But *that* was the gentleman who offered me a gold coin the night o' the big ball at Fairfield if I'd clear out of my room so's he could bed one of the serving maids! And he's the *bridegroom?*" he marveled.

From the stairs Carolina found her voice. She might be no help at all in clearing Kells of piracy charges, but of this slur at least she could clear him.

"No, Rye didn't want the room for a serving maid," she corrected the man before she thought. "It was for me." She stopped. For the moment Kells was forgotten. All heads had turned toward her, and a sea of faces was staring up at her, open-mouthed at this frank admission in a day when aristocratic girls were sheltered and led virgin to the marriage bed.

"Oh, God," moaned Fielding, and Letitia shushed him and moved swiftly toward the stairs.

Carolina's face had gone scarlet. "But we didn't actually *use* the room," she hastened to add. And to their disbelieving expressions, "No, you don't understand. On Tortuga, we—"

"Not another word, Carolina!" cut in her mother's crisp voice. "He is gone, you can stop defending him!" Gathering up her wide lavender skirts, Letitia sped up the stairs and stepped in front of her blushing daughter. "Carolina is obviously distraught," she told the company. "She spent the entire night last night in tears at my bedside, wondering if she should marry the brute who has just departed! Her feeling of loyalty to him is quite unfounded and I will not have her tell lies to save what shreds of reputation Rye Evistock may still possess. Rye Evistock . . . Captain Kells—indeed I do not know what to call him!—has fooled us all. Come along, Carolina!"

Letitia moved inexorably forward, dragging a dazed Carolina with her.

As her mother was about to drag her down the corridor, Carolina turned to call down to the servant who had seen Rye leave. "The man with the sword— where did he go?"

"Into a longboat, last I seen," was the response and Carolina heaved a deep sigh of relief before her mother jerked her forward, train and all, down the empty upstairs corridor.

"I was about to say that Rye and I were married in a 'buccaneer's wedding' on Tortuga before we left there," complained Carolina when they were alone at last in her mother's room and she had tossed onto the bed the long strand of island pearls that had been her wedding circlet.

"Carolina, I know what you were about to tell them." Letitia whirled to face her daughter. "And believe me, it was best to keep silent!"

"But—"

"I know *all about* your 'buccaneer's wedding' on Tortuga."

"Sandy told you?" gasped Carolina.

Her mother nodded grimly. "We have few secrets from each other, Sandy and I. Especially about you. He also told me the wedding was not legal. It does not count!"

"*It counts to me!*" cried Carolina. "I vowed to be Rye's wife in Tortuga and his wife I will be forever!"

"Nonsense," said her mother in a weary voice. "Can't you see that what just happened downstairs changes everything? Stay here—I will say you are indisposed. Latch the door, talk to no one, while I try to get rid of our guests. Then I will think what to do."

"No, I can't just sit here and look at four walls," objected Carolina restlessly. "I have to know what is going on, whether Rye made good his escape. . . ." *And if he did not, I must hasten to his side. With a pistol hidden beneath my skirts!*

"He will have got away clear." Letitia was managing to hold on to her temper, but only just. "Sandy saw to that. But if you come downstairs, you will be forced to answer the questions of the curious—are you ready for that?" she shot at her daughter.

"No." Carolina shuddered.

"Then don't come down," she said sharply. "I will send Virginia up to you. And I will come myself if there is any news."

Virginia arrived in a dither, to tell Carolina that Lewis Burwell and Ralph Wormeley had been telling everyone they really ought to clear out, that the family needed to be alone at such a time. People had been departing, some reluctantly, for this was as juicy a scandal as anyone could remember. But most of the river barges were already pulling away, taking with them the wedding guests. There would be stories told at the Raleigh in Williamsburg this night!

Carolina ignored Virginia's meant-to-be-soothing chatter. "Any word about Rye?"

Virginia, with a pitying look, shook her head. "It's too soon."

Of course it was. Carolina knew that. But she couldn't help asking, and she knew she would go on asking. Until she knew he was safe.

"I'm going downstairs," she told Virginia, for indeed she was so upset she could hardly keep still. "I don't care what anyone asks me, I'm going to be where I'll know what's happening."

Virginia accompanied her anxiously down the broad empty stairway where they found that the last guests, the Montrose family, were just leaving. Sally Montrose, in her pink bridesmaid's gown, was just going through the door, and she turned and gave the distraught bride an avid look that said plainly, *Not only a buccaneer but a buccaneer with a wife!* Then Sally's frowning mother was jerking her through the door and Carolina and Virginia were alone in the great festive hall, decorated for a wedding destined never to be.

They found a family conference going on in the large dining room where sunlight streamed through the tall windows. Save for Della and Flo, who had been summarily banished from the proceedings and now were indignantly walking about the garden in the company of a nurse, the entire family was gathered around the long dining table which was heaped with confections and topped by a bride's cake that must have weighed more than forty pounds. Fielding and Letitia were there, Aunt Pet was there. And surprisingly, Sandy Randolph was there.

Carolina walked past Aunt Pet, who sat back exhausted in her stained gray skirts, without speaking, and approached Sandy Randolph.

"I want to thank you for saving Rye's life," she said softly. "I know you did it for me."

That face with coloring so startlingly like her own, hardened. "I did it on your mother's behalf. To rid you of him," he said briefly.

"Oh, surely you can't believe—"

"There had been rumors just before I arrived in Tortuga that Kells had attacked an English ship," was Sandy's terse response. "Once having met him, I was prone to believe him when he said he attacked none but the Spanish. But"—his face hardened—"I would believe Petula against the world."

Carolina swung around on Aunt Pet, who was now munching sweetmeats as if her life depended on it. "How can you be so sure the ship that attacked you was Kells's ship?" she demanded.

Petula chewed valiantly for a moment. Then, *"I* did not read the name *Sea Wolf,"* she admitted, almost choking. "And I think it is really too bad of you, Carolina, not to greet me when I shortened my stay to come back for your wedding!" She looked aggrieved.

Carolina hardened her heart. "You came back and *spoiled* my wedding!" she said bitterly. "Why could you not have remained in your open boat rowing about at sea for a few minutes longer?"

Aunt Pet gasped. "Oh, for shame!" she cried. "That you should wish such a thing!"

"I do not really wish it, Aunt Pet," groaned Carolina. "And I am truly glad to see you. But *how could you*

accuse Rye of such a thing? And you say yourself that
you did not see the name *Sea Wolf!*"

"No, but a crewman seated near me peered toward
the pirate vessel as we rowed away and he said that
in the light of the fire from the *Ophelia* he could make
out the name *Sea Wolf* painted upon her hull."

Again Carolina felt that light breath of cold caress
her. "But Aunt Pet, anyone could paint a name on a
ship!" she cried, remembering that the real *Sea Wolf*
now bore the name *Sea Waif*. "And what makes you so
sure the captain was Kells?"

"They called him Kells," said Petula flatly.

"Perhaps you misunderstood. Perhaps it was Mells.
Or Bells."

"Carolina, Petula has been through enough," reproved Letitia. "Do not bait her in this fashion."

"I am not baiting her!" flashed Carolina. "This
foolish old woman has just ruined my life and perhaps cost my lover his! Dare I not question her? Oh,
Aunt Pet—" She sank down on the rug beside the
older woman, unmindful of her bridal finery. Nor did
Letitia reprove her this time as she clutched those
travel-stained skirts. "Aunt Pet"—her voice turned
wistful—"I cannot believe that Rye would sink your
ship. Or set you adrift. Indeed when I was his guest"
—she carefully did not say "prisoner"—"on Tortuga,
I know that he was most gracious to captured Spanish
ladies—"

"Indeed! He married one," Letitia cut in ironically.

Carolina ignored that. "He returned them in style to
Havana. Indeed it is possible that he suffers from *too
much* gallantry toward women, that he would take such
chances on their behalf. Is it not possible that you are
mistaken? That the man you saw—in near darkness,
you admit—was not Kells?"

The room was very silent. Still chewing, Aunt Pet considered.

"No," she said at last, and there was finality in her tone. "It is true I did not see his face clearly or hear his voice, but he was of the same height, he had an arrogant bearing like your late"—she sniffed—"bridegroom. And his men called him Kells. And you all freely admit that he was at sea at the time the poor little *Ophelia* was attacked—he had the opportunity and he took it!"

"And the woman?" Carolina heard herself ask.

"The woman? Oh, you mean his wife? I could not see her clearly either. She was standing on Captain Kells's other side, away from me as our longboat pulled away. But I saw her skirts blow and I saw her hair, which was pale blonde and piled up—fashionably, I thought, though rather windblown."

Fashionably . . . windblown . . . Carolina moistened her lips. "And you say she was his *wife?*"

"How do I know whether she was his wife or no?" burst out Aunt Pet, aggrieved that Carolina, who had always been her favorite among Letty's daughters, would talk to her thus. "I remember, I was so distracted, I thought at first she was one of our passengers being detained for who knew what purpose, and I called out to one of the pirate crew, 'There is room for that woman too in our boat!' And he called back in very surly fashion, 'She doesn't go with you. She's Captain Kells's wife.'"

Not his woman—*his wife.* But of course Kells was known to have married her on Tortuga, so an impersonator would have found some blonde woman to impersonate her too.

"Aunt Pet," Carolina said sadly. "I hope you realize

that you have ruined my life by bringing these charges against Rye."

"Ruined *your* life?" Aunt Pet was so indignant that she threw down her sweetmeat and glared at Carolina. "It was *my* life that was in jeopardy! I am shocked to hear that you would consort with buccaneers on Tortuga—but to have brought one home with you!" She rolled her eyes to the ceiling as if seeking celestial aid.

"I did not bring him home—*he* brought *me!*" Carolina corrected her sharply. "And I met him in Essex— not Tortuga." *But it was on Tortuga that I found him again, so in a way it was Tortuga that gave my life meaning. . . .*

"He is a terrible man!" cried Aunt Pet. "His men swarmed aboard and took all our rings, our jewels, the provisions we had on board—even our luggage!" Her voice grew waspish.

Nearby Virginia muttered, "They got the silver chamber pot!" And was silenced as Letitia gave her a dangerous look.

"They 'got' the amethyst and pearl pin my mother gave me!" cried Aunt Pet in a passion, for she had heard Virginia's aside to Carolina.

"Well, I must go." Sandy rose with a sigh. "I only stayed to explain what I know of the man and why I think you would do well to lock your daughter up." He looked straight at Letitia. "She will try to find him again—I am sure of it."

Carolina scrambled to her feet, uncaring that she heard a rip in her handsome white satin gown. "I will see you to your barge, sir!" she flashed. "And you can tell me to my face what it is that you have been telling my mother behind my back!"

Letitia groaned. All of a sudden her dark blue eyes focused with burning intensity on the great cake dominating the table, dominating the room—so patently a wedding cake, mocking them all.

"Sandy," she said between her teeth. "Give me that sword-cane of yours—blade out."

He gave her a startled look, but he flicked out the sharp blade and surrendered the sword-cane to Letitia.

"The sight of that enormous cake is driving me mad!" she cried with sudden vehemence. And brought the blade of the sword-cane down upon the cake, splitting it in half. And down again.

The cake lay in ruins.

Virginia stared at it in awe.

"Thank you, Sandy." As if suddenly drained, Letitia handed him the sword-cane and sank back down upon her chair.

Sandy Randolph stood looking down on it in a bemused way as he cleaned the cake from the blade, dipping a napkin in wine to do the job. "Blood I might have thought to clean away, but never did I dream it would be cake!" he muttered.

And then he bowed and departed, with Carolina following him out to the hall, to the front door, her wedding gown trailing.

"You didn't really mean any of that, did you?" she asked him anxiously. "You were just talking for effect? Oh, Sandy, take me with you. Please, please—help me find Rye again."

He turned and took hold of her wrist. The grip of his fingers felt like steel and the countenance she looked up into was a wintry one. "You would be wise to forget Kells," he told her. "For it is unlikely that he will cross your path again. And if he does, I will deem it my duty to remove him from it. With this." He patted his sword-cane. "Or a pistol."

She recoiled from him. "I can't believe that you would—"

His voice came from between clenched teeth and rubbed her nerves raw. "Can't you take it in, Carolina, that you have been deceived, duped by this buccaneer —no, by God, this *pirate!* He's unworthy to be called a buccaneer! Setting a woman like Petula adrift in an open boat!"

"Rye didn't do that!"

"That's what *you* say, because you are enamored of him—but the facts show otherwise."

"Say what you mean," she panted. "Call me 'his woman'! For that I will continue to be!"

Sandy considered his rebellious daughter, standing there furious in white satin—the very picture of himself. His expression was grim.

"And you may not be his *only* woman," he told her evenly. "Have you never asked yourself why they call Kells the 'Petticoat Buccaneer'?"

"I did not know he was called that!" cried Carolina, trying to wrest her arm away. "Indeed I do not believe he is!"

Sandy Randolph sighed. "No, I suppose none would care to call Kells that in his hearing—or in yours, lest you might tell him and he wreak vengeance upon them. His reputation for gallantry—which you were so quick to defend—is well known. Still you must have noticed the unusual flag he runs up his masthead when he is about to assault a Spanish vessel?"

"I have never been with him in a sea battle!"

Sandy passed a hand across his forehead. "No, of course you have not. I had forgot you are a woman. It is well known that while other buccaneers may run up a skull and crossbones or a plain red or black flag to make known what they are, Kells runs up a woman's petticoat."

"A—a petticoat?" she faltered.

"Yes. It is of heavy black silk, very rich. *And when Kells attacks the ships of Spain he flies no other flag.* Dare you ask yourself why?"

And Spanish ladies were given to wearing heavy rustling black silk petticoats. . . .

"There was a Spanish girl once, he told me."

"A Spanish *wife* by his own admission—did he tell you that as well?"

Carolina's suddenly flushed face told Sandy he had not.

"I thought it was a surprise to you," he said dryly. "And hardly a welcome one."

Carolina felt humiliated. *Why had not Kells told her?* "But—but that was long ago," she protested.

"Or maybe not so long ago. And maybe not one Spanish girl but a dozen! You hardly know this man, Carolina!"

"I know him!" flashed Carolina, bent on defending Rye. "I have looked into his eyes and I have read there the truth!"

"Bah!" said Sandy Randolph disgustedly. "You are young, you know little of truth—and nothing at all of the world!"

"No, but I am learning!" she cried. "And from such men as you! I would not have thought it of you, to lie about him!"

"Lie?" Sandy gave her a look of such amazement that she knew he must have been telling her the truth as he knew it. "I have no reason to lie to you! The truth speaks for itself. Kells has had another wife—he said so."

"A dead wife!"

There was a look of complete cynicism that she had sometimes seen on Sandy Randolph's handsome unhappy countenance. He was wearing it now.

"Or perhaps a living one?" he suggested softly.

"Damn you!" cried Carolina violently. "I will not listen to you!" A sob broke from her lips and she fought to tear her arm away, but still it was firmly held.

"Letty," he called. "Look to your daughter!"

Her mother appeared, frowning, and escorted Carolina back to the dining room where Aunt Pet was still eating ravenously. Carolina did not look back at Sandy Randolph's departing form. Her eyes were filled with tears. Sandy had been—so briefly—a real father to her, but now that he believed Rye capable of doing terrible things, now that he had threatened Rye's life, he had sunk back into the pack so far as she was concerned. Let him go back to Tower Oaks—or to hell! She would not seek him out again!

"Carolina, you must apologize to Petula," said her mother as they reached the dining room door.

"I will apologize to no one!" gasped Carolina. "I am going upstairs to my room and rid myself of this—this awful dress! I should never have come back here, never!"

She turned and ran.

Her mother's gaze was speculative as she watched her go.

Chapter 12

Later that afternoon Virginia came up to inform Carolina cheerfully that Aunt Pet had eaten so much she had developed a stomachache and had gone off to bed, and that Fielding and Letitia were holding a counsel of war downstairs.

"Care for some wedding cake?" she asked Carolina, taking a small bite of one of the pieces she had brought up on a plate.

"It would choke me," said Carolina bitterly.

"It's very good," Virginia observed tranquilly. "And there are some forty pounds of it going to waste on the dining room table. Along with hams and what have you. I suppose Mother felt that if people ate before going it would be too much like a wake!"

"I'm going downstairs and get a slice of ham and some Sally Lunn," said Carolina, rising.

"Mother told me to watch you," sighed Virginia. "*She* thinks you'll run away."

"I won't run away," Carolina said resentfully. "But only because I don't know where to run!"

"I told her that." Virginia shrugged and continued to munch. She was gaining weight and with it her old personality was coming back.

But food was not Carolina's real reason for going downstairs. Promising Virginia to return shortly, Carolina slipped off her shoes and padded down in her stocking feet toward the library—that was where Fielding and Letitia usually had their family conferences. A servant had just left with a tray and the door was ever so slightly ajar. Carolina inclined her ear to that door.

". . . get her married to anyone who will take her," Fielding was saying angrily. "And as soon as possible."

"We must not lose our heads," Letitia said on an acid note.

"Lose our heads? We have already lost what little reputation we had left!" snarled Fielding. "You with Randolph's brat, fighting his battles for him with the Bramways! And now *she*—"

"Fielding," Letitia cut in coldly, "I will pretend I did not hear that remark about 'Randolph's brat.' Whatever you may think, if we are to continue living together as man and wife, we cannot have *that* between us."

"Oh, God." Fielding bent his head and groaned.

"The situation is easily rectified," his wife said soothingly. "This man Kells—or Rye Evistock, if that is truly his name—is lost to Carolina. He will never come back. But Ned Shackleford has always wanted her—you saw how he pursued her at the Fairfield ball. And Ned is not married yet. True, he has only a modest fortune and cannot give her the emeralds of the Incas or the gold of Mexico lifted from Spanish galleons. He cannot give her the life of adventure, living always on the brink, which she seems to desire—"

"*You* desired such a life once!" he interrupted hoarsely.

"Yes—well, I was young and foolish then," was the cool response. "But in his favor, Ned Shackleford *does* have an aunt in England. He and Carolina could be married here and sail for England and ride out this scandal. And when it is forgotten—"

"Forgotten?" rasped Fielding. "It will *never* be forgotten! She is a scandal throughout the Tidewater."

"*We* have been a scandal throughout the Tidewater before," his wife reminded him serenely (Letitia was always at her best in a crisis). "And yet we have always managed to get through it!"

"But not like this," he grumbled.

"Nonsense! Carolina is a young girl. She has made a mistake—as young girls often do. But it has not sullied her beauty nor made her old before her time. Indeed, in certain quarters this 'scandal,' as you call it, may have added to her luster! Everyone was talking about her emeralds—and she still has them. A handsome dowry in themselves."

"I cannot believe you would take it so lightly," croaked her husband.

"I do *not* take it lightly, Fielding!" Letitia rebuked him. "I am facing the facts—as you doubtless will, presently."

Outside, listening, Carolina found herself leaning against the wall in horror. *She* was facing the facts too. And those facts had made her forehead and her palms damp. They were calmly planning to marry her off to someone else, those two, just as if Rye did not exist! She pressed her hands to her temples where pressure was building up. Oh, she must do something—*now!*

When she went back upstairs, Virginia had gone, presumably back to her own room. Glad to be alone,

Carolina sat there glaring at the chair where her wedding gown reposed—her mother's creation, not her own. *She* had been wed in an ice-blue gown on the deck of a buccaneer ship in Cayona Bay—*wed in her heart, wed forever!*

But as she sat there, unbidden she began to shiver. *I had a wife. But she is dead in Spain. . . .* The words drifted aimlessly through her mind. Rye had never admitted he had a wife. What else had he not told her?

And then, sitting there on the blue and white coverlet of her big canopied bed with her hands clenched, she pushed that thought away from her as unworthy. The main point was, *had Rye got away?* All else could be sorted out later.

She sat there for a very long time. The sounds of the household changed, became evening sounds. Virginia stopped by to ask her if she would not come down to dinner. She told Virginia moodily that she did not care to.

"I think you might," Virginia said with an owlish look. "They are deciding your future down there. And I was right," she added. "They *did* get the silver chamber pot." She laughed. "Poor Aunt Pet, she had managed to smuggle it through Customs long ago, but when the pirates attacked the ship she didn't have the presence of mind to hide it under her skirts again!"

"They have already decided my future," Carolina said moodily, ignoring this talk about chamber pots—she had more important things to think about just now! "Virginia," she said in a wistful voice, *"you* don't believe Rye sank the *Ophelia*, do you?"

"Oh, no," said Virginia lightly. "But then I wasn't asked. And now that they all know he's Kells, they'll believe anything!"

That, Carolina thought bitterly, *was indeed the up-*

*shot of it. Those who once would have given him the
benefit of the doubt would believe anything of him now.*

"You had better eat something," advised Virginia.
"Keep your strength up. Suppose they've caught him?"

Carolina, whose gaze had been dismally focused on
the Turkey carpet, now looked up. Virginia met her
gaze calmly. She had steadied, had Virginia, now that
the worst had happened. "I know how you feel," said
Virginia with a rush of sympathy. "But I think you
should come down."

Carolina did so. She looked at them all accusingly,
feeling they were all her enemies. From the dining table
they looked back at her: Fielding with concealed fury,
Aunt Pet with indignation, her mother with resigna-
tion, and the younger children with wild curiosity.

Most of the meal was spent curbing that curiosity as
first Flo and then Della shot avid questions at their
elders. Questions which were parried warily.

"Carolina," said her mother, noting her daughter's
unhappy silence. "It's not the end of the world, you
know." She was speaking from down the long dining
table which had now mercifully been cleared of most of
its delights, which were being devoured by the servants
in the kitchen as best they could—though even their
stout appetites could not make much headway against
such a hoard.

"It's the end of the world to me," Carolina said
bitterly. She lifted her head and fixed Fielding with a
hard look. "Rye was planning to pay off some of your
debts as a parting gift," she said scathingly, "because
you had set no objection to his marrying me. Did you
know that?"

Fielding only growled but he pushed his thin-sliced
ham away from him as if he had suddenly lost his
appetite. Carolina took a dainty bite of hers. She was in

a vengeful mood and food was giving her strength. "He did not want you to lose this house," she added with a shrug.

"Carolina," her mother said dryly, "that will be enough of that."

Carolina turned to Aunt Pet. "I had asked Rye to give you a silver washbowl on my behalf, to go with your silver chamber pot. But now you won't be receiving it."

Aunt Pet's face flushed with indignation and something very like regret. She had always yearned for a silver washbowl and now—she turned upon Carolina.

"It would be enough if he would just return my silver chamber pot!" she announced waspishly, and both Della and Flo giggled so loudly that their mother commanded them to leave the table.

"*Now* have you finished?" She turned to Carolina.

"Not quite," said Carolina. "I had also planned, as soon as Rye and I were in residence in Essex, to arrange for you, Mother, to visit me. I realize it is an arduous journey to make alone, and—since he had come to Tortuga at your request, believing he must rescue me—I had thought that Sandy Randolph might come along to protect you along the way."

Fielding flung down his napkin with a curse and nearly overturned his chair as he stalked out of the room.

"Carolina," said her mother in a voice of menace, "if you are hoping to be turned out of the house by this behavior, you may as well disabuse yourself of the thought. You are going to stay right here where I can watch you. And tomorrow your father will seek out Ned Shackleford—"

"My *father*," said Carolina heavily, "is already on his way to Tower Oaks. Not that I care about him either!"

Aunt Pet choked but Letitia ignored her. She leant forward. "How did you learn about that?" she demanded, and when Carolina did not answer, she turned upon Aunt Pet. "Did *you* tell her, Petula?"

Red-faced, coughing, unable to speak, Aunt Pet shook her head. She was rewarded by being thumped on the back.

When Aunt Pet was able to take a gasping breath again, Letitia turned her attention again to her daughter—after one quick glance at Virginia across the table. Virginia's guilty knowledge showed in her eyes.

"Carolina," her mother began with a sigh, "I had hoped for you never to know. It is true I went away with Sandy, it is true you are his daughter. But Fielding took me back, and Fielding has brought you up as his own."

"He has always hated me!" flashed Carolina.

"All these years he has allowed you to live in his house," her mother continued inexorably. "Allowed you to wear his name. Would you shame him now?"

"Only if he tries to force me into marriage with Ned Shackleford or some other choice of yours!"

For a long time Letitia studied her. "I see you are going to be difficult," she said in a remarkable understatement. "But I think not *too* difficult."

Carolina, who had hoped to gain a reprieve with the barbs she had hurled at them, said coldly, "May I be excused?"

"From the table, yes," her mother said, frowning. "But not by me if you say a word to Fielding about Sandy being your father—not *ever!*"

Not for worlds would Carolina actually have done that but, perversely, she preferred her mother to think she would. Without a word, she flounced from the table. Virginia rolled her eyes.

Carolina passed Fielding in the hall. He turned away and did not speak to her. He was heading back toward the dining room.

Head high, Carolina gathered up the full skirts of the blue linen dress she had changed into after ridding herself of her wedding gown, and climbed the stairs to her bedroom. Gradually the sounds of the house died away and Virginia came upstairs and joined her in her room. Virginia had a couple of white linen napkins over her arm and she was carrying a plate piled high with food—ham and Sally Lunn and big slices of wedding cake.

"I thought you might be hungry," she declared cheerfully, "since you hardly touched your dinner downstairs. Mother thinks it best that I sleep in here with you tonight," she added.

"She *would!*" exclaimed Carolina. "And no, I am not hungry! Mother has asked you to guard me, Virgie, to see that I do not escape. Admit it!"

"Oh, I freely admit it." Virginia set the plate down on a little table and tossed the napkins down beside it. "Consider me your 'constant companion,' I think was the way Mother put it."

Carolina regarded her sister darkly.

Virginia returned that look blandly. "I was the last to come up," she stated. "I told Mother I wished to find a book to read in the library before retiring so I am the last to bed."

"What were they saying about me downstairs—if you chanced to hear?"

"Oh, I chanced to hear. I didn't go to the library for a book—I stayed outside the dining room door and eavesdropped shamelessly. They were saying that if Ned was agreeable to their plan, he could have you without a dowry—provided he would agree to a shipboard marriage ceremony performed by the captain of a ship of their choosing."

A ship of their choosing . . . In spite of herself, Carolina shivered. A captain who would *declare* her married, whether or not she said "I do!" And once emboldened by a shipboard wedding ceremony, however fraudulent, Ned would be hot to claim his marital rights. He was stronger than she was, he would overpower her. . . .

"They are determined for you to be gone to England," said Virginia. She sounded indifferent.

"Oh, how can you be so calm about it?" cried Carolina. "They are ruining my life!"

Virginia shrugged and strolled to the window. "The fog is coming up from the river," she remarked casually.

"The fog is always coming up this time of year when we get unseasonable weather with the promise of rain," Carolina declared heatedly. "What difference—" She stopped suddenly, intrigued by her sister's mocking expression. "Virgie, what do you know that I don't?"

"That Rye Evistock is still here," Virginia said placidly. "He never left. I saw him distinctly—standing between two tree trunks, looking up at the house after the guests had gone."

"Virgie!" Carolina scrambled up from the bed. "Why didn't you tell me?"

"Because if you'd known, it might have affected your behavior at dinner," her sister said sagely. "I wanted you to act completely natural—and you did!" She chuckled. "I was sworn to secrecy as to your parentage after you left. And the huffy way you left the table made Mother certain that you had no immediate plans for escape. She told Aunt Pet so. She said it was not knowing where to turn that was making you insult everybody!"

"Ha!" said Carolina. But she looked at her older sister in amazement. Clearly there were depths to Virgie that she had not plumbed! Then her mind flitted back to Rye, out there somewhere in the fog. *He had stayed, he was waiting for her!* "I must go downstairs," she said. "He'll be expecting me!"

"Not just yet," counseled Virginia. "Let the fog thicken a bit. And put on your emeralds—it would be a pity to leave them behind! As you will have noted, I'm already wearing my traveling clothes."

"Oh, Virgie!" Impulsively, Carolina hugged her. "You really are planning to go with me!"

"Yes," Virginia said. "Under the circumstances, I think you might need someone. Now dress so you'll be ready."

"I'll go in what I'm wearing. I've plenty of clothes aboard the *Sea Wolf*—I mean the *Sea Waif.*"

"Is that how you think we'll be going?" wondered Virginia curiously. "Because word arrived right after you went upstairs that the *Sea Waif* had sailed."

Carolina's heart skipped a beat. "I don't know *how* we'll be going," she admitted. "And I don't care, so long as it's with Rye!"

She had already adjusted the heavy emerald necklace around her neck, and the ear bobs were in place when a new and dreadful thought occurred to her.

"Fielding will have locked the front door and like as not pocketed the key!" she cried. "How will Rye get in?" For she knew that her mother would have seen to the back doors, under the circumstances.

"Through a downstairs window I found obligingly left unfastened," said a deep familiar voice behind her, and Carolina turned to see Rye standing in the doorway holding a naked blade in his hand.

"Oh—Rye!" Carolina's whispered greeting had all the joyousness of a shout. She flew to him, threw her arms about him, and was welcomed there as he gave her a great hug.

Behind her Virginia held up the scabbard that she had salvaged from the hall and brought to Carolina's room earlier. "'Twas I who left the window unfastened," she admitted modestly. "And—you might have a use for this?" She proffered the scabbard.

Rye flashed a smile at her as he detached Carolina's arms from around his neck. He sheathed his sword, buckled it to his belt. "Aye, I do," he agreed. "And for a dozen such sisters-in-law, were I lucky enough to have them!"

Virginia flushed with pleasure. "I saw you earlier, standing between the tree trunks. What puzzles me is that Burwell's servant insisted you had been rowed away in a longboat."

"I was—but I got out upriver a ways and walked back."

"I thought you must have," Virginia said, smiling. "I've put Carolina's pearls in this velvet bag." She held it up for their inspection. "I was afraid she'd go off and forget them."

"What would we do without you, Virgie?" murmured Carolina.

"I don't know," Virginia replied composedly. "But you aren't going to have to find out since I'm going with you!"

Carolina turned to Rye. "We received word that the *Sea Wolf* had sailed," she told him anxiously.

"But only for a short distance," said Rye. He laughed. "None cared to pursue her, to learn that! And

by now she will have sailed back. The longboat left—
but it has now returned. It's waiting for us just beyond
the landing."

Carolina's silver eyes were flashing with joy. "Virgie," she cried. "Help me wrap up that food. We'll
bring it along—Rye must be starving!"

"I thought he might be," was the tranquil response.
"That's why I brought the napkins!"

PART TWO

The Petticoat Buccaneer

A thoughtful maid is she tonight,
An age-old puzzle this. . . .
Can she who's held her virtue light
Distract him with a kiss?

Spring 1689

Chapter 13

The lean gray *Sea Waif*—looking more *Wolf* than *Waif*—cut the water like the reckless lady she was, heeling before the wind. On her swaying decks, beneath the clouds of billowing canvas, gray too against a black night sky radiantly sprinkled with stars, stood Rye and Carolina and Virginia.

Shrouded by a white blanket of fog, the longboat had waited for them. Through that fog, across the lawns of Level Green the two girls had run, skirts hitched up, with Rye bounding along beside them. A quick smothered greeting, the girls were lifted into the boat, the buccaneers bent their broad backs to the rowing, and the longboat had made its silent way down to the river's mouth with hardly the splash of an oar to mark its passage. Rendezvous with the ship had been made near the mouth of the York. There the fog had lifted and the rakish *Sea Waif* had spread her canvas wings and flown them across the smooth surface of the Chesapeake.

Now they were beating their way into the open sea aided by a stiff breeze. And their captain, who had tossed aside his satin coat and stood in shirt and trousers smiling down upon the gleaming fair hair of the girl he might have lost this day, had ordered a keg of ale to be broached for all hands.

"I can't believe it," Virginia was marveling as they stood, the three of them, along the portside railing. "I can't believe we're really on our way! I kept thinking something would go wrong." Since so much had, in her life!

Carolina, leaning against the broad chest of her buccaneer, letting her hair blow and feeling the cambric of his white shirt smooth against her face, gave her sister an affectionate look. "We're for England, Virgie —nothing can stop us now!"

God willing, she would be right, thought the tall captain at her side. Thought it ruefully, for there was much that could "stop" a ship on the ocean sea: storms; floating wreckage that loomed out of the dark and stove in the most seaworthy hull; English warships that might desire to send a boarding party, some member of whom might chance to recognize the famous Captain Kells and remember that there was a hue and cry for his arrest in Williamsburg; Spain's Vera Cruz galleons with their mighty fore and aftercastles and captains thirsting for his blood—and he short-handed and with a woman aboard he would not risk. . . . But God willing there would be none of these. The Vera Cruz galleons would cruise the Caribbean where they belonged, the British warships would be off on other business, the storm gods would hold back their lightning bolts and still their winds to let a man for whom women had never been lucky before pass by with his lady.

"Aye, we're for England," he agreed in his deep resonant voice.

"And you won't try first to find the ship that was passed off as the *Sea Wolf* or the man who said he was Kells?" Carolina asked anxiously.

Not with you aboard, he might have answered, and it would have been the truth for he would not risk her. But he chose to amend the statement. "Not with so much treasure aboard," he said briefly. "I've taken much of mine to England already, but the men haven't and they're eager to set foot on English soil as rich men—and *then* straighten out whatever's gone wrong here."

"You're not planning to *come back here?*" she breathed, afraid for him.

"Not for a time at least," he told her soothingly. And that too was the truth, for a hurried conference with his officers and crew had reached agreement all round that they would sail to England first and then later rendezvous and sail back to the Caribbean and wipe the seas clean of whoever had dared to impersonate them. For other survivors of the *Ophelia*'s sinking had reached Yorktown and their stories had made it clear to these buccaneers that their names were known and being used along with their captain's and the ship's.

Just why this was being done was not so readily apparent for a ship must make port somewhere, it must be careened and its hull scraped to keep it seaworthy— and there were too many men scattered throughout the Caribbean, buccaneers and others, who knew the lean *Sea Wolf* by sight and would not easily mistake another ship for her, many men who knew her captain and would never dream of mistaking *him!* The sun-darkened faces of the *Sea Wolf*'s officers and crew had darkened still further at the thought of other men attempting to steal their names and commit crimes under those names, but all had agreed: home and family first, and stash their treasure. *Then* back to sea and straighten out the mess they'd left behind them.

Carolina, forgetful of the fact that if Rye failed to return and straighten things out, the pardon he had been at such pains to secure would be worthless, leaned against him, happy and content. Once in England she'd find ways to keep him there, she promised herself.

Their first night together on board ship was glorious —a wondrous reunion of few words but murmured endearments, of blissful touchings and caressings and tender sighs for they had been so near, so very near to being wrested apart forever. The magic of that reunion engulfed them both and made questions unnecessary.

But . . . now that she had him safe, now that he was back with her again, there was something troubling her.

And that second night, lying back luxuriously in the great cabin, still basking in the glow of a silken joining that had been all she would ever desire of heaven, she asked him about it.

"Rye," she began, "tell me about Spain."

Spain . . . For a treacherous moment he thought of Spain, land of a lost love. *His* Spain was not the haughty iron-fisted Spain where a yellow-haired king in plain black velvet had worked himself to death in a cell-like office in the Escorial's vast palace monastery— and along the way suffered defeat by England and the destruction of his vast Armada; nor was it the corrupt misgoverned Spain of Philip's successor, the old-before-his-time Charles II. It was a Spain such as he had first seen it, divorced from politics, a pleasant land of wheat and cattle—and fighting bulls. There in the province of Leon a golden city had waited for him— Salamanca, its old stone buildings mellow in the golden sunlight that struck silver from the Tormes River flowing by. Salamanca with its cork oaks and its storks' nests and its magnificent private houses. . . . *And in one of those courtyard houses at the edge of storied Salamanca he had thought for a time to live always— with the fifteen-year-old girl who had won his heart.*

"I think," he said slowly, "that it is not about Spain you wish to hear."

You are right, she thought. *It is about the woman I wish to hear!* But when she spoke, her voice was hesitant. "You told Aunt Pet you had been married before. Was that true?"

She was lying naked beside him as she spoke, and moonlight streamed in upon her gleaming body through the bank of stern windows of the great cabin. The night was quiet; there was no sound save the creaking of the great ship as it rode the water. Beside her Rye lay on his back with one long arm stretched across her slight body caressing the rounded curve of her hip, his fingers straying occasionally to the whiteness of her inner thigh.

"Yes," he said, his dark head turning toward her. "It is true, Carolina."

Her voice was troubled. "Why did you not tell me? Why did you let me find it out *that* way?"

"It was so long ago, I never thought it would trouble us," he told her moodily. But there was another reason as well. Even now it was hard for him to speak of her without remembering the radiance of her glowing dark eyes, the scented midnight of her hair, the way she had sighed when first he had kissed her in an arcaded patio redolent of flowers. . . . For years her memory had been the shrine at which he worshipped, her purity the standard by which he measured other women.

Now he gave the girl beside him a restless look. "Old wounds are best forgotten, Carolina."

Old wounds . . . Lying there in the moonlight, Carolina felt a shadow of something gossamer pass over her naked form, like a warning. Perhaps she should not ask—but she could not help it.

"Tell me about her, Rye," she said in a low voice.

He frowned and ran restless fingers through his dark hair. *She* was the lady of his heart now, this woman of starlight beside him. She deserved the truth from him—and the truth she would have, since she desired it.

He folded his long arms behind his head, lying naked and straight beside her, a lean handsome animal, a vigorous man in his prime. "Very well, Carolina, I will tell you. What do you wish to know?"

"Everything."

He sighed. "Where shall I start?"

"At the beginning," she said, and hoped she was not opening a Pandora's box that would unloose troubles upon her cloudless world.

"At the beginning . . ." he repeated thoughtfully. And now, for this bride of his heart, he relived the nightmare once again. "My uncle trained me in navigation and the ways of the sea," he told her. "When I was twenty I sailed with him on a merchant voyage. There was a great storm and we sighted a Spanish galleon—going down. Nothing could save her." *Like a bird with broken wings, disappearing beneath the waves.* "We saw a man clinging to a spar. We tried but we could not reach him and he was too exhausted even to catch the rope we tossed him. I leaped overboard with a rope lashed around me and managed to get an arm around his body and we were both dragged aboard." *It had been a foolhardy venture because their own vessel was about to be swamped by the pounding seas, and the rope—a fragile lifeline at best in such a tempest—could have snapped at any time.* "He was an old man and frail," he said, excusing his foolhardiness.

Her heart warmed to him as he spoke. How characteristic of him, to take such a risk! "So you saved his life?" she asked softly.

"Yes, and Don Ignacio Saavedra was very grateful. He had been a passenger on the ill-fated galleon and indeed had expected to die like the rest—for he was the ship's only survivor. He spoke English passably well and he asked me if I would come home with him to Spain. He said he had no son of his own and that he would be honored if I would become his son. I was young, reckless, of an adventurous turn of mind. I was hot to see Spain. My uncle pointed out that I was an Englishman, a heretic so far as Don Ignacio's country and his church were concerned. Don Ignacio shrugged that off. He said that in six months' time he would have me speaking good Castilian—for he was from Castile although he had married an heiress in Leon, and now that his wife was dead he still resided in her old family home in Salamanca. He said he would pass me off as a long-lost distant relative and I was to pretend a throat injury until I had mastered the language—he would tutor me in private. For himself he was not very devout although his family back in Castile had been. Indeed, his only brother had once considered studying for the priesthood. He said he would teach me the ways of the church so that I could pass for what I was not. At twenty, such an offer was too tempting to resist. . . ."

Something dreamy in his tone told her how he must have felt at twenty, flying into the face of danger, visiting worlds undreamed of in his native England. . . . The winds of other lands had called to him—*perhaps,* she thought fearfully, *were calling to him now*.

"But your uncle?" she protested. "Did he not object?"

"He knew I was but a younger son—the third of my father's four sons, and thus unlikely to inherit. He told me that Don Ignacio was a rich man and that this was a great opportunity for me if I could adapt to the ways of an alien land."

And so, when they chanced upon a Portuguese fishing vessel near the Azores, his uncle had set him and Don Ignacio aboard and the fishermen had been persuaded to sail them to La Coruna. From there they had made their way on horseback to the ancient city of Salamanca on the right bank of the Tormes—beautiful Salamanca, ravaged by so many invaders throughout the centuries, where Hannibal's feet had trod and later the Roman legions, the Goths, the Moors.

And there in the sunny courtyard of Don Ignacio's villa on the outskirts of Salamanca, the young Englishman had met Don Ignacio's daughter Rosalia. She had been fifteen then, untried, beautiful—they had fallen in love. Carolina could almost see Rosalia in her high-backed Spanish comb, languidly waving her fan in the shadow of the cork oaks. There was a richness in Rye's voice when he spoke of her that made Carolina wince inwardly. *She was wonderful,* that richness said.

"You were—lovers then?" Carolina heard herself ask—and was ashamed at the catch in her voice.

He shook his head. "Spanish customs are very strict. A stroll in the courtyard—her duenna always present . . . a serenade beneath her balcony at dusk . . . through the iron grillwork she tosses me a rose. . . ." *And a look from her dark eyes more glorious than any sunset. . . .* His heart remembered the whispered vows of young lovers as a sleepy duenna dozed in the sunlight by a tinkling fountain.

It all sounded so very romantic, it was painful for Carolina to hear. "And so you were married?" she murmured.

"In Holy Mother Church," he said ironically. "I, a sometime Englishman and a heretic, took solemn vows under a false name, for Don Ignacio had christened me 'Diego,' the name he would have given to a son of his own. I chose my own last name. I chose 'Diego Viajar'—Diego the Traveler."

"But Don Ignacio could have had other sons," she objected, for this recital was becoming painful for her.

"No, his young wife had died in childbirth. He mourned her—and was still mourning her. Even though he had been urged to do so, he had refused to remarry. The estate in Salamanca would go to Rosalia," he added absently.

Not to Diego then. . . . Rye had worn so many identities—English, Irish, and now, she had just learned, Spanish. She was hanging onto his words, almost afraid to hear what was coming next.

"Don Ignacio had a brother—Carlos," he said abruptly. "Carlos had left Castile some years earlier and had made his home with Don Ignacio in Salamanca, but Don Carlos had influence at Court and had been sent out to Peru two years before. He had left behind him, as souvenirs of his stay at Salamanca, a mistress named Conchita no older than Rosalia—indeed Conchita must have been a mere child when Don Carlos first bedded her—and several illegitimate children got on various serving wenches. Don Ignacio, with his kind heart, was caring for them all, even old Juana, Conchita's mother, who had been mute since birth. Don Carlos was a few years younger than Don

Ignacio and in better health; he had expected when Don Ignacio died to become Rosalia's guardian and gain control of her fortune. Someone must have written to him in Peru about me for he returned post haste, but he was too late—he rode up covered with dust just as Rosalia and I were coming out of the cathedral into the sunlight—man and wife."

For a moment in her mind Carolina saw the scene as *he* must have seen it then: the glare of the sun on the red tile roofs and white-walled buildings of the town, the gloom of the high-vaulted ceiling of the great Romanesque cathedral they had just left. She imagined Don Carlos, a richly dressed Spanish grandee, travel-stained and weary, galloping into town on a lathered horse and coming to an abrupt halt before the twelfth-century cathedral. Saw his chagrin as he viewed a younger Rye—Don Diego Viajar, Diego the Traveler—stride out of the old church beside Don Ignacio's daughter, the white lace of her mantilla spilling down from a high-backed Spanish comb over her dark hair. . . . It was a beautiful and a painful picture.

"Did Rosalia know you were an Englishman and a heretic?" wondered Carolina—for she had heard such things meant much to Spanish girls.

Rye frowned. "No. Her father had asked me not to tell her. He said it would only worry her, that she was a woman and should not be troubled with such matters. He said that I was Diego now and I should remain Diego. I did not like deceiving her but it was his wish and I honored it."

So Rosalia had not known. She had gone into marriage believing her Diego to be one of her own—just as *she* had been about to enter into wedlock with him at Level Green without knowing there had been a wife before her. And Rosalia somehow had ended in tragedy. Carolina told herself she would sort all that out later.

Rye's next words rocked her.

"I never knew if Don Ignacio was poisoned or not," he murmured. "But he had a violent seizure at our wedding feast and died almost immediately. When I took Rosalia weeping from his bedside, we found ourselves in an empty house—empty save for Don Carlos and those who had followed behind him. Don Carlos had driven away the servants. That left him in full charge. . . ." Rye's face in the moonlight seemed carved in granite. There were terrible memories flickering in his gray eyes. "He had brought his men with him. They seized me and whisked me away to a wine cellar where they entertained themselves by recounting to me all the delights of the Inquisition which I would soon enjoy."

The tortures of the Inquisition were well-known—and gruesome.

"And you never saw Rosalia again?" Carolina whispered.

"Oh, yes, I saw her again. The following evening they got me up out of the wine cellar and took me to a room that opened onto the courtyard and tied my wrists to the rusty iron grating with strong leather thongs so that I could view the dusky courtyard—so that indeed I could not turn away from it. 'Now, Englishman,' said Don Carlos—I do not know how he had learnt I was English; Don Ignacio must have told him in confidence just before the wedding feast when they were closeted together, believing the information was safe with him—'Now you will see what happens to those who marry heretics like yourself—and afterward

239

I will deal with *you!*' He waved his arm and across the courtyard I saw Rosalia brought out of the house by two of his men. She was still wearing her white wedding gown, still shrouded in the heavy white lace mantilla she had worn in the cathedral. I called to her but she did not answer. I think they must have gagged her for I could hear her moan but not her voice." He fell silent, remembering.

"What—what happened?" quavered Carolina, for she saw beads of sweat on Rye's forehead now and realized that his breathing had changed.

"Don Carlos took out his sword," said Rye. "And he turned to me with a laugh. Then he strode across the courtyard and thrust the naked blade through her body." *The anguish in his voice told better than words the way the red blood had run down that chaste white gown, the way that proud dark head beneath the enveloping white mantilla had fallen forward as a girl who had never known a wedding night collapsed upon the stones of a courtyard in Salamanca far away.*

"No!" The word was wrenched from Carolina. *How could I have asked him to remember this?* she was thinking.

She did not have to ask him what happened then. Rye told her.

"I must have gone mad," he said thickly. "I remember cursing him from that empty room where I was shackled—for the guards had gone away and left me. I remember Don Carlos swaggered toward me carrying his bloody sword." His face seemed carved in stone as he felt again his grief and rage at the sight of that slight crumpled figure, lying so still, a mound of white across the courtyard in the shadows of the cork oak, but his voice strengthened as through him surged the memory of the fiery need for vengeance that had possessed him at that moment. "I remember his face and his white teeth as he stood before me laughing. . . ."

Carolina shuddered.

"And then—the grillwork was rusted and old, the mortar crumbling for Don Ignacio was never one for repairs—I wrenched the grillwork loose and slammed it into his face. I remember his look of surprise when he fell—and I was tumbling through the window upon him, beating him to death with that iron grille to which I was still shackled."

"Did you—kill him?" she whispered.

A terrible smile lit his dark countenance. "I did," he said softly. "I killed Don Carlos before his men could reach me. I remember hearing a scream. Then one of them struck me from behind and I remember nothing more until I woke, covered with my own blood, at the bottom of a cart with a load of straw on top of me."

"Who had saved you?" she wondered, awed.

"Old Juana had come to my rescue. She could not tell me how, for she was mute and she could not write, but she was leading the donkey that pulled the cart, and when I peered out at her she waved to me to stay hidden. Juana tended my wounds as tenderly as if I had been her own, and she took me in this manner all the way to La Coruna. . . ."

"Where you made your escape?" she breathed.

He shook his dark head soberly. "I was not yet to escape that cursed land. Several prisoners had escaped from the jail the day we arrived in La Coruna and when we reached the waterfront, the entire area was being systematically searched. We were caught in the open and there was no escape. I was hauled out of the cart, seized by a dozen men, the old woman was questioned. When she did not answer she was thought insolent and despite my cries that Juana was mute and *could not* answer, she was struck such a blow as sent her staggering backward where she fell beneath the wheels of a passing wagon. I believe she did not suffer—the heavy wagon wheel passed over her head and crushed the life from her instantly."

Carolina, caught up in his narrative, gave an involuntary moan.

"The authorities assumed I was in league with the escaped prisoners since I had been found hiding in the cart. And since *their* crime had been heresy, I was promptly hauled before the Inquisition—"

"Where they discovered you were English?" she guessed.

"That they never discovered. I staunchly maintained I was a Castilian vagabond and had been merely sleeping in the cart and been wakened by the sounds of the soldiery. Naturally I was not believed. There was some talk that I might be an emissary of the Devil himself." He gave a short mirthless laugh that chilled her. "I was sentenced to death by burning at the next *auto-da-fé*—and would have gone to my death in flames had not Spain needed strong backs to row her galleys even more than she needed human torches to subdue the multitudes who were being ground down by the price of bread even as gold and silver poured in from Spain's colonial empire. My back was broader than most, my sinews commanded attention—so my sentence was regretfully commuted to life as a galley slave."

A living death . . . she had heard it called that.

"How did you escape them, Rye?" she asked anxiously.

"I didn't—not then. I was chained to an oar of *La Fuerza,* one of the smaller galleons of the Spanish treasure flota sailing to Porto Bello to bring back the gold and silver from the mines of Mexico and Peru. A great storm came upon us in the Caribbean and the ships became separated. *La Fuerza* was badly damaged, barely afloat and rudderless when we chanced upon two buccaneer vessels from Tortuga. They boarded us and the situation was wild, for *La Fuerza* was well manned and there was fighting all over the ship. In the confusion, we galley slaves were stealthily running the long chains through our leg irons so that we could free ourselves. I had just threaded that chain through my leg shackles and freed my legs when the fighting spilled over into the galleys. The chain was still in my hands. The captain of one of the buccaneer ships was being hard-pressed by two Spaniards and was about to be run through by a Spanish blade when I launched that chain at the pair of them and by a lucky stroke struck them both down. It was at that moment that a cheer rose from the deck above—the Spanish captain had surrendered his vessel. Captain Reynard— whose life I had saved—freed all the galley slaves, had our leg irons struck off, and when he learnt that I was a navigator, he put me in charge of bringing back their prize, *La Fuerza*—if I could keep her afloat—and allowed me to select a crew from among the galley slaves."

"I should like to thank Captain Reynard," Carolina murmured.

Rye flashed her a grim smile. "So would I," he said. "More handsomely and more tangibly than I was able to do at the time. But his officers and those of the other buccaneer vessel chafed at lingering with the disabled *La Fuerza* when there might be other crippled galleons in the area, easy to pick off. They forged ahead, leaving us to limp along—and half a day away they chanced upon a pair of carracks that made short work of them. Captain Reynard died without ever reaching Tortuga."

His words brought home to her with force how short was the life expectancy of a buccaneer and she gave silent fervent thanks that Rye was a buccaneer no longer.

"We were alone upon the horizon until we sighted another ship of the scattered *flota—El Lobo,* The Wolf. She had escaped the storm with relatively little damage. Since we were in some danger of sinking, it occurred to me that we could use a more seaworthy vessel. I held a council of war. There was a chance we could take *El Lobo* and have a ship of our own—but we were not in sufficient strength nor had we a maneuverable vessel; we must do it by a ruse. We donned Spanish uniforms. When *El Lobo* hailed us, we duped her into believing we were the Spanish officers and crew, survivors of a battle with the buccaneers. In my good Castilian Spanish I requested a boarding party to help us assess our damage—and when they came, we forced them at gunpoint to call for other boats to be sent with men 'to aid us in our repairs lest we sink at once.' As each boatload arrived, we clapped them in irons. By a stroke of luck, *El Lobo*'s captain became curious. He himself arrived. That was all we needed. A party of us accompanied him back on board his vessel. I had a pistol pressed against his back and in fear for his life he gave such orders as left us in command of the ship. We took *El Lobo* without firing a shot."

Carolina was so proud of him it shone in her eyes.

"As a galley slave I had steadfastly kept the name 'Diego,' but now I had a thought for my family back in England and I passed myself off to the buccaneers as an

Irishman named Kells. Now I had a ship of my own under me and I was towing a prize. When we sailed into Cayona Bay, I was already Captain Kells and *El Lobo*, which we later altered and refitted to more rakish lines, became the *Sea Wolf*." He turned to look at her sternly and there was a leaping hellish light in his gray eyes though his voice was soft. "And ever since the night I sailed *El Lobo* into Cayona Bay, I have sought vengeance against Don Carlos and his kind."

And so had begun his private war with Spain. A battle that had raged ever since. Rye did not have to tell her that whenever he boarded a Spanish galleon, he saw Rosalia's face.

Carolina's lips were dry.

"And that is why you fly Rosalia's petticoat when you fight the ships of Spain?" *A salute to a lost love. . . .*

He nodded grimly. "That is why. Although the petticoat is not Rosalia's and never was. It came from a trunk of clothes making the passage by galleon from Cadiz to Panama—I intercepted the shipment."

So the petticoat was symbolic. But the woman—he wore the woman in his heart like a flag.

There was a knock on the door. "Cap'n," said a brusque voice, "the wind has changed and there's dirty weather ahead."

"I'll be right there." Rye was up and dragging his trousers over his lean muscular thighs.

Carolina watched him go. She sat in the bunk, feeling the lurch and roll of the wooden ship beneath her, and thought about the terrible story she had just heard.

A bride he had never bedded, a woman he had loved so deeply that he had spent all these years avenging her. . . . A woman whose name, just the mention of it,

245

*made him restless, unhappy, a woman he had cared for
too much ever to forget. . . .*

Carolina bent her gleaming head and covered her
face with her hands. With all her heart, she wished she
had never asked Rye about that other woman long ago
in Spain.

Chapter 14

The night wore on with the roll and pitch of the ship growing ever more pronounced as the storm increased its fury. The lamp swung precariously, but Carolina, tossed about, took no notice. Rye had not returned and as the storm worsened, an idea occurred to her. She would look through Rye's things; she would see if there were any mementoes of that Spanish girl of long ago!

It seemed safe to do it now for Rye would be fully occupied on deck with green seas slashing over the side and the *Sea Wolf* driven like a white-winged bird before the wind. She leaped up and began to open his chests, which were ranged about the cabin, and tumble their contents. Chest after chest disappointed her and she was about to give up her search when suddenly she found two tall-backed Spanish combs intricately carved of tortoise shell. She grasped them speculatively and was studying them beneath the lamp, asking herself for the tenth time if these combs—so obviously meant to be worn by some lady of Spain—could possibly have belonged to Rosalia, when there was a sound behind her.

Carolina whirled guiltily to see that Rye had come into the cabin. His clothing was soaked and he tossed back his wet dark hair with a shake that sent droplets flying.

"I came to see if you were all right—" He stopped, amazed at the confusion of opened chests and piled up goods about him. "Did the storm overturn these?" he demanded.

"No, I—I was looking for something." Carolina's face flamed.

Rye glanced at the two combs, held stiffly in her slender hands. "Ah, so you found them," he said. "I had intended those combs as gifts for you but in this welter of stuff I had forgot where I put them." He cast another thoughtful glance about him. "I will be on deck until the storm eases off," he said abruptly—and was gone.

Carolina was left with her embarrassment and the two Spanish combs. They were beautiful and delicately wrought but they conjured up unhappy thoughts: of a younger Rye strolling through a sunlit garden in Salamanca, his gray eyes drinking in the beauty of another woman who wore a comb like this one. Of Rosalia in her wedding gown with her white mantilla held up by a comb like this one. Of the memory of a lost love that these combs would conjure up.

She cast the pair of combs away from her with a shiver, then scooped them up and hid them away in the deepest corner of one of her own chests. She would never, *never* wear them! A reminder of Spain and Rosalia she would not be!

And now that her search had turned out to be

fruitless, she began to feel ashamed of herself and sought out Virginia to see how she was faring.

Not very well!

Carolina had been flung about mercilessly as she sought Virginia's cabin. She arrived there to find Virginia clinging to her bunk, moaning and desperately seasick.

"Go away and let me die in peace!" croaked Virginia.

Carolina, a remarkably good sailor herself, had forgotten that Virginia was not a good sailor. Now she remembered guiltily that when they were children Virginia had often been sick just making the trip across the Chesapeake to Aunt Pet's.

The storm did not abate and neither did Virginia's seasickness. She lay, weak and retching, in her bunk, while Carolina—afraid that her frail sister would lose all the gains she had so recently made and sink back toward death again—tried desperately to make her comfortable.

"You should try to eat *something*," she told Virginia in a troubled voice during the days that followed.

Virginia turned away with a shudder. "I may never eat again!" she gasped.

"Oh, Virgie!" Carolina cried in panic. She turned Virginia's limp body back toward her so that she could mop her pale face with a damp cloth. "Virgie, if you die on me on this voyage, I swear I will never forgive you! Oh, Virgie"—her voice broke—"I *need* you!"

The white face so close to her own broke into a weak smile. "I promise not to die," whispered Virginia. "If only this miserable storm will end so the world isn't going every which way!"

And the following day it did.

They had been driven far south, Rye told Carolina.

"The storm must have visited the Virginia Capes too," Carolina said, trying to look on the bright side. "In the Tidewater they may decide we're all dead and forget about us!"

Rye gave her an ironic look. "Little chance of that," he said dryly. "When a man carries treasure, the world tends to seek him out!"

They were not to know—not yet—that the freakish path of the storm that had driven them so far off course had struck only a glancing blow at the Virginia Capes before it swirled south, driving them before it—or that other ships that had sailed past Yorktown into the Chesapeake a full two days after them had missed the storm altogether and were having fair sailing across the broad Atlantic.

It was mere chance, but it was to alter their lives, for on one of those London-bound ships was a gossipy lady from Williamsburg, a friend of Amanda Bramway, who had drunk in delightedly the scandalous story of the disastrous wedding at Level Green, as Amanda Bramway had told it. . . .

But of course, they did not know that then. And as the weather cleared and murky skies changed to blue, as they struck out again for England, as Virginia sat up and, under Carolina's coaxing, began to eat again, new hope surged through Carolina.

"I have a wonderful feeling about what lies ahead!" she told Virginia breathlessly one day as they stood by the railing looking out over a wide blue ocean. Overhead the seabirds screamed, swooping down past the billowing white sails to dive for the ship's garbage that the cook was just then throwing over the side. Alongside the hull a pair of dolphins were playing joyously. The wind was steady and a sparkle of white spray blew upward, causing Virginia to step back and Carolina to shake out her blonde hair with a laugh. "Everything is going to be all right," she told her sister confidently. "What does it matter after all that Rye and I couldn't be married at Level Green? We'll be married in Essex—and after *that* we'll straighten everything out!"

Her sister gave her an affectionate look. Dear headlong Carolina, always so sure things would work out. Virginia held back a long sigh as she turned back to gaze into the unfathomable blue distance. Nothing, *nothing* had ever worked out for her. . . .

But time and the sea were both passing rapidly now. The weather continued fair, the wind held. They passed the Scilly Isles with their treacherous rocks and boiling seas, they came smartly around Lizard Head at the southern tip of England, they sailed past Plymouth, where Francis Drake had sallied forth to meet the advancing Armada, past the Eddystone Rocks, past Torquay with its terraced houses and spilling banks of flowers, past Lyme Regis where the young Duke of Monmouth had made his ill-fated bid for a throne, past brooding Corfe Castle and the Isle of Wight, past Hastings where in a single bloody battle England had changed hands. The *Sea Waif* was marching up the English Channel toward the Straits of Dover. They would soon be coming round Margate and sailing up the broad mouth of the Thames.

And at last, with London but a day's sail away, Carolina, lying in bed beside Rye while the pale moonlight streamed in through the stern windows and made her blonde hair seem to have a cool glow all its own, repeated to Rye what she had said to Virginia on a spray-washed deck.

And Rye, looking down into her sparkling eyes as he delicately stroked her slim body to passion, smiled down at his lovely mercurial lady.

"Aye," he agreed huskily—for just to look at her made him feel a stirring in his loins, an overwhelming urge to sweep her up against him, to hold her, to have her. "We'll be married when we reach England."

They would have been less sanguine about their future if they could have heard a conversation that was even then going on in London.

There were two participants in that conversation—a man and a woman—and this was no chance meeting, here in an upstairs room of The Shark and Fin, for the tall well-dressed man seemed out of his element in this dingy waterfront inn that catered to sailors and street bawds—and the woman had come here in the night at no small risk to herself.

The woman had come in with an impetuous rush. She was hooded and cloaked and wearing a black face mask—not too unusual in itself, for not only prostitutes but many aristocratic ladies now customarily wore face masks when out in public. She had not arrived unaccompanied. Outside the closed door stood a darkvisaged servant who would have died for her—and the lady knew it. Now he stood frowning guard over the bedroom door through which she had vanished. His name was Sancho and he had been long in the service of her husband's family—and hopelessly in love with her from the day she had first crossed his vision.

It was a love never to be, of course. Nor even to be mentioned. Sancho had long ago accepted that fact. And it was to Sancho's credit that he did not understand what was afoot here—if he had, even *his* blind devotion to the lady might have faltered.

For the lady was the wife of Spain's ambassador to England. Her husband was the Duke of Lorca, scion of one of the oldest families of Spain and patrician confidante and advisor of that last of the Spanish Hapsburgs, Charles II, the dull-witted and sickly King of Spain.

His Duchess was here tonight on a mission all her own. She had been a bewitchingly beautiful girl when the elderly Duke of Lorca had got her at sixteen fresh from a convent and she was now, in her early twenties, a flamboyantly beautiful woman. Her dark eyes flashed behind her mask as she entered. She tossed back her hood with a shake of her thick shining black curls—which supported no high-backed Spanish comb or mantilla this night, for the Duchess of Lorca was endeavoring with all her might to look English. With a graceful nervous gesture she tore off the black mask that covered almost her entire face, and the man who stood by the hearth—cold at this time of year despite the damp rising from the river—feasted his gray eyes on the creamy smoothness of her skin.

It was he who spoke first. "You were not wise to come here tonight—"

"Hush," she interrupted. "No names. Even the walls may have ears."

He shrugged. If the walls had ears tonight, they were both in deep trouble—the kind they were not likely to survive—for knowledge of their enterprise would have put both their handsome heads on the block. Hidden away in the wine cellar of this very inn (with the bought connivance of the landlord), sandwiched in between giant hogsheads of ale and well guarded, lay the lady's gray-haired husband, the Duke of Lorca himself. And despite being bound hand and foot, despite his age and enforced inactivity of late, the Duke had kept up a steady deadly flow of invective during his waking hours whenever his gag was removed so that he might eat or drink.

The Duke of course did not know it was his young wife's machinations that had brought him to this pass. He *had* quickly learnt that to attempt to shout brought instant retaliation from the impassive rogue who guarded him—a rough return of the gag to his mouth without so much as a sip of water. That water was left tantalizingly near the wine cellar's single guttering candle and the Duke of Lorca was not allowed to touch it until by his moans he made clear that he had seen reason and would be quiet if allowed to drink.

This dispensation had not kept him from muttering in a low venomous tone all the curses he could think of—in Spanish, of course—and since his captor did not know Spanish any more than the heavyset and heavily scarred innkeeper who came down occasionally to bring up ale or wine, those mutterings were ignored.

How long he had lain there in the wine cellar, the Duke of Lorca did not know. In fact it had been a very long time, and only an iron constitution inherited from forebears who had fought alongside El Cid, had saved his strength from failing up to now. He had been brought here, heavily drugged by a potion slipped into his Madeira by the dainty hand of his wife—but he did not know that. He was at a loss to explain—and indeed no one had bothered to explain it to him—how he could have gone to sleep in his big carved bed in a fashionable town house in this—to him—barbaric English city, this London, and waked up dazed, with a mouth dry as cotton, in this dark cellar, a prisoner of total strangers.

The pair in the room above were just then deciding his future.

"There is news?" demanded the man restlessly. "Is this why you take such a mad chance as to come here?"

"Not the news you seek," said the Duchess. "I would have you remember that things move slowly in Spain."

The Englishman who faced her—and who was desperate for money indeed to have entered into such a plot with this beautiful but, he suspected, unreliable woman—sighed. He was well aware that things moved slowly in Spain. The several months that had already passed had proved that!

"Is he still well secured?" The Duchess was speaking of her husband.

The tall Englishman nodded absently. In an effort at disguise he was raffishly dressed in a puce coat several sizes too large for him with wide fraying cuffs and tarnished gold braid. And his deliberately mismatched trousers of an off shade of green were a trifle too tight and tended to bind his well-shaped thighs. One of his faded garters had lost its rosette but his black boots— he had found no others to his liking—were his own and held an incongruous mirrorlike sheen. But his shabby clothing, marking him for a down-at-the-heels gentleman though they might, could not conceal the arrogance of his stance or the excellence of his figure. And the rather ratty sand-colored wig he had purchased at random to conceal his own dark hair rode atop a dissolute face that would to its dying day be attractive to women.

"And he is in good health?" she persisted, noting as she spoke the masculine lure of his physique.

"As good as could be expected."

"You have looked in on him, have you not?" she asked sharply.

"No, I did not want him to be able to identify me." *In case things go wrong.*

"The difficult part is over," the reckless lady said with a shrug. "What could go wrong now?"

Everything, he thought, studying her. Had she been a man, she would probably not have lived past her teens, he thought. Quick to anger, she would most likely have died as the result of a duel, for she was always tempted to exceed her capacities and would probably have flared up, unwilling to admit that she was overmatched.

He had tempered her wild scheme with common sense. *He* had arranged for the capture of the Duke from his bed by stealth and by night. *He* had made arrangements with the greasy innkeeper of this filthy establishment, who, despite the rats that ran about and the reputation for harboring cutthroats and thieves to prey upon the sailors who came ashore, had also a reputation for keeping his given word—if paid enough for so doing. *He* had urged that she put out a story that while visiting in the country the Duke had suffered a wrenching fall and would be absent from the Court for some time.

Now the tall Englishman fingered the jewel of price that gleamed from the froth of lace at his throat. It was a ruby—at least it had been a ruby until he had pawned it and substituted a red glass fake. The real ruby had been a gift of the Duchess of Lorca. He wondered if she would notice the difference.

She did not.

"We will hear soon enough," she told him haughtily.

Soon enough for whom? he wondered. *Certainly it could not come soon enough for him! She* was still quartered in her town house "awaiting news" but *he* was quartered here in this accursed inn, in hiding from the world he knew. And his crew was becoming restive—and no wonder!

"Then if not to the ransom, to what do I owe the honor of this visit?" he wondered. "I would remind you there is danger in this charade that we are playing."

Her light shrug spoke volumes. She had broken the bonds of convention many times, had the young Duchess. Most recently by stealing out by night in this foreign city, and thus meeting an Englishman whose carriage had chanced to careen into hers near Charing Cross. While the wheels were being unloosed they had fallen into conversation. The Englishman knew a wild wench when he saw one—and he saw one in the Duchess. When their paths had chanced to cross three nights later at a ball, it had been too much. They had danced the night away, kissed behind the hangings of an alcove. One thing had led to another. There had been clandestine meetings, wild protestations of love in the upstairs rooms of one inn and another.

That was six months ago.

Now they were engaged in a deadly plot which could bring them both to ruin and death.

It had all seemed so devilishly simple—at first. Now he could see from the way she was hesitating to bring up the next point that it was becoming considerably more complicated.

"I have brought you something," she said, and produced a small vial.

He recoiled from her. "I have told you I will not murder the old man!"

"But if he is not dead," she said plaintively, "how can I become a widow? And a widow I must be if we are ever to have any peace. His sons back in Spain would not care where I went but my husband would pursue me until the end of time!"

There was that, of course. The Englishman considered her critically. Beauty she had and to spare. And fearlessness, there was no doubting that. She was devious and wily. But she had no more compassion than the hard stones of the country that had bred her. He would as soon be mated with a pit viper.

His caressing smile bore no trace of what he was

thinking. "There will be some other way," he said firmly. "Something that will not, *cannot* connect us with the deed."

Her white teeth flashed prettily at that implication of assassins yet to come. He was too squeamish, this Englishman, not fierce enough—for all his formidable breadth of shoulder. But he was learning. He had fallen in with her schemes thus far. And he would fall in with this one too—in the end. She pressed the vial into his unwilling palm.

"Take it anyway, *querido,*" she urged in her softly accented English.

She desired most ardently to become a widow.

But not to marry this Englishman—as he thought. It was something else entirely that the lady had in mind. The Duchess of Lorca considered that she had had an abominable life—and she meant during her projected widowhood to correct that. Taken from a convent at the age of sixteen, her father dead, a guardian for her appointed by the king himself, she had found herself immediately betrothed to an elderly nobleman whose youngest son was many years her senior—indeed he had grandchildren nearly her age! And she with her budding breasts and her bright young dreams and her waist that a man could easily span with his two hands! Angry and rebellious, she had considered escape. But then the thought had flitted into her mind that married to the Duke, she would become not only a Duchess— she would be presented at the Court near Madrid. The Court would be filled with courtiers . . . and she would find someone. Someone younger, handsomer, more desirable than the gray-haired Duke of Lorca.

So she had pretended to desire the match.

She had married the Duke meekly, with eyes cast down. She had been the very soul of compliance on their wedding night. The Duke, inspired by her beauty, had called her (as Henry the Eighth had once called a bride he would later have beheaded) his "rose without a thorn." She had lain by his side in bed and listened to his quiet snoring. Lain there with her young body still pulsing and unsatisfied from his too abrupt lovemaking, and stared up wide-eyed at the moon above the tiled roofs.

From that moment she had hated him.

And it had been a shock of earth-shattering proportions when the Duke had told her calmly that he did not intend to take her to Madrid with him. Far better for her to stay in the country in "less sophisticated" surroundings. Indeed, he had said loftily—and meant it—the ways of the Spanish Court, strictest in all of Europe, were so loose that they would shock her.

She had wept. She had fallen to the floor at his feet in her wide-skirted black silks and thrown her arms despairingly around his knees and wailed that she could not bear to be parted from him. Not for a day, not for an hour. She would *die* if he left her!

The heart of the elderly Duke had been touched by such simple childish devotion. He had graciously consented to take her with him.

And once at the Court at El Escorial near Madrid, the enchanting young Duchess had flowered. She had swiftly learned the drifting walk of the Spanish Court ladies—and their graceful gestures and artful use of a flirtatious fan. She had learnt that the flattery of the elegant courtiers was just that—flattery.

Her brief exciting affairs with the numerous courtiers who had succumbed to her charms were legendary— although the Duke of Lorca was happily unaware of them. But . . . there was always the chance that he would find out. And a Spanish grandee such as the

Duke of Lorca could mete out summary justice to an erring wife.

But not if he were dead!

The Duchess was determined to have her freedom.

At any cost.

This now was the cost, this devil's pact with an impoverished Englishman who, in his conceit, thought she was enamored of him. So much the better! He would be putty in her hands, she told herself confidently. And at some point—where and when she desired it—he would use that vial of poison.

And she would be free!

The Englishman in whose hand she had pressed the vial of poison that was to kill her husband knew nothing of this, of course. It would have amused him if he had. For it was in his mind to enjoy the Duchess's delightful body and eventually to leave her somewhere. Perhaps in Italy, perhaps somewhere else—whenever he grew tired of her.

As he had left so many other women when he grew tired of them.

For the titled Englishman who faced her in that low-ceilinged shabby room at The Shark and Fin was also a snob. He considered Spain, for all her might, a barbarous country. He had been married once before and his wife had been not only an heiress but a flower of the English aristocracy—dead now, alas. Although he had made many rash promises to a variety of women—promises he had never intended to keep—it had never even occurred to him to replace her with someone he considered beneath his own station (and to him all foreign nobility ranked several steps lower than that of England). And certainly not with a foreigner. Especially one from England's fiercest enemy, Spain!

Still, it was only good sense to let the Duchess think so, since she so obviously desired him. Indeed she was moving toward him now with a certain light in her eyes. An elegant companion in bed she certainly was, and he was abruptly aware of the bed immediately behind him. He little doubted they would be tumbling about in it soon. But now he must try to discourage her from further visits that would endanger them both.

"You could have been followed," he said bluntly— and set the vial aside on a table.

"I was not," she scoffed. "Sancho kept close watch. He is very reliable. Nobody saw me leave—I went to bed early and left my bedchamber door locked. My maid will keep it locked until I return."

"Why do you take these risks?" he demanded.

"Do you not know, *querido?*" She flashed him a dazzling glance from those glowing almond-shaped eyes, a fierce proud look that, even though he knew her for what she was, heated up his blood. "It is because I love you, and I would not have anything happen to you, that I hastened here to bring you the news."

He retreated from her a step but he came alert. "What news?"

She sighed. "You will have to go to sea again. This man Kells whom you are impersonating so brilliantly may be in England soon—and if he is caught and hanged here, all our plans would go awry."

"How do you know this?"

She shrugged. "I am out. I hear gossip. There is word in the town that a talkative woman has arrived from Virginia and spread the word that the redoubtable Captain Kells tried to marry a Virginia girl under the name 'Rye Evistock.' Have you heard the name?"

"Rye Evistock . . ." The tall Englishman rolled the

name over his tongue. "Yes, I think so—an Essex family, I believe."

She nodded impatiently. "But his identity was discovered in time to stop the wedding. It seems he claimed to have procured a king's pardon from the Governor of Bermuda—which means your efforts so far may have been in vain, my love."

The man before her ripped out an oath. His chest in the ill-fitting puce coat seemed to expand with his anger. "I told you it was too soon for the *Alicia* to attack English ships!"

"For the *Sea Wolf* to attack," she murmured, reminding him that they had rechristened the *Alicia*. She gave a fatalistic shrug. "But it might *not* have been too soon. These things happen, *querido*."

"What else do you know that you have not told me?" He ground out the words.

"The wedding was to take place in the bride's house on the York River"—she pronounced it awkwardly—"but when the bridegroom's real identity was discovered, he escaped. The girl disappeared too and it is thought that they may have returned to the Caribbean."

"Or perhaps to Essex if 'Rye Evistock' actually is the fellow's real name," he growled.

She nodded cheerfully. "Just so. But his pardon will not cover any crimes committed *now*. So, *querido*, you must arrange one."

"I have already attacked two peaceful merchant ships to please you," he said in exasperation. "And found little enough loot for my pains. Am I to make war for a few trinkets and a silver chamber pot?"

"Well, English merchantmen do not carry the gold of the Indies," she pointed out reasonably. "And anyway, your crimes must be against England—not Spain. Although," she added wickedly, "I realize how you must hunger to hurl yourself against the treasure *flota* now that you are 'Captain Kells'!"

The Englishman passed a weary hand over his eyes. Did this Spanish seductress really think that he had ever had any intention of going up against one of Spain's great carracks or galleasses with their multi-storied castles fore and aft and their decks of guns? It was bad enough that he must pretend to be this Irish buccaneer who just might after all be an Englishman named Rye Evistock, bad enough that he had had to recruit men to play the parts of Captain Kells's ship's officers—for they too were well known by sight. Careful descriptions of them all had been obtained by the Duchess—who had pumped those descriptions from returned Spaniards who had enjoyed an enforced stay on Tortuga—even of the Silver Wench. Indeed, a stripling member of his crew, wearing a silver-blonde wig, had played *that* part, though not too well. Bad enough that he had been forced to voyage about off the Virginia coast, taking and sinking two small unarmed English vessels, all the time fearful that every sail that appeared on the horizon might be that of a real buccaneering vessel or—perhaps even worse—the whipping canvas of some vast galleon with guns beyond number.

All that was bad enough—and now she dared to jibe at him!

She saw the anger in his face and shook her black curls at him in reproach. "All this I do only that we may be together, my pet," she told him plaintively. "And now that you are warned that this buccaneer, this Kells, may shortly be among us—"

Her chiding words had brought him up short. He had forgotten for a moment why he was supposed to be doing all this. Not for the gold—for *her*.

"I will check into this matter of Rye Evistock," he promised hastily.

"Yes, find out if there really is such a man and if so"—she frowned—"you must find a way to capture him. To be dealt with later."

He looked down at her in amazement. She was so matter-of-fact about "capturing" a famous buccaneer who had eluded the combined might of Spain all these years!

"I will do my best," he promised ironically.

"Oh, I know you will, my darling," she purred. Now that their business was over, she advanced on him with that faint, delicious swagger that had heated so many other masculine breasts. Her bustline—slight by English standards but ample according to Spanish fashion —was thrust forward to make the most of what she had, and her long black skirts swished seductively across the floor. "I intend to go to the play tomorrow," she told him, looking up at him through her dark lashes. "Will I see you there?"

"I don't know," he said restlessly, certain her love of the theatre would endanger them both. "I must look into this Rye Evistock matter—it may take time."

"Then we must make the most of what little time we have, must we not, *querido?*" She smiled flirtatiously and turned her back toward him, lifting up her thick black curls from the nape of her neck with both hands. "You must help me with these hooks. . . ."

She would not have liked his expression had she seen him stare at the sleek feminine back beneath those hooks which he hastened to undo. It was at the moment grim, to say the least. He would rid himself of this disastrous wench, he was promising himself even as his fingers touched the almond-pale silk of her skin. As soon as the ransom was in his hand he would rid himself of her. He would find a way to do it, even if he had to drop her off in some Caribbean hellhole. For it had come to him—and the thought had sobered him—that he was not the aggressor here; the Duchess had woven her web and lured him into it like a black widow spider.

And that was what she obviously wished to become: a widow, with her bright eyes watching mockingly from behind the swaying web of her intricate black lace mantilla. . . .

His uneasy thoughts tore at him.

And then as he eased down the dress from her pale body and felt the smooth silk of her bare shoulders beneath his hands, as he let his questing palms slide down those shoulders until he found her soft slight breasts, he felt a familiar tug in his groin. With a low growl in his throat he spun her around to face him and buried his face in her white upflung throat. He slipped an arm about her shoulders and the other below her knees and scooped her up and deposited her in the bed upon the straw-filled mattress.

Lust, he had often told himself, *was as good as love—and far less entangling.*

Somehow he did not find it so tonight. The news the Duchess had brought worried him, the vial she had brought distressed him, the thought of going on with her into the distant future was suddenly a terrifying one.

"What is the matter?" demanded the soft voice of the ardent woman beneath him. "You—stopped."

He realized then that he had broken the rhythm of his steady thrusting within her. His thoughts had brought him up short.

"I thought I was hurting you," he muttered.

"Never!" Her slender body arched up temptingly toward his.

He seized her more roughly then and got on with it. She was after all a lustrous piece, and many a man would give his strong right arm just to hold her as he was holding her now, to lie on her breast and strain the more fully to possess her. And yet, possessing her, he felt of a sudden a great loneliness and realized that he had never fully loved a woman, not even his young wife, dead these two years past. Somewhere out there, there was a woman—there must be—who would fill all voids, who would dim all others in his view. Forever.

But certainly *he* had never found her!

And then the Duchess's demanding body was straining against his with mounting passion and he heard the small strangled cry in her throat as she quivered with tension, with desire, her arms wrapped round his neck. He forgot his loneliness then—perhaps all men were lonely, he thought—and abandoned himself to the lady's undoubted charms.

Lust, after all, was better than nothing.

BOOK III

The London Lady

Married in Fleet Street, legal or no!
Parsons all waiting, kiss me quick and go!
Though such brides are joyous, their future is dim
But Carolina doesn't care—she has him!

PART ONE

The Fleet Street Bride

The lady in her satin gown
Her feelings now must hide
As she is carried through the town—
Naught but a Fleet Street bride!

LONDON, ENGLAND

Summer 1689

Chapter 15

Carolina had not realized how excited she would be at seeing London again. Memories assailed her as the *Sea Waif* made her stately way up the Thames, past the Isle of Dogs where those three little wooden ships, the *Susan Constant,* the *Godspeed* and the *Discovery,* had set out for Virginia in December some eighty-odd years ago—and so made a place for her ancestors. The grove of Spanish chestnut trees at Greenwich Palace brought back memories of Thomas, her first love, and the aching desire she had felt for him. But those memories dissolved when she turned to look at the tall stalwart man beside her. Here was no slippery Thomas, pursuing every skirt in sight—here was a man to live for, to live *with.*

As familiar landmarks drifted by, she was busily telling Virginia about them: There was the massive bulk of St. Paul's Cathedral destroyed in the Great Fire of London more than twenty years ago and rebuilt at such cost! And there was the Tower of London where queens had been imprisoned—and later lost their heads!

And there—ah, there were the Inns of Court. And that was Gray's Inn where her school friend Reba's cousin George had studied law. Carolina's silver eyes sparkled, for it was in an ice-green satin suit belonging to Reba's cousin George that she had slipped out a window one snowy night at Mistress Chesterton's School for Young Ladies and first met Rye Evistock.

"You need not tell your sister everything in great bursts," Rye told her affectionately. "We will be staying in London for a few days before we go up to Essex."

Carolina could not have been more delighted. That would give her time to show Virginia all her old haunts—all those places that had once meant something special to her: the Whispering Gallery at St. Paul's, Highgate Hill where the Bow Bells had called to Dick Whittington, Drury Lane Theatre where she had attended plays with her schoolmates and later with Thomas.

Being back here made her think of Reba, her auburn-haired roommate from Miss Chesterton's school. It had been a long time since she had given much thought to Reba. Indeed when Reba's mother had caused her servants to seize Carolina and summarily force her aboard a ship bound for the Colonies, Carolina had been very angry with Reba for not taking her part. She had thought never to speak to Reba again. But now she felt differently for, after all, had not Reba brought her and Rye together? No matter why she had done it, it was at Reba's home in Essex that she had fallen in love with Rye and he with her. . . .

When she had last seen Essex it had been a winter wonderland of snow and ice. She wondered what it would be like now in the full bloom of summer.

They took rooms at a good centrally located inn, the Horn and Chestnut, whose painted swinging sign outside displayed a horn of plenty spilling out chestnuts—and it took Carolina rather by surprise when Rye told the innkeeper their last name was Smythe. Even Virginia blinked to learn that she was to be known as Rye's sister Virginia Smythe for the duration of their stay in London.

"Just until I hear from my younger brother Andrew in Essex," Rye told the girls when they were gathered together in one of the two adjoining rooms they had secured upstairs and were sorting out their luggage. And Carolina realized that this was but an example of the eternal vigilance that had kept him alive throughout his buccaneering days in the Caribbean. "You will have plenty of time to sightsee," he added. "For I'll be busy this next few days with the unloading of the ship, making sure that everybody has collected his portion and gets off safely."

She knew he would help all those who didn't know how to deposit their gold with a goldsmith, under a false name if necessary. And see all those off to visit their families who still had families in England. Rye was very reliable, she thought warmly. He never forgot old friends.

"The landlord tells me today's the day for Swan Upping," he told Carolina. "Perhaps you might want to take Virginia up the Thames to see that."

"Oh, yes, please let's do!" cried Virginia, for Carolina had told her how the graceful long-necked birds who floated in frosty beauty upon the Thames were considered the property of the Crown unless they bore the marks—nicks in their bills actually—of either the Vintners or the Dyers who had had royal permission for over two hundred years to keep swans upon the

273

Thames. Once every year on a summer's morning members of these two ancient "livery companies" would start upriver from Old Swan Pier near the Tower of London, marking swans as they went. These were jolly occasions and very popular with the public.

"And perhaps tomorrow," added Virginia shyly, "we could visit the booksellers' stalls that you said are congregated around St. Paul's?"

Carolina smiled at her sister. Virginia would never change. Even here with all of London about her to be explored, she was bound to have her head in a book!

Rye left them at the inn and they promptly headed out, having changed to light calico dresses that blew in the breeze. They hired the boat of one of the watermen to take them along, following after the Swan Uppers, who were presided over by the royal Keeper of the Swans as the cygnets were rounded up from London Bridge to Henley.

"'Tis said swans mate for life," the waterman told them thoughtfully as they viewed the beautiful long-necked white birds, excited by all this activity. He shook his head in wonder. "'Tis more than can be said of men!"

"Indeed it is," echoed Virginia and Carolina threw her sister a compassionate look. Life had not been very kind to Virginia; she hoped all that would change now that they were in England.

"Just think," murmured Virginia, letting her fingers trail over the side of the boat to ripple through the water. "Anne Boleyn drifted down this very river on a barge to her coronation at Westminster—and *her* husband wasn't faithful either."

Your husband wasn't unfaithful—he just didn't love you, Carolina thought with a pang.

"I wish you could be here during a frost fair," she

said, to change the subject. "Stalls are set up and hawkers run about and everybody is dancing on skates and they roast whole oxen on the ice! But then," she added lightheartedly, "perhaps you *will* be here if the river freezes over this winter, for Essex is not so very far from London."

Rye had sent a message to his younger brother Andrew on the day of his arrival and Andrew arrived the very next evening on a lathered horse. He looked worried. He was a tall, thin young man with a slightly stooped appearance which came, Carolina suspected, from habitually having his head bent over a book as he rode or walked. He had forgotten to pack any clothing —not even fresh linens, which Rye good-naturedly supplied him from his own luggage—but his saddlebags were bulging with leather-bound volumes.

"I thought I might find time to read a bit in London," he told them apologetically, running his bony fingers through his lanky, carelessly cut dark hair.

"Perhaps you will let me look at some of your books?" asked Virginia eagerly. "For I have nothing to read and although Carolina had promised to take me to the book stalls around St. Paul's today, we were sidetracked by the dress shops and, I am afraid, have rather overspent!"

Rye gave his young wife an indulgent look. "Ever extravagant!" he said lightly. "What would you have done had you fancied a poor man?"

"I'd have found a way to make him rich," Carolina said pertly, but her attention was focused on Virginia and Rye's younger brother Andrew. Indeed she could tell from the sudden tension in the way Virginia was standing that she was not unattracted to him.

"Mistress Virginia," said tall Andrew with a sudden flashing smile that was reminiscent of Rye's wolfish grin, "I would be honored to escort you to the book stalls around St. Paul's. And Mistress Carolina too, of course," he added hastily. "And as to my own books, you may have of them what you will. They are at your disposal, every one."

Virginia flushed happily and bent over to study the covers of the books he had brought with him, raising her head eagerly to ask Andrew questions about each. They were soon so engrossed in their literary discussion that neither one of them heard Rye suggest it might be time to go down to supper.

But as Carolina and Rye were moving from the room, Andrew suddenly roused himself from his discussion and said, "I've come bearing bad tidings, I'm afraid. Word is out all over Essex that you're none other than Captain Kells and you'll be arrested if you go in that direction. Indeed, 'tis a good thing that you're here under the name of Smythe, for I hear the word is well out in London too that the noted Captain Kells may be coming home to England. . . ."

"Say rather notorious, Drew," Rye amended in an ironic voice. "But tell me, how did word get about so soon?"

"Some gossipy visitor from the Colonies, I'm told." His brother frowned. "She leaves for Nottingham but before she goes she tells a wild story that's being repeated everywhere about a wedding that did not come off. In Williamsburg, I believe she said?"

"No, on the York," said Carolina bitterly. "And I'll warrant it was Amanda Bramway who gave her all the gory details. That woman cannot get over the fact that Mother took Fielding away from her!"

Andrew looked properly mystified and Rye muttered, "Family matters, Drew. I'll explain it all later—

just remember to call me 'Ryeland Smythe.' Well, now that you've properly impressed Mistress Virginia here"—he slapped his brother lightly on the back—"tell me how things are at home, Drew. How's Father?"

"About the same. Takes little interest in what goes on and lets Darvent and Giles have their way about things."

Rye frowned. "I'm sorry to hear it—though it's no more than I'd expected, of course. I'd hoped to go up there and see if I couldn't straighten things out once again, set them on a right course for a change, but I see it's not to be." He sighed. "Well, why don't you take Mistress Virginia downstairs, Drew? Remember we're all named Smythe though we've kept our given names for convenience's sake—and I'll follow with Carolina as soon as she's put away her purchases."

Carolina had already put away the things she had bought, so she knew that Rye's words were just an excuse for having a word alone with her. She turned to him expectantly as Andrew closed the door behind himself and Virginia.

"This means," said Rye, looking down at her gravely from his great height, "that we cannot be married in Essex."

"But surely here in London—" she protested.

"Nor in London either. You heard what Drew said. The word is out. In London as well as Essex. If I tried to get a marriage license or have the banns cried, I'd be arrested."

Carolina turned and walked to the window, where she stood looking out. The disappointment at his words went through her so keenly that she realized with shock just how much she had been counting on this wedding, this *reaffirmation* of Rye's love for her. His recital on ship of the details of his first tragic marriage to the young Spanish girl, Rosalia, had affected her more than she cared to admit. And now it was beginning to look as if she was to be always a mistress and never a bride!

"We *shall* be married!" She swung about accusingly. "You promised me we would be married when we got to England!"

"Carolina—"

"There is bound to be some place!"

"There is," he said coldly. "St. James's in Duke's Place, which claims it does not come under the Bishop of London's jurisdiction. We could be married there—for a price—no questions asked. I'm told they'd even predate the certificate."

Carolina's eyes widened. "Is it legal?"

"'Tis said to be perfectly legal," he said coolly. "And we could be married there, say, the morning of the day I sail back to the Caribbean. Just before boarding, so that there may be no hue and cry after me should the prelate decide to make a few extra guineas by telling the authorities who it is who's just been made a bridegroom!"

But that meant waiting. . . . Carolina's soft lips formed into a pout. She wanted to be married *now*.

"We won't wait for that," she declared. "I know a place we can be married where there's no waiting."

He sighed. "Where?"

"Fleet Street," she told him promptly. "Virgie and I—"

"You'll stay away from Fleet Street," he interrupted. "Just south of it is the area they call 'Alsatia' and it's peopled by cutthroats and thieves. They'd as soon cut your purse as look at you. I'll not have you going there alone."

Carolina tossed her fair head. "Virgie and I just *happened* to stroll through there today. I remembered you had said you were taking some money to deposit with the goldsmiths—"

"On Lombard Street."

"Well, I thought you might be taking it to Child's on Fleet Street. I remember being told Nell Gwyn had banked there." She had recalled school friends telling her of seeing a coach carrying that famous actress and one-time mistress of the king pull up before No. 1 Fleet Street and watching Nell herself descend, laughing, to go into the bank. "Anyway," she defended, "we were perfectly safe, no one accosted us."

"You should not have gone there unprotected at all! Indeed the denizens of Alsatia can come up to Fleet Street, cut a purse or two and then find legal sanctuary in Whitefriars Priory and refuge from justice!"

"I shall try not to need sanctuary!" Carolina cried, exasperated. It took an effort not to stamp her foot. "I am only trying *to tell you,* Rye, that as we were walking along Fleet Street, we saw two couples pounced upon by ministers who jumped out of doorways and offered to perform a wedding ceremony on the spot for five shillings! And I want to be married there tomorrow morning!" she added recklessly.

"A Fleet Street marriage? You want a Fleet Street marriage?" He stared at her. "You cannot be serious! D'ye not know they're none of them legal? They publish no banns, require no licenses! Indeed most of these alleged 'clergymen' are prisoners from Fleet prison who bribe the warden to let them live outside the prison walls!"

"They are marriages nonetheless!" snapped Carolina, who had been driven too far. Why couldn't Rye see that she *needed* this ceremony to tell her that she meant as much to him as had that long-ago Spanish girl whom he had married proudly in a great cathedral? "The banns and the license I do not care about! Indeed you can be married as 'Ryeland Smythe' and I as 'Christabel Willing,' but at least it will be a proper wedding ceremony."

"No more a 'proper wedding ceremony' than was our buccaneers' wedding in Tortuga!"

"But this is different," she wailed. "Rye, you *promised* me!"

They were still arguing about it when they went down to dine on shrimp pie, stewed eels in parsley sauce with shallots, pease and comfits and steaming hot cups of that expensive "China drink"—tea, which, the laughing serving girl assured the ladies with a flirtatious toss of her head at the gentlemen, cost more a pound than enough geneva (referring to gin) to make a whole party tipsy!

"Yes, tea is so dear that the merchants do adulterate it with all manner of dreadful things," said Virginia, eyeing the steaming brew warily.

Carolina gave her sister a warning kick under the table. Virgie had been about to say that tea was often adulterated with floor sweepings, and she did not want Rye diverted from talk of marriage to talk of adulterated tea!

"Indeed, 'tis true, Mistress Virginia," agreed Andrew soberly. "Tea is adulterated with practically anything that will go unnoticed—even floor sweepings, I'm told!"

Virginia gave her sister a vindicated look and Carolina glared at both Virginia and Andrew with equal hostility. They were soulmates, those two, she decided impatiently, both of them staring suspiciously into their teacups!

Rye tasted his Canary and declared it to be but a mixture of rough sherry and malaga. Carolina might have observed that he was too used to the best wines Spain could provide, but the flirtatious serving girl was hovering over them and she kept silent.

Andrew turned brick-red as the girl leaned over to pour him some wine and her low-cut blouse fell open to reveal a pair of plump breasts, and beside him Virginia was scarlet with embarrassment. *How alike they are,* thought Carolina, suddenly amused. *Cut from the same cloth.* She wondered if they realized it yet. In time they would, she was very certain. It was hard to realize that Andrew was Rye's brother, they were so different. Except when they smiled—then their white teeth flashed in much the same way, transforming alike Rye's saturnine countenance and his brother's owlish one.

Thoughtfully Rye fingered his glass of Canary and looked across the table at his brother. "My lady is in mind of a wedding, Drew." He sighed. "She yearns to be a Fleet Street bride."

"On the morrow!" said Carolina promptly.

Andrew looked at her aghast. "But Fleet Street weddings are—"

"Illegal?" she supplied sweetly but her silver eyes were stormy. "That's what you were going to say, weren't you, Andrew?"

"Well, yes, I—"

"Forget your warnings, Drew," Rye cut in. "If it's a wedding we must have, a wedding is what we'll get. Tomorrow morning."

Carolina was hard-pressed not to throw her arms around his neck.

Her eyes were still glowing when next morning the four of them took a carriage to Fleet Street where an unsavory lot of "ministers" were hawking the virtues of the married state. Rye looked about him in some distaste.

"Well, you can see what's offered," he said politely as several of the "ministers," scenting business, converged on them. "Pray select a parson of your own choosing."

Carolina ignored the irony of his tone and promptly chose the one that seemed cleanest and best spoken. "I am Mistress Christabel Willing and this gentleman by my side is Ryeland Smythe," she declared in a ringing voice. "And we are here in Fleet Street this morning to be wed."

"Ye've come to the right place, my lady," boomed the "minister" of her choice, who had more than a trace of yesterday's gravy on his shirt front. "And would ye be taking a wedding parlour at the tavern yonder for your wedding breakfast? Brandy is provided by the landlord without charge," he added slyly.

"No, I—I thank you, but the marriage ceremony will be enough," said Carolina, flushing under Rye's derisive look.

It was swiftly over. Their vows were spoken firmly before a worried-looking Virginia and a completely puzzled Andrew, the five shillings paid, and a grubby piece of parchment with a completely illegible signature was stuck into the bride's hand.

"'Tis your proof, my lady, that ye are now legal wed!" the "minister" with the gravy-stained shirt said with a chuckle.

Carolina flushed again and turned away, hurrying to the waiting carriage.

"Satisfied?" asked Rye sardonically as he reached out an arm to help her ascend into the carriage.

"Yes," she said defensively, tucking the scrawl of parchment into her velvet purse. "And now should the landlord demand proof that we are man and wife—"

Rye snorted. "Should our landlord be so imprudent as to demand proof that we are man and wife, I'll rearrange his teeth for him!"

"Carolina," said Virginia hastily. "Rye has forgotten to kiss the bride."

"The bride ran away before she could receive her wedding kiss," said Rye, bending over to press a light kiss on Carolina's hot cheek.

"And we forgot the ring!"

Carolina held up her finger with the large square-cut emerald conspicuously displayed.

"Oh, yes, of course," said Virginia, who had been upset by the whole odd ceremony. "I forgot you already had one!"

And then they were dropping Rye at the waterfront near where the *Sea Waif* lay at anchor. Before they could tell him good-by he was hailed by a jolly ship captain from Jamaica whose acquaintance he had made the day before.

"Did ye hear what has happened to me?" cried the captain, aggrieved. "I spent the night ashore. My ship was anchored upriver a ways and during the night she was cut adrift by the River Pirates. They ran her aground, they did, and while the mate slept they broached the barrels of the rum I was carrying and did siphon it off into skins! I'm told these blasted River Pirates have special funnels for the work and can do their mischief in dead of night while the crew sleeps all unknowing! I'm missing a quantity of rum," he added, "and the owners will be sorely tried to discover I've come up short. Mind you," he cautioned, "that it does not happen to you!"

Rye's grim smile betokened what would happen to a crew of "River Pirates," however seasoned, if they were so unlucky as to try such tactics on a ship manned by buccaneers fresh from their wars with Spain in the Caribbean.

"I am sorry to hear of your trouble," he sympathized. "But my crew sleep like cats with one eye open and would pounce upon these River Pirates before they had a leg over the railing!"

"I am glad to hear it." The captain from Jamaica shook his head in wonder—and went his way.

Carolina, who had been a bit shaken by the tawdriness of her Fleet Street wedding, which had seemed— once it was underway—a very mockery of the wedding vows, had regained her composure and flashed a smile at Rye as the carriage left him and turned and went its way.

Its "way" meant to the book stalls around St. Paul's, for this was the place Virginia most yearned to see in all of London and Andrew too was eager to view the publishers' newest offerings. He diverted them by telling them how all the publishers had carefully stored their books in St. Paul's for safekeeping when the Great Fire had raged through London. And how they had watched in horror the resultant holocaust as the great cathedral burst into a veritable inferno, its lead roof tiles running red like molten lava cascading down Ludgate Hill, its stones bursting and booming like cannon as the belching flames consumed church and statues and books alike in its uncaring red grasp.

Carolina was hardly listening—she had other fish to

fry. There was one place she had wanted to go ever since they had arrived in London—and she had no desire to take a disapproving Virginia or a worrisome Andrew along with her.

"I think I'll just let you two browse around St. Paul's," she told them, "and let this carriage drive me about the city for a while. After all, 'tis been a long time since I've seen it and then only as a schoolgirl!"

Virginia gave her a doubtful look, but such was her interest in the offerings of the book vendors that she would have accepted practically any excuse to have a go at them.

"Will ye be all right, Mistress Carolina?" wondered Andrew doubtfully, not sure he should allow her to wander about unchaperoned.

"I'm sure I will be," Carolina told him sweetly. "I've walked these streets by night—and in men's clothing at that!"

She was delighted by Andrew's shocked expression but the carriage driver turned to give the blazing beauty in the back of his carriage a sharp look and she heard him chuckle. He at least was well aware that some of the wilder London ladies occasionally went out on the town dressed in satin breeches and tricorne hats!

Carolina had determined that she would stop by Mistress Chesterton's school—that school that had since become a gaming house when scandal had roiled about wild Jenny Chesterton's pretty ears. And she had been certain that Virginia—and certainly Andrew as well—would violently disapprove of her visiting a gaming house even in the morning!

As a matter of fact, she wasn't sure how Jenny Chesterton would receive her. She remembered all too well how irritated the young schoolmistress had been when Thomas had somehow got around her and had managed to take Carolina away from the school on all sorts of delightful excursions.

She remembered Thomas now with a sudden pang. She had been so in love with him then—and he had turned out so badly. But now she had Rye and—her brows lifted wryly as she glanced down at the velvet purse containing her marriage "certificate"—now she was at least a Fleet Street bride!

MISTRESS CHESTERTON'S GAMING
HOUSE
LONDON, ENGLAND

SUMMER 1689

Chapter 16

Sure that Rye would disapprove, Carolina hesitated a little to go calling on Jenny Chesterton. As she puzzled over whether to do it, she stopped the carriage and bought some gilt gingerbread from a bawling street vendor whose cries overrode even the din of London. But she blushed and shook her head when another hawker dashed up to offer her some Venus cockles. "To please y'er man if not y'erself!" he urged her with a leer—for Venus cockles were said to arouse lust.

"Drive on," Carolina told the driver firmly, munching the gingerbread as he threaded the carriage warily through the medley of vehicles that surrounded them. Not only every sort of conveyance but every sort of person seemed to be out on this brilliant day of summer sunshine: smiling farm girls come to market with a goose or a brace of chickens or a basket of eggs; drunken rakes just roused from a rendezvous and sent home, or cast out by gaming houses that needed to sweep and clean up before another day's "business" began; clerics in robes and an occasional monk or nun; bankers in long velvet cloaks too heavy for the weather; tradesmen and hawkers and chimney sweeps—and here and there an occasional well-dressed lady like herself who got more than a passing glance from the men as they rode by.

Finally, tired of driving aimlessly about, Carolina directed the driver to that familiar brick building where she had attended school when first she had come to London, a green girl from Virginia's Eastern Shore. So much had happened to her since. . . . She sat for a few moments studying that plain brick facade where one snowy night, dressed in a borrowed ice-green satin coat and breeches she had been let down by a bevy of schoolgirls upon a rope to the icy street below. And gone to an inn to look for Thomas—and found Rye instead.

She had been but a schoolgirl then. She was so much wiser now.

A group of children carrying paddle-shaped wooden hornbooks skittered by, the boys laughing and throwing their caps in the air, the girls more circumspect, pattering along with bright eyes sparkling and petticoats flying. Had she ever been that young? wondered Carolina, remembering the unhappiness of her early years on the Eastern Shore.

As she watched, two giggling off-duty chambermaids came out of the servants' entrance of the house. They gave the handsomely dressed young woman in the carriage a speculative look, then passed on by, talking and smothering their laughter. They were wearing so much cheap red ochre on their faces that they looked like prostitutes. Carolina remembered her roommate Reba's oft-repeated remark when viewing such girls: "Ochre costs but a penny," she would murmur, "but would you think they'd use so much of it?"

Reba . . . she wondered what had happened to Reba. Had her termagant mother forced her into marriage at last?

Well, there was one way to find out. Carolina alighted from the carriage and bade the driver to wait. Yet still she found herself hesitating. Jenny Chesterton might have greatly changed. . . .

As she stood there uncertainly looking up at the building, a handsome coach drew up—one she recognized immediately. That green and gold coach with the Ormsby arms painted in gilt on its side with its resigned-looking liveried coachman and two footmen—both of the latter just alighting—were well-known to anyone who had attended Mistress Chesterton's school. For Jenny Chesterton was Lord Ormsby's longtime mistress and every girl in the school had watched bright-eyed for that coach—since it usually meant that they were to be sent out for some outing while Jenny Chesterton entertained dissolute Lord Ormsby.

Thinking it might be easier to breeze into the hall along with the two footmen, who were both wearing Lord Ormsby's green and gold livery, Carolina hurried forward just as the first footman banged the heavy iron knocker.

The door was opened immediately by a neat little maidservant whose eyes rolled as the clamor within the house burst out upon the street.

Carolina took in the whole scene before her in a single dizzy moment. The lower floor of the house had been handsomely converted to a gaming establishment —and no doubt the second floor as well—for there was a tipsy gentleman in pea-green satin perilously hanging onto the banister at the head of the stairs.

"Milord!" cried one of the footmen, racing past Carolina and up the stairs toward the gentleman who waved a vague hand at him and toppled slowly forward to be caught—just in time—in a pair of muscular arms.

Lord Ormsby's weight, however, was not inconsiderable and the footman staggered backward as his master's body plummeted down upon him. For a moment the two teetered like dancers on the stairs.

Before they could well right themselves, Jenny Chesterton's form appeared behind them. She was clad in her favorite peacock-blue—this time a robe that had fallen open in the front to reveal a shockingly sheer chemise. And she was holding in each hand a highly polished boot.

"And you may tell Lord Ormsby, when he is sober enough to take it in, that the next time he leaps into my bed with his boots on, I shall tear off his wig and hurl it through the window into the street!" she cried fierily, lifting her skirts dramatically to display a bruised lower calf. "You may tell him I'll not endure such treatment!"

The other footman, who had not been so fast to move as had his companion and so had missed the impact of Lord Ormsby's falling body, now leaped nimbly forward to catch Lord Ormsby's boots which the lady at the top of the stairs hurled down with some force, one by one. He was young and Carolina could see how red his face was and how shocked his expression—probably new-hired. It came to her with some amusement that the poor lad would not keep his innocence long in Lord Ormsby's employ!

To her left was what had once been the drawing room of the establishment where elderly Mistress Chesterton, who had established the school—and after her death her niece Jenny Chesterton, who had inherited it—had stiffly entertained the parents of the students over tea. Now Carolina saw that a fancily dressed young fellow in crimson was lying beneath one of the tables. He had obviously slid there from his chair last night, drunk. Now, aroused by all the commotion, he was shaking his head and endeavoring without success to rise. As he moved, his foot struck an empty wineglass which rolled across the floor until it came to a halt at a table leg. Not all of last night's patrons had been cleared out, it seemed. . . .

Carolina would have left at that point, but as she turned to go she found her way out was blocked by the two footmen supporting Lord Ormsby, wig askew, whose bones seemed to have turned to butter and who was now tittering uncontrollably.

At that moment, the former headmistress, peering down the staircase, discovered her.

"Who is that?" she called. And then, with a gasp, "Why, 'tis Carolina Lightfoot, is it not?"

Carolina, just beating a hasty retreat, paused and admitted it was she. She realized a shade too late the folly of her having come here—since she was known at the Horn and Chestnut, which was, after all, not so far away, by the name of Smythe.

"Well, do come up, Carolina," the former headmistress said laughingly. "Things have changed a bit here, have they not?"

Carolina, lifting her pale blue linen skirts to move reluctantly up the stairs, agreed that they had. "I think one of your patrons is trying to leave," she said as she reached the head of the stairs. "But he's under a table and can't seem to find his way out."

"The servants will take care of him," said Jenny airily. "Poll!" she shouted down the stairs. "Poll, we've a leftover from last night—get him up, get him out!"

Running her gaming establishment had coarsened

Jenny Chesterton, thought Carolina. The headmistress *she* had known had kept a semblance of good breeding at least. Jenny looked much the same, yet there was the puffiness of dissipation under her eyes, and her figure had slipped a bit; her bustline which had been so trim hung lower now, her waist was not quite so slim.

"Do you—ever see any of the girls?" Carolina asked awkwardly when Jenny did not invite her into one of the gaming rooms to sit down but simply leaned against the banister considering her and scanning with an appraising eye the rich lace that spilled from her sleeves.

"You mean my former students whose parents withdrew them in such a hurry?" Jenny Chesterton shrugged. "Very rarely—they don't come calling at gaming establishments!" Her mobile mouth quirked into a wry smile.

"I thought perhaps Reba—"

"Oh, you mean the Fleet Street bride?" chuckled Jenny, still lolling against the banisters.

"The—what did you say?"

" 'The Fleet Street bride' is what I call Reba. Yes, of course I see her. Or didn't you know she's staying here?"

"Reba? Here?" gasped Carolina, amazed at her good luck for it was really Reba she had come to inquire about. "Oh, where is she? Can I see her?"

"Certainly." The former headmistress made an expansive gesture and pointed. "Her room is upstairs at the back and she doesn't get up early—she'll still be in bed."

"Oh, thank you! I'll just run up and say hello." Relieved that her awkward interview was at an end, Carolina picked up her skirts and dashed up the stairs.

She found Reba quartered in a shabby little room at

the back of the house. It brought to mind the days when Reba, who had been the fashionable school's wealthiest student, had commanded the best front room. Times had certainly changed!

Carolina knocked on the door. She wasn't quite sure how she felt about Reba, who certainly hadn't stood up for her in Essex. And when a sleepy irascible voice, unmistakably Reba's, said, "Go away, whoever you are, and let me sleep!" she almost did just that.

Then curiosity overcame her.

"Reba," she said hesitantly. "It's Carolina. I—"

"I said *go away!*" Reba's voice rose savagely and something struck the door. Suddenly her tone changed to disbelief. "Carolina, did you say?" There was the patter of feet slipped hastily into slippers, and the latch was lifted. "Carolina, it *is* you!" she cried and grasped Carolina by the elbow and hurried her inside.

One look about that drab little room, and all Carolina's resentment toward Reba fled—she remembered only Reba's generosity with her wardrobe at school and felt dismay that she should have sunk so low. She was so startled to find that Reba was actually *living* in what once had been the servants' quarters that Reba had to ask twice, impatiently, "How on earth did you get here?"

"I was in London and I thought I'd stop by and say hello to Jenny Chesterton and ask her about you," Carolina said. "And she told me you were upstairs!" She could see that Reba was still her slender fashionable self, wearing an elegant embroidered satin robe which seemed strangely out of place with her drab surroundings in this tiny bare room. Her thick auburn hair was disheveled from sleep but her brassy bright russet eyes were shining with interest as she studied her friend.

"You look wonderful, Carol!"

Carolina had to bite back the urge to say *"You don't,"* for there was a sullen expression around Reba's mouth, and her pretty face—never soft at any time—looked hard in the morning light. Instead she said vaguely, "Oh, that's probably because this dress is new. I bought it yesterday." She looked deprecatingly down at her pale blue linen with its big white lawn sleeves and flowing lace. "I was surprised to find you here at Jenny's, Reba," she admitted.

"Yes—well, it's a long story." Reba was dressing rapidly as she talked. "Let's go out to a coffeehouse, Carol, and talk over the cups. I hate this place." She looked around her with distaste at the dingy walls, low ceiling and bare floors. "Here, will you help me with these hooks in the back? Now that I no longer have a maid to help me, some of these dresses are just too much! I don't know what the dressmakers were thinking of!"

They were thinking you'd always have a maid to dress you, thought Carolina. *So what matter if you couldn't reach the hooks?* She was dying to find out why Reba was living in a gaming house instead of in her parents' elegant home in Essex, but she bent her energies to getting Reba's green silk dress decently hooked and soon they were clattering down an empty stairway. Jenny Chesterton and the maid who had let her in had both disappeared somewhere, and so had the man who had been crawling around the floor half-drunk, Carolina noticed as they went out.

"Your blue hat is a perfect match for your dress and so are your shoes and gloves," style-conscious Reba remarked, looking at her friend as they climbed into the waiting carriage and Carolina told the driver to take them to the nearest coffeehouse. "I'll warrant it cost you a pretty penny to match them up," she added shrewdly.

Carolina was glad to slide into a discussion of clothes and how dreadfully much things cost because it had come to her unhappily that she had so much to hide she couldn't really enjoy her meeting with her old roommate from school. But after the carriage driver was dismissed (by Reba's airy, "Oh, pay the man! You can always take a hackney coach back to wherever you came from when we've done!") her curiosity overcame her.

"Reba," she began hesitantly, "Jenny Chesterton called you 'the Fleet Street bride.' Are you really? A Fleet Street bride, I mean?"

"Yes, I am and Jenny never lets me forget it," said Reba in a resigned voice. "She thinks it's hilarious." She took a long swallow of coffee. "You see, Robin came back—"

"Your marquess?" cried Carolina. For Reba had considered herself betrothed to the Marquess of Saltenham—until he had gone away and deserted her. "You mean you've actually *married* him?"

Reba gave her a jaded look and stirred her coffee. "Well—in Fleet Street," she said.

"But where is he? And why are you living at Jenny Chesterton's if you're—"

"Because Robin went away again. Leaving me no money—nothing. Oh, Carol, it's a long story. After you left—"

After your mother had me dragged aboard a ship and sent back to the Tidewater! thought Carolina.

"—Mother dug up a 'suitor' for me—oh, the worst you could possibly imagine!"

Carolina could imagine some pretty bad ones, but she forbore saying so. "What was wrong with him?" she asked mildly.

Reba lifted a disdainful shoulder. "He was dreadful! He was fat—simply huge. Mother called him portly but he was *enormous*—three chins, no, four! He'd have *squashed* me if we'd ever gone to bed together! He couldn't drink without spilling his wine—or eat without dribbling gravy down his shirt! When he laughed his stomach shook like jelly and he *insisted* upon calling me 'his little Rebakins!' Can you imagine going through life as 'little Rebakins'?" She paused in solid fury and Carolina tried not to laugh.

"I take it," she said in a smothered voice, "that you did *not* marry him?"

"No, I did not indeed! Even if he *was* a baronet! My mother would sell me to the Devil if by doing so I'd gain the title of 'Lady' before my name!"

Carolina knew that to be true. Reba's mother was the worst termagant and social climber she had ever seen. "But surely if she knew that your marquess wanted to marry you—"

"Oh, he didn't—and he hasn't." Reba sighed. "Except for Fleet Street." She swallowed the rest of her coffee at a gulp, looked around her restlessly and said, "I think I'll have them put some brandy in the next cup."

Carolina gazed at her friend sympathetically. This was obviously a tale that one needed fortifying to tell.

"He has hoodwinked me again," Reba explained ruefully. "I do not know why Robin can always fool me, but he can. I childishly believe everything he says—like that wild tale that when his wife died he'd come back and marry me!"

Carolina doubted if the Marquess of Saltenham had

ever really made that specific promise but at least Reba had deluded herself into believing he had. "But he *did* marry you," she pointed out. "At least in Fleet Street."

"Oh, yes. At least in Fleet Street—and that is why my mother has disowned me. She considers me 'ruined' and she thinks I sold out too cheaply. And *that* is something she cannot forgive."

Carolina remembered the harridan who was Reba's mother. She could well believe it!

"You see," confided Reba, sipping the coffee and brandy that had just been brought, "we were all to leave Essex for Bath because that is where that repulsive suitor mother had dug up for me has his 'seat.' But the night before we left we had a visitor and he mentioned casually that he hoped to collect some bad debts—notably those from the Marquess of Saltenham, which were considerable, and I said, 'Oh, is he back in London, then?' and our guest said indeed yes, and storming through the town like the rakehell he was. So the next morning before the family was up, I put what clothes I could into a saddlebag and rode for London."

Carolina studied her friend curiously, trying to imagine Reba leaving most of her fine clothes behind and fleeing the great house her father had bought in Essex, mounting a horse and riding away into the dawn from all the luxuries that meant so much to her. She had somehow never imagined that Reba would run away. Stand and fight perhaps—but not run away.

"And you came direct to Jenny Chesterton?" she hazarded.

"Yes, I did." Reba nodded vigorously. "I asked her where Robin Tyrell might be living now—I was sure her friend Lord Ormsby would know—and she was glad enough to tell me. She said I might bring Robin to her gaming house now that he was in funds again! So I betook me to his inn and told him that I was quite desperate—indeed that I had run away from home lest I be forced into marriage with a monster, and that I did not know where to turn."

Reba's russet eyes sparkled and her face flushed, seeming to cast rosy highlights onto her auburn hair.

"And of course he took you in at once?" Carolina divined dryly.

"Oh, yes, at once. And at first it was all very comforting. I told him of course that I couldn't live with him at an inn. And"—she cast a quick surreptitious look at Carolina's new clothes—"he found a glorious place for us on London Bridge, a tall house built on one of the sterlings and overlooking the river to the east. He had half the tradesmen in London busy redecorating it. I spent positively *days* with the drapers and bought all my dishes fresh off a ship—delftware."

"Then Jenny was right? He was in funds, I take it?"

"Oh, yes. At least at first."

"And so you gave lavish dinner parties and invited all his friends?" asked Carolina, amused.

"N–no," admitted Reba, avoiding Carolina's gaze. "Robin wouldn't have people in and he refused to go out, he said he'd rather have me all to himself. At first that made me happy, because I knew Mother would never find me hidden away like that—but whenever I mentioned marriage, Robin would always turn me off and talk about something else. Until finally in desperation I mentioned Fleet Street and he was willing enough to go there."

Carolina felt a little chilled. "And then . . . ?"

"And then nothing." Reba's voice went flat. "One day he just—left. He suggested I go shopping and as you know, I never could resist that. When I got back he wasn't there—and all his things were gone. He had paid up the rent for a month—I'll give him that—but there wasn't even a note. I looked for him everywhere but he seemed to have disappeared."

And that was doubtless the usual fate of Fleet Street brides, thought Carolina, unnerved.

"Did you—go back to Broadleigh then?" she asked, using the name of Reba's father's house in Essex. "Or did you try to join the family in Bath?"

"Oh, they were back from Bath by then."

Carolina waited. The serving girl brought more coffee laced with brandy. Reba tossed it down at a gulp. "I went back to Essex—at least I tried to. But I was turned away at the door. Even poor old Drewsie wasn't allowed to speak to me!" (Carolina remembered Drewsie, the housekeeper at Broadleigh. *The only person I can confide in,* Reba had called her.) Reba sighed. "So I came back to London and the rent was due and I had no money and I didn't choose to go on the streets for a living, so I bethought me again of Jenny Chesterton who had turned a scandal that ruined her school into a tidy business."

"But only because Lord Ormsby backed her," muttered Carolina.

"No matter how she got the backing," Reba countered realistically, *"she got it.* And so I went to see her again and she has given me employment—of a sort. At least, I get bed and board and such tips as the gentlemen care to give me." Seeing that Carolina was looking at her in horror, Reba gave a short laugh. "Oh, don't look so shocked, Carol. I'm not a prostitute—not yet anyway! I'm a sort of—shill. I egg the gentlemen on, to bet more recklessly. They play all manner of card games at Jenny's—whist, primero, cribbage, ombre— and of course most gentlemen like to dice."

"You play, then?"

"Oh, yes."

"But—but don't you lose sometimes?"

"Oh, if I play I only play with *their* money," said Reba indifferently. "And I'm not allowed to keep my winnings if I do win. Jenny comes round afterward, after the tables have closed for the night, and gets it from me."

"Then you don't have to—" The words stuck in Carolina's throat.

"I don't have to sleep with them, no. And I wouldn't in any case. Rather than do that, I'd sell myself to the highest bidder! And there'd be bids too," she added thoughtfully. "But I can't seem to forget Robin. I keep feeling he's coming back, that I'll see him again."

There didn't seem much chance of that but Carolina didn't say so. "What do you see in Robin?" she asked. "You were angry but not really broken up when he left you before."

"I know." For a moment a baffled look passed over Reba's countenance. "I've asked myself that very question. Robin grows on you—at least he does on me. And"—she sighed—"I would *so* love to be a marchioness!"

But somehow that last did not ring true. Carolina guessed that Reba had fallen in love, really in love for the first time—and she just couldn't give up. Her marquess enjoyed sleeping with her and Reba kept feeling sure that next time, *next time* he'd propose. . . .

"I'm a Fleet Street bride too," she confided, to make Reba feel better, for misery usually loves company.

"You're—!" Reba's laughter pealed. "And I sit here feeling sorry for myself!" she gasped, still laughing. "And here we're in the same boat!"

"Well, not quite," said Carolina uncomfortably, noticing uneasily that Reba's sudden shout of laughter had caused heads at nearby tables to turn in their direction. "We're still together."

"For the present!" was Reba's sardonic comment.

Carolina's face reddened. Reba had a right to jab at her.

"Well, why don't you bring him to Jenny Chesterton's?" prodded Reba.

"Oh, I—I don't think he'd go."

"One of those, eh? Pious about everything except making an honest woman of you?"

Carolina thought in panic of her buccaneer, whom she must not betray by her casual talk. "I—suppose you could say that," she lied.

Reba noted the reluctance of her manner. "Well, there's something wrong with all of them," she said flippantly. "Robin is a rake. Your—what's his name?"

"Ryeland Smythe," supplied Carolina promptly. After all, she had married Rye in Fleet Street under that name!

"So you are Mistress Smythe now." Reba smiled broadly. "I can see it won't do to introduce this upright gentleman to a woman who's a shill at a gaming house!"

"Oh, I'm sure he'd like you," Carolina said hastily. "It's just that—"

"I know," interrupted Reba. "You don't have to explain. They're all like that." Her auburn brows drew together in a deep frown. "Men! I hate them!"

All except Robin, Carolina thought pensively. *And that's because you're in love with him.* She wondered if Reba, under her defiantly hard exterior, would ever admit that even to herself. . . .

"Perhaps your mother will change her mind and forgive you," she said, feeling helpless.

"Only if I bring in Robin," said Reba. "When

Mother found out I'd been married in Fleet Street and was living with a man in London, she sent me word never to darken her door again. The only way I could ever go back there would be as a bride—a marchioness."

Which they both knew was never going to happen. They fell silent, toying with their coffee cups.

"Well, tell me how you met this Ryeland Smythe," said Reba, breaking the silence.

I met him at a gaming table at an inn, Carolina thought. *In an ice-green satin suit that you lent me—a suit that belonged to your Cousin George!* "I met him on shipboard." She was fabricating quickly. "He was traveling with his sister. She doesn't really approve of me, so that's why . . ." She let her sentence trail off unhappily, hating to tell Reba these lies.

"She doesn't approve of you? Say no more!" echoed Reba, again draining her cup.

"Reba, could I lend you some money?" asked Carolina after she had paid for the coffee and they were outside trying to hail a hackney coach for her.

Reba shook her head. *Reba had always been proud,* Carolina remembered with a sigh. *"Haughty," the girls had called her in school.*

"Well, isn't there something I can do?" she asked just before she clambered into the hackney coach that pulled up beside them.

"Not unless you can find Robin for me and persuade him to marry me!" said Reba with a puckish grin.

I wish I could! thought Carolina.

Reba said good-by and turned away, walking back toward Jenny Chesterton's. From the coach Carolina watched her go, stared at her straight-backed form until she was out of sight. That slight swagger wasn't fooling her. Reba needed help and needed it badly. But she wasn't going to accept it—not from her. At least not in the form she had offered. . . .

Carolina leaned back and thought about that as the twisted streets and alleys of busy London jolted by. Poor Reba, waiting for a man who was never coming back to her—or if he did, would only leave her again. . . .

Carolina was very quiet that evening at dinner, only picking at her bullace cheese and strawberries and completely ignoring her delicate and tasty Dover sole. Asked how she had spent her day, she said vaguely that she had been shopping for ribands but had not liked the selection. She dared not tell them where she had really gone.

"If you're tired of the fare here," Rye suggested, noticing how she hardly touched her dinner, "we could go to Greenwich for whitebait tomorrow."

"Yes, that would be nice," she agreed in a flat voice, for her visit with her old school friend had depressed her and not even the promise of such a popular delicacy as whitebait could bring a smile to her face.

Not for worlds would she have admitted to Rye when he gave her a puzzled look that night before they went to bed that her sadness stemmed from having—on the day of her own Fleet Street wedding—met another Fleet Street bride.

PART TWO

The Ambassador's Lady

An old love may be half forgot
When a hot romance is new,
But when that old love returns again
Will it be off with the new?

LONDON, ENGLAND

Summer 1689

Chapter 17

As it turned out, they did not go to Greenwich to eat whitebait after all. For the next morning, while Rye was still occupied with matters regarding the *Sea Waif* and her crew, Andrew hired a carriage and took the girls sightseeing again through London's half-moon streets and serpentine alleys and long tortuous lanes.

They passed Newgate Prison and watched in horror as a cartload of bawds was driven in, one of them sobbing as if her heart would break, one doing a drunken jig and almost toppling out of the cart, others waving and throwing up their skirts, and one calling out plaintively to Andrew that she'd give him a better time than ever those whey-faced wenches with him could if only he'd rescue her from this cart! Andrew's face reddened and he drove smartly past. They clip-clopped round the cart to the accompaniment of raucous female laughter.

"Those women were—awful," breathed Virginia once they'd gone by.

I've seen worse on Tortuga, Carolina thought ruefully. *At least this lot looked relatively clean!* It came to her suddenly how much broader her experience was than Virginia's. "We should take you past the debtors' prison, Virgie," she murmured. "Fleet Prison."

Andrew gave her a nervous look. "I'm afraid Mistress Virginia would be shocked by what she might see outside its gates," he interposed hastily.

"Why? Why would I be shocked?" demanded Virginia, fascinated.

"Because 'tis said to be the greatest brothel in London," Carolina told her demurely.

Virginia gasped and Andrew promptly launched into a determined—and much safer—discussion of London's Wall, which left Carolina yawning. "And there's another famous place you might like to see, Mistress Virginia," he suggested with a chiding look at Carolina —and drove them to Moorfields. Before the entrance to Bethlehem Hospital on Moorfield's southern side, he drew up.

"This is the famous Bedlam, where the lunatics are housed," he told them, and with a wave of his hand indicated the large figures that hovered over the gates. "One represents Melancholy—the other Raving Madness," he told them grandly.

"Bed—Bedlam, did you say?" gasped Virginia. She caught Carolina's twinkling glance and suddenly both girls burst out laughing.

Andrew looked hurt. "'Tis considered an interesting place," he said, offended.

"I–I'm sure it is, Andrew," gasped Virginia, laughing so that tears ran down her cheeks. "It's just that we know of another place called Bedlam, Carolina and I!" And she went on to tell him—rashly, Carolina thought —how their first home on Virginia's Eastern Shore had been nicknamed Bedlam for the wild goings on between their parents.

Andrew, whose world was rather narrow and whose breath was quite taken away by Rye's exploits, blinked at this startling recital. "You have an interesting family, Mistress Virginia," was his wary comment as they rode away.

But this breath of air from across the seas seemed to limber him up, and he spent the rest of the morning regaling them with stories of the infamous Moll Cutpurse, whose real name, he told them, was Mary Frith. And when Virginia learnt that *The Roaring Girl*— Dekker and Middleton's play about this famous pipe-smoking wench who wore men's clothing and was not only a thief but an accomplished forger as well—was playing this very day at Drury Lane, she could not wait to see it.

"Well—I don't know if Rye will want to appear in such a conspicuous place," Andrew said doubtfully. "Things being as they are."

"Oh, of course he will," Carolina put in with vigor, for she knew the reckless gentleman in question very well and little doubted that he would stick at attending a public performance. "Perhaps we can persuade him to rent a periwig for the occasion," she suggested roguishly.

Andrew gave her a helpless look. He was endlessly amazed at the difference between the two sisters— Virginia so studious and demure despite her occasional biting wit, and Carolina so lighthearted and devil-may-care. As different as he was from his brother, he would come to realize, for Andrew was a homebody who had never ventured farther from home than London and was intimidated by beautiful women, while Rye had ever had a restless foot and an eye for spectacular beauties.

When they returned to the inn and suggested that periwig to Rye, he snorted. "We will attend the play if you like," he said with a shrug. "I don't expect to be recognized—I'm not that well known in London. God knows I've spent little enough time on English soil these years past."

"You see?" Carolina turned to Andrew with a puckish grin. "Your brother not only will attend—he refuses a disguise!"

Andrew's response was a worried frown.

"Oh, buck up, Drew." Rye clapped his brother jovially on the shoulder. "I'm not caught yet—nor will be if I can get my business here attended to and get back to sea to straighten matters out. Remember I've a pardon for all I've done."

"But not for what this other fellow's done that's now attributed to you," Andrew said, sighing, and Virginia nodded solemnly.

"Let's have no long faces for our outing," laughed Rye. "The girls are probably set on seeing the play because they've bought new dresses and they want to show them off. They'll be so ravishing that none will notice us, Drew!"

"Should we wear face masks?" asked Virginia, big-eyed, for this would be her first London play.

"No, I wouldn't bother," Carolina told her carelessly. "It's mainly prostitutes who wear masks—those and women who attend the play with someone other than their husbands!" She laughed.

Virginia colored to her ears at the word "prostitute" and when Andrew gave Carolina a reproving look, Rye quirked an eyebrow at him in amusement.

"I think we've taken in two babes in the woods," he

murmured to Carolina when they went upstairs to dress for the play.

"Yes, they do seem to fit together, don't they?" said Carolina, once they were in their own room. She was donning, as she spoke, an elegant ice-green gown, narrow-waisted and with an enormous gauzy skirt. The satin bodice was moulded to her delicate breasts and waist like her own skin, and the elbow-length sleeves were embroidered heavily in silver threads with an enormous spill of nearly transparent silver lace falling from the elbows. She caught the skirt up in wide panniers at each side to display her ice-green satin petticoat frosted with silver embroidery, then pirouetted before the mirror and looked over her shoulder at Rye with satisfaction. "Do I meet your approval?" she asked.

"Ah, you do." His hot gaze roamed over her. "Still—that dress is a bit low-cut for wearing in public. 'Twill attract attention."

"Just so it attracts *your* attention." She laughed and gave a little twitch of one almost bare shoulder that set the gauzy lace of her cuffs atremble. She was setting pale green brilliants into her fair hair as she spoke.

"To squire such a lady is worth taking chances," he admitted with a rueful grin. "Are you ready?"

Carolina nodded and swept out on Rye's arm to join Andrew—soberly dressed like Rye, although in shades of brown rather than shades of gray—and Virginia, very excited in olive silk.

"The real Moll Cutpurse prowled the area they call Alsatia, just south of Fleet Street," Rye told Carolina as the four of them arrived in a hackney coach at the theatre and he handed her out. "After you've seen the play, you'll know why I didn't trust having you stroll about Fleet Street without an escort."

Carolina tossed her head and the corners of her expressive mouth curved into a smile. For last night's wooing had convinced her that she was more than a Fleet Street bride to this complex husband of hers. They had lain close together in the warm darkness, shared lovers' dreams, and she had felt soothed and comforted from any of the day's rebuffs. Tonight she might be only a Fleet Street bride, but tomorrow—ah, tomorrow . . . on some lovely tomorrow she would be married properly in a tall church in Essex and be acknowledged to all comers as the mistress of his heart!

But outside the Drury Lane theatre something happened that was to erase both the night before and Moll Cutpurse from Carolina's mind.

They had barely alighted in the milling raucous crowd that always congregated at the theatre entrance just before the performance. Well-dressed dandies mingled with merchants of the town, apprentices stared at silken ladies and ogled giggling street girls—a motley crowd. Suddenly, just behind Carolina, someone in the crush rudely jostled his neighbor, who was just then in the act of taking snuff.

"Ho, there!" cried the jostled gentleman wrathfully. "Y'dare to shove me, sir? Ye've made me drop my snuffbox!"

Before an apology could be offered he gave the culprit a hard shove—which sent him, off balance, hurtling against Carolina's back. Beside Carolina a sumptuous lady all in black and with a large black mask covering her face clear to her brunette curls had just bent down to brush an invisible fleck from her rich taffeta skirts. Carolina lost her balance and went ricocheting past her—and in reaching out in an involuntary effort to regain her balance, her fingers caught in the edge of the dark lady's mask and jerked it from her face, knocking it to the ground.

Rye's arm had gone out instinctively to catch Carolina about the waist and beside him Andrew had already turned and was berating the man who had done the pushing. The crowd was shoved backward as there was a struggle to retrieve the snuffbox, which had been kicked away under somebody's buckled shoes. Carolina was aware of a musky odor of exotic scents, very distinctive, from the lady's black taffeta gown as she went plummeting by. She heard a tow-headed orange girl say, "Lor', look at that!" then looked up into the orange girl's face and saw her staring at the mask—and at the lady who had lost it.

Supported by Rye's strong arm, Carolina snatched up the mask from the floor and, with a word of apology, proffered it to the lady, who was a ravishing brunette, slender as a reed, with thick shining dark hair and large almond-shaped eyes flashing beneath high-arched dark brows. Her nose was aquiline, her lips perhaps a trifle too thin, her demeanor imperious—and she wore a startled expression which Carolina attributed to having the mask suddenly dashed from her creamy features.

The dark woman snatched the mask from Carolina's fingers. Carolina twisted upward and Rye automatically gave her aid with a lifting movement of his arm. But as Carolina's head swung round, she saw that Rye was not looking at her. He stood transfixed, staring at the dark woman, and he had gone very pale beneath his tan.

A moment later the mask was back in place, the dark lady turned without a word and the swarthy man with her guided her on by.

Rye, who had been occupied with rescuing Carolina as the struggle went on behind them, now turned his

frowning attention to those who had made the distur-
bance in the first place. He would have reached out a
rough hand to chasten someone but Carolina, realizing
that if there was a general brawl they might all be
hauled before a magistrate and Rye's true identity
discovered, clung tenaciously to his arm.

"Let us not attract attention," she said quickly.

They were the right words. Abruptly Rye remembered where he was and who he was and that there was
a price on his head.

"Did you know that woman in black?" Carolina
asked him as they moved on into the theatre. "You
turned pale back there and the woman whose mask I
tore off looked so startled."

"No, I could not have known her," he said slowly.
"And I don't wonder that she looked startled at having
her mask ripped off. But—she bore a striking resemblance to someone I once knew, and for a moment I
thought I had seen a ghost."

Rosalia. He did not have to say it.

And just the sight of someone who "bore a striking
resemblance" to Rosalia was enough to make him
blanch. To Carolina that was a bitter thought.

The play and Moll Cutpurse went by Carolina in a
blur. Around her the audience was large and noisy,
talking, eating oranges, stamping their feet. Somewhere, not far off, Carolina spotted the dark lady
seated beside the swarthy man. The fabrics she wore
were elegant but her effect was somehow inconspicuous
—as if the wearer wished to escape notice. Carolina
could hardly take her eyes from her—and twice she saw
the lady's dark head swivel around and that featureless
black mask turn in their direction. Could the woman be
staring at Rye?

During an intermission, when Virginia was vivaciously discussing the play with Rye and Andrew, Carolina found an orange girl at her side—and remembered that this same tow-headed orange girl had been crying "Oranges, oranges!" nearby when Carolina had knocked off the lady's mask.

Under pretext of selecting an orange, Carolina leaned toward the orange girl. "That lady in black over there just behind that man in green and purple," she muttered. "Who is she?"

The orange girl turned and shot a lazy look in the direction Carolina indicated. She shrugged. "How should I know?"

Carolina felt for a coin in her purse. She displayed it. "She is the one whose mask was knocked off outside the theatre. You were standing nearby." She was still talking in an undertone. *"Can you find out for me who she is?"*

"Oh, that one?" The orange girl took the coin with a laugh. "I know who *she* is because I have seen her before. In a coach and without her mask. She is the wife of the Spanish ambassador."

"Do you know her name?"

"No, I don't—and I don't have no way to find out. Why don't you ask her yourself?" With a mocking look, the orange girl turned and sidled away from Carolina, loudly offering her wares, "Oranges, oranges!"

The wife of the Spanish ambassador . . . This woman could have known Rye in Spain, then. As Carolina watched, the dark lady—who seemed to be arguing with the swarthy man beside her—gave her head an angry toss and beckoned to a tall thin orange girl who swayed toward her through the crowd, carrying her small basket of China oranges on a graceful arm.

Covertly Carolina watched the brief conversation the

dark lady had with the orange girl, watched the girl turn to glance in Rye's direction and then nod, watched her wend her graceful swaying way toward them, saw her offer an orange to Rye, saw him shake his head—and then the girl leant closer and muttered something and Rye took out a gold coin and gave it to her. And was rewarded with an orange.

Carolina felt her heart sink down to her slippers. One did not pay in gold for a China orange.

One paid in gold for . . . what? For a lady's address?

She was so upset she could never remember afterward what the rest of the play was about.

She did see the elegant masked lady and her frowning escort leave abruptly. Rye did not seem to notice.

Carolina wanted to turn and rage at him, to demand to know what was going on. But she knew it was no use—he would not tell her. There was a shuttered look in his eyes when he turned to offer her the China orange.

Carolina took it. It might have been delicious, but to her it tasted as bitter as a half-ripe persimmon.

And then the play was over and they were struggling out with the crowd, picking their way over discarded orange peels and crushed baubles and forgotten broken fans, and making their way back to the inn.

Carolina was very silent that night at dinner. She was waiting for the expected to happen—and it did.

Directly after dinner, when they had gone upstairs, Rye excused himself. "I have to see one of my men," he explained to Carolina. "He has sent me word that he got home to find his wife had run off with another man and he needs help in finding a place for his children. I think perhaps my London agent can help him."

"Then why have you slipped two pistols into your belt and thrust a dagger into your jackboot, if you are going to meet a friend? And carrying a sword-cane as well as a sword?"

So she had noticed his heavy armaments. . . . "I am to meet him in a bad part of town," he said briskly. "Alsatia. He has lodgings there. Buccaneers grow used to living in odd places," he added pleasantly. "And this poor fellow doesn't realize that he has chosen to live among cutthroats again. Don't wait up for me, Carolina. I may be late."

"Late . . ." Carolina repeated woodenly. "No, I will not wait up." She did not meet his eyes.

But after he was gone and she was alone in the big square bedchamber, the best the inn had to offer, the low-ceilinged room seemed suddenly so barren and lifeless without him that she turned and fled to Virginia's room—and found her sister not only awake but brushing her strawberry-blonde hair vigorously.

"Oh, Carolina, what a day it has been! Isn't London wonderful?" Virginia's dark blue eyes were shining.

Until today Carolina had thought so. Now she gazed pensively at Virginia. "You've only seen it in good weather," she said. "Wait till the fogs roll in."

Virginia spun around from her brushing, and her long hair streamed away from her in a shining mass. "Oh, I wish it were winter!" she exclaimed. "For Andrew has told me that when the Thames freezes over and the frost fairs are held, that coaches go out on the ice and the printers from London Bridge go down upon the frozen river and set up their presses and print your name and the date right there while you're on the ice! He tells me that Charles II and Queen Catherine both had it done—the printers charge a small fee of course. And he tells me that next winter we will all come down into London by sleigh and attend a frost fair and I will have a printed souvenir to take home!"

If you ever go home, thought Carolina. *For London seems to have cast its spell over you!*

"And you were right, Carolina!" Virginia put down her brush. "There *are* men in England who find me attractive!"

"Rye's brother?" Carolina guessed with a wan smile.

Virginia nodded her head vehemently. That brisk shake set her strawberry-blonde curls in motion—Virginia had started curling her hair again, Carolina noticed with approval, since they had arrived in London. "Yes, Andrew told me the women he had met before were so shallow, so unlettered." She blushed. "I am glad he has not found that to be the case with me!"

I am glad too, thought Carolina. It was wonderful to see Virginia brought to life again.

"Andrew is the most interesting man I've ever met!" Virginia told her in an animated voice. "He loves books and he *talks* about them—with *me,* a woman! I'm so used to hearing men tell me everything is above my little head and beyond my poor female understanding! But Andrew doesn't feel like that at all." She blushed. "Do I sound very silly?"

"No." *You sound like a woman in love.* Carolina didn't say that, of course. It was plain to her that Andrew and Virginia *were* falling in love, more each hour. But they didn't know it yet. Some day—perhaps in Essex—it would burst upon them with all its radiance and their lives would be changed forever.

"Here, have a sweetmeat." Virginia proffered a box. "Andrew gave them to me."

"Oh, Virgie!" Carolina gave her older sister an impetuous hug. "I think it's wonderful!"

"What? That I asked you to have a sweetmeat?" asked Virginia with a wicked grin. "You're always imploring me to eat—and here I am, stuffing myself!" She popped a sweetmeat into her mouth.

"Yes—that too," Carolina said, smiling.

"Well, 'tis plain a woman does not have to be parchment thin to hold Andrew's interest," admitted Virginia. "Or beautiful. He is interested in things of the mind. He has written a group of essays on the future of man, which he has promised to read aloud to me when we get to Essex—oh, I can hardly wait! Someday he may even publish! And he is writing me a sonnet, did you know that?" she added proudly.

"No, I did not." Carolina's gray eyes had gone misty.

"Yes, he is working on it now. He said he would not rest until he had finished it and I am to hear it tomorrow." Virginia munched another sweetmeat. "And do you know, he told me he thought me much too thin? He said that winters were cold in Essex and that being too thin himself, he feels every blast of wind go through his very bones." She gave a schoolgirlish giggle.

Carolina, watching her sister affectionately, thought with deep relief, *I have done the right thing. I have brought Virgie to safe harbor. They will be a couple of scholars, these two—wrangling happily over Latin translations and obscure meanings. And once in a while Virgie will spice up Andrew's life with some wonderfully trashy novel—indeed they should get on famously!*

She didn't say any of that, of course. She said instead, "I am glad to see you are eating well again. Andrew is right, you must keep up your resistance if you want to survive the snowy Essex winters." She remembered an Essex winter . . . at Christmastide . . . and a man who had fallen in love with her. And left her in anger in a maze.

She felt somehow as if she were in a maze again, but this time in a London maze without grass, where the cobbles were slippery underfoot and there was no guarantee she would ever find her way through it. Life was like that, she supposed.

"Andrew has been telling me about the family seat," confided Virginia, taking another sweetmeat. "Will you and Rye live there after—" She paused, seeking words.

"After we are legally married?" Carolina supplied coolly.

"Well, I didn't mean it quite that way!" protested Virginia.

"I don't know where we will live," Carolina said briskly. *Or if we will ever be legally wed,* she told herself silently. Fate seemed always bound to intervene. . . .

"It would be wonderful if you do decide to live in Essex," Virginia said shyly. "For I promise to visit you endlessly—oh, Carolina, I have never felt so at home with anyone in my life as I do with Andrew! We can talk for hours about books, about anything, and never run out of interesting things to say!"

Carolina personally considered Andrew a rather dull stick—well-meaning but dull. She gave her sister a wistful smile.

"Perhaps we will live in Essex," she murmured. "Who knows?"

And suddenly Virginia's perpetual munching and her bright-eyed happiness were too much to bear. For a nameless fear had settled over Carolina—she chose not to give it a name. Not yet.

"Get your beauty sleep, Virgie," she counseled as she left. "So you can fascinate Andrew tomorrow!"

When Carolina got back to her room, Rye was still not back. She climbed into bed. There was no sense waiting up even though she ached to do it.

She was still not asleep when Rye came in. He closed the door behind him softly, then muttered a curse as his scabbard clanged against a chair leg in the darkness.

Given such a good excuse as that, Carolina sat up.

"Rye!" she exclaimed, as if he had just awakened her. She ran combing fingers through her long hair in the moonlight. "It must be late, where have you been?"

"My business took longer than I had expected," he said, and as he crossed the room toward her the moonlight struck his face and she saw that he looked haggard—as if he had been through some great battle. "And afterward, we sat about the common room of his inn and quaffed some wine. I had a bit too much."

"Oh," Carolina said blankly.

"I'm sorry I waked you," he said, as he crawled into bed beside her. "It's late. Go back to sleep."

So Rye had seen a face that reminded him of his lost love and he had gone out and tried to wash away the memories with strong drink. . . .

Carolina lay back, entirely miserable.

The incident had served sharply to remind her that she had no real hold on him, that she was only—just as was Reba—a Fleet Street bride.

Chapter 18

Rye was gone when Carolina awoke the next morning. She dressed abstractedly, her mind still on the events of yesterday. She was still hooking up her creamy bodice when there was a knock on the door. It was a plump smiling serving girl collecting the laundry.

Carolina piled her own rolled up laundry into the girl's arms, then picked up the shirt Rye had flung upon a chair last night. As she handed it to the servant girl there came to her a faint musky odor of exotic perfume —surely it was the highly distinctive scent she had noticed yesterday as she plummeted past the Spanish ambassador's wife at Drury Lane! She stiffened and would have bent to sniff the fabric but that the girl was eagerly snatching it from her hands, exclaiming over the fine fabric. The girl smelled so strongly of bacon grease and onions from the kitchen that Carolina's sense of smell was immediately overpowered.

By the time she trailed down to breakfast, Carolina had persuaded herself it was all her imagination. She had been thinking so fiercely about that incident of yesterday—which had made such a sharp impression on Rye that he had stayed out half the night drinking—that her senses had played a trick on her.

She did not mention anything about the incident to Virginia, who in any case was entirely wrapped up in the sonnet Andrew had composed for her, reading it raptly and exclaiming her delight.

The sense of foreboding that had come over Carolina outside the theatre at Drury Lane clung to her all that week. But although she had taken to guiltily sniffing Rye's shirts, there was no further whiff of that strange musky perfume and eventually she dismissed it from her mind.

Rye was very busy. He was provisioning the ship for the return voyage to the Caribbean. Carolina did not see much of him because he was not only busy by day, he was trying to round up as many of his officers and men as possible—and getting them away from home and family was proving difficult.

He would come home late, harassed by the day's problems, be preoccupied at dinner, then often make some excuse and be gone for a large part of the evening.

Even Virginia, caught up in her own affairs, remarked it.

"Rye is leaving you alone a lot these days, isn't he?" she asked commiseratingly one day when they were upstairs, freshening up for tea which would be drunk downstairs with Andrew, Rye being as usual absent.

Looking into the mirror as she combed her hair, Carolina gave a sober nod. It was true enough—anyone could see it.

"Well, I suppose he *is* occupied with important

things," Virginia turned her head about to view her strawberry curls. "But—I am glad Andrew is not so busy. Did you know he has written me another sonnet? And he keeps telling me how much I will enjoy living in Essex and that the family seat is very old and there are such romantic stories about it. Oh, I can hardly wait to see it with him!"

Neither can I, thought Carolina sadly. *With Rye. But when will that be? He is going to sail away soon and leave me here in London. I suppose I will go on to Essex, but what will Essex be without him? What will any place be without him?*

She finished her combing and they made their way down the wooden stairway of the inn, deciding as they went that they would like to go to a music hall that night.

But when, over teacups, they broached the subject to Andrew, he seemed embarrassed and muttered that he was not much of a dancer. And Virginia—a Virginia more vivacious and self-assured than Carolina had ever seen her—tapped Andrew lightly with her fan and told him *she* would teach him to dance, indeed she would make him an expert!

Carolina was astonished to hear it, for Virginia herself was no expert dancer. But looking at her sister's flushed happy face and shining eyes, she decided that love would blind Virginia to her own shortcomings just as it would blind Andrew to her mistakes. She looked about her restlessly for their company was becoming tedious—it was not much fun for her always to be the "extra girl" with Rye occupied elsewhere.

They remained there, whiling the afternoon away in the low-ceilinged common room of the Horn and Chestnut. The common room was not crowded at this time of day and they were alone save for two tables of gentlemen, leaning back and smoking their long clay pipes and casting occasional covert glances at the blonde beauty in the cream-colored gown.

For her part, Carolina kept casting covert glances through the small-paned window at the street outside, hoping to see Rye's tall form striding along it.

Across the table Virginia and Andrew had drifted into an animated discussion of the book reviews in the London papers. Virginia was fascinated.

Carolina was not. She glanced at the red and white satin bindings of the new books Virginia had bought that morning and which now reposed on the table before them—and thought silently that she preferred the older green and purple velvet bindings embroidered in silk at the edges that she had found in Ralph Wormeley's library back in Virginia—and the fine leather-bound volumes. She did not say that, however.

And anyway they were off on another topic now. Andrew was telling Virginia that writing a book was such a risky venture that many writers now prepared a prospectus and circulated it to prospective buyers so that they might know in advance how many copies to have printed—Dryden had done it, and others. An edition might be a hundred copies!

Carolina sighed. She was restless, her feet wanted to dance. Rye had promised to be home early—what could be keeping him?

And then she saw him, walking briskly toward the inn door. As always, her heart leaped at sight of that lithe masculine figure, the sureness of his movements, the confident way he carried his dark head. She melted at the white flash of his smile as he came in, spied them sitting there and hurried over.

"'Twas difficult," he told them, "but I managed to get away. What festivities have you ladies planned for the evening?"

"A music hall," they both answered at once, and he laughed.

"You want to go dancing?"

"Yes," said Carolina, her gaze suddenly challenging. "We have not danced a step since we have been in London."

"I had forgot," he murmured. "You were deprived of balls in Essex when Andrew reported it unwise to go there. . . ." His gaze was warm upon her, like a caressing hand, but there was a wistfulness in it, too, that puzzled her. "Of course, I will take you dancing—and Andrew here will squire Mistress Virginia. You will both wear your best gowns, and give a sailor happy memories to dream upon when he puts to sea. . . ."

At that mention of his impending journey, Carolina caught her breath. "But that will not be for a long time, Rye!" she protested.

He was about to speak but the serving maid appeared with more tea and there was much discussion about whether the ladies should stay and drink theirs or dash out and buy riband rosettes to wear upon their dancing slippers.

In the end the rosettes won and Carolina had no real chance to speak to Rye about his plans, for he was already dressed for the evening and downstairs conferring intently with Andrew when the two girls breezed merrily back into the inn with their purchases and dashed upstairs to dress.

Carolina felt that it was their first really gala evening in London. She wore her emerald necklace and emerald earbobs, careless that they would attract attention wherever she went. The flawless skin of her swelling young breasts would attract attention too in the low-cut silver-frosted ice-green gown she wore—the same she had worn to Drury Lane. Its gauzy billowing skirts and drifting lace made her look like a great silver-winged moth as she floated down the stairs beside a more prosaic Virginia dressed in a rich umber-hued gown with bronze lace overlay, which also was cut fetchingly low.

Both gentlemen rose from their table in the common room at their approach. Rye's gray eyes glinted at sight of his lovely lady, but Andrew looked positively dazzled by the sight of Virginia's elegance as she approached him with her head high, walking more confidently than Carolina had ever seen her.

"Mistress Virginia," Andrew said humbly, "your beauty overwhelms me."

Virginia flushed with pleasure and gave her fan a saucy flirt.

"Your costume needs only one small item to make it perfect," Andrew told Virginia earnestly. "This." He stepped behind Virginia and fitted around her neck a dainty gold necklace with a topaz pendant that flashed from the cleavage between her breasts.

Carolina guessed where Andrew—whose clothes were just short of being threadbare—had gotten the necklace, and flashed Rye a grateful look. He smiled blandly back at her, unwilling to admit that the necklace had really come from him.

For a man whose apparel up to now had been unremarkable, Rye's garb was singularly conspicuous this night. As if to honor his lustrous lady he was sporting a splendid gunmetal satin coat, wide-cuffed and trimmed in silver braid and a plumed tricorne. He seemed to pay no attention to the fact that he might at any time be recognized. Indeed he seemed blithely not to care and his rich laugh rang out as they made the rounds of the music halls. It was as if a great weight had been lifted from his body, leaving him carefree.

It was a wonderful evening. Carolina was sure there was not a music hall in London they missed, and they swirled to popular music, sometimes played by tipsy musicians. They laughed and drank delicate sparkling wines and watched Virginia exclaim endlessly over her topaz necklace—and danced some more. And after it had grown late they took a moonlight boatride on the Thames, drifting along the silver ribbon of the moonpath. . . .

Carolina, letting her hand drag in the cool water over the boat's side as they drifted along the moonlit river, wondered if Rye had received some new information that had made him feel safer. Had he been cleared, and the pirate who had dared to impersonate him off the Virginia coast been caught and brought to justice?

No, if that were true, surely he would tell her. She stole a covert look at him as he leaned back, relaxed, gazing at the dark London skyline drifting by. Perhaps he was saving such wonderful news for tonight—when they were alone, their bodies pressed close together in the big bed at the inn. Her lovely face softened at the thought and she leant against him the more luxuriously. The ghost of a contented sigh escaped her lips and she moved slightly against him, feeling with a little thrill the slight pressure under her breasts of the long arm he had thrown carelessly about her.

He bent his dark head and his face lost itself in her lemon-scented hair.

"Did you enjoy the evening?" he murmured.

"Yes—oh, yes." She snuggled the closer, tinglingly aware of that long hard body she rested against. "It's late, Rye. I–I think we should go home."

He gave a low laugh and nuzzled her ear. "And I wonder what we'd be doing there?"

To her chagrin—and his delight—Carolina blushed. "'Tis late," she repeated virtuously, hoping the other occupants of the boat did not notice her embarrassment. "Honest folk should be home abed."

He chuckled. "And we are honest folk and 'tis late indeed." His long fingers were toying with a lock of her fair hair as he spoke, and the back of his hand was brushing the back of Carolina's neck as he did so, making little ripples of feeling race up and down her spine. He sighed. "'Tis time to end this boatride, Andrew, lad," he called over his shoulder to his brother. "My lady is for bed."

"Aye," agreed Andrew absent-mindedly, for he was deep in a discussion with Virginia as to whether Christopher Marlowe had really authored some of Shakespeare's plays, and the two of them hardly noticed whether they were on land or sea.

As if she weighed nothing, Rye lifted his lady out of the boat when they reached the shore where their hackney coach was waiting for them—although Carolina had protested that the night was so fine she would rather walk. But Rye insisted that the waterfront by night was too dangerous a place for her, with thieves and cutthroats leaping up out of alleys to plunder the unwary. She had no doubt he had experience of such things. "But was it so much safer in Tortuga?" she murmured humorously against his coat.

"Did I ever take you walking through the town there by night?" he countered—and she had to admit he had not.

She let him hand her in then and snuggled against him dreamily as they clattered back to the inn.

The downstairs of the Horn and Chestnut was only

sparsely populated as the four of them swept through it, and there was nothing to remark this evening's end from any other, save that before their door Andrew suddenly detached himself from Virginia to wring Rye's hand.

"What was that about?" Carolina asked Rye when their bedroom door had closed behind her, then before he could answer, "Oh, I suppose he was thanking you for giving him the topaz pendant for Virginia?"

"Perhaps," said her tall lover, looking down at her inscrutably from his great height. "I think tonight we will have a candle," he said, pausing to light one as he spoke. "I would like to watch my lady undress. . . ."

Carolina flushed but she made no demur to the candle, and by its flickering flame she took off first the emerald necklace and earbobs. They cast brilliant green lights that seemed to dazzle her eyes and turn their silver-gray to silver-green as she laid the jewels carefully on her bedside table top.

Across the room Rye had removed his sword and loosened the lace at his throat. He looked very commanding, standing there, she thought, and as always she thrilled to the sight of him. The world might know him as a dangerous buccaneer and the best blade in the Caribbean, men might take heed and warning from the cold eyes that lit his sun-darkened sardonic countenance—but *she* knew him as a lover, a man who would dare anything, risk anything—for her.

Gracefully, knowing she was being watched, she took off first her high-heeled satin dancing slippers, and then her sheer silk stockings, pulling up her skirts to reveal long silken legs as she did so.

Rye stood by, undressing desultorily, watching her with hot appreciative eyes.

"Turn a little," he said. "So that the candlelight

strikes golden on your breast—I want to remember you thus."

Carolina gave him a startled look. "But I will be here in plain sight," she protested. "There will be no need to remember me!"

"Even so," he said, smiling.

She turned about as she was bid and the candlelight sparkled in her silver eyes, turning them to gold. It gilded the long pale hair she now let down into a white-gold shower that spilled like cascading water over her slim shoulders. She would never know how lovely she was at that moment, but the very sight of her made him catch his breath.

"I will need help with these hooks," she said.

He stepped forward with alacrity, still feasting his eyes on her, and swiftly unfastened the hooks of her bodice down the back—and even as she would have eased the sleeves down from the point of her shoulders he said, "Here—allow me," and did it for her, stroking down the sleeves caressingly as he brought them sliding down her slim arms. And then, standing behind her, he cupped his hands beneath her breasts as her tight bodice fell away from her slim torso.

"How good these pretty things must feel to be released from their satin prison," he murmured in her ear as he toyed with her breasts.

"Rye," she said breathlessly, for she could feel her senses quiver with each tweaking touch of her sensitive nipples. "Rye, in another moment one of us will step on my gown and tear it—you must let me undress."

He laughed, but he let her go and stood back to watch her step at last out of the glamorous panniered ice-green gown. It slid in silver-frosted luxury to the floor and glimmered there.

Carolina lifted her eyes to his and saw that miraculously he had divested himself of coat and shoes and stockings whilst she was easing her gown from her body. He looked so strong and sure standing there in trousers and shirt, his sun-darkened skin dramatic against the white cambric and froth of lace. More the buccaneer she remembered from Tortuga, less the English gentleman he had become in the Colonies and in London. He was marvelous—and he was *hers*. Her heart went out to him and for a moment all that she felt for him was reflected in her luminous silver eyes.

Briefly her fingers hesitated at the riband drawstring that held up her delicate white chemise.

"Rye," she asked softly. "Have you something to tell me?" For all this evening she had sensed a difference in him and she hoped against hope that he would tell her that he had somehow straightened out his difficulties, that he would never leave her.

Did his lean body tense? Or did she only imagine it?

"Nothing that won't keep till morning," he said cryptically. His keen gray eyes were moving leisurely up and down her slim form, almost naked to his gaze in the near transparency of her sheer chemise.

So he wanted to make love first and then awaken her with his good news, she thought contentedly—and with the thought she pulled the white riband drawstring.

The delicate fabric seemed to collapse about her, slithering down her body to lie in a fluffy white heap around her slender bare ankles until she stood quivering in the light of that single candle, naked to his burning gaze.

"God, you're lovely," he said huskily. "And never lovelier than tonight. No, don't move. I want to view you just as you are."

He was divesting himself of his remaining clothing as he spoke, but his hot gaze never left her. She could feel its pressure, as if he would devour her with his eyes. Up and down his gaze swept her, moving from throat to breast, from breast to hip, from hip to thigh—and back again. It was like an intimate caress. Carolina felt her own woman's body grow taut and expectant under the intensity in his eyes.

Her heart was pounding as his trousers were flung away. And then in a single long step he was beside her. With one hand at the small of her back he bent her resilient form backward, so that her neck arched upward, swanlike, for a long delightful kiss. His warm lips brushed teasingly over hers and then settled down to enjoy. The tip of his tongue roved over her mouth and then probed artfully inside, exploring what—although surely by now familiar ground—was an ever new and absorbing adventure.

And then inexorably his dark head was moving downward, his lips brushing lightly across her pulsing white throat, moving across the satin smoothness of her bosom to the delicate swell of her breasts. His lips danced tantalizingly over their soft smooth rounded surface and he nipped and nibbled at her nipples while she started and writhed in his arms, making soft blurred protests never meant to deter him.

His wandering lips passed on, seeking new delights, moving down to her waist, across the sleek, yielding flesh of her stomach. He set his strong teeth lightly into one hip, laughed softly as she quivered in whispering protest—and moved on, exploring forbidden places, bringing forth shivers and sighs.

He cradled her soft buttocks in his two hands and lifted her—with her arms twined round his neck and eyes like stars on a misty night—to the big bed. They sank into it together, rapt in each other, alone in the world.

All his masculine arts he used tonight, bringing to her woman's body a glow of passion, a stirring yearning. Accomplished lover that he was, he took no heed of his own wants or needs but drove her ever onward, spurring her desire until she almost wept and clung to him, moaning softly.

Then and only then did he deftly enter her—and she was more than ready to receive him. She welcomed him with every fiber of her being, clung to him, ran her slim white fingers over his naked back. His long muscular legs pressed tight against her yielding thighs. His grip upon her grew of a sudden tighter, his lips more urgent, and they were drifting together in a rhythmic mating dance somewhere beyond earth, beyond time, where the world had no meaning and nothing mattered beyond this night and this moment.

But even this was not to end it. On and on he led her, skillfully spiraling to the highest vault of heaven, leading her up a golden stair where they shimmered, disembodied, creatures of feeling, creatures of light.

Their pleasure became a tumbling torrent of madness, a whirlwind of ecstasy until—lost in each other—the world seemed to shatter about them into shards of sweetness, and the glow they felt was so beautiful it was not, *could not* be real.

Shimmering down from the heights, still held loosely in his arms, Carolina wondered if ever before in time there had been such a lover.

Rye leant over then and with his fingers snuffed out the bedside candle. "We have no need of light tonight, Carolina—you make your own light for me," he murmured.

And with that he began to make love to her again—even more slowly, more magically this time. And their desire became a raging torrent, and the torrent a mighty ocean until in a last vast tidal wave of emotion they were swept away again and washed up on some distant shore together—fulfilled.

Moments passed, moments of golden afterglow.

Then Rye lifted himself on one arm and smiled down upon his lady. Her dark fluttering lashes opened and she smiled up at him lazily. And opened her arms to him in a mocking gesture of surrender.

"My Colonial minx . . ." he murmured and bent to plant a last kiss upon the pulsing pink-crested tip of each of her delicious breasts.

Carolina stretched luxuriously, deliberately tempting him.

"Go to sleep," he said with a low laugh, and rumpled her hair. And more softly, "And dream of me."

Carolina did. All the cobwebs with which the week had been plagued had somehow been swept away tonight, and she went to sleep knowing that her fears had been unfounded. Rye had not meant to neglect her—he had merely been occupied with other things. And he loved her. So much. He had proved that tonight, with the delicacy and ardor of his lovemaking.

She nestled down into the bed, a woman secure.

Her dreams were lovely ones, adrift in the arms of love—and she awakened to the scraping of boots and the light clank of a scabbard that hit the door as it was opened.

She sat up, startled. It was still dark, no candle had been lit, but the door was open a bit and a man's tall figure was discernible against the dimness of the hall.

"Is that you, Rye?" she said, confused.

"Yes," came Rye's voice. "I am sorry I woke you."

"But—why rise so early?" She was leaning on her elbow now, peering at him through the darkness.

"I sail with the tide at dawn," he said simply. "I had

thought it best to let Andrew tell you, but since you are awake I will tell you myself." He closed the door and crossed the room to her, bent down and took her in his arms. The cloth of his coat brushed her naked breasts and his shoulder-length dark hair spilled over her cheeks to mingle with her own blonde tresses as he embraced her. "I will eat a quick bite of breakfast downstairs," he said, "and be gone. 'Tis best you go back to sleep."

"Oh, no!" she cried, distressed, trying to struggle up. "I'll dress and have breakfast with you."

"No." He shook his head with decision. "My breakfast already awaits me downstairs for I left strict instructions."

"But you can't go! You have not yet rounded up all the men you need," she protested. "They are still straggling in and you are still short-handed—you told me so!"

"I will pick up the men I need in Plymouth," he said.

"Wait then—I will have this last breakfast with you."

"No, Carolina." He pressed her gently back upon the bed. "Once dressed and breakfasting downstairs, you will be wanting next to accompany me to the docks—and I have no desire to have you bid me a weeping farewell dockside. Better far to remember you like this." His hands slid down her bare body, for she had felt no need of a night garment on this warm night.

"Oh, Rye," she whispered, straining against him. "I don't want you to go!"

"Nor have I any wish to leave you," he sighed. "But I go because I must, Carolina. Let me remember you like this."

"Then take me with you!" she wailed.

He sighed. "This is why I had hoped to be gone

before you waked. There will be danger where I am going, Carolina, and I will not drag you into it."

"But—"

"Andrew will take you and your sister home to Essex and there you will await my return. Should aught happen to me, Andrew will have a way of finding out and my London agent will see that you are well provided for. Meantime, I have given Andrew a sum of money and I have left a purse of gold on the table here which should be enough for your needs."

He would have risen then but she clung to his sleeve and brushed aside the pale shawl of her hair that kept her from seeing him in the darkness.

"But you cannot leave me here!" she cried desperately. "I belong beside you, whatever happens!"

"Nonsense." His voice roughened. "You belong where you are safe."

He was deaf to her pleadings, to her threats. She could almost see his face in the darkness turn stony as he repeated, "Andrew will look after you." He opened the door and closed it behind him. With finality.

He was gone.

Carolina, left behind in the big bed, knew it was useless to rail at him, to run after him. But perhaps there was a way!

She scrambled up and dressed with nervous haste, donning the first thing that came to hand—the dramatic gown she had worn last night. Her fingers stumbled over the hooks but at last she got enough of them fastened for decency, although they weren't all hooked. She ignored the panniers and let the dress flow free from the waist. With fingers made awkward by hurry she got her hair into some kind of semblance of neatness. Her legs were at last encased in stockings, her feet shod in last night's dancing slippers when she reached the door.

Ah—there was one last thing she must do!

She sat down at the little portable writing desk and opened its slanted top, took out inkwell and quill and parchment. To Virginia she penned a brief note.

Rye has changed his mind, and he is taking me with him. No time to pack. Please take my things to Essex—and wear anything of mine that you choose. Wish me well.

She signed it with a flourish—*Carolina*. And she slipped the folded note under Virginia's door. Rye had left her a purse of gold and now she snatched it up for she would need money for her fare to the dock—and that was where she was going, there to melt into his arms and let her warm body persuade him where her arguments had not, to take her with him on this doubtful venture to find that other "Captain Kells" who prowled the Caribbean pirating ships in another man's name.

But she must be careful. Rye might hesitate to leave her standing alone and unprotected in a ball gown at dawn on the docks, for fear something might happen to her. That alone might be sufficient to persuade him to take her along. But downstairs over his breakfast he would merely drag her back upstairs and lock her in.

She slipped the small bag of gold coins into her velvet purse. Then she stole from the room and took up a position at the head of the stairs from whence she had a clear view of the inn's front door.

Rye had eaten quickly. In only a few moments she saw his tall form go striding out into the street. She fled down the stairs after him, and as she reached the door she heard him hailing a hackney coach outside.

Breathless, she waited until the clatter of the horses' hooves across the cobbles told her he was gone. Then she ventured outside and hurried to another of the hackney coaches that waited patiently for passengers outside such a popular inn.

"Stay behind that coach just ahead," she told the driver. "We are going to the docks."

Rye had not seen her come out of the inn, she was sure of that. Indeed he had not looked back at all. He had clapped his tricorne hat more firmly on his head in the brisk morning breeze that swept in over the Thames and sprung into the hackney coach with determination —all that she had seen through the crack of the door. And now his coach was jogging over the cobbles just ahead with her own following sedately behind it.

On through a sleepy London they clattered, a London just rising, with hawkers just starting out on their rounds, and apprentices running so as not to be late, and yawning chambermaids carelessly throwing slops out of second-floor windows into the gutters of the narrow streets.

They had reached the docks now with dawn just pinkening the eastern sky, and she saw Rye alight and pay the driver. Before her lay a forest of ships, at anchor in the Thames. Her eyes picked out among them the lean lines of the *Sea Waif*—and she wondered for a moment if Rye would have the name changed back to *Sea Wolf* once he was at sea. But chiefly her mind was on what to say to him, what torrent of words could be so persuasive as to make him change his mind. She would throw herself into his arms first, of course— and cling to him sobbing. She had got as far as that.

She decided it was best not to follow too near in the coach, for he well might fling her back into it with a brusque order to the driver to "Return the lady to her inn!" Rye had dismissed his own hackney coach and Carolina shrank back when he glanced briefly in the direction of her conveyance. Then she leaned out and hissed at her driver to pull up and wait.

She was about to leap out of the coach impulsively and run to his side when another coach pulled up—this one a private coach, black with a coat of arms glittering on its side.

Rye's attention was now centered on that coach—indeed Carolina had the sudden feeling that he might have been watching it arrive when his gaze had swiftly raked her own less splendid conveyance. To her surprise, he stepped forward and opened the door and a lithe lady swathed in black allowed herself to be helped down. She arched her neck to look up at him and the black lace mantilla that covered her head blew back from her face to reveal a beautiful imperious countenance that Carolina had seen once before.

It was the face of that woman whose mask she had knocked off at the theatre, that woman at sight of whom Rye had turned ashen and muttered to her curious question that he thought he had seen a ghost. It was the wife of the Spanish ambassador he was helping alight upon the London docks at dawn!

Rye's back was to Carolina and she could not see his expression but the woman—before she adjusted her mantilla to cover her features again—had smiled up at him with a look of languorous appeal.

Stiff with shock, Carolina watched him take her arm and guide her to a waiting longboat, saw him lift her carefully in, saw her settle those wide black taffeta skirts around her, saw the two of them—along with the lady's boxes—rowed out to the waiting *Sea Waif,* saw them go aboard.

It was only then, when they had disappeared from view on board the vessel, that the full import of what she had just seen crashed in on her.

Rye was running away—and with the wife of the Spanish ambassador!

The Fleet Street bride had gambled—and lost.

Summer 1689

Chapter 19

When, outside the theatre just before the performance of *The Roaring Girl,* Carolina had inadvertently knocked off a passing lady's mask and revealed the face of Rosalia to him, Rye Evistock had felt such a shock go through his tall frame as even a Spanish rapier run through his body when he had near lost his footing on the deck of a dying galleon had not been able to give him. Almost he had gasped her name.

But then—with the same lightning swiftness that had characterized him that day on the galleon—he had got hold of himself. On the galleon's deck he had let himself fall backward away from the blade and even as he did so, another buccaneer had slashed with a cutlass at his Spanish attacker's throat. The fellow had fallen backward, choking and spurting blood, and had lost his grip on the rapier. The battle had surged past them and Rye had seized the blade and carefully withdrawn it from his body.

The feeling of quivering pain that had shuddered through him then had been much the same as he had

342

felt when the beautiful arrogant face before him—so patently Rosalia's in every detail—had denied him recognition. That olive-toned high-cheekboned face had neither flushed nor assumed an added pallor. That aquiline nose had seemed to lift to a slightly haughtier manner. Those large dark eyes in which he had once thought to drown had shown no visible recognition. Those thin expressive lips he had on privileged occasions kissed had not by so much as a quiver told him she remembered.

And like that long-ago wound taken on the deck of a Spanish galleon, he had wanted at the moment nothing so much as to crawl away and find a convenient hole to die in.

For at sight of her all his memories had come rushing back to overwhelm him, memories as vivid as if they had happened but yesterday and he was once again that counterfeit Spaniard, Diego Viajar, protégé of kindly Don Ignacio Saavedra, and madly in love with Don Ignacio's young daughter, Rosalia.

Those memories had held him rigid for several heartbeats while his arm automatically rescued Carolina from falling, but he had stared white-faced at this suddenly resurrected Rosalia—and seen in her no sign at all that she knew him.

Then the lady had snatched up her mask, replaced it and swept on beside the swarthy dark man who looked at Rye Evistock darkly but also without recognition. The man was Sancho, whom the Spanish ambassador's lady had long ago charmed to her will.

It was not Rosalia, of course, Rye told himself. How could it be? Had he not seen Rosalia die, crumple in her wedding gown to a mass of bloody white lace beneath Don Carlos's sword in that twilit courtyard in Salamanca?

There was a glaze of sweat on his brow now.

No, it could not be Rosalia. A kinswoman perhaps but not Rosalia. And so he had muttered in answer to Carolina's anxious query that he must have seen a ghost.

The ghost of first love, ever sweet. And haunting him once again. . . .

He had sat beside Carolina in the theatre numbed with shock, watching the play, and observing how once or twice that same masked lady's head swung round in his direction. And he was not to know that the masked lady was a superb actress, or that her performance outside the theatre just now had far outstripped anything that a swaggering "Moll Cutpurse" might do on stage. Caught breathless by the sight of him after all these years—and looking so lean and fit and dashing—she had nevertheless instantly steeled herself to show no trace of recognition of this man she had long ago indiscreetly married—for that was the detached way in which she thought of that burst of young love now across the years. It could never have worked. He had not been what he seemed—an English heretic, not even a Spaniard, marrying her under a false name and with her fool of a father's connivance! Her uncle had been right to try to kill him! But he had somehow escaped and she had always wondered what had happened to him for it had been as if the River Tormes had swallowed him up.

But gradually her curiosity—that curiosity her old duenna back in Spain had so often warned would be her downfall—overcame her and she whispered a message in her softly accented English into the ear of an orange girl and watched while that message was delivered.

Did she see those broad shoulders tremble at the words the girl uttered? She did not. Nor did his gaze stray to her masked face after hearing them. Indeed, he had bought an orange and was coolly proffering it to the blonde beauty at his side!

The ambassador's lady sat back, frowning behind her mask. There was no guarantee that he would even come tonight! Her chagrin spoiled the play for her and she rose to her feet, brusquely announcing to Sancho that they were going home.

Sancho, at least, was relieved.

But to Rye Evistock, pondering as he sat beside Carolina while *The Roaring Girl* thundered on stage, there was no relief. He had been sent a taunting message—and he was aware that it might be a trap. With restless fingers he loosened a cravat that had become suddenly too tight.

"Come to the side door of the Spanish ambassador's residence an hour before midnight," the orange girl had whispered. "A servant will let you in."

The Spanish ambassador's residence! Until the moment he had seen Rosalia's face, Rye would have laughed at the idea of going to the Spanish ambassador's residence for any reason whatsoever. Why, that would be to put his head in a noose! He would be promptly spirited away to Spain and there done away with. Speedily. And probably with torture.

But the possibility that this woman really was Rosalia haunted him. Perhaps she was only someone got up to look like Rosalia—if she were, they had done a noteworthy job! For everything—and he remembered everything about her—was exactly as he remembered. A little older—but then she would be a little older now. And still that same flawless pale olive complexion, still those same big dark eyes fringed by a forest of dark lashes. . . .

Suppose it *was* Rosalia? Impossible but—suppose it was? The thought tantalized him, tormented him.

And—he cast a quick glance down at Carolina's blonde head as she applauded Moll Cutpurse's on-stage antics—if it was Rosalia, then he had a lawful wife, and where did that leave him with this blonde beauty he loved so well?

The more he thought about it, the more harshly the truth struck him. *If Rosalia were still alive, he had to know it—indeed he had no choice in the matter!*

And so it was that he stuck two pistols in his belt, slid a long Italian dagger into one stiff jackboot, and with his basket-hilted sword swinging reassuringly against his thigh and his competent hand grasping a silver-headed Malacca sword-cane, he let himself out into the London night and made his way on foot to the Spanish ambassador's residence. He was more than an hour early, and he sank into the shadows across the street and watched.

For the plotters—if plot there was—would expect him to be prompt, as befitted Rosalia's hold on him. If this was an attempt on his life, then his enemies must know about Rosalia—how else would they have used an exact double as bait? There were candles still lit in the Spanish embassy. He watched as one by one they went out.

Across from him his view commanded not only the front entrance of the big brick house but the alleyway to the side as well. There was indeed a dark doorway there, inviting him to slip inside.

At eleven o'clock precisely—told by the gold watch he carried—he made his move. Nothing untoward had happened so far. There had been no sign of unusual activity inside the building, no contingent of armed men had clattered up and surrounded the house.

Which was not to say that inside the place was not crawling with armed men, all waiting to seize the redoubtable Captain Kells and carry him back—alive or dead—to Spain.

Like a shadow Rye Evistock moved toward that dark doorway. He cursed inwardly as his sword made a small sound against his jackboot—and promptly steadied it with his sword-cane. The amount of armament he wore was indeed impressive, but if this should be a trap he was walking into, then he meant to sell his life dear.

It was no surprise when the door swung silently open for him as he reached it. A single stocky form—it was Sancho for the ambassador's lady trusted no one else—beckoned him into the dimness where a single small window lit the narrow stairway leading up, then glided before him, nodding that he was to follow.

With misgivings, Rye did just that.

The stairway led half a flight to the ground-floor level—for there was an imposing half flight leading up to the main entrance—and then another twisting flight to the second floor that opened onto a more spacious corridor. Here would be the bedrooms.

He had rather expected to be received in some out-of-the-way corner, but to his surprise Rye was discreetly ushered down that empty corridor into a large room where a branched candelabrum gave ample light to illuminate the elegant furnishings, the dark red damask draperies that hung over the tall windows, upholstered the heavy carved dark furniture and canopied the tall thronelike bed that dominated one end of the handsome room. His booted feet rested on a rich carpet the Moors had brought with them to Spain. And off to his right was a mirrored dressing table filled with jars of pomades and powders.

He was in a lady's bedchamber.

And the mistress of that bedchamber was rising to greet him. Rising from a graceful lounge she had had transported from France. She was wearing a splendor of a robe, of almost paper-thin crimson velvet which suited her wild nature far better than the somber black fabrics she was constrained as a Spanish aristocrat to wear by day. The robe was cut daringly low and she had eased it down farther so that it showed not only a wide creamy display of upper breasts but the tips of her pale shoulders as well. Her hair was not piled high as she had worn it at the theatre—she had changed it several times before deciding on the coiffure she had worn when she had known Diego Viajar back in Spain, the spilling curls of a young girl that now cascaded black as night down upon her shoulders and the crimson velvet that covered her upper arms.

The door was silently shut as Sancho withdrew.

The woman in crimson took a step toward Rye, moving hesitantly, almost fearfully, across the rich maroon carpet with its geometric designs.

"Diego?" Her timid whisper penetrated the stillness. And then, as she peered up toward the tall man who seemed at this point rooted to the carpet, her face broke into a brilliant smile of recognition and she opened her arms and flew toward him. "Oh, Diego"— that breathless joyous note in her voice still managed to carry an unmistakable note of yearning—"it really *is* you!"

This was no trick, no trumped-up wench out to make

him believe the dead had come back to life. This woman before him was Rosalia. He knew that voice, that face, that slender body.

Goaded by memories, he took a step forward. Rosalia swayed toward him and his world stood still. Time spun back, back to a golden courtyard in Salamanca when young Diego Viajar had thought to wed a Spanish lady and spend his life in sunny Spain.

"Oh, Diego!" Her voice was a prayer. She went straight into his arms, and around her those arms involuntarily tightened. She lifted her face, lips parted. Her dark-fringed eyes, staring up at him, were pleading, willing him to love her and—just as he had done before—he lost himself, drowning in their dark depths. "Diego"—her voice broke—"I have found you again! At last—"

Her words were cut off as abruptly his lips crushed down on hers. In that embrace there was no past and no tomorrow, only an achingly wonderful return to yesterday. He did not even question that she was wearing nothing beneath the velvet gown. In the heady circumstances of her return to him, it seemed natural—right.

She was moving subtly backward as he embraced her and he moved with her as she went, his thighs moving against hers—for the Duchess of Lorca was tall. She melted against him, moving with the elegant grace of a flower swaying in the wind, and the musky lingering scent of her perfume—that perfume he remembered so well—filled his nostrils. Her slight breasts were against his own and through the velvet he could feel the swift beat of her heart.

"Oh, Diego," she murmured ruefully as the unyielding metal of his two big pistols pressed into her flesh. "You need not have come to my chamber armed. . . ."

"*You* have disarmed me," he muttered thickly.

And it was true.

The wheel had gone full circle in a world gone mad.

Across the years a dead woman had come back to claim him.

THE LONDON DOCKS

Summer 1689

Chapter 20

Carolina's thoughts roiled like a black whirlpool as the hackney coach jolted her away from the docks, away from the sight of Rye and that woman—together! And as the coach rumbled back over the cobbles toward the inn, those thoughts engulfed her in grief and fury mingled with a terrible sense of loss.

It was all clear to her now, clear in a naked brilliant clarity without joy or light. A knowledge of the soul, intuitive, devastating:

The shadow of an old love had come between them. A woman who bore a close resemblance to his lost Rosalia had crossed Rye's path and he had left all to follow her. So deeply had Rosalia's memory been etched upon him that it was enough to make him throw his life away—for that was what it would mean if either Spanish or English authorities caught up with him now. One did not lightly flee with the wife of the Spanish ambassador. . . .

Yet Rye had been willing to risk all that just to spend his days with a woman who reminded him of Rosalia.

Thinking about it, Carolina's world cracked—and fell in broken shards about her.

Her thoughts rushed on.

Rye had been too much of an English gentleman to coldly tell his new American love that he was leaving her. He had chosen instead to let her down gently, to send her to Essex in the care of his brother. *Ah, it was the coward's way!* she thought hotly, the nails of her clenched hands cutting into her palms.

And he had sailed away with the shadow of his bride of yesterday. . . .

Her mind saw them again in those last moments when he had lifted the ambassador's lady up, steadying her with his hands as she mounted the ship's ladder. Her dark hood had fallen back and in the distance the sun had glistened on the midnight of her hair just as it had turned Rye's thick dark hair to bronze. The sun had bronzed their dark clothes too, making them seem for a breathless second in time to be a clinging statuette carved by the gods—of a piece, perfect together.

Not till then was Carolina aware that she was crying.

And what would this woman's fate be? she asked herself as the hackney coach rumbled along. Would Rye tire of her eventually? For was she not a chance-met stranger? What could Rye see in her except her resemblance to a dead woman? And if he did tire of her, what then? Ah, he would be too chivalrous to return the ambassador's lady to Spain and a husband who would no doubt kill her! He would—she thought about that, trying to concentrate on it to somehow escape the hurt that ached through her—he would not desert her . . . not entirely. He would find her some pleasant island, or some pleasant Colonial Spanish city. Or perhaps a place on the Continent where no one would ever guess the beautiful olive-skinned lady was the runaway wife of Spain's ambassador to England.

And there he would leave her. Waiting. Just as he had left *her* here. Waiting.

And he would never return.

She wondered for a cold moment how many women he would run through like that in the course of a lifetime. The thought chilled her.

Well, *she* would not be one of them—waiting endlessly!

Her blonde head came up and she dashed away her tears angrily and took a look out at the district they were going through. Shops, half-timbered houses, narrow dirty alleys—it all went by her in a blur.

They had reached the inn now, and she sat there numbly looking up at the edifice she had left so blithely a short time before. She felt older now—older by a thousand years. And wiser. So much wiser!

And it was dreadful how much it hurt to be so wise!

She stared up blindly at the second-floor windows while the driver waited patiently to be advised of her wishes. Virginia was up there, fast asleep—dreaming perhaps of Andrew. She wished she could tell Virgie good-by but she dared not. For that would bring a storm of questions, and in her anxiety Virgie would run and rouse Andrew and Andrew would rush in and try to circumvent her plans.

Her plans? As if she had any! she thought hollowly.

But one decision she had made as the coach lurched from dockside to inn—she was *not* going to Essex.

Rye was her past now, he had left her for another woman. She would not pause to mourn him, she would fly far away—and perhaps if she ran far enough and fast enough she would be able to escape the vivid memories of him that would come crowding in to torment her. Memories too of those two figures there by the *Sea Waif*'s rakish side, gilded by sun and . . . probably . . . happiness.

Her lovely face grew haggard at the thought.

"Drive around," she leant out to tell the driver in a ragged voice. "But—away from the docks, anywhere we cannot see the Thames." Because she could not bear to look upon that wide silver expanse of river and imagine the lean *Sea Waif* winging down the ebb tide, carrying the lovers to some distant shore. . . .

The driver gave his changeable passenger a strange look but his passenger paid no attention. Through Cheapside they went, through the Poultry and Cornhill, past Moorgate, skirting the London Wall. Still the beautiful lady sunk in thought did not stir. The driver shrugged his shoulders in his worn coat. The sun had risen, it was a beautiful day, and if his odd cargo chose to spend her day wandering about the city without looking at it, why should he care, so long as she had gold to pay for it?

Inside the hackney coach Carolina could feel herself shiver although the warmth of the day had already reached her.

At least she had done one good thing, she told herself: She had made Virginia a gift of Essex. Virgie would read the note she had left, she would show it to Andrew, they would have no reason to doubt it—and even if they did, they would have no way to ask Rye; he would have sailed away. Indeed Andrew would probably chuckle and say something like "I did not think Rye could bear to be so long parted from his silver wench!"

And how wrong he would be! Her heart bled.

But Virginia would go on with him innocently to Essex. She would wear Carolina's beautiful clothes and flash Carolina's jewels—she would be received with open arms no doubt by Andrew's threadbare family. And as time went by she and Andrew, who shared so much, would come to share something else—ardor. They would realize they were in love.

And this time everything would be right. Virginia at last would have found safe harbor.

And in time perhaps even they would cease to speculate about what had happened to Rye and Carolina, adrift on some nameless sea. Although of course the emerald necklace, the rope of pearls would remind them. But Rye, she felt in her sinking heart, would never return. And everyone would assume that she was still with him. . . . They would both sink into obscurity and be forgotten—and maybe that was just as well.

Nevertheless the thought made Carolina's eyes grow moist, and that annoyed her. Was she really fool enough to care about being remembered? No! She had a life of her own to live—and now that Rye had gone off with another woman, she would live that life as she pleased!

Carolina squared her slim shoulders, gave her blonde head a rebellious shake, and leaned out to instruct the driver.

"Take me to Jenny Chesterton's gaming house," she directed.

The driver nodded and shrugged. This new and strange destination for his elegant passenger seemed to him of a piece with this aimless driving about London. At least Jenny Chesterton's establishment was nearer the stables where he kept his horse than Moorgate was—Old Dobbin here would be glad of this change in direction!

Inside the hackney coach, trying to push away the heartbreak that had come upon her with the dawn,

Carolina leaned back and tried to tell herself that she was lucky to have found Rye out *now,* instead of later. Her expression had grown ironic. It would be good to talk to Reba, who was as unfortunate as she—one abandoned Fleet Street bride could console another!

As it turned out, consolation was not immediately in order. Carolina had not had time to alight in front of the familiar plain brick building before two boxes came flying out the front door, one of them spilling its contents of ribands and gloves into the street. And after them came Reba, elegant in russet silk—but stumbling onto the cobbles from a firm push given by Jenny Chesterton, still in her dressing gown, who stood hands on hips and squalled, "And don't come back! You hear me?"

"I demand you give me the rest of my clothes!" Reba, having regained her equilibrium, whirled upon Jenny.

"Demand, do you? When you've caused my first-floor gaming rooms to be wrecked? You're lucky I don't call a constable and have you taken up for it!"

Carolina spilled out of the coach to grasp a shaking Reba by the arm. "Whatever is the matter?" she cried, her own troubles sinking for the moment into the background at sight of all this commotion.

"Oh—hello, Carolina." Reba acknowledged her friend, then stooped to rescue several pairs of kid gloves and some orange ribands that had spilled onto the cobbles. She looked up as the front door was slammed with force. "Well, I suppose that ruins my gambling career," she grumbled.

"But you didn't *have* a gambling career!" cried Carolina, bewildered. She snatched up Reba's other box. "Oh, do come along. We'll have some coffee in the nearest coffeehouse and you can tell me all about it."

The hackney driver had not stirred from his perch to help either lady. His brows were lifted in amazement. He'd have a rare old story to tell his Lottie tonight, he would! Couple of wild ones had invaded his hack. Wouldn't be surprised if they insisted he drive them to Hell and demand the Devil let them in!

"Since you're going to ask me anyway, I might as well tell you." Reba sighed as she climbed in beside Carolina and they sat with her boxes on their laps. "Last night Bertie—that's Lord Grymes—came rolling in deep in his cups and I saw a chance to make my fortune. Whist, primero, cribbage, ombre—I play all the card games, but whist is my specialty. And so we sat there gambling for small stakes—and Jenny Chesterton chose to overlook it. But as I began to win his jewelry—the diamonds from his cuffs, the ruby at his throat, his watch—she began to take notice. Bertie hates to lose, and Jenny's had to throw him out before. And all of a sudden he staggered to his feet and roared that I was cheating him out of the family jewels!"

"And were you?" asked Carolina resignedly, for she knew Reba of old. Reba seldom made these little distinctions—she tried to keep the cards stacked in her favor.

"We-ell . . ." Reba shrugged. "Nothing too flagrant."

"But Jenny Chesterton had noticed?"

Reba nodded. "And suddenly she grabbed me by the arm and yanked me from my chair, tearing my sleeve. Well, Bertie is very unpredictable and at that point he seemed to rear up and he fixed her with a drunken leer and he said, 'Are you attacking this young woman, madam?' And with that he overturned the table and began kicking the chairs apart. He's very strong and there was chair stuffing all over the floor. And as he careened around with several gentlemen who were already the worse for drink themselves trying to control him, they broke up quite a bit of furniture. And also confused everybody's bets, for money and cards were all on the floor by then. So when they finally got Bertie quieted down, quarrels broke out as to wagers and who owned what was scattered on the floor. At that point several actors from the theatre came in—Jenny doesn't usually allow them inside her doors but I guess she was rattled by all that had happened—and they began scooping up the money. When the players protested they calmly insisted they'd dropped it, and a general brawl broke out and the whole first floor was wrecked.''

"But that was last night. Why should Jenny throw you out this morning if she didn't last night?"

"I think she smouldered all night," Reba said frankly. "And if her lover, Lord Ormsby, had been willing to foot the bill for the damage, she might have forgotten about it. But I could hear them quarreling downstairs this morning and he told her that her damned gaming house was becoming a drain on him and he'd have no part of any refurbishing and stalked out." Reba shifted the heavy box on her lap. "And at *that* point Jenny came charging upstairs and told me *I'd* have to pay for the damage!"

"And of course you couldn't," Carolina said resignedly.

Reba shrugged. "Of course not. And she raved and said she'd have my clothes then! That she'd sell them and use the money to repair her rooms since Lord Ormsby wouldn't!"

"Do you think she will? Oh, here's a coffeehouse—driver, let us off here."

"Who knows?" said Reba as they alighted, carrying the boxes. But when they were inside, seated at a small table by a window that looked out upon the street, she said meditatively, "I don't really think so. Jenny isn't that vengeful. But I don't think she'll let me come back and stay there for I broke one of her cardinal rules—no gambling on my own account." She looked up suddenly at Carolina. "You look pale," she commented. "And your hair's a mess!"

"I don't wonder," Carolina said with a short laugh. "I got a small shock this morning. My—lover"—she was reluctant to mention Rye's name—"went off with another woman."

Reba gave her a pitying look. "I'm sorry to hear it," she said sincerely.

"Don't say 'I told you so,'" said Carolina with a grimace. "I don't think I could bear it." Her coffee was so hot it burned her tongue—she swallowed it anyway.

"No, I won't. I'm as big a fool as you are." Reba's voice was bitter. "Some people never learn and I suppose I'm one of them. Well"—her quick glance shrewdly appraised Carolina's handsome gown—"at least he didn't leave you empty-handed!"

"No, that was not his intention," Carolina said in a small voice. A biting pain went through her heart. He had tried to provide for her, damn him, when all she really wanted was for him to love her!

Suddenly through the window she saw Andrew striding along, peering about him—and beside him Virginia in a light summer dress, looking upset.

Carolina choked on her coffee and bent her head as if to collect something she had dropped on the floor.

"Reba," she hissed in panic, "if those two people come into the inn you must help me get out quickly before they see me!"

Reba turned to scan the pair on the street. "They're going on by," she said. "I don't know the woman, but the man—" She gasped. "Why, it's Rye Evistock's brother—I can't think of his name. You can sit up now, they've gone."

Carolina straightened to see Reba staring at her. Her russet eyes had widened as she leaned forward.

"Ryeland Smythe," she murmured. "And that was Rye's brother you're hiding from! There *isn't any* Ryeland Smythe—you married *Rye Evistock* in Fleet Street!"

Carolina's deep flush gave her away.

Reba's mouth had opened as well as her eyes, and suddenly she threw back her auburn head and her laughter pealed. "We're a pair of fools, Carol!" she gasped, when she could speak again. "Robin seduces me and deserts me—and what do I do? I take him back the moment he returns and go through a meaningless ceremony with him in Fleet Street! And *you*, Carol— Rye left you standing lost in a maze in bitter cold at my home in Essex a year ago last Christmastide. You thought at the time he had left you there in a thin gown in the hope you might freeze to death!"

"He had reason to hate me then, I suppose," Carolina said dully, bent on giving the devil his due. She might also have protested that wasn't really what had happened, but then she would have had to explain about Tortuga, about Rye's other identity as Kells—for Reba plainly hadn't heard about that. But something held her back. She told herself it was because the Crown might seize her emeralds but she knew it was more than that—she had not yet shaken off the fierce loyalty that had bound her to him. "I suppose I deserved that—in Essex," she sighed. "For what I'd done to him!"

"Oh, we're both getting our just desserts," Reba agreed airily. "And I don't like it a whit better than you do!" She rested her chin on her hand and looked out the window. Suddenly she stiffened. "Good Lord!" She leaned forward, almost pressing her nose against the pane as she stared into the street. "That's Annette Osborne out there," she whispered. "I'm sure of it!"

Carolina was drawn to look at a thin young woman walking unsteadily by. Bravely gowned in red, she seemed very frail. There were dark circles under eyes that seemed vacant, without hope. But her thin cheeks wore vivid spots of rouge, her pouting lips were reddened and her hair, which seemed to have no luster of its own, was dyed a brilliant red.

"But that's a prostitute out there," protested Carolina.

"Nevertheless. It's also Annette Osborne."

"Who is Annette Osborne?"

"She's a girl I knew in Bristol before we came to Essex. She's a couple of years older than I am, a merchant's daughter, very strictly brought up. Mother was always saying 'Why can't you be more like Annette Osborne?' I used to hate her! *Then* Annette fell in love with one of her father's clerks and her family wouldn't let them get married, so she ran away with him. We heard later that they'd been married in Fleet Street. Her parents might have taken her back but that was the last straw. . . ." Reba was staring in horror after the passing woman, who plodded on out of their range of vision. "Annette's aged ten years," she muttered. "She looks terrible!" She shuddered and turned to Carolina. "Let's hope the same fate doesn't overtake us," she said ironically. "To the future!" With a sardonic gesture she raised her coffee cup.

"Well, I don't know about you but I'm *positive* that such a future will never overtake *me!*" said Carolina vigorously. "Because I'm not going to stay here and let this city grind me down!"

"Do you have a place to go?" asked Reba conversationally.

"No," admitted Carolina.

"But weren't you staying at an inn?"

"I was—until this morning."

Reba gave her a jaded look. "They put you out because you couldn't pay?"

"No, I can't go back there because Rye's brother and my sister are staying there!" blurted out Carolina.

"Oh, I see!" Reba's auburn brows shot up. "But what about your clothes?"

"I don't care about my clothes," Carolina said stubbornly. "I'm not going back for them. I left a note," she added.

"Burned your bridges. . . ." mused Reba. "Well, what now?"

"I think Andrew and Virgie are searching the town for me," Carolina said uneasily. "The anxious way they were looking about as they passed here told me that. I want to get away—right now!" She put a hand impulsively on Reba's wrist. "Oh, Reba, don't stay here waiting for a man who will never come back! Come away with me."

"Where?" demanded Reba.

"To America."

Reba laughed. "Back to 'Bedlam' in Virginia? I doubt your family would welcome me—an impoverished cast-off, slightly used!"

"I wasn't thinking of going back to Virginia," said Carolina, choosing her words carefully. And all of a sudden she wasn't. She wanted to try a new life—far away.

"Any particular place?" Reba asked indifferently. Her speculative gaze was still noting passersby.

"Yes," Carolina said on inspiration. "Philadelphia. I have a sister there—at least that's where she was when she was last seen. Penny. She's the one who left her husband, you remember I told you about her?"

"Oh, yes." Reba sounded amused. "She ran away to the Marriage Trees with him and then decided she didn't want him after all."

"Well, he *was* a terrible dolt," Carolina said.

"Aren't they all?" Reba sighed.

All except one, you mean, divined Carolina. *And that one is Robin Tyrell, Marquess of Saltenham. Ah, Reba, you're still in love with him.*

"You didn't want to marry Robin just to become a marchioness, did you?" she asked her friend quietly.

"No. Actually I just wanted to be his wife." Reba looked down into her empty cup and laughed. "There must be something more potent than coffee berries in this brew—that's the first time I've ever admitted *that* to anyone!"

"I think I always knew it," murmured Carolina.

So for all her attempts not to show it, Reba had really been in love all along. But Carolina, younger and less wise in those days, had seen only Reba's hard-polished exterior—she had never looked below the surface or seen beneath the banter. *Trouble,* Carolina thought grimly, *was giving her insight—although perhaps a trifle late!*

"Reba," she said quietly. "I once cost you half your

wardrobe—and you've never reproached me for it. Let me make it up to you now—let me pay your passage with me to Philadelphia."

Reba turned to consider Carolina, a twisted smile upon her lips. She turned the coffee cup restlessly in her hands. Then, "Well, why not?" she said briskly. "We certainly can't make any bigger fools of ourselves there than we already have here!"

THE SPANISH AMBASSADOR'S RESIDENCE
LONDON, ENGLAND

Summer 1689

Chapter 21

Within the Duchess of Lorca's bedchamber the man who had called himself Diego Viajar embraced the bride he had not held in his arms all these years past. Outside the bedchamber a shadow skulked.

That shadow was Sancho and his ear was pressed to the bedchamber's oaken door. He could hear little within—a man's voice, murmuring, rich in tone, an elegant rustling murmur that would be the Duchess of Lorca's. And then—just as he had feared—a faint sound as a booted foot came up against the corner of the thronelike bed, a little breathless tinkling laugh. And then only—could he really hear it or did he only imagine it?—the tantalizing rustle of straining bodies sliding along a coverlet.

Half sick with murderous envy, Sancho's stocky form leant against that thick door. Beads of perspiration dotted his dark brow and his palms, pressed against the wood, were wet as well. It took all the will power that was in him not to fling wide the portal and burst in upon the lovers, to make short work of the man with the long knife he carried, and crush the erring Duchess in his arms.

He had felt that way about every lover she had ever had. For Sancho's love of the young Duchess—though silent and never alluded to—ran deep. He would have died for her.

Unfortunately, the Duchess did not care, accepting such loyalty—indeed such debasement, for Sancho had for his lady's sake betrayed the Duke of Lorca again and again—as merely the just due of her beauty, her queenly femininity.

In Spain she had been more circumspect—most of the time. Sancho had even dared to hope that those swift almost absent-minded smiles she sometimes gave him held a deeper meaning. He had sweated blood trying to shield her clandestine meetings from discovery. It had eaten into his entrails that it should be so, but he had been ever mindful of the fate that would await the reckless Duchess should her affairs be discovered: Death. Or a life spent forever locked away in a convent. Or perchance some more cruel imprisonment, lying chained in some out-of-the-way stronghold of the Duke's. The possibilities were endless—and unthinkable. Sancho, swallowing his pride, lowering himself to treachery to his sworn lord, the Duke of Lorca, had bent his considerable efforts to shielding his mistress.

In Paris, when the Duke of Lorca was sent to the Court of Versailles as ambassador to France, Sancho had foreseen a welcome end to the young Duchess's passions. But Sancho's relief had been of short duration.

In Paris, the Duchess of Lorca had discovered the French courtiers. The new palace of Versailles had sparkled with them: young gentlemen in richly embroidered satins, resplendent with gold and silver braid, gentlemen wearing black patches and sometimes powder and paint, gentlemen who took snuff from a variety of intricately decorated snuffboxes—and favors from any source offered. One such source was the bright-eyed young Duchess of Lorca who moved excitedly from the gilded Hall of Mirrors to the fabulous Orangery—and lingered on one of the splendid staircases leading to the Swiss Lake while the lounging courtiers, who seemed always to follow her about, closed the distance. The young Duchess was accounted one of the most brilliant jewels in a startling array of such gems that roamed the palace gardens at Versailles and there were wagers made behind ringed hands and wafting fans as to who would be her latest "conquest."

But the Duchess of Lorca, dragging her slender fingers in the Grand Canal from one of the Venetian gondolas placed there by Louis XIV, had at last been sated by all this attention.

Eventually she had come to England at the side of the Duke of Lorca who, having exchanged the post of Ambassador to France for that of Ambassador to England, kept his graying head bent over cranky missives from Spain inveighing him to do better with this barbaric heretic country to which he had been sent. The harassed Duke had given little thought and no attention to the affairs of his beautiful young wife—indeed he would have paled had a whisper of them reached him.

And that they had not reached him was due in part to the Duchess of Lorca's own careful machinations—but largely to Sancho, who guarded his lady's reputation as zealously as a husband and would have found a way to stick a dagger into anyone who made free with it.

England had been at first a respite for Sancho—and

then had come those meetings with the Englishman the Duchess visited by night at the Shark and Fin. Sancho had no idea that the Duchess was involved in the Duke's disappearance—indeed he had been duped into believing that it was love that took her to the Shark and Fin.

Now there was this other Englishman, met outside the Drury Lane theatre, at sight of whom a slight tremor—not overlooked by Sancho, who had been guiding her through the crowd at the time—had gone through the frail form of the Duchess.

And now this latest Englishman, in response to an invitation sent via an orange girl at Drury Lane—was here in that most holy of sanctuaries, the Duchess's bedchamber. No other man save the Duke had ever violated that particular female domain—and since he was her husband Sancho had grudgingly accorded him that right. Sweating and with the blood pounding in his head, Sancho was undergoing the agonies of the damned as he envisioned what was going on within.

What was actually happening there would have plunged the knife even more deeply into Sancho's aching heart.

For Diego and his lost lady, time had swept back and both had for the moment forgotten that they had other loves and other ties. For them the candlelight had turned into the golden sunlight of Salamanca where as young lovers with all their lives ahead of them they had kissed and exchanged whispered vows in the shadows beneath the stirring rustle of the palms.

Never had the Duchess of Lorca had so exhilarating a lover. And she who had reveled in every vice of the vice-ridden French Court found herself moaning in enjoyment against the hard body of the Englishman and willing him with every fiber of her being on to even more stupendous efforts.

Until at last with a sigh she slipped away from him and lay on her back, mentally comparing his performance with that of the other Englishman at the Shark and Fin—no mean lover he, either!

But now at her side a silent Diego had heaved himself up on an elbow and was looking down at her quizzically. Even now he was regretting his impetuosity. It was as if all those nights in his buccaneering days when he had brooded about her as he stared down into the phosphorescent waters of the Caribbean had converged and overpowered him.

He had seen before him only Rosalia—his lost Rosalia, his bride of yesterday. And he had claimed her without thought.

Now that the first gust of passion was over, there was the world to reckon with.

"Rosalia," he said on a half sigh. "I should not have taken you like this. . . ."

"Why not?" The Duchess lay beside him with her slight figure naked to the candlelight. Her rose-tipped breasts were gilded to russet by the candlelight and golden flames danced in her dark eyes. "Did I ask you to desist?"

"No," he said thoughtfully. And he was wondering as he spoke, *Why not?* For surely the intervening years must have meant something to her—as they had to him.

His hand reached out almost involuntarily to touch with marveling fingers those rosy nipples, rising and falling.

"But it cannot be you," he said soberly, studying the flawless skin revealed to him. "For I saw you die of a swordthrust in your father's courtyard in Salamanca."

The Duchess laughed and rolled over so that her silken body was half atop his own. She had in mind other delights in which she would instruct him. . . .

But that light laugh had jarred him. And now, almost instantly, even as he smelled her heady perfume and felt her soft flesh pressed against him, sanity returned and he put her from him, unclasped her clutching hands from his body, untwined her slender arms and stared into her face. She was—*but she could not be*—Rosalia. And by the slight rejection implicit in his gesture, he was telling her that despite his sudden almost involuntary taking of her, they were no longer young lovers—other loves, other entanglements had intervened.

The lady's husband, for example.

Realizing that now was a time for talk, just as a moment ago had been a time for sighs, Rosalia sat up in a lithe gesture that rippled the crimson velvet of the robe that had fallen away from her even though its sleeves still encased her upper arms. She allowed the robe to hang open as she spoke, intending to incite him to further passion by the sight of the smooth creamy skin of her torso.

"What is it that disturbs you so, Diego?" she asked in a solicitous voice. And wistfully, *"Why* cannot it be me?"

It would have been less than gallant to have told her that what disturbed him was the sudden vision of a pair of silver eyes or the trusting smile of the girl he had left at the Horn and Chestnut.

"Because I *saw* you die," he repeated bluntly. "I killed a man because I saw him run a sword through your body. I saw you fall to the courtyard in your blood-stained wedding dress. Frail as you are, you could not have survived it! Yet here you are today as lovely as ever—your body unscarred." His puzzled eyes traced down that pale expanse from breast to hip of the woman before him.

The Duchess shuddered delicately, a movement that rippled the pallor of her stomach. "I did not see that terrible scene in the courtyard, Diego. They told me about it later. Much later. I almost went mad to hear it. . . ."

"Not see it?" he exclaimed. "How so? For you were assuredly *there*, Rosalia!"

She shook her dark head and made her voice sad for his benefit. "No, Diego, you are wrong. I had already been spirited away. The woman you saw in the court-yard was my uncle's mistress, Conchita—old Juana's daughter. He killed her for her indiscretions—he be-lieved Conchita had taken a lover while he was away. But he sought to torture you as well as her, so he had her dressed in my wedding gown, which his servants had already stripped from my back. Conchita was about my size and height, she was gagged so that she could not speak, and with my white mantilla draped over her head so as to conceal her face, across the courtyard at dusk she must indeed have *seemed* to be me but I was already far away."

In truth Rosalia had watched the whole scene from the window of a nearby locked room—a vantage point from which the young Englishman could not see her. Watched in terrified silence because her uncle had told her that the heretic dog of an Englishman who had pretended to be Spanish and had wed her under that pretense must die, and that if she so much as made a whimper of sound she would die too. She had shivered to see fifteen-year-old Conchita die. She had seen the iron grillwork burst forward, seen a maddened Diego suddenly overwhelm her uncle, seen two of her uncle's men rush forward and deal the young Englishman a terrible blow—only then had she screamed. But it was best that her tall Diego not know that. He might wonder where was her courage that she had not cried out to him earlier.

Now her pale hands were pressed against his chest. Somehow they had found their way beneath his coat and were quivering against the white cambric of his shirt. Rosalia was a very convincing actress.

"They told me you were dead, Diego—and I fainted," she said simply. That much at least was true. It was only later that she had learnt the young Englishman had escaped. But by then she had had time to consider. Life with a heretic Englishman would be impossible in Spain. She had been glad he was gone and she did not have to deal with him. She did not tell Rye any of this of course.

"Once in the convent, my future was controlled by distant kinsmen whom I hardly knew and who were deaf to my appeals." She sounded aggrieved. "I was told I must marry, that I was not to"—she batted her eyes at him with a piteous expression—"to pass my life in grief and prayer."

Caught in a crosscurrent of turbulent emotions, Rye felt her last words strike him as solidly as a blow. For no sooner had he left the embrace of his old love than a bright vision of his new love had risen up to reproach him. And now he was presented with a picture of his bride of yesterday, inconsolable, cloistered away, *passing her life in grief and prayer*. The thought stunned him, and he gathered her to him, cradling her, as if to shield her from a cruel world.

"Oh, Diego!" Stimulated by his touch, her soft voice grew wild with grief. It was totally convincing. "If only I had known you were still alive, I would have plunged a dagger in my breast rather than let them force me into marriage with the Duke of Lorca!"

Every word bit into his heart, telling him how remiss he had been *not to make sure,* hammering into him guilt that he had allowed this to happen to her. It was because of his negligence that Rosalia, with whom he had once knelt before an altar and vowed eternal love, had been coerced into a loveless marriage. Now he flayed himself. *Why had he not made sure?*

"You were forced into this marriage?" he asked hoarsely, rubbing salt into his wounds.

She nodded, blinking her dark eyes as though fighting back tears, and his arms tightened about her. "Yes—*forced,*" she whispered. "And I have been miserable with him ever since. He is Spain's ambassador to England now, Diego. That is how I come to be here in London."

As a buccaneer, Rye had good reason to know the name of Spain's ambassador to England, but he saw no need to mention it.

"In what way has the Duke made you unhappy?" he growled, pushing her away from him and frowning down into her face. It was hard for him to hold back the anger that ripped through him that Rosalia, whose dreams had been shattered along with his in far away Salamanca, might be mistreated now. For long ago though their alliance might be, he still felt a heart-tugging responsibility toward this woman whom he had loved as a half-fledged girl—a woman who had gone into his arms without question this night and seemed to love him still.

Rosalia tugged her robe around her and sat shivering for a moment. Then, "The Duke is very—repressive," she said with an outward gesture of her arm that parted her robe and brought her small bare breasts again into view.

Rye ignored the display, fighting to retain logic in this scented overheated atmosphere.

"And yet I saw you attending the play at Drury Lane this evening?" *Something I doubt you could have done in Spain,* his tone implied. *So he must be a lenient husband as the dons go.*

"Ah, that is only because"—she leant forward again and her dark curls brushed his broad chest invitingly—"because he was not here to prevent it." She was trying to look innocent and almost succeeding.

"And is he perchance in the next room wondering that he hears a man's voice in his wife's bedchamber?" Rye asked grimly.

She moved pettishly away from him at that remark. "There is no need to fear the Duke, Diego—"

"I do not fear him for myself," he corrected her gently. "I fear him for you, Rosalia. A Spanish grandee is unlikely to overlook finding a man in his wife's bedchamber!"

"But he is gone," she said—and remembered to make her voice sound bitter. "He has been kidnapped and is being held for ransom! That is the reason I am allowed so much freedom of movement. No one dares protest for I say that I *must* go out, I must move about the town so that his captors will be able to reach me in some public place with their demands—after all, they would hardly dare come here where they would be seized!"

Rye cast a look around him. There was more than one door to the room. "Seized by whom?"

"By my husband's retainers, of course. They had mounted a guard until today, when I dismissed them."

"You dismissed them?" he demanded incredulously.

"Yes. Sancho is quite sufficient to guard me. He is the man who let you in and he is entirely trustworthy."

"But why did you dismiss them?"

"Because I have now heard from his captors," improvised the Duchess, for Diego, found again, might prove to be the perfect solution to a knotty problem. "A note was slipped into my hand in the crowd at the theatre, telling me where the ransom is to be delivered."

"And where is that?" he said, sensing that this might be the real reason she had sent for him. Perhaps she did not trust the people around her, perhaps she needed someone to hand over the ransom for her, someone who would have no ties with Spain but feel allegiance only to her, someone trustworthy.

"In the Azores," she said.

"The Azores! But they are far out into the Atlantic!"

"I know," she said, pouting. "But what place more likely for a *pirata* to demand money than far out at sea?"

"A pirate? What pirate?"

Her white teeth ground slightly. She was the picture of disdain as she spoke. "That abominable Captain Kells."

If Rosalia had suddenly dashed a bucket of cold water over him, she could not have astonished him more. Rye sat at gaze, staring at this fragile elegant woman who had once held his heart in the palm of her delicate hand.

"Not Kells," he said definitely, leaving the bed and rising to his feet, fastening his trousers. "Some other buccaneer perhaps might hold the Duke for ransom—but not Kells."

"Certainly Kells!" she flashed, annoyed that Diego would dispute her statement, annoyed even more that he had not flung himself on his knees and kissed the hem of her robe and wept at his good luck in having found her again. Instead he was calmly adjusting his trousers, preparing to leave her! "Why not Kells?" she demanded. "All London knows this Kells is really a renegade Englishman named Rye Evistock," she added spitefully, eager to assure him that Kells was not Irish but one of his own countrymen!

He was tempted to tell her through clenched teeth, "Because *I* am Kells and *I* did not take him!"—but somehow he bit back the words. It was a dangerous admission to bandy about in the house of Spain's ambassador—even if that ambassador was at the moment absent. He cast a sudden thoughtful glance at the door, beyond which—though he did not know it—Sancho listened. "Because Kells is not known to have carried his trade as far as London," he told her flatly.

She shrugged her indifference. "One place is as good as another to these *piratas!*"

Her sneering tone told him they were worlds apart.

"I can bring you only danger here, Rosalia," he said courteously, preparing to go.

"Oh, what of that?" she scoffed.

"The possibility of discovery—and disgrace—should concern you," he pointed out soberly. "But if you should have need of me, I am now called—"

"Oh, I know what you are called!" she interrupted, annoyed that he should be leaving—and so soon. She had hoped for a long evening of intimate joinings! "Sancho has had you followed. You are Ryeland Smythe and you are staying at the Horn and Chestnut with a party of friends."

The words, *Sancho has had you followed,* rang warningly in his mind. "Would Sancho be the heavyset fellow who squired you to the theatre?" he asked, for he had been escorted upstairs in nearly total darkness and could not be sure.

"Yes. A servant only," was the careless response.

Outside the bedchamber door, Sancho's shoulders writhed and the tiniest of groans escaped his lips. *Oh, that his mistress should use him so when his heart beat only for her!*

Rye told himself that he would be careful of this Sancho and be on guard against sudden discoveries. He thought back but he could not recall an indiscretion that would bring his real identity to light.

"How is this ransom to be delivered?" he asked, mindful that somewhere a man who pretended to be himself was waiting—for a ransom. "Will your man Sancho deliver it?"

"Oh, no," said the Duchess. "I must take it myself— when I can find a suitable ship to take me there." She sighed, for finding a suitable ship was indeed one of her problems.

The man before her frowned. "Surely Spain must have many ships at your disposal for such an important mission."

She could hardly tell him *why* finding a ship to carry her was difficult. That ship must not be a warship of Spain—indeed must not be Spanish at all. For in case the Englishman at the Shark and Fin bungled it—and he might—she would have to take matters into her own hands. She had not gone this far down the road to allow things to slip now. And no tales must ever reach Spain of how the Duchess of Lorca had murdered her husband and taken off with his ransom!

Rye had only been considering the possibility of trailing Rosalia's ship to this impostor's secret lair. Now, taut with the possibility of something far more satisfying, he leaned forward, his gray eyes intent. "Is it possible that you are afraid this ransom will be seized by some rapacious grandee for his own ends?"

Her nod and sigh were answer enough.

"For then"—he shot at her—"I must offer you my services. I have a ship even now lying at anchor in the Thames and I would carry the ransom to any place you would suggest and exchange it for your husband."

Rosalia's dark eyes gleamed. She had known indeed —for Sancho had told her—that the man before her captained a ship now lying at anchor in the Thames— but she had thought she must bring this up herself. Now this fool of a Diego had thrown the information in her lap!

"Oh, Diego," she breathed, *"would you* take me to him? Would you carry me and the ransom to the place this *pirata* names?"

Rye was nonplussed by this sudden request to carry her aboard his ship, but his blood was beating fast at the thought that he might be able to capture his man directly—instead of sailing endlessly in search of his tormentor. His gray-eyed gaze was steady on the beautiful face before him.

"I will take you to this Captain Kells, Rosalia," he promised calmly. "But only you. I will not take Sancho or any other."

"But—" she began, for Sancho had figured prominently in her plans. It was Sancho she had intended should carry back a story making her the heroine of a tragedy in which her husband was unfortunately killed. Sancho was her chosen witness for she could influence his tale!

But her Diego was shaking his head firmly. "I will carry only you to this rendezvous, Rosalia. No others in your train."

Rosalia pouted—then she smiled up at him. "Not even a maidservant?" she asked wistfully. "To dress me and do my hair?"

"Not even that," he said, for two women would be hard to keep track of on board ship. He could keep the knowledge of his real identity from Rosalia, he was fairly sure of that—but it might be more difficult to keep a chambermaid, of whom one of his men might grow enamored, from learning that their captain was none other than Kells the buccaneer.

"Ah, well . . ." she said, then flashed her brilliant smile at him again. "I will let you know," she purred, sidling up to him and putting her arms once more around his neck, "as soon as the ransom arrives."

This time he put her from him almost absently. A few minutes ago she had been Rosalia, his lost love. Now she was the wife of the Spanish ambassador, from whom many things must be kept.

"What is this ransom to be?" he asked.

"Fifty thousand pieces of eight."

It was a vast sum but Spain would soon be asking that much for his own head! He gave her a quizzical look. "Is that all?"

She hesitated. "And a necklace," she admitted. "Of diamonds and rubies. From the Far East."

If he was surprised that some faraway sea rover would have such detailed knowledge of the Duke of Lorca's wealth that he would know precisely what to ask for, he did not show it.

"It is worth a king's ransom!" she declared pettishly, annoyed by his level gaze.

Or an ambassador's, he could not help thinking.

"I am surprised these fellows would demand your jewels," he said slowly, thinking better of her now, for she had seemed not to have any feeling at all for a husband housed, perhaps, in the foul hold of a ship, kept from sunlight, lost to hope.

"Oh, they are not *my* jewels! They are the de Lorca jewels—one of my husband's kinsmen is bringing them from Spain." One of the Duchess's main complaints against her absent husband had been that she was not allowed to wear the de Lorca jewels which were indeed worth a king's ransom in any country—and her anger showed in her voice.

Rye hid a smile. He understood the situation. Suddenly Rosalia seemed a lot older. And far less innocent.

He chided himself for thinking that. Perhaps the Duke of Lorca had been truly cruel to her—in ways she preferred not to describe.

The thought hardened his strong jawline and made his voice gentle when he spoke. "You will let me know when the money and jewels arrive?"

"Oh, of course I will." Such a consummate actress was Rosalia that there were real tears trembling on her lashes as she spoke. "Sancho will bring a note to you at your inn."

He would be on the lookout for Sancho, the lean buccaneer told himself as he took his leave. In more ways than one!

And so—in a life that was stranger than that of anyone he knew—Rye Evistock, that one-time Diego Viajar—committed the ultimate folly. He had agreed to carry Rosalia and the ransom to some as-yet-unspecified place in the Azores and then exchange that ransom for the body of the Spanish ambassador, spirited away from London to some "dark hole" as the pouting Duchess now put it.

"It is not that I love him, Diego—God forbid," she

told him plaintively. "I have never loved anyone but you. But the Duke married me unaware—unaware of you, for my kinsmen frightened me so much, I was afraid to tell him about us. They said that you were dead and gone and that to speak of you would bring ruin to us all! And although the Duke is a cruel man and I do fear him, still I feel duty bound to save his life now. Oh, surely"—her voice grew pleading—"surely you can understand that?"

"Diego" could. On first seeing the Duchess, he had been overcome by memories. At her first touch, he had been carried back to Salamanca and the rapture of first love. Now on reflection what he felt toward the young Duchess was more like duty. Indeed, retrieving her husband for her was in the nature of a last gesture to an old love—an old love he had always felt he had somehow failed. He would make it up to her now. He would take her to this rendezvous as he had promised her he would—and that he had other reasons of his own for doing that, she need not know.

It was Sancho who let him out, a Sancho whose eyes glittered in the dimness and whose hand longingly caressed a dagger. How he yearned to drive it into the heart of this dog of an Englishman who had so lately been with the lady of Sancho's dreams, enjoying her charms! But his devotion to his master's unfaithful wife kept Sancho silent, and it was with only a guttural grunt that he saw Rye Evistock from the house and went back to knock on the door of the Duchess's bedchamber to learn if there were further instructions.

He found the Duchess seated cross-legged on a red upholstered stool with her arms in her lap. She appeared lost in thought. Her small white teeth were pressed into her soft lower lip and her dark eyes were narrowed. Sancho's discreet knock brought from her an absent "Enter." Not till she saw who it was did she bother to pull her crimson robe around her, and Sancho's dark face flamed at the sight of so much beauty carelessly revealed.

"The Englishman is gone," he reported in a reproachful voice.

"Good." The lady nodded, noting with spiteful pleasure the anguish of his tone. To torture him, she stretched and again let her robe fall open. "This Englishman, this Ryeland Smythe, is the answer to everything, Sancho," she told her hot-eyed henchman. "We will use him and then," she said contemptuously, "we will throw him away."

"That is what you said about the other Englishman who has now sailed away," muttered Sancho.

"Ah, yes," said the Duchess airily. "They will dispose of each other. It only takes planning, Sancho—careful planning." To rowel Sancho further, she stretched out a languorous bare leg. "I brushed my ankle against the Englishman's scabbard just now as he departed. Would you tell me if it is bleeding?"

Half suffocated by desire, Sancho sank to inspect the slender leg the Duchess had extended. He trembled violently as his fingers touched her ankle. "It is not bleeding," he reported in a smothered voice.

"Good," said the Duchess, rising with a benign smile. "That will be all. Good night, Sancho."

Her smile deepened as he went out with shoulders drooping. It was such delightful sport, tormenting Sancho, who could not conceal his dumb helpless worship of her!

When she went to bed that night, the Duchess of Lorca was well pleased with herself.

But for Rye Evistock it was a bad night. What he had done with Rosalia had seemed at the time so natural, so

predestined even. But now as he strode out into the
street, their lovemaking assumed a new perspective.
Faith, he had done no very honorable thing! It seemed
to him that he had cuckolded an old man when that
man was being held a prisoner. Worse, he had betrayed
the shining girl who waited for him at the inn.

The golden sun of a Salamancan courtyard sank
behind the rooftops of a crooked London alley, and a
brighter shaft of light laid bare his shrinking soul. He
was tormented by new visions: of a girl in white who
had tossed him a sword above the heads of the wedding
guests, who had chosen to escape with him to an
uncertain future, who waited for him now, knowing
nothing of what had transpired between him and the
Duchess of Lorca.

He could not face her.

And so he spent most of the night getting royally
drunk in a waterfront tavern. And as he drank and
thought, it was ground in on him the more that there
was no shirking his obligations here. Rosalia had
reappeared in his life as if she had never been away.
She had said she loved him. And he was bound to
her—bound by his own vows, freely given long ago.
Rosalia had a right to his protection, a right to his
strong arm supporting her for as long as she wished.
She had a right to his love.

Indeed she had the prior claim.

He went home to Carolina that night a chastened
man.

He was not good enough to share her bed, he told
himself as he opened the door hours later. Not good
enough to brush the hem of her skirt!

And so it was that Carolina thought he looked
haggard when at last he crawled into bed beside her and
turned his back.

He was not fit to touch her, was what he was telling himself.

Carolina, of course, had misunderstood.

But even strong drink had not been able entirely to push his problem away from him. He lay silent beside her, but he slept little. For he knew he was faced with a terrible decision—a decision that would alter all their lives.

A choice.

Rosalia, to whom he had given heart and hand in Salamanca, Rosalia who had endured all these years—terrible years, to hear her tell it—without him.

Or Carolina, whose silver shimmer invaded all his thoughts.

Rosalia—and honor. Or Carolina—and love.

Bitter though the choice would be, he still must make it.

BOOK IV

Revenge!

Her eyes stare into the darkness
But she does not find him there.
He trampled her heart with his buccaneer boots
And left her the empty air. . . .

PART ONE

The Counterfeit Buccaneer

Life's a joyous banquet—
She's demanding her fair share.
Let good girls go to heaven—
Bad girls go everywhere!

Summer 1689

Chapter **22**

From the beginning the voyage had been a disaster.

They had not cleared the harbor before the Duchess of Lorca had lost her mantilla to a sudden gust of wind. It had gone overboard and floated away while the Duchess wailed.

Another mantilla had been found in her luggage and she had subsided—but only temporarily.

Before nightfall she was insisting that she needed—*indeed must have*—a maidservant. Did Diego—she insisted on calling him that—really expect her to do her hair *alone?* With her own hands? It was very tedious, she was not used to such tiresome work! When Rye remained adamant she threw things around the great cabin—which the cabin boy, who was awed by her beauty, picked up most willingly at her direction.

It was then that she conceived the idea of using the cabin boy for a hairdresser.

When Rye came suddenly into the cabin, looking for his charts, he was treated to the astonishing sight of young Johnny Downs, red-faced and intent, trying desperately to comb the tangles from the Duchess of Lorca's long black hair with a silver comb.

"Johnny," said Rye weakly, almost disbelieving what he saw, "get you aft. You're not in training to be a lady's maid."

Stung, Johnny dropped the comb and shot from the cabin like an arrow from a bow. He quaked lest the men discover the feminine task to which he had been put and was relieved when, later, his captain did not mention it.

But Rosalia, left alone with Rye, had turned to him with a frown. "The boy had some talent," she complained, shaking out her curls.

"Not on my ship," said Rye.

Rosalia decided to charm him.

"Would you care to see the ransom?" She smiled, rustling to her feet in her black taffeta gown.

What buccaneer would not? Rye watched with interest as she extracted a small teakwood box, heavily chased and silver-trimmed, from among her effects and opened it.

Even he—used to treasure—was taken aback at the sight that met his eyes.

Huge rubies of a somewhat uneven Oriental cut but of a pigeon's blood glow met his gaze—and among them, set in heavy gold, diamonds. The necklace Rosalia held up to his gaze seemed to him enormous.

"I am told the diamonds are from Tibet," she said carelessly. "The rubies of course are from India."

"The Duke's wealth is indeed phenomenal," said Rye with feeling.

She shrugged. "He will not miss it. He keeps it hidden away never to be worn. Here, I shall try it on for you and you shall see what it looks like when it is worn around a lady's neck." She gave him a provocative look. "Will you work the clasp for me, Diego?"

Rye lifted the necklace, marveling at its weight, and clasped it around her neck. It sparkled there like blood on snow, the rubies flashing redder than any sunset.

"Amazing," he murmured. "All the thieves in Europe would have followed had they known gems like these were on the march!"

The Duchess was not listening. She was studying the necklace in the mirror, turning this way and that. She meant to have it for herself. She had always meant to have it, ever since the day she had first seen it back in her husband's forbidding fortress in Castile. A day when he had been pleased with her and had let her try the necklace on. She had teased him to give it to her but he had remained adamant. Upon his death, the necklace would go to his eldest son, he had insisted.

And be worn by his son's insipid wife! the young Duchess had thought, enraged. From that moment she had sworn a silent vow that she herself would one day possess the necklace.

What she did *not* tell Rye was that, in accordance with that vow, she had among her effects a duplicate silver-encrusted box which contained a copy of this necklace, looking equally majestic against the box's dark red velvet lining. The reason for her delay in setting out was that it had taken a sweating London goldsmith this long to duplicate in glass the stones of the de Lorca necklace.

How she meant to use the duplicates was as yet unclear to her. But it was part of her plan to let Rye see and hold the necklace so that when at last he handed it over it would be familiar to him—he would not stop to examine it, would not guess that it was not the original.

She herself would have that—for she wanted that necklace more than she would ever want any man!

She put away the necklace and gave him a sidewise look. "You will be dining with me tonight, Diego?" she purred.

Rye saw that look in her eyes. It made him wary. "A quick meal only," he said. "For I must study my charts tonight."

"*Study your charts?*" Her tone was derisive. "But your ship's master has told me you know these seas as well as any man!"

"He gives me too much credit," Rye said shortly.

"Do *I* give you too much credit, Diego?" She looked wistful and moved over to stand before him. She sighed and put her palms against his chest. "Or have you forgotten our night together in London?"

"I wronged you there," he muttered. "You should rather rebuke me for it."

"Rebuke you?" She laughed, and her hands began to wander lightly over his chest. "Rebuking you was not what I had in mind!"

Rye sighed and took her hands, put them back at her sides. For him the vision of Carolina was at the moment very bright.

Rosalia decided to try persuasion. She moved still closer, so that her breasts brushed his chest. She pouted and looked up at him through the dark shadow of her lashes. "I am restored to you and yet on our first evening at sea you would spend it with your *charts?*"

"Better that than we run aground," he said grimly, but he was aware of her allure, the way his body was answering hers.

"Oh, Diego." Her voice rose to a wail. "You are my *husband* and I have found you at last! We are running away together, away from everything I have known. I have entrusted my very *soul* to you, Diego! Would you spend this—our first evening—with your charts?"

"No." He sighed, and pulled her toward him.

She came into his arms, moaning, and tangled her fingers into his dark hair, pulled his face down to hers.

A hot wench was Rosalia, and tonight she meant to lead him down all those paths that had been omitted in that one encounter in London. . . .

For Rye the night was a revelation. He had somehow assumed that in his adventurous life he had sampled all the vices. Rosalia seemed to know a few more. He woke feeling somehow disturbed. Surely the aging Duke of Lorca could not have taught her all that? But courtiers . . . perhaps at the dissolute French Court?

She lay beside him, sleeping tranquilly, her dark hair spread about the pillow.

Yet Rosalia's amorous night did not deter her from wanting to make changes in the ship. By the following day there were more complaints lodged by the Spanish lady. The Duchess was not fond of English cooking. No, she had lost her taste for Spanish dishes as well. Could they not pick up, say, a French cook on their drive down the Channel?

She was very much put out when Rye did not accede to her request. She slammed her cabin door and deprived him of her company.

It was a relief.

Yet Rye, sometime later, watching a cormorant swoop and dip about the white shrouds that filled and billowed above him, was forced to admit to himself that he was not the same man he had been when, as Diego Viajar, he had set out to change his life, to become in all ways Spanish—a fit husband for Rosalia. It was unreasonable to expect that Rosalia, young and unformed when he had wooed her in Salamanca, would remain unchanged by all that she had encountered.

That Rosalia had indeed changed, he saw with regret. Along with her petulance, there was a cynical worldliness about her that he did not remember. He preferred her the way she had been. But now, standing upon the open deck as they beat their way down the Channel, his lean face softened as he remembered her in other days. Shadowy pictures flitted by him, infinitely sweet.

How once she had slipped from the shadow of a cork oak and thrown her slender arms around him, her hands pressed over both his eyes, and said with the breathless innocence of a child, "Can you guess who this is, Diego?"

Her small young breasts—the almost unformed breasts of an aristocratic Spanish girl brought up in a steel corselet that caged her womanliness to make her fashionably flat—had pressed like fire against his back and he had answered hoarsely, "I cannot guess. Let me hold your face in my hands that I may the better reflect." And she had laughed and slipped around in front of him and he, with eyes closed, had held her narrow face in his hands and—for the first time—kissed her lips.

It had been a miracle, that kiss, to a healthy young man long at sea who had already become enchanted by her tantalizing smile—usually seen from behind the iron grillwork when he looked up from the sunlit brilliance of the courtyard. For even though they took their meals together in the cool, vaulted dining room of her father's house, there seemed always to be a duenna lurking about to keep wayward young Rosalia from smiling overmuch at the young man Don Ignacio had brought home with him.

But she was the Duchess of Lorca now and he was once again masquerading through her life—this time as Ryeland Smythe, captain of the *Sea Waif*.

The visions died—to be replaced by thoughts of Carolina and how she was faring in Essex. For Rye had no other thought than that Carolina and Virginia had accompanied Andrew to the family seat in Essex. He wondered yearningly how she was and if she missed him. His lean face grew melancholy as he thought of her, wishing it were she sailing with him and not the complaining Duchess.

Rosalia satisfied his body, but not his soul. He was not the first man to find himself in that predicament, he guessed grimly.

Weighed down by guilt, he quickly put that thought away from him.

He had taken a wife for better or for worse. And even though it was for the worse, he had taken her for life.

So be it.

And then, just this side of Plymouth Sound, three of his crew members came down with an unknown malady and Rye, already short-handed and unwilling to venture into the broad reaches of the Atlantic with a possible epidemic on his hands, put into harbor at Plymouth Hoe and waited for what seemed an endless fortnight until no new cases of the disease had appeared and his men were better. He used the time to good purpose for he picked up the men he needed from the Plymouth waterfront taverns and sailed at last with a full crew.

And unknown to him as his ship lay at anchor in Plymouth Hoe, and as he fought in turn his conscience and his heart, a merchant ship called the *Mary Constant* had sailed past him, rounded the Lizard and Land's End and sailed out into the broad Atlantic.

Summer 1689

Chapter **23**

A fine fresh wind was blowing from the North Sea and the good ship *Mary Constant* had taken that wind in her sheets and was running before it. She had driven past Gravesend and out of the mouth of the Thames last night. Now in morning's pale light, with the sea a gray white-capped glimmer enclosing her fat wooden hull, she stood off Sandwich making for Deal and the Strait of Dover. The fair county of Kent lay off her starboard bow and the distant coast of France was somewhere off to larboard.

On the *Mary Constant*'s spray-splashed deck stood the two girls who had once been roommates back in Miss Chesterton's select school for young ladies—eons ago, they would have told you.

"He's a nice old man, our captain," murmured Reba, who had sensibly changed to a sleek bronze broadcloth whose wide skirts, now whipping in the sea breeze, had bands of stiff black braid at the hem. She was holding on to a ratline with one hand as she spoke and shading her eyes against the sun to look upward at the topgallants flashing as they caught the wind.

Carolina had also been holding onto the ratlines, looking up at the billowing topgallants. Now her fascinated gaze came down to focus on Reba. "How do you know?" she wondered—for stout, red-faced, smiling Captain Dawlish with his worn clothes and quaint bluff manners hardly looked the kind of man to frequent such a fashionable gaming establishment as Jenny Chesterton's.

"I met him once when I was a little girl," replied Reba, pushing back the locks of auburn hair that were blowing over her face. "He doesn't remember me, of course—I've grown more than a dozen inches and filled out since then! But I remember my father introducing us—he was the captain of my father's very first ship, Carolina, and he looked just the same then. The *Mary Constant,*" she added in a bored tone, "is my father's ship. I thought you knew that."

Carolina, who had paid for their passage with the gold Rye had left her, considered how thunderstruck the smiling little captain would be—how indeed he would blanch—if he knew that he was carrying the owner's daughter overseas without that owner's permission.

Captain Dawlish could not know that Reba was Jonathon Tarbell's daughter of course. Both girls were using false names—Rebecca Jones and Carolina Smythe. They had thought it best to travel incognito under the circumstances—Reba because Captain Dawlish would probably promptly return her to her father, Carolina because she did not want the Lightfoots of Level Green ever to hear about her misadventures; she wanted to lose herself completely and begin again.

Arranging passage to Philadelphia on the spur of the moment had proved impossible. No ship was leaving for Philadelphia until the end of the week. But Reba's sharp russet eyes had sighted the *Mary Constant* lying at anchor in the Thames and she had immediately brightened.

"There's our ship, Carolina!" she had muttered in triumph. "And she's about to leave for *somewhere*—that's plain enough!"

Rather against her will, Carolina had let Reba arrange to have them both rowed out to the soon-to-depart vessel, and over the ship's side they had dickered with a surprised Captain Dawlish, who was quick to admit that he had room for two more female passengers. Indeed there was a widow, one Mistress Wadlow, even now occupying a cabin that would accommodate three.

"So now there's no going back," Reba had muttered as, with Carolina's gold coins, she struck the bargain.

"I hope you realize we're going to Bermuda—not Philadelphia," Carolina had replied in an undertone as she prepared to climb the ship's ladder.

"And from Bermuda we can get passage to Philadelphia easily, I would imagine," Reba had countered—and once aboard had gone along with Carolina and her boxes to greet the woman with whom they would share accommodations on this journey.

Mistress Wadlow had proved to be a fragile, perverse, talkative old woman from Cambridge who had taken passage to Bermuda so that she might see her daughter's new grandchild before—she told them dramatically—she died.

"But you'll have many years yet!" declared Carolina, scandalized. She believed people should make plans to live—not plans to die. "Indeed you appear to be in good health."

"No, no, it is not my health. My health is fine."

Mistress Wadlow's birdlike voice rose to shrill over Carolina's. "I had my fortune told before I left Cambridge and the fortune-teller told me I would never see England again, that something tall and black would rise out of the sea and would stand in my way!"

"And yet you took passage anyway?" marveled Reba, who had grown up on tales of sea monsters.

"Aye." Mistress Wadlow sighed and her thin jowls shook as she shrugged. "I'm counting on the sea monster to appear on the *return* journey, so I may never come back from Bermuda! For I don't like my son's new wife and I've been living with them in Cambridge, you see. And besides," she added with a flash of candor, "my son didn't want me to go and I wouldn't put him above bribing that fortune-teller to frighten me out of the trip!"

The two girls exchanged startled glances.

"My elder sister once made the voyage to Bermuda," Mistress Wadlow added. "And after ten years of living there she decided to come back to England and—wouldn't you know?—the ship sank with all hands. But she had many adventures on that first crossing and she wrote me all about them."

She promptly embarked on the telling of all of them, her flow of words checked only when she paused to draw breath. When finally she stopped to answer a knock on the door, Reba leaned over and whispered in Carolina's ear, "Now we know why her daughter went to Bermuda. She *fled* to escape this torrent of words!"

"Shush, she'll hear you," muttered Carolina, who had taken a liking to this kindly, half-innocent, half-worldly old woman, fleeing a distasteful daughter-in-law to the shelter of her own flesh-and-blood daughter. The situation had been reversed with her own parents

—her mother had fled the scorn of her in-laws. But Carolina herself had never felt truly welcome at home when she was growing up and she sympathized with little Mistress Wadlow.

Mistress Wadlow even talked and muttered in her sleep, her gray head tossing on the pillow. And now, after having passed a restless night listening to her jibbering while the *Mary Constant* fought her way valiantly through the shipping down the Thames, the two girls had escaped their talkative cabin mate, who was still dressing, and had come out on deck for a breath of fresh air. In the early morning light other passengers were stirring, some lounging by the rail watching the Kentish coast sliding by on their right. Soon there would be little groups of passengers cooking over small fires made on the deck—fires which must be watched carefully lest they set the vessel afire.

Carolina had last night taken off her ice-green satin gown—the glamour of which had quite stunned the stout little captain when they had hailed his ship as it was about to depart. She had folded it away carefully in one of Reba's boxes. Reba had generously offered Carolina one of the two dresses she had been able to bring along, aside from the handsome russet silk in which she had come aboard—for Reba had not gone back to try to collect her things from Jenny Chesterton; there had not been time. The dress Carolina had borrowed from Reba was a pale yellow sprigged muslin with three-quarter sleeves which she wore over a sunny yellow linen petticoat—crushably thin and also borrowed from Reba. The gown was tight-bodiced and narrow-waisted and mercifully cool for a sunny voyage. The skirt was split down the center in front so that it might be gathered up on either side into panniers, the better to display the petticoat. But Carolina had not bothered to tuck it up—indeed on this windy day that overskirt, which was trimmed in narrow lemon-yellow braid, was a help in keeping her petticoat from flying up and displaying her pretty legs (and she had already noticed with some dismay how bright were the smiles of the male passengers and how dark the frowns of the female passengers when this happened!).

Reba had generously offered her the dress this morning so that she would not have to "wear out" her beautiful ice-green satin on this long voyage. At first Carolina had hesitated, for the sprigged muslin was a lighthearted dress indeed—not one to be worn over so heavy a heart as her own. Then with a little laugh she had accepted both dress and petticoat.

"Once again I am wearing your wardrobe, Reba— just like in school," she had told her friend ruefully.

And Reba had shrugged. "But who's paying my passage?" she had countered.

Now both girls offered a tempting sight to the strolling passengers who paced up and down the slanting deck for exercise. Like bronze and yellow fall chrysanthemums blowing in a brisk early autumn breeze, they swayed as they clung to the ratlines and talked, occasionally pausing to fight down the voluminous skirts that blew up to reveal a froth of white lace-trimmed chemise skirts. They were so conspicuous as to be the subject of frequent comment among many of the *Mary Constant*'s passengers.

"I still say that for two girls with *their looks* to be traveling alone means that they're no better than they should be!" insisted one of them—a Mistress Hedge— tartly. She looked balefully at the ship's rail where Carolina and Reba were now leaning on their elbows, staring out to sea. "*And* with such fine clothes!" she added spitefully, casting an annoyed glance down at her own plain mouse-colored gown and then back at the late arrivals.

"Come along, Nettie." Her husband, John, hurried her past the two flowerlike young figures. "And speak more softly or they'll hear you." He winced as his wife turned again to glare at the offending pair.

"And the way they answer a body!" Nettie added with indignation. "I asked the red-haired—"

"Auburn," corrected her husband gently.

"I might have known *you* would notice that, John! As I said, I asked the *red-haired* one with the hard face where she would be staying when she got to Bermuda and she said she didn't know. Then I turned to the white-haired one—"

"Silver blonde," murmured her husband with an appreciative glance at Carolina's shimmering locks, blowing wildly in the sea wind.

His wife sniffed her disdain.

"—And I asked *her* where they'd be staying and *she* said she didn't care!"

Nettie's husband hid a smile. "Perhaps they thought it none of your affair," he suggested cheerfully, taking a deep breath of the bracing sea air and peering up at a couple of gulls, noisily chasing each other about the rigging. It was a beautiful day, a day made for sailing, and the white sails of the fat merchant ship *Mary Constant* billowed gaily overhead.

"Nonsense!" his wife snapped. "They were just trying to put me in my place!"

Which would have taken some doing, thought her husband gloomily. *Certainly he had never been able to do it.* He managed another quick look at the two girls as he and his wife turned about and began to walk the ship lengthwise in the opposite direction. "The Beauties" was what the male passengers privately called the dazzling pair who had boarded just before the ship cast off, but to his mind only one was a real beauty—the blonde with the sad preoccupied expression.

"Impudent, they are!" declared his wife, incensed.

"Unhappy more like," he said with sudden insight. "The blonde's eyes are red-rimmed, didn't you notice? She looks as if she might have been crying."

As indeed she had. For last night Carolina had dreamed of Rye. She had lain in her bunk, somewhere between sleep and waking, and of a sudden as she drifted off into dreams, it had seemed to her that she was on board the *Sea Wolf* once again. She had nestled the more contentedly into the bunk and the creaking of the merchant vessel's heavy timbers had become the straining of a buccaneer ship's sturdy timbers as she cut into the blue waters of the Caribbean, eager to be unleashed against some mighty galleon three times her size and triple her guns . . . a great ship flexing its muscles even as her valiant captain might flex *his* muscles.

And with the thought, her buccaneer had appeared suddenly before her. "Kells," she had murmured in a soft rich voice and opened her white arms to welcome him.

"Christabel," he had answered, calling her by the name she had used on Tortuga.

He had come to her willingly and lain down by her side. Her clothes had magically disappeared without so much as a belt being unbuckled—but then magical unreal things happen easily in dreams. Carolina's thin chemise had sped away from her on a shaft of moonlight, becoming, somewhere out there beneath the stars, the white wingspan of an albatross soaring across the blue and endless depths of ocean.

"Kells," she had murmured again, and sighed as his long body warmed her, as his deft hands caressed her. "Hold me," she had whispered, and her arms had gone round his neck. As his grip on her tightened she had strained toward him, feeling the hardness of his rib cage and another hardness, more intimate, that she met with a glad sigh.

She had lain in his arms all night—but only in her dreams. Morning had found him gone. Morning had found Reba vigorously brushing her thick auburn hair and saying curiously, "Who is this Kells? You were babbling about him all night!"

And then Mistress Wadlow, who had wakened in time to hear that, had sat up and interrupted with a shudder, "The child must have been having a nightmare. For the only Kells I've heard of is a notorious pirate."

"Buccaneer," corrected Carolina absently.

"I see. There's a difference?" asked Reba politely, for she had never been one to worry about such fine distinctions. A sea rover was a sea rover as far as she was concerned.

"Oh, yes, there's a difference," said Carolina. And while Mistress Wadlow made chirping sounds indicating she'd like to interrupt, Carolina went on to educate both of them in Caribbean lore and to explain to her that the buccaneers were really privateers who attacked only the ships of Spain while pirates preyed on anyone.

"And how did you learn all this?" Reba asked with lifted brows.

Carolina could have reminded her that she might have learnt it from Rye's own lips that Christmastide in Essex but she chose not to. "Everyone in Virginia knows the difference," she said with a shrug. It was not quite true but would serve well enough for the moment.

"I expect," piped up Mistress Wadlow, who was panting as she struggled into her stays, "that Captain Dawlish is keeping his fingers crossed and hoping we can make port safely, for beyond the Azores I'm told the sea grows wilder and is filled with hunting ships." Her faded blue eyes grew saucerlike in her thin face.

Carolina sighed. At that moment, still under the spell of last night's vivid dream, she would have given almost anything to see just *one* long gray hunting ship—the *Sea Wolf. But of course that is not to be,* she told herself sadly. *Never again.*

She turned resolutely toward Reba. "There's little use putting your hair up so elegantly. The wind on deck will only blow away the pins."

Reba turned to give her a quelling look. "There's *always* good reason to look your best! After all, you never know what will happen or who you'll meet."

Carolina shrugged. They had already met all the passengers and Reba had considered none of the men worthy of her steel. As for anything "happening," the best they could hope for was fine weather—the worst, to meet a Spanish galleon or a storm at sea. For herself, she hoped for an uneventful voyage.

Nearby Mistress Wadlow, who had now found her breath again, was saying much the same thing.

"I don't know why I let you talk me into this," Reba complained when they were at last out on deck, leaning against the portside railing as the wind bellied the canvas and the vessel heeled before the breeze. Reba was having trouble finding her footing but Carolina had become used to having a vessel's swaying deck beneath her feet and felt a kind of kinship with the ship as the sails cracked and the ratlines hummed.

"You'll get your sea legs soon," she promised Reba. "And remember it won't be forever. We'll reach Bermuda and then—" She had almost said "home." But Philadelphia, which was to be their eventual destination, was not home. Home was the Tidewater—no, it was not there either. Home was a man's arms, held wide and welcoming. Home was a buccaneer ship or a white red-roofed house overlooking Cayona Bay or a great house in Essex that she had never seen—home was where Rye was, wherever he might be.

And now she knew she could never go home again. Not to those warm strong arms.

She could never forgive him. Her pride would not let her.

Not that he was likely to ask her to forgive him. She had been cast out from paradise.

But the days on shipboard were long and monotonous. They had passed Dover before Reba, who for so long had bottled up her love for her errant marquess, began to talk.

"I don't know when I first discovered I loved Robin," she confided to Carolina as they walked up and down the deck of the swaying ship, listening to the great sails crack in the wind, and trying to hold on to their flying skirts and ignore the admiring smiles the seamen sent their way at sight of dainty ankles suddenly in view.

"In Essex I didn't believe that you really loved him at all," Carolina admitted.

"I don't think I did—then," Reba confessed with a sigh. "He was so handsome and I was so thrilled at the idea of being a marchioness and"—she flushed as she turned to Carolina—"I wanted to be considered, well, ahead of the pack. I pretended more experience than I had."

Carolina had long suspected as much. She nodded to two tradesmen who were just then passing by, lost in talk of cargoes, their steel-buckled shoes sparkling in the sun. "So there never really was anyone but—your marquess?"

Reba nodded. Her face, once so pretty, had grown melancholy, Carolina thought. "Oh, if only I could make you see him as I did, Carolina! So tall and straight, so magnificent! With those eyes that roved over you and"—she shivered—"stripped you down to your chemise and then threw *that* away!"

Carolina was used to a pair of eyes like that. She sighed too.

"And I believed everything he said," mourned Reba. "Do you know I was really under the impression that *I* had seduced *him?* It wasn't until he left me—for the second time!—that I began to realize what had actually happened."

"I don't understand why he didn't marry you after his wife died," Carolina said soberly. "You told me he was desperate for money, I remember." She bit her lip for she had not meant to suggest so bluntly that Reba's marquess might have been persuaded to marry her for her dowry.

But Reba, absorbed in her own thoughts, seemed not to notice. "I *do* think I could have landed him if I'd had time. But I was afraid to let Mother know how I was living—and I suppose that cast doubts on my dowry in Robin's mind. And I was so happy with him that I didn't want to risk—well, losing him."

Which you well might have, if you'd pushed for

something more than a Fleet Street marriage, thought Carolina grimly. *And you wouldn't even have had the little you got!*

"Oh, Carolina, you should have seen how happy we were!" Reba murmured dreamily. "Robin had found us that little place in Hanging Sword Alley and we almost never went out at all." She shivered deliciously, remembering.

"Hanging Sword Alley?" Carolina turned in surprise. "But that's off Fleet Street near Whitefriars! I thought you told me he found you a house on London Bridge with a watergate, high up on one of the sterlings!"

"I lied," Reba said cheerfully, and when Carolina blinked, she frowned at her. "Well, after all, Carolina," she complained, "there you were back in London looking wonderful and wearing new clothes and there *I* was, staying at Jenny Chesterton's, feeling utterly bedraggled. I didn't want to admit that Robin had only found me a bare little two-room place in Hanging Sword Alley! A tall house on London Bridge sounded *much* more impressive!"

"Indeed it did," Carolina agreed dryly, remembering that she had envisioned Reba to have been dashing about London with a coach and six. "But why didn't he take you out?" From what she had heard of Robin Tyrell, Marquess of Saltenham, he was a man who enjoyed the gaiety of nighttime London.

"Well, he *said* it was because I was his new bride. . . ."

A Fleet Street bride, Carolina thought sardonically.

"And of course he was fast running out of money. But—" Reba hesitated, then with a shrug admitted the truth. "I think it was really because he was afraid we'd be seen together, and my father might hear of it and storm into London and force him to marry me in a church—without any dowry at all!"

"If you thought that," said Carolina, knowing how Reba's mind worked, "I'm surprised you didn't get in touch with your father."

"I did write to him," Reba said frankly, "one night while Robin was sleeping. But the chimney caught fire before I could get the letter posted. We all ran out into the night to save our lives, and I think maybe Robin found the letter for I know I never did. It disappeared —perhaps into the fire. It was only the rooms on our floor that were damaged. We moved into other rooms downstairs the next day. And the next day"—her hard young face clouded—"was the day he left me."

Carolina was not surprised. From what she had heard of the rake, Robin Tyrell, he was entirely capable of that. For all that Reba had been his willing playmate, he had still blasted her young life—and apparently he did not care.

"I'm sorry," she said softly.

"So am I!" Reba's hard shell was back, protecting her inner hurt. "After all, I had planned to become a marchioness!" Her brittle laughter caught suddenly on a sob and she snatched for a kerchief and violently blew her nose. "And—and there was something else, Carol, something I haven't told you. Robin had found himself another woman—I'm sure of it. Twice he had come home reeking of her perfume!"

Carolina turned her face away. She did not want Reba to see how bleak her expression was at that moment. She looked up and traced the pattern of a hunting gull winging through the sky, wings glittering white against the blue.

"Do you think women are always fools?" she asked quietly.

Reba hesitated a moment—then she gave a frank answer. "Where men are concerned—yes."

"I don't understand men who just—walk away." There was pain in Carolina's voice.

"*I* do," Reba said bitterly. "They think they've found something better. At least *newer*. I suppose it amounts to the same thing."

Was that it? Was that really it? Oh, she couldn't credit it! Rye had given her no sign that he had ceased to love her—except possibly his preoccupation with matters concerning the ship and his men, and long evenings away from her. *Spent with the Duchess of Lorca?* The thought seared her.

"We're going to have to find a new life, Reba," she said tiredly.

"Yes." Reba sounded sad. "But I'd give my eye teeth for the old!"

Carolina said nothing for Reba had voiced what they both felt.

"At first I thought I wouldn't," Reba said, sighing. "But now I know that I'd take Robin back. No matter how many other women he had."

"*I* wouldn't," said Carolina bitterly—but she knew it was her pride speaking. She desperately wanted Rye back—as desperately as ever Reba wanted her Robin.

But . . . there was another woman standing squarely in her path.

And suddenly, with a force so great that it lent venom to her voice, Carolina wanted revenge. Revenge upon the dark and lovely Duchess of Lorca. Revenge upon the woman who had stolen her lover!

"I'd *never* take Rye back," she choked.

411

She found herself brooding about that as the *Mary Constant* slipped through the Strait of Dover and into the English Channel. Through the choppy waters the stout little merchant ship drove, with France somewhere off her port bow and the south of England off to starboard. Hastings, where England had changed hands during the Norman invasion, drifted by, and Dungeness and Beachy Head, as Kent gave way to Sussex. Hampshire's New Forest, ancient hunting ground of the West Saxon kings, where two of the Conqueror's sons had met their deaths and where a scant four years ago the wild young Duke of Monmouth had been seized in full flight after the disastrous Battle of Sedgemoor, passed by on her right—but it meant nothing to Carolina. History was marching by her in a line of bright beaches and green forests and towering rocky cliffs, but all she could see was one dark face and a pair of gray eyes that had smiled on her for a season. She felt ten years older by the time they reached Torquay with its terraced gardens and cascades of flowers, and passed by Plymouth Sound where in Tudor times the English fleet had waited to do battle with the mighty Spanish Armada.

"That's Plymouth Hoe over there," Reba told her, shading her eyes against the sun to look across the shining waters of the Sound. She studied the port. "All those ships . . . I wonder if any of them belong to my father?"

She sounded homesick already, and Carolina turned with Reba to study the harbor with its forest of sails.

She would have been thunderstruck to know that the beautiful Duchess of Lorca, who had become such an obsession with her, was at that very moment sulking on the deck of one of those distant ships or that Rye had gone down into town to see how his men were faring. . . .

And then their westward voyage continued, Plymouth disappeared from view, Devon gave way to Cornwall, they were rounding The Lizard, passing Land's End, the jagged rocks of the Scilly Isles disappearing off to starboard. Before them stretched the broad reaches of the Atlantic.

The voyage seemed interminable to the two girls, with no young people on board and little to do save eat and sleep. Blue skies alternated with gray as the ship cut a white wake through a trackless ocean, and day followed monotonous day. The passengers, tired of hard ship's biscuits and mouldy cheese and cramped quarters, had grown quarrelsome. Even Mistress Wadlow, whose disposition was even despite her tendency to talk everyone to death, had grown petulant. This morning when her comb caught on a tangle in her gray hair, she had thrown a dozen hairpins on the floor and stamped on them.

Although it was already dusk on a damp day with a fog bank nearly obscuring their vision, Carolina and Reba had as usual remained on deck where the air was better than it was in their stuffy cabin. And there one of the "mercantile gentlemen," a Mr. Souers, had found them and was now waxing expansive about his crossings, which had been many.

"We are nearing the Western Islands," he told them, airing his knowledge. "The Azores—Isles of the Hawks." Eager to impress such pretty young creatures, he went on. "When I made this crossing nine years ago there was a great volcano in the Azores belching smoke and blackening the sky. I can still hear its thunder!"

Reba shuddered and glanced uneasily at the cloud

bank which obscured the direction in which Mr. Souers was pointing.

"Oh, look," she cried. "There's a ship. It just shot out from behind that fog bank and it seems to be heading this way. Do you think it's English?"

In silence they all three studied the approaching vessel, indistinct in the dusk but coming up fast. It looked rather like the *Sea Wolf*, thought Carolina forlornly, and felt a twist of pain in her heart.

"I can't quite make out her flag," Mr. Souers said, straining forward. "Perhaps the captain with his glass—" The words died on his lips.

From the approaching ship had come another kind of thunder.

For at that moment a shot skimmed across the *Mary Constant*'s port bow and struck the water just ahead of them.

They were being commanded to stop.

Chapter 24

Around the two girls and the tradesman, who a moment ago had been standing upon a peaceful deck, the ship seemed suddenly to erupt into frantic activity.

"Do you think she's a Spanish ship?" cried Reba.

"No, that's no galleon," rumbled Mr. Souers. "More likely a pirate." His Adam's apple seemed to be hopping up and down with his increasing anxiety. "Where's the captain? What does *he* say?"

As if in answer, Captain Dawlish came running down the deck, bawling orders as he ran. His usually ruddy face had taken on a grayish cast and he came to a sharp halt before the two young women, crying to them to get below, "For can't ye see, the devils yonder have raised a black flag and we've no guns to compete with theirs!"

What with first Reba and then Mr. Souers constantly jostling her to get a better view of the oncoming vessel, Carolina scarcely had a chance to study it, but at the captain's mention of a black flag her heart lurched. Pirates? Here in these comparatively northern waters?

It seemed incredible to Carolina, who had somehow associated piracy entirely with Caribbean waters and the coast of the Americas, that out here in the middle of nowhere Mistress Wadlow's worst fears had become reality—the *Mary Constant* was about to be attacked by pirates.

Not that they were to see that attack. All the passengers still on deck were busy scurrying for cover and spurred on by the captain's whiplash words, Mr. Souers promptly grasped both girls and hurried them below to find Mistress Wadlow wringing her bony hands and bemoaning ever having taken this voyage.

"Oh, the fortune-teller warned me!" she cried tragically. "I should have listened, that I should! And now we'll all be walking the plank!"

"I never heard of anybody being forced to walk the plank," Carolina told her energetically. "That's a myth to frighten children, Mistress Wadlow."

"Oh, lor'," gasped Mistress Wadlow, envisioning other ends if not that one. "How much time do you think we have to live?"

"They won't kill us," cried Carolina. "It's ransom they're after—and jewels and gold." This remark was meant to be soothing but it only evoked from the older woman a rolling of faded blue eyes and a gasp that if that was true and they had no jewels and gold, *even worse* might happen to them!

Carolina was about to retort that buccaneers did not rape the women they captured, but set them on ships to return home again, when she was brought up short by the realization that these men bearing down on them were not buccaneers—they were pirates, and who knew what might be their fate?

Reba kept running to the cabin door, opening it a crack and calling out in a piercing voice, "Is there any news? Does anyone know what ship it is that fired on us?"

On one of those penetrating calls, she was answered. White-haired Mr. Patterson, who owned a plantation on Sandys in the Bermudas, was hurrying by and he paused to report, "We have not yet been able to make out the name of the vessel but we think she flies a black petticoat for a flag—which would mean that her captain is a man named Kells."

Carolina's world did a dizzy turnaround. The next moment her flying feet reached the door. "I want to see it!" she cried breathlessly. "The ship!"

But at the doorway, a shocked Mr. Patterson pushed her back inside the cabin with a firm hand. "This is no time for sightseeing!" he admonished. "The captain does not want any of the passengers on deck—and especially the women," he added on an ominous note.

"Why not?" cried Carolina. "What harm if we—"

"There may yet be fighting," he interrupted her tersely. "I have come below for my fowling piece in case the captain decides we should try to fend them off."

"*A fowling piece?* When they'll have twenty pounders aimed at our decks? Tell the captain—"

She got no chance to finish. Mr. Patterson gave her a wounded look and cut into her words. Plainly he was a man intent on doing his duty—nobly, whether he had the proper armaments for it or not. "Keep the wench inside," he instructed Mistress Wadlow and Reba. "It would seem they are about to board us." And he shut the door in Carolina's face and stalked away.

Reba seized her by the wrist and Mistress Wadlow clawed nervously at her sleeve, dragging her back from the door.

"Oh, for pity's sake, Carol!" cried Reba in exasperation.

Carolina desisted—and stood trembling. At that moment it was difficult for her to think coherently. A lean gray ship had come suddenly out of the fog—and now they were telling her that ship flew a black petticoat, the symbol of the feared Petticoat Buccaneer!

All that Sandy Randolph had said about Kells that day at Level Green was coming true, she realized, stunned. He had fired across the bow of an English ship; he was about to board her.

"About to board us!" Mistress Wadlow gasped, echoing her thought and even Reba shrank back. "And he says it's Captain Kells," she whispered.

But Carolina, hearing Mistress Wadlow wail that name, stood bemused. No matter how calamitous the circumstances, her heart for a moment soared at the prospect of seeing Rye again—and then it plummeted. She would see Rye again—but with another woman at his side. A woman at the very sight of whom he had been struck speechless. A woman whose very shadow reminded him of his one great love—Rosalia. A woman who had been able to make him forget her. . . .

Around her now all was excitement. Mistress Wadlow, now that the situation had grown desperate, had suddenly recovered her wits and was pouring out a torrent of words. They must put on their best chemises, their best petticoats, their best silk dresses—two or three of them if possible. They must hide about their persons any jewels they possessed. (She was tearing into boxes, rummaging, slipping on extra garters and extra silk stockings and a brace of petticoats even as she spoke.) And over the top of all that clothing, she insisted, they must wear their plainest, drabbest gowns.

"There is no chance our bodices would hook over such wads of cloth," Carolina responded absently. She was grappling with larger problems than what she would wear to be captured!

"But you must *make* them hook!" exclaimed Mistress Wadlow. "So that we will be *overlooked.*"

"There is no chance at all that we will be overlooked," sighed Reba. "My hair is too red and I'm too tall to go unnoticed. And Carolina is a blazing blonde that *everybody* notices! We are *certain* to be singled out. Oh, just this once to be mousey!" She looked very frightened.

"Well then, there's a way!" Mistress Wadlow was proving to be nothing if not resourceful. "I am bringing a trunkful of widows' weeds to Bermuda for a friend of my daughter's who is very large and will pay handsomely for them. We will wear *those* over our clothing. Surely even pirates will respect mourning!" She was scrabbling through a large trunk as she spoke. "And that way we can swathe our heads and faces in heavy black veils." She tossed a black gown and petticoat and several thick black veils in Reba's direction.

Reba caught them. She looked undecided for a moment, then she began putting on the mourning garb with feverish haste.

"Wait, you're not putting on extra garments beneath!"

"I would rather let the pirates have my wardrobe than be dragged off to Tortuga to wear away my life in some brothel!" she retorted scornfully. Smoothing down a black petticoat over her slender hips, she turned anxiously to Carolina, who had not moved but stood with her head bent, her hands clenched together. "Wake up, Carol!" She gave her friend a rude nudge.

"This is no time for wool-gathering! You haven't even begun to dress—you must hurry!"

Carolina eluded Reba's grasp and shook her head almost dreamily.

"There is no need for all this furor," she told them almost brusquely. *"I* will speak to Kells."

"You'll speak to . . . are you out of your mind? Oh, you'll do no such thing, Carol. Here, put on these mourning clothes. At once!" Taut with excitement, she tried to drape a black garment over her friend's head.

Carolina pulled away. "No, thank you. I'll wear what I have on to face these sea rovers. No—no, I won't. I'll put on my pale green satin." She turned about to find it.

"Oh, Carolina, don't do it," begged Reba. "I realize you look ravishing in it, and when you smile you could melt a stone, but these pirates may rape you and then cut your throat—don't *inflame* them!"

But Carolina had already peeled down to her chemise and was slipping the silver-frosted petticoat over her head. "I doubt I will inflame Kells," she added sardonically. "But one can always hope for the best."

"Mistress Wadlow, help me with her—she's mad!" Reba turned to appeal to the older woman who already looked like a stout bereaved widow in thick black silks with a long black trailing veil that shielded her face and gray hair.

"Perhaps she is right," sighed Mistress Wadlow. "As lovely as she is, nothing may happen to her. But I can't think she'd care to take the chance."

"Nor can I!" Reba was almost dressed in stiff taffeta mourning garb by now. "I must say, Carol, that I consider you a perfect fool," she told her friend in a huffy voice. "Mistress Wadlow is right, we might escape notice as mourners. After all, even pirates must have some respect for death since they have constant brushes with it!"

"Oh, 'tis true death is always with them," agreed Carolina, feeling her confidence return as she patted the bodice of her low-cut ice-green gown with its enormous gauzy skirt down around her perfectly formed bust, easing out any wrinkles of the bodice from around her narrow satin waist. She flicked out the great spill of silver lace from her elbows and it glimmered around her pale arms. "But I do not think you need to worry," she added calmly.

She was about to tell them why when there was a sudden jolting jar as the two hulls crashed together, and they almost lost their footing as the shock sent them all staggering across the room, clutching at each other to stay upright. There was a clamor on deck as grappling irons bit into wood and armed men swung over onto the deck of the helpless merchantman. They heard shouts, and the sound of feet pounding. Then the door to their cabin burst open and several raffish looking fellows, naked to the waist and armed with pistols and cutlasses, surged through.

Mistress Wadlow screamed.

Reba shrank back a step and involuntarily clutched the older woman. The two of them looked like witches, standing there swathed in black, thought Carolina dispassionately.

She frowned at the strange faces of the men, then took a truculent step forward. Her swirling ice-green gown drifted around her ankles, her delicate chin was lifted, and the face she turned to these rough-looking interlopers was quite haughty.

"You will take me to Captain Kells," she said in a ringing voice. *"At once,* if you please!" And she heard Mistress Wadlow give a little bleat of protest.

All the men were momentarily dazzled by her beauty. The tallest of them whistled in amazement as he peered down at this imperious vision, and the stout fellow beside him muttered, "Kells will certainly want to see *her!*"

Behind him the others nodded in agreement.

"Ye'll come along with me, ladies," the tall fellow told the pair of ebony-garbed mourners, gesturing curtly for them to precede him. "But *this* lass"—he indicated Carolina with a jerk of his head—"will stay here."

"No, I will not!" flashed Carolina. She tried to step forward but he pushed her resolutely back.

"The cap'n's busy just now," he explained, and the thought flashed through her mind: *He must have seen me on Tortuga—he seems to know who I am!*

She would have protested further but the cabin door was closed abruptly in her face and she heard a key turn in the lock. It would do no good to call after them, she knew. There was nothing to do but wait.

Alone now, gorgeously clad and facing the tumultuous thought that she would soon see Rye, her mind simmered. What would she say to him? Dear God, what would she *not* say to him? Would she upbraid him for sailing away with the Spanish lady? Or . . . would she falter when she was confronted once again with that loved face? Would she forget all the angry words that now came so readily to mind and fly disgracefully into his arms, ready to forgive?

Alone and desperate, Carolina fought a heavy battle with herself. Every fiber of her being wanted to forget the past, to tell Rye she would forgive him. . . .

But how could she, when the beautiful Duchess of Lorca even now undoubtedly occupied the great cabin of the *Sea Wolf*? When she knew that Rye had come so recently from the embrace of those creamy arms?

Through the closed door she heard all the sounds of a ship being rifled for gain. Doors slammed, feet pattered about, there were shouts, protests, the sounds of heavy objects being dragged. She wondered absently whether the pirates would set fire to the *Mary Constant*—and hoped they would not, for she was a good ship and Captain Dawlish an able captain who was proud of his vessel. Barely a fortnight ago, finding her alone on deck, he had regaled her with tales of the wild storms his little vessel had weathered—and he had assured her in his gruff voice that they'd make landfall safely in Bermuda. How sad it would be for him if the last he saw of the *Mary Constant* was the sight of her in flames, burning to the water line, as he himself struck out, heartsick, in an open boat for some distant island in the Azores!

Time passed with maddening slowness.

And then there was a booted step outside. A crisp commanding step.

She guessed that Rye had come for her and in sudden panic she turned about, so that she would be standing defiantly with her back to the door when he entered. She would wait to hear his voice—surely that would tell her his temper—before she whirled to face him. Not only that, her heavy pale blonde curls and the sleek ice-green satin lines of her back would present an alluring picture. Besides showing her captor a certain disdain which he well deserved!

Behind her the door opened. She could feel her heart pounding as those booted feet entered the room.

"My lady," said an amused masculine voice. "I beg you to turn about so that I may see your face."

As in a dream, Carolina swung about.

Before her was a tall dark-haired man with gray eyes. *Hunter's eyes*, she thought, *seeking their prey*. And curiously empty. He stood easily before her, clad in French gray satins heavily encrusted with silver embroidery. A swatch of frosty mechlin at his throat, a delicate spray of mechlin at his cuffs, dripping down over fine slender hands. It was a dissolute face that she looked into, a face charged with recklessness—but it was a face no woman would soon forget.

As she turned about, he made her an elegant leg and bent in a formal bow so low that his dark hair almost swept the floor.

"Permit me to introduce myself," he said coolly. "I am Captain Kells."

Like a strange hot sighing wind, those words went through her. They were words she had heard long ago—from Rye Evistock on Tortuga. But this smiling adventurer who had straightened up to look down into her face, gone suddenly so pale, was a total stranger, a man she had never seen before.

"Who—who did you say you were?" she whispered, feeling her knees waver beneath her.

"Kells. Captain Kells. But do not be frightened," he told her in a more soothing voice, seeing how stunned she looked. "I have no desire to harm you." He was scanning her features narrowly. "Might I know your name?"

From her spinning world, Carolina sought for an answer. It would not do to give her real name, she felt. And now she was sure that the pirate who had given her such a strange look before locking her in had *not* seen her on Tortuga—that there was some other reason for his singling her out. Best to stick to the name that would appear on the list of ship's passengers.

"My name is Smythe," she told him through stiff lips. "Carolina Smythe."

"Smythe . . ." He pondered. "In truth, Jonas did not lie. He told me you were a silver wench—and a witchingly beautiful silver wench you certainly are! Mistress Smythe, will you take the arm of a sea rover and allow me to escort you to the *Sea Wolf?*"

Carolina could not trust herself to speak. In silence she took the gray satin-clad arm proffered her, in silence came out onto the deck to observe the activity that was still going on as stores were being transferred across the rails which had been lashed together.

"Where—where are the passengers?" she asked fearfully, looking about her, for they were nowhere in sight.

"Have no fear for them, dear lady," said the tall man by her side. "They have all been put into boats, unharmed, and are at this moment rowing with all their might toward the Azores which lie in that direction." He waved a casual hand and the lace at his cuff fluttered.

"But the Azores stretch out interminably with leagues of empty sea between!" protested Carolina, heartsick at the thought of Reba and the rest adrift on an endless ocean. "Indeed they could miss them altogether!"

"There will be no difficulty," he assured her. "The distance to the nearest island is but short, and Captain Dawlish is in command of the boats. All have been provided with lanterns and he will guide them safe to shore."

"I wish I could be as certain," said Carolina bitterly. But she allowed him to lift her over the side and onto the *Sea Wolf.* He lifted her in a light gesture which proved his strength, and once set down upon the deck of his vessel she saw that it was not the *Sea Wolf* at all—indeed not even a very good imitation. The lines were slightly different, the decks not as clean-scrubbed, the brasswork not polished half so bright as the ship she remembered from her days in Tortuga. And—surprisingly—the crew that grinned at her as she was lifted aboard did not look half so dangerous as the buccaneers she was used to rubbing elbows with on Tortuga.

She was perplexed, looking around her. What manner of men were these? Surely not buccaneers!

In the distance she saw a young stripling striding along in a dress. In his hand was clutched a blonde wig. And she thought with a sudden start, *He is imitating me! He is supposed to fool people into thinking he is the Silver Wench!*

It was all part of the charade the tall debonair captain was playing, and somehow the realization made her less afraid of him although she knew she *should* be afraid because she was completely in his power.

"Then I am the only passenger you—kept?" she asked.

"You are indeed the only one." His gaze, which at first had passed over her as sharply as a blade, had turned caressing. He was regarding her now with a leisurely, catlike look. "And I have come to invite you to share my humble repast."

Invited to break bread in the great cabin of the masquerader! Carolina remembered vividly the last time she had boarded the real *Sea Wolf*, fresh from Tortuga, remembered the wild wedding ceremony, the cheering buccaneers, the flash of cutlasses, the church bells clanging discordantly from shore . . . so long ago, so far away.

She took a deep breath. This was another *Sea Wolf* and this was another Kells. She must not confuse the two.

It was a shock to Carolina to realize how like the real *Sea Wolf* this ship must look from a distance. From up close there were many differences and she observed them without comment. She could not help but notice the openly curious stares of his men.

"That's Lars Lindstrom," he said affably, nodding toward a tall blond man as they passed. "And over there is my ship's doctor—Dr. Cotter." He indicated a dour fellow who gave them a lowering look as they went by.

Carolina's breath caught in her throat. This game had been very well planned indeed. And with knowledge. Someone had known that Lars Lindstrom was an officer aboard the genuine *Sea Wolf* and Dr. Cotter indeed her ship's doctor. But the impersonation was not perfect. This "Lars Lindstrom" in no way resembled the real Lars other than by being blond, and the real Dr. Cotter was half a head shorter and a deal wider than the dour fellow who was passing himself off as Dr. Cotter.

It occurred to her to wonder uneasily why *she* had been kept aboard when the other passengers of the *Mary Constant* had all been put into boats, but when she voiced her query as they walked along the deck she received a courtier's bantering answer.

"I heard of your beauty, dear lady—my men were stunned by it. And I thought to give myself the signal delight of sharing my repast with you this night. After all, I am a man long at sea, and living always in a hellhole such as Tortuga, I have need of fair companionship."

427

She gave him a scathing look. In need of fair companionship he well might be, but living in the hellhole of Tortuga he certainly was not—for there the real Dr. Cotter would have denounced him and the real Lars Lindstrom would have cut him down with his cutlass for this charade!

"I am honored, sir," she said dryly, with the faintest curtsy.

He smiled. "Spoken like a lady. And yet you signed the passenger list as 'Mistress Carolina Smythe, sempstress.'" He was regarding her keenly as he led the way to the great cabin.

So he had scanned the passenger list before he came for her. . . .

"I will have need of your skills this very evening, dear lady," her captor was saying. "For I have burst a seam in one of my coats while attempting to climb this cursed rigging, and 'twill need a skilled sempstress to set it right."

Carolina, who could not so much as stick a needle into a piece of linsey-woolsey without pricking her finger, gave him a helpless look. "Perhaps after dinner," she suggested vaguely. "I could take the coat back with me to my cabin and work on it by candlelight." She hoped she would be able to somehow mend the break in his coat seams without spattering the material with her blood!

"Ah, yes, to your cabin . . ." he murmured thoughtfully.

"I *am* to have a cabin? Or am I too to be set adrift?"

"Of course you are to have a cabin, dear lady," he soothed. "I shall clear out my ship's doctor and give you his quarters."

And I shall find a way to barricade my door, Carolina

428

thought uneasily. *In case your ship's doctor finds in the middle of the night that he has forgotten something and returns to look for it!*

"My cabin, dear lady. Enter!" He flung wide the door and Carolina looked around her curiously.

Here at least no effort had been made to copy the interior of the great cabin of the real *Sea Wolf*. Indeed the place was entirely different from that sumptuous interior that Carolina had grown to know—and love. Yet this great cabin had a careless splendor that took away her breath. The green hangings over the bank of stern windows looked new and were of rich brocade yet they had already been allowed to become water-stained. The furnishings had once been exceedingly handsome—chairs in gilt, an oaken table fit for banqueting—yet the oaken table top was scarred as if many a tankard had banged down upon it, the gilt chairs were chipping and their gold velvet seats looked somewhat moth-eaten. A handsome Turkey carpet in rich bronzy red covered the floor (Carolina imagined slipping about on it during a storm!). The brasses were not highly polished and Carolina realized that this man did not run a tight ship. Indeed the deck had been a shambles compared to the real *Sea Wolf,* rigged always for swift and silent running and prepared at any moment to do battle with the best Spain had to offer. Through the hangings that obscured a curtained alcove she glimpsed a bunk on which a coverlet of some rich stuff—she thought it was embroidered with gold threads—had been carelessly thrown and now tumbled half off a bed of white linen. And below just a tiny bit showed of what just might be a silver chamber pot—she wondered suddenly if it was Aunt Pet's! Handsome masculine clothing was flung carelessly about on chairs and she almost stumbled over a pair of fine polished boots.

Plainly this particular captain, while possessed of sumptuous tastes, cared little for order.

"I am not by nature neat," he told her with a deprecating smile. As he spoke he reached out with a booted foot and casually kicked both boots under the table on which they were to dine, for Carolina could see that it had already been set with a pair of blue and white delftware plates, some handsome silver salts, a couple of blackjack leathern tankards, massive silver spoons, some wicked-looking knives and—surprisingly —forks.

Her winglike brows elevated at the sight of those forks. For forks were still quite new and fashionable and most of the population still made do with knives and spoons and their fingers, endlessly wiping them off—in the better houses at least—on a succession of linen napkins.

Her captor noted the direction of her gaze. "I simply could not put to sea without forks," he said wistfully, and she was again besieged by curiosity about him.

"I am surprised your delftware plates have survived," she observed. "For they must crash to the floor during storms at sea!"

He sighed. "Indeed they have, dear lady. These two are all that remain of the dozen I sailed with. They were"—his lips quirked in a wry smile——"the gift of a lady."

"And these furnishings?" she asked, with a sweeping gesture. "Were they also the gift of a lady?"

"Ah, no, these odds and ends came from my country house at—" He paused suddenly and gave her an odd smile. "You ask direct questions, dear lady."

"It is a bad habit of mine," she admitted.

"But useful, I'll be bound," he murmured, pulling back her chair with a flourish.

"Sometimes," she admitted demurely and settled her skirts onto the chair's gold velvet seat with more confidence for suddenly she had lost her fear of him. He had a rag-tag crew, his ship was improperly run, he had put to sea with delftware plates to slide off the table and break whenever the weather turned foul—yet his voice and manner proclaimed him a gentleman, he had furnished this cabin with fabulous "odds and ends" from his country house, and he had set to sea with forks—oh, surely she had nothing to fear from such a one!

"I am afraid we will have to make do with these blackjack tankards," he told her ruefully, pouring Canary wine into the black leathern tankard before her. "All the crystal goblets suffered the same fate as the delftware plates. Their fragments were long since thrown into the sea."

Carolina, lifting the tankard to her lips, remembered the jewel-encrusted gold goblets from which she had drunk wine in the cabin of the real *Sea Wolf*—goblets seized from the might of Spain.

"The wine is delicious, sir," she commended.

"The best Spain had to offer at the time," he murmured absently. His eyes never left her face as he raised his tankard to his lips.

"You seized it then from a Spanish galleon?" she made bold to ask, for she could not credit it that this raffish ship had ever taken anything more dangerous than an unarmed merchantman.

He chuckled. "I am afraid not. The wine too was the gift of a lady."

Spanish wine, she thought and was hard put to keep her brows from lifting again in astonishment.

"Actually," he said, "I prefer a good Bordeaux, but the lady's husband preferred to stock the wines of his country."

The gift of a married woman? And a Spanish woman at that? Carolina was fascinated.

"Allow me to propose a toast," he said. "To the most beautiful woman it has ever been my privilege to gaze upon."

Carolina's heart quickened. "And who might that be?" she asked coolly.

He chuckled. "I think you know," he said, and took a long draught of the wine before setting the tankard back upon the table.

Chapter 25

Now that it was clear that the man who sat across from her was courting her favor—and courting it indeed like the gentleman he appeared to be, Carolina studied him frankly.

Blatant masquerader that he was, still this fellow who lounged opposite her in silver-encrusted gray satin might easily, at a distance, be mistaken for Rye. He stood as tall as Rye—and as straight. He was of a slightly narrower build and had not Rye's breadth of shoulder or depth of chest beneath that satin coat, but his hips and flanks as he strode along beside her to this cabin had had a wiry grace. And the sweeping bow he had made to her had the easy grace of a courtier at the Court of St. James. His shoulder-length hair was his own and it was as dark as Rye's, but while Rye's was of the deepest richest brown imaginable and only appeared black in some lights, this man's thick hair was truly black and had more of a bluish sheen. The face that looked so boldly into her own was smiling and lightly tanned—not so deeply tanned as Rye's which had been bronzed by the fierce Caribbean sun. A narrow aquiline nose, a mobile mouth with a slightly jeering twist, a pair of arching, quizzical dark brows beneath a surprisingly high forehead confronted her.

But his eyes were what held her attention. They were a murky gray, lighter in color than Rye's and curiously flat. Empty eyes. She could read nothing in them or tell whether there was even a soul behind them.

Those eyes fascinated her.

"And *you* are Captain Kells," she murmured ironically.

That slightly jeering smile flashed again. "Aye," he said coolly. "But as I told you, dear lady, there is no need to be affrighted by the name. 'Tis well known that Captain Kells never does harm to women."

Yes, she thought with an inner sigh, *that was well known of him. He did not damage their bodies—it was their hearts he left in disarray!*

She did not challenge his statement, but sat at gaze, studying this tall languid impostor in his elegant gray satin.

Gray, she thought stabbingly. *Someone must have told him that Kells always wears gray. . . .*

Her gaze, which had drifted to his satin coat, moved up again to that dissolute reckless face. For all the emptiness of those strange gray eyes, there was heat in the look he gave her.

"Perhaps you should show me the rent in your coat that I am to mend," she suggested hastily, for she had seen his eyes stray from a consideration of her breasts in her low-cut gown and wander briefly in the direction of his curtained bunk—and she wished at all costs to forestall any discussion of *that.*

"After supper will be soon enough," he told her

carelessly. "More wine?" Without waiting for her answer he was filling her black leathern tankard.

Carolina decided to jolt him from his present line of thought. "I'd have thought you would have taken more goblets than you could well use—from some Spanish galleon," she said curiously.

He had the grace to wince. "I have not been so fortunate with Spanish ships of late," he told her—and stopped as the cabin boy brought in their dinner.

Dining with him was a treat after the monotonous fare aboard the *Mary Constant*. There was fresh fruit, fresh fish, and bread and cheese of a more recent vintage than anything she had tasted in weeks. She suspected he had picked up fresh supplies in the nearby Azores. She felt guilty to be enjoying all this food while the crew and passengers of the *Mary Constant* peered past their winking lanterns, hoping to sight shore.

That thought crispened her voice when next she spoke. "I am surprised not to see any navigational equipment," she declared tauntingly, for she remembered how the great cabin of the real *Sea Wolf* had seemed to be littered with it.

He gave her an uncomfortable look; then his face cleared. "No. . . . Regardless of anything you may have heard to the contrary, dear lady, I do not do my own navigating."

So he knew that Kells was a navigator, she thought grimly.

She toyed with her food, too disturbed to eat heartily.

"From whence do you come, dear lady?" he asked her at last. "For I would think that surely the men of your locality are remiss if none of them has asked you to wife."

"Oh, but one has." She gave him a mocking look. "I

435

am a Fleet Street bride—if you chance to know what that is."

"I know very well," he said. "You are from London, then?"

"No." She sighed. "But I have been living in London of late."

"And your Fleet Street husband?"

"Has left me," she said with a shrug. "For another woman."

Those empty eyes widened. "I am indeed surprised," he murmured. "For a man to leave such a wench as yourself—!" He poured her more wine.

"There are many kinds of men," she said bitterly, for the wine was beginning to warm her. She took a long draught of it.

"Doubtless that is so." He watched her carefully. "And women also, of course."

She decided to throw caution to the winds. "Who are you?" she demanded. "For you are assuredly not Kells."

His hand, which had been lifted to pour more wine into his tankard, was arrested midway and for a moment remained very still as those empty gray eyes considered her. A wry little smile seemed to play about his lips.

"And what makes you say that, Mistress Smythe?" She noted that he had abandoned the half-bantering "dear lady" with which he had been addressing her.

"Because I have seen the *real* Captain Kells," she declared recklessly.

He set the wine bottle down carefully and let his fingers drum lightly upon the scarred table top. "And where was that?" he asked at last.

Ah, it would not be wise to say that she had known Kells on Tortuga! Such caution as still remained in her reckless heart forbade that. "On the street in Charles Towne," she said clearly. "He was pointed out to me."

"And in what way do I fail to resemble him?"

"His shoulders are broader," she said instantly. "His hair is more brown and your faces are nothing alike."

A slight laugh escaped him. "You are a shrewd observer, Mistress Smythe, and the only person on board this vessel who has had an actual view of the buccaneer in question!"

So he admitted it! She sat back, amazed.

Thoughtful now, he poured his wine, leaned back and drank some, and then said meditatively, "So you viewed Kells once in Charles Towne. . . . You did not meet him, perchance?" he shot at her.

"No," lied Carolina through stiff lips. "I did not meet him."

"Too bad," he said with a sigh. "It would have been helpful if you could have pointed out his mannerisms and gestures—perhaps a characteristic turn of phrase."

"I did not meet him," she repeated woodenly. *And she would stick to that,* she told herself. *Whatever happened!*

"But you mention Charles Towne . . . and your name is 'Carolina Smythe'—I take it then you are from Carolina?"

She nodded. One place was as good as another to claim for this impudent fellow!

"Why do you call yourself Kells?" she shot at him.

He laughed, fingering his tankard. "Can you not guess?" he asked softly. "Is it not perfect to fly another man's flag, assume another man's identity, take what you will of life—and leave *him* to pay the piper?"

"But you have not taken so very much of life," she observed crushingly. "You have found no very good quarry—a handful of merchant ships perhaps."

"Three, to be exact," he murmured, "counting the *Mary Constant*."

"And the first Spanish carrack to pass your way would blow you out of the water," she hazarded.

"All true." He looked up thoughtfully. "But how do *you* know what quarry I have found?"

"It is common knowledge throughout the Colonies that Captain Kells has turned from plundering the ships of Spain to plundering anything that floats."

"Ah, yes." He grinned at her engagingly. "And there's the rub, isn't it? Your tone tells me that you resent the fact that a man such as myself—not even a sailor by trade—should pretend to be such a famous buccaneer?"

"I wonder why you do it."

"And I have told you."

"I think you have not," she said daringly.

He was watching her closely and now his grin deepened. "I like you, Mistress Smythe," he said. "And I think that perhaps you have not told me the whole truth either." He rocked back in his gilt chair. "But perhaps as the evening wears on, we may get to know each other better."

"I am not a sempstress," she said stiffly—for certainly he would find that out soon enough.

"I guessed as much. What are you?"

"I was a schoolgirl and a runaway. I was married in Fleet Street and deserted in London—surely such a story as mine is familiar to anyone who knows the city! I had enough money to leave London and I am now—or I was before you interrupted my journey—making my way to Bermuda and thence to America."

"Where in America?" he asked idly.

She gave him a frank answer. "I had thought of

Philadelphia," she said, "because I have a sister there. But I really do not care so long as I put enough distance between myself and the man who betrayed me."

"But we are betrayers all," he murmured, watching her narrowly as he balanced his gilt chair precariously on its two back legs.

"You will bring yourself down if the wind comes up," she told him resentfully, indicating the way he was sitting.

He laughed and brought his chair back onto its four legs with a slight crash. "Right enough, dear lady. And now that you know my well-kept secret, what am I to do with you?"

"You might put me ashore on the nearest island of the Azores," she said resentfully. "So that I might join the other passengers of the *Mary Constant* and continue my journey."

"No." He gave her a sunny smile. "I hardly think I will do that. Tell me about this man who deserted you."

"I do not want to talk about him!" she flashed. "Indeed I have forgotten him already!" Her flushed face gave that the lie.

He sat studying her—and she could not know that he was wishing at that moment that *he* could have been the man to bring such fire to those silver eyes, to have made those beautiful breasts in their ice-green satin prison rise and fall so rapidly. He leaned forward and offered her more wine.

She took it readily.

"He was a betrayer," she said, her voice trembling. "He made me believe that he loved me."

"And then he left?"

"And then he left with another woman!"

"Ah, yes," he said in a consoling voice. "And

doubtless you seek revenge?" His face was amused, but Carolina, perturbed at the thought of Rye's faithlessness to her—and faithfulness to the memory of someone else!—missed the implication.

"I seek a new life," she muttered—and recklessly drained her tankard.

"Mistress Smythe," he said suddenly. "I believe that you are nobody's fool, and so I will lay my cards face up upon the table."

Carolina was feeling a little dizzy from so much wine swallowed so fast and she peered at him, wondering if he was making sport of her.

"It is important that my impersonation of this buccaneer Kells be letter perfect," he explained. "And I am told that he has a mistress—perhaps she is his wife, I am not sure. The Silver Wench, they call her, though her name is Christabel Willing. My cabin boy—the stripling who served us just now—has been constrained to put on female clothes and wear a blonde wig to make himself appear to be this Silver Wench, but he will not bear very close inspection."

Well, he had fooled Aunt Pet! thought Carolina.

"When my men told me we had truly a 'silver wench' aboard the *Mary Constant,* I gave thought to yet another impersonation. You are a most amazing beauty, dear lady, and surely no hair could be more like spun silver than your own. Mistress Smythe, will you play the part of Kells's woman, this Christabel Willing? Will you be my Silver Wench?"

Carolina gaped at him. This fake buccaneer was actually asking her to play *herself?* Suddenly the humor of the situation struck her and she began to laugh uncontrollably, rocking in her chair.

Across from her the tall man in gray looked faintly

hurt. "I have said something amusing?" he asked ruefully. "Faith, I'd have expected you to be scandalized or affrighted or scornful—even avid! Anything but to be overwhelmed by mirth!"

But then he did not know the circumstances! Carolina was sent off into gales of laughter again.

"What—what would I have to do?" she gasped when she could speak.

Those empty eyes upon her were very steady but the dark brows above had drawn together in a frown. "Very little, really," he said slowly. "There is to be another ship coming soon to these waters. It will bear a lady. And there may well be witnesses aboard who will stare through a glass at my ship and report later everything they see. And they will expect to see a woman at my side and—this is as much for the lady's protection as my own—that woman beside me had best not be a cabin boy got up as a female. *You,* dear lady, could pass yourself off as this Silver Wench without causing disbelief."

Indeed I could! she thought irreverently, managing this time to repress her wild laughter.

"But why should I do it?" she said, cavalierly overlooking the fact that she was entirely in his power.

Another smile, this one mirthless, quirked his lips. "For gain?" he suggested. "Or doesn't gain interest you, Mistress Smythe?"

Carolina gave him an irritable look. "There are some games I could not in honor play," she told him evenly. Her tankard made a small definite sound of finality as she set it back upon the table.

If she had surprised him by that flat statement, he had the grace not to show it.

"But then I take it you are already dishonored?" he

hazarded. "By a Fleet Street alliance from which the bridegroom has already flown?"

A shiver of revulsion went through her. He was right to twit her, she thought bitterly. Hers was no very blameless life!

"You say you seek a new life," he reminded her. "Remember, money can bring you that."

"Is that what *you* seek?" she asked bluntly. "A new life?"

He sighed. "No, I seek only to repair the old one. I am in sad financial straits, Mistress Smythe, and beggars cannot be choosers."

"You do not need *me* for your schemes," she said coldly.

"Ah, but I do." He leaned forward earnestly. "I need you quite badly, Mistress Smythe. Will you not do it as a favor perhaps for your host? Remember, one favor begets another."

She considered him. An attractive man, certainly, and he had offered her no harm. And yet indirectly he was the cause of all her troubles. If this man had not pretended to be Kells, had not taken Aunt Pet's ship and sunk it off the Virginia coast, she would be legally married now to Rye Evistock.

But perhaps Rye would have left her anyway, once he had laid eyes on the Spanish ambassador's lady who looked enough like his lost Rosalia to turn his face ashen! The thought brought sudden tears to her eyes, which made them dazzlingly bright. The man before her was quite dazed by them.

"Faith, you're a beauty," he murmured. "This Caribbean wench, whatever she is like, could not have half your looks."

Ah, but she has, thought Carolina.

"And if I do as you ask?" she said slowly.

"Ah, then I promise to show you all deference and set you ashore at any place you desire—once the deed is done."

Once the deed is done. "What deed?" she asked impatiently.

"Why—the rendezvous I told you about. With the lady."

"It is all very strange," she complained. "I do not know what I am getting into."

"You will not be getting into anything," he corrected her. "For like myself, you will have assumed a new identity. Mistress Smythe will become on the instant"—he snapped his fingers—"transformed into Mistress Christabel Willing, the Silver Wench of the Caribbean."

And for that she could later be called to account. Carolina realized on what thin ice she was treading.

"I have seen *her* too," she told him recklessly. "This Christabel Willing, this woman they call the Silver Wench."

"You have?" His eyes lit up. "You have actually *seen* her?"

She could see that he was impressed. "Yes. She was with Kells in Charles Towne. I got a very good look at her."

"And does she resemble you?" he cried, rapt.

Carolina shrugged. "Enough," she admitted. "We are of near the same size, our hair is the same color. Perhaps our eyes as well," she said grudgingly.

He was lost in admiration. "So you have seen her, you know how she walks, how she carries her head? Ah, you will be invaluable in this venture, dear lady!"

"I am not your 'dear lady,'" said Carolina—a trifle

unevenly for she was feeling the effects of the wine. "And I must know more of what I am getting into if I am to become this Christabel Willing."

He hesitated, frowning. Then, "Why not?" he said blithely. "For you will be as committed as any of us, once the venture is well begun. I will tell you, dear lady, that locked in a cabin of this ship there is a certain gentleman whom I now hold for ransom."

In the name of Captain Kells. . . .

"And who is this gentleman?" she interrupted. "He must be some very great lord if he can afford to pay such a ransom as would merit all these preparations."

"Indeed he is." The voice of the man across from her had gone languorous. He leant back and toyed with his tankard, his amused gaze considering her. "His wife, dear lady, is even now on her way to pay this ransom, which is to be fifty thousand pieces of eight and a ruby necklace beyond price which has long been held by his family."

"But who is this man? You must tell me if I am to help you, for I could be trapped into saying the wrong thing at the wrong time." Her lovely face was serious now for she most earnestly desired to know what sort of trap was planned—and who was most likely to fall into it.

He leaned forward and there was a gleam like that of distant candles in those strange empty gray eyes of his.

"He is the Duke of Lorca, Spain's emissary to the Court of St. James. And the lady who carries this treasure to me is his Duchess."

For the moment Carolina was rendered absolutely speechless. She felt as if a great thunderbolt had just split open the skies.

"This woman who is bringing you the ransom is *the*

Duchess of Lorca?" she heard herself say incredulously. "Oh, no, it cannot be!"

He laughed. "Indeed it can, dear lady. And make no mistake about it. The lady is sailing toward our rendezvous at this very moment, for it is she who has planned the whole thing!"

"She is—she is your confederate?" gasped Carolina, her head whirling with this new knowledge.

He nodded. "She is a most unusual lady," he added with a grand gesture. And then, giving her a level look, "She fancies me."

"These delftware plates, this wine—they are the gifts of the Duchess of Lorca?"

"The same," he told her, smiling. "She desires to leave her husband who is elderly and, I gather, tiresome. And she has chosen this novel way to do it. It would seem that she has heard of this pirate Kells—"

"Buccaneer," she murmured in correction.

His dark brows lifted but he went on. "She has heard this man Kells discussed at great length by various aggrieved dons whose ships he has plundered. They have quite a dossier on Kells in Spain, it would seem. She had noted his description well and when we met, she realized how closely I fitted it. We became— friendly." His tone implied just how friendly! "And she realized I was in sore need of funds for I made no bones about it. She seeks a new life."

"With you?" whispered Carolina, who felt the windows of hell had just opened wide and all the troubles of the world flown out toward her. "She seeks this new life *with you?*"

"So she says," he declared urbanely.

Suddenly joy washed over Carolina. *This* was why Rye had run away with the Duchess. Not for love—to get at the man who had dared to impersonate him! Her heart soared.

But it was a flight of short duration for his next words dispelled that illusion.

"The Duchess has kept everything about the kidnapping secret—not even the Crown knows of it, only his family back in Spain who after all must come up with the ransom. She plans to dupe some ship captain into bringing her to the rendezvous—and then he will be a good witness to the crime committed by 'Captain Kells.'" He chuckled. "And who can disprove it? We will all go back to our own lives again, this ship will become once again the *Alicia*—*nothing* will be traced to us. You see how foolproof it is?"

Oh, yes she saw! The Duchess planned *to dupe some ship captain*—and she had done it! Rye had run away with a woman who cared nothing for him, who was callously using him for her own ends. The Duchess had seen the impression she had made on him that day at Drury Lane, she had connived to meet him again, she had entrapped him on a sea of memories! *Oh, Rye, Rye, you have thrown me away for nothing!* Carolina thought wildly. So tightly were her hands clenched that her fingernails bit into her smooth palms. *And that woman, who had stolen from her all she held most dear, was even now sailing toward a rendezvous in the Azores and a reunion with the lover who would shortly replace Rye!*

Ah, but she would not. . . . The Duchess of Lorca, whom Carolina now hated with all her heart, would not gain what she sought. *She* would not allow it!

Filled with fury and indignation, Carolina unclenched her hands and leant back in her chair to give the lamplight a better chance to highlight the pearly tops of her breasts in her low-cut gown. The pose she had chosen was a seductive one—and she knew that too. That this masquerader was attracted to her was very obvious from the sudden softening of that hard dissolute face before her.

"But if I became your Silver Wench"—her voice held a soft note of complaint—"would that mean that I would shortly be deprived of your company, whenever this Spanish lady chose to join us?"

She could see his chest expand in his gray satin coat as he took a deep surprised breath. He leaned forward and there was laughter low in his throat.

"Dear lady," he said, and his gaze was lazily tracing the curving line of her throat, lingering over her delicately moulded breasts as he spoke. "Our fortunes are all on the knees of the gods. Who knows what will happen? The night is soft. Shall I sail you ashore to a black sand beach to discuss it?"

Tense as she was, Carolina could feel her heart stirring. For not only did she feel rage to make her quiver, but the man before her was an interesting fellow—one who in other days would have made her heart beat faster on his own merits and not merely as an instrument of revenge.

"Why?" she murmured in some surprise. "Are we then so close to the Azores?"

"To one island at least," he told her, smiling. "We can reach it before the moonlight has departed."

Carolina lifted her tankard in a mocking salute—and it was a salute to a nameless future and a farewell to her past. "To black sand beaches lit by moonlight!" she said and touched her tankard to his.

"And to silver wenches gleaming upon that sand," he murmured. He pushed back his chair and went up to give the order to take them to shore.

Carolina remained at the table, trembling slightly.

For her the cards had long ago been dealt, far away in a sunny courtyard in Salamanca, Spain. She would play out this hand and when it was over, she promised herself, she would have stolen away the Duchess of Lorca's lover—even as the Duchess of Lorca had stolen *her* lover away!

When the man who pretended to be her buccaneer returned, she looked up questioningly. She saw that he was carrying another bottle of wine, and a crooked half smile played over his mouth.

"Dear lady," he said whimsically. "It seems that I was wrong—as I so often am on matters nautical. We cannot make the black sand beach by moonlight's end. Indeed I find that there is a dangerous channel which lies between here and there that is best negotiated by daylight. I have said it is no great matter, we will reach the black sand beach by tomorrow's moonlight. And so, dear lady"—he threw his arm wide in an expansive gesture that included the curtained bunk—"the night is ours to do with as we will."

Carolina drew a quick ragged breath and the blood seemed to race to her head.

The moment was upon her.

PART TWO

The Silver Wench

How will I face the morning?
For that's when my tears will start. . . .
How will I square with my runaway pride
That I let you break my heart?

1689

Chapter 26

This too attractive man who called himself Kells was looking down at her now with hot eyes that seemed to disrobe her.

"More wine?" he asked softly.

And Carolina, her throat suddenly gone dry, nodded. In that moment she almost sprang away from him in revulsion, she almost cried out, *No, I will never lie in that sumptuous rumpled bunk with you for I belong to Kells—the real Kells, not the imitation!* But the moment passed. She took the wine with shaking fingers.

"'Tis the best the Duke of Lorca's cellars could offer," observed her newfound captain, standing close by. "Furnished by his Duchess." He gave a wry laugh.

Carolina, who had just taken a sip of the strong wine, choked. And as she tried to catch her breath, there rose up before her a vision of the Duchess of Lorca as she had seen her that day at the theatre—regal and elegant in rustling black. And masked, as if to hide the soul. She seemed to see a mocking smile on that challenging olive-skinned face, a derisive smile that she had not seen at the theatre.

It was that sudden stabbing vision of the Duchess that made up her mind for her. Like a burr beneath a saddle was that vision. Her heart lurched and then it was off and running. *The Duchess should not have them both!* She might have snared Rye but when she arrived in the Azores she would find *this* tall Englishman had another lady in his heart—and in his bed.

Recklessly Carolina swallowed down the rest of the wine, felt it burn down her throat.

She set down the blackjack tankard and rose sinuously, pretended to lose her balance.

Gallantly he stepped forward and caught her against his chest.

"I think I have had too much wine," she murmured with a little laugh and looked up at him, saw the delight in his eyes as she continued to lean against his broad chest.

This would be the most cold-blooded thing she had ever done in her life, she knew. Back in London she would promptly have struck down anyone who even hinted that she might do such a thing. But now she had a heart full of fury to drive her onward. Not only would she drive a wedge between the Spanish duchess and this cat's paw of hers, this man who pretended to be Kells, but she would in her own way get even with Rye. In a way too she was punishing herself for being fool enough to love a man who did not love her when she leaned against the stranger's chest, and in quite another way she was assuaging her feminine pride which had been struck a blow as well as her heart when Rye had left her.

It was a tantalizing woman, a seductress who smiled

up through a fringe of lashes and trailed experimental fingers down her captor's chest.

"Did you say," she murmured, "that I was to occupy the doctor's cabin?"

"Only if you wish to," he answered, smiling down at her, and she could feel his urgent masculinity in his very gaze. "I had hoped you would prefer better quarters." With a gesture of his arm that rippled the froth of lace at his wrist he indicated the great cabin that surrounded them.

She gave a low laugh. "You are right," she said. "I *do* prefer the best. And it would be naughty of me to disturb the doctor's sleep, would it not?"

His face burned suddenly for he had not expected this lustrous wench to fall so readily into his arms. It was a triumphant moment.

"I will see to it that we are not disturbed," he said hoarsely and moved to the cabin door and locked it.

When he turned she stood bathed in the golden glow of the lamplight—a spot she had deliberately chosen. She was running her slender fingers in leisurely fashion through the pale blonde ringlets at her neck—and letting him view her tempting figure in profile. She turned sinuously, in a gesture designed to emphasize the feminine beauty of her lines, to show him the grace with which she moved. For she was out to lure this man, to so stun him with the fiery femaleness of her that he would forget his Spanish duchess.

She stood there posing, as if undecided.

"Perhaps I should not. . . ." she murmured, to goad him.

"Why not?" he asked, coming quickly to her side.

"Well, my wedding vows may have been taken in Fleet Street, but I still am a bride, for all that." She sighed.

"All this heat over a wandering husband?" he said lightly and those gray eyes narrowed. He laughed. "Permit me the honor of helping you exact your revenge!"

She gave him a sudden frowning look. "Revenge?"

"Of course," he said lightly. "Do unto him as you tell me he's already done unto you." His smile broadened. "Take a lover. Myself, for example." He made her a courtly bow. "At your service, Mistress Willing. Unless"—he rose from his bow smiling wickedly—"I find you un-Willing."

She ignored his pun. "It would be a lovely revenge, would it not?" she murmured. "Still . . ."

He sensed that she was wavering and he put his arms around her as if to keep her there. "I will make you forget him," he said urgently.

"Will you?" She gave him an oblique look. "But then it could all end so badly. . . ."

"What are you saying?" he asked, puzzled.

"I am saying"—her hands had slid beneath his satin coat, she was unfastening his shirt as she spoke, her slender fingers moving delicately, ruffling the hair of his chest—and causing his body to lurch as he responded to her touch—"that if I find that bed attractive"—she nodded significantly toward the bunk—"that I should take it amiss if I were to be pushed suddenly out of it for another, be she titled or no!"

His rich chuckle interrupted her last words. "If you are speaking of the Duchess—"

"I am, of course."

"You need have no fear. My interest in the lady has run its course. There have been too many others before me and there will be too many after. The Duchess of Lorca is not a woman to be faithful to one man for long.

454

I dare say that by the time her ship arrives she will have found some new lover."

"But if she does not?" Those small, softly moving hands held him off when he would have drawn her close.

"It will make no difference," he said thickly.

"Then, my captain"—her dazzling smile promised endless delights—"I think we have struck a bargain."

That it might prove an empty victory did not even occur to her. The wine had warmed her, perhaps clouded her judgment, but her resolve was firm. She would conquer him as he had never been conquered before!

He took a step toward her but she waved him away. *Not yet . . .* her slight shrug seemed to be saying. She moved toward the bunk so that again she stood sideways to him and with a little sidling gesture kicked off her shoes.

"These are so tight," she murmured, and of a sudden she had pulled her satin skirts and petticoat up over her smooth white knee and had bent to unfasten one green rosette garter, half-seen in a white froth of chemise lace. Then slowly, with infinite care, she slipped off her silk stocking and stood contemplating it for a moment, then tossed it lightly over a chair. Standing now on one bare foot, she lifted her other foot to the edge of the bunk, tossed her skirts lightly up over a bent knee dusted with gold by the lamplight, and with great care removed her other rosette garter, held it up as though to inspect it, then tossed it onto its mate on the seat of a nearby chair.

"I could help you with that," he said hoarsely, for he had stood rooted in his tracks, watching her.

She laughed. It was not her usual laugh—indeed it

could have been some other girl laughing. "No, you would tear my stockings," she objected. "And they are my only pair."

"I will buy you more stockings than you can ever wear!" he protested gallantly.

She gave him a mocking look. "But not tonight . . ."

He subsided, watching the sheer silk slowly leave her leg.

The last stocking removed, she turned to face him, smiling, as with both arms behind her she struggled with the hooks that ran down the back of her bodice to her waist. This pretty exercise, she knew, caused her round breasts to move and ripple beneath the ice-green satin, their pearly bare tops gilded by the golden light.

She could see him take a deep breath and guessed that it took an effort on his part to keep from pouncing on her then and there.

But she wanted to drag this out, she wanted him to savor the moment, she wanted to build up the tension so that when at last she was in his arms they would be fevered arms yearning to possess her—so that she would seem to him more than a woman when he took her at last, she would seem to him a goddess!

At last she sighed and moved toward him, turning about to present her back to him in a little gesture of mock defeat.

"Hooks have always given me trouble," she murmured. "And these down the back of this bodice are entirely beyond me. Could you—?"

He could. He did. His fingers trembled with anticipation as he unfastened the last hook and eased her bodice away from her smooth pale back, tantalizing in the lamplight through her sheer chemise.

She felt the ice-green satin bodice slide away from

her. She told herself dreamily that this was the only logical course of action to take, the only way. And besides, she was a woman of tinder, and she was catching fire at his touch.

She turned to him, smiling, and let him receive full force the splendor of her eyes, silver and luminous and golden-flecked in the yellow glow of the lamp. Half out of her satin bodice now, she reached up and pressed both palms against his chest.

"I am not wrong about you, am I?" she murmured.

"Wrong?" His tense face showed some alarm, for he wanted this splendrous wench to come to his arms willingly, desiring him. "How so, dear lady?"

"You are not owned by this"—her voice flicked the word contemptuously—"this duchess? You are not her little lap dog to be ordered about?"

Her words stung him. "I am nobody's lap dog!"

She laughed that she had drawn fire, and traced little patterns on his face with the tips of her fingers. "I am glad to hear it, my captain." She had decided to call him "my captain" for it would have jarred her to call him "Kells." "For myself, I like a man of strength—and independence."

"You're an impudent wench," he muttered and would have wrapped his arms about her on the instant but that she struggled away from him, protesting, "You will tear my chemise! And where in these godforsaken islands am I to get another?"

He desisted then, gentleman that he was, and stood at gaze, watching her slither out of her dress, unfasten the waist of her petticoat, delicately step out of it, turn with a smile, then fold it carefully.

She wanted him to wait. She wanted him to be impatient. She wanted him to fall in love with her.

Whether she broke his heart was of no consequence. All that mattered now was to erase the Duchess of Lorca from his heart and from his thoughts!

"Turn off the lamp," she insisted. "I am shy."

Her previous boldness had given that the lie and he protested that he was eager to see the chemise—which hid so little, sheer as it was—fall from her shoulders and leave all revealed.

She pouted prettily. "You are wicked," she murmured and slipped behind the curtain of the bunk.

A minute later a pale arm came out with the chemise dangling from her fingers. She leaned far out—far enough that her long fair hair, which she was unloosing with her other hand, streamed down over her shoulder, and the bunk's curtain for a moment did not obscure one beautiful naked breast.

He must have ripped off his clothes, she decided, for his naked form was beside her almost before she had closed the curtains over the alcove that hid the bunk.

Every artifice Carolina possessed she used that night. Bent on enchanting him, she was laughing and playful, by turn teasing and passionate. Her hands, her lips, were everywhere—promising untold delights. He himself was an experienced lover, she was to learn, but there was that about her that drove him wild. A certain storminess of the spirit perhaps, that was communicated to him through her soft open lips, her firm agile young thighs, her slender amazing body that seemed to match him, stroke for stroke, heartbeat for heartbeat.

She knew it wasn't right, she knew she was making love for all the wrong reasons—in her heart she knew it. But lying in that tumbled bunk she wasn't listening to her heart. She was listening to her brain, which told her—cold-heartedly, ruthlessly—that in this simple way she could achieve vengeance.

And then her woman's body took over, her sensuous physical self, that self that loved life and loved men and loved sex. Her female body let itself go in a wash of pleasure, of passion, of release. . . . And it *was* a release. She had a beautiful sense of unreality lying there beneath him, of floating somewhere between heaven and hell, and the glow that surrounded her now was a fragile thing—like sheerest crystal, it would break at a single strong beat of the heart. But that break would come in the morning when she had had time to think—not now, not in these breathless moments of passion when their strong young bodies strained together in silent bliss.

There was about her tonight a wild tenderness for she had never played at love before. Love had always come first with her, the most important thing in her life—and now she brought to their joining a kind of teasing half commitment that intrigued this jaded roué.

What a courtesan she would have made! he thought. Half child, half woman, all female. All desirable.

He spoke little. He was not a man who talked while making love. But he knew the moment when her fiery spirit joined with his in a reckless rhythmic race to the heights, he knew from her involuntary quiver and from the soft moan in her throat when she had reached the brink, and exultation filled him, that he could enthrall this woman of light.

He let her go with a kind of wonder.

She lay against his damp body, cradled in the crook of his arm. "You are tired?" she murmured impudently. "Rest a few moments—it will refresh you!" She buried her face against his chest.

"Witch!" he accused her, laughing. "Insatiable witch!"

She sat up and swept aside the curtains of the bunk. "It is warm—I would seek the sea breeze."

Naked, she strolled through the moonlight toward the bank of stern windows that let in the soft breezes that caress the Azores.

Feeling strangely content—and yet excited as well— her captain lay on his side, holding open the curtain of the bunk with one hand, and watched her, marveling at the beauty of her body, at the cleanness of her lines, at the subtle grace with which she moved.

"Wonderful," he murmured, not realizing he had spoken aloud.

She turned then and the breeze took her hair, blowing it in a disheveled cloud of light around her face.

Lying there, he knew he would never forget that sight; it would be with him always: the wild haloing tendrils of white-gold hair blowing about that smiling face and perfect body in the moonlight.

It was a good thing her eyes were shadowed for they were not smiling. They were the haunted eyes of a woman who seeks—and does not find. She had reveled in his masculinity, for he was a magnificent animal— although not quite so magnificent as one she had known. But now she felt again restless, unsatisfied. And somehow cheated.

She wondered if it would always be so.

Perhaps . . . if he made love to her again? Perhaps that was the answer. Perhaps *that* would still this restlessness of the heart.

"Come here," he said hoarsely and she moved toward him, a golden moon-washed temptress, endlessly enticing.

This time she did not reach up and draw the curtains of the bunk. This time she let his hot gaze scan her up and down at close range, acknowledged with a slight deprecating movement of her shoulder his murmured, "Lord, you're beautiful. I've never seen anything like you."

"You are prejudiced toward women you've made love to," she said calmly—and they both laughed.

It was a laugh that broke the ice for them, and this time his lean body bore down upon her in a spirit of lighthearted camaraderie as well as passion.

"Impudent wench," he said as his hard masculinity found its goal and he felt her body stir again with desire. "I'll make you cry 'Enough!'"

She was but a breath away, matching her throbbing rhythm to his own.

"Will you, my captain?" she murmured with a tantalizing smile. "You can try!"

And try he did. It was sheer exhaustion that pulled them apart at last and left them lying side by side on the damp sheets of the bunk, their bodies warm and touching in the afterglow of passion.

"Dear lady," he murmured tiredly as he drew away. "There is no one like you—anywhere."

Carolina did not answer. She lay staring upward into the darkness.

Someone else had said that to her once.

And *he* had proved untrue.

Chapter 27

Carolina woke in the great cabin with the sun streaming in over her naked body—and at first she was bewildered and did not know where she was. Pulling aside the curtains of the alcove, she sat up and looked about her. She was alone. The man who masqueraded as Kells had gone off somewhere—and closed the bunk's curtains when he left.

Silently she lay back, remembering last night.

She had done what she had never before thought conceivable: She had broken her vows, she had let another man make love to her.

Not that Rye's vows counted for much, she told herself with a curl of her lip. But her own vows—both those she had taken on board a buccaneer ship in Cayona Bay and those she had taken again before a smirking fellow in Fleet Street—*those* vows she had taken in her heart and had meant to keep. Always.

A shudder went through her. She felt dishonored, vile.

Trembling, she turned over and pressed her face into the pillow, wishing she could end her life.

But . . . it was not in her to run away in that fashion. Indeed she would have called that a coward's way. Whatever she had done, she must face it, live with it. She alone was responsible for what she did.

For a long time she lay in silent aching misery face down in the bunk, half smothered by the pillow.

It was there the tall Englishman found her. He paused as he entered the cabin door to drink in the beauty of the girl lying naked, face down on the bunk with her disheveled pale hair spread out in a gleaming mass around her. His hard eyes softened at the sight. Last night she had been wonderful, driving him on to new feats of passion.

Now in morning's light her smooth young body had all the fresh dewy loveliness of a very young girl, an appealing innocence that made him suddenly wish to shield her from life's hurts.

Such thoughts were a new experience for him.

He moved toward the bed, leant over and passed a caressing hand down her spine—felt her quiver at his touch. Carelessly, he played with her buttocks.

She turned over abruptly and sat up, facing him. Her eyes were very bright but he did not guess it was the shimmer of tears that made them so.

"Good morning," she said—and eluded him when he sat down on the bed and would have caught her to him.

"Good morning," he said, adding a little wistfully, "Would you not like to go back to bed for a time before breakfast? You were up late."

Late indeed! But this morning a reaction had set in and she did not want the touch of his flesh—it would only serve to remind her of what she had become.

"No, I am going to dress," she announced briskly. "And I'm ravenous. Cannot that cabin boy who blushes so prettily whenever he looks at me, be persuaded to bring us some food, my captain?"

"Breakfast you shall have, dear lady." Her captain rose as briskly as she. He went out while Carolina took a quick sponge bath in the basin she found in a small cupboard and looked about for something to wear for she did not wish to spend the day on deck in this elaborate gown.

She noticed now what she had somehow missed last night. Reba's boxes and Mistress Wadlow's had all been brought to the great cabin and stood inconspicuously in one corner—obviously someone believed that they belonged to her! Ah, he had been very sure of her, this masquerader! she thought grimly. Or perhaps *all* the luggage from her cabin on the *Mary Constant* had been gathered together hastily and brought in this morning while she was asleep. . . .

In any event, she folded away her ice-green satin and dressed herself instead in the sprigged yellow muslin she had borrowed from Reba. The dress seemed to impart to her a gaiety she did not feel and she looked a carefree lass indeed when "her captain" and the cabin boy returned, bearing food and drink.

His eyes lit up at sight of her, standing so jauntily.

"Faith, you'd grace any board," he murmured appreciatively as he seated her at the battered oaken table.

"I think it is a courtier speaking," she said dryly.

"And you have heard many courtiers speak, I don't doubt?" he teased.

So he was still curious about her, still did not accept her story entirely at face value. . . . Perhaps it was women like the Duchess of Lorca who had made him so distrustful.

The thought of the Duchess hardened her weakening resolve. She gave him a shadowed tantalizing look from beneath her lashes. "Perhaps . . ."

He studied her as they ate. It was pleasant to breakfast on eggs and delicious little hot cakes. She wondered whimsically if this pirate who could not face going to sea without forks had brought along some treasured cook from his country house as well! Oranges, bananas and pomegranates filled a large tarnished silver bowl at the center of the table—another gift, no doubt, of the Duchess of Lorca, Carolina thought resentfully. Considering its condition, it had been cherished no better than her memory had been last night!

Still, one could not be sure, she thought as she bit into the juicy flame-orange pulp of a pomegranate. And she must find a way to bind him to her if she hoped to rout the wily duchess!

"I am surprised you could be persuaded to turn to piracy since you have told me you are in truth no sailor," she commented.

His graceful shrug rippled the flowing cambric of his white shirt. "I took what was offered," he responded with equal frankness. "Had an opportunity even half so good turned up on land, I would have preferred it."

"Yes," she laughed. "I cannot see you dining eternally on mouldy sea biscuits as one must on long voyages! Indeed, I am sure you must have scurried here to the Azores as fast as you could, to get away from a tiresome ship's diet!"

"Indeed you are right." He smiled on her with perfect candor as he lazed across from her. "I sailed direct to the Azores under a mountain of canvas and then did a bit of prowling round about the islands to see if there was some easy prey to be pounced upon."

"And found the *Mary Constant*," she said ruefully.

"To my infinite relief!" He lifted his tankard of wine. "A toast to your eyelashes, dear lady!"

"It is too early to toast eyelashes," she objected, giving him a challenging look.

He was very striking this morning, she thought, and he did not look tired despite his efforts of the night before. In deference to the weather, which was warm, he had removed his satin coat and was dining in shirt and trousers. The ruffled cambric of that shirt was spotlessly clean and well pressed. She little doubted that he had found some island woman to do his laundry—and possibly to share his bed.

She voiced the thought.

"The laundry, yes—the other, no," he said with amused regret. "For these Portuguese guard their women well. Indeed they shroud them from head to ankle in a black hooded cloak they call a *capote e capello*—and all you can glimpse of them is a pair of bright eyes or perhaps a smiling wind-burned face as they turn away from you."

"Then I should *hate* life on the Azores," Carolina said with feeling, shuddering at the idea of having her lithe young body enveloped day and night in a long black hooded garment!

"Oh, I am sure there are island beauties under the cowls," he said with an impudent grin. "Do you think I should search them out?"

"Not on my account," she said—and he laughed.

"No, I rather think you are a woman who jealously guards her own." He regarded her narrowly.

I was once, but perhaps I am changing. . . .

"The ship has been in motion ever since I woke," she observed. "We are obviously heading somewhere."

"For Pico," he said. "It is one of the islands in the Azores' central chain."

Restless, and wishing to avoid going back to bed with him in her present mood, her captain had no sooner laid down his napkin than Carolina expressed a desire for fresh air.

As she came out upon the deck, with the tall Englishman just behind her, Carolina saw past their stern the sails of the *Mary Constant*. Unharmed, the fat little merchant ship bobbed nearby, looking as if her passengers might be gone down somewhere below and would at any moment return. It gave Carolina an odd turn to see the ship riding there, looking so innocent— as if she had never been plundered by pirates, her crew and passengers set adrift. She could almost believe none of this had ever happened and that a moment from now she would wake up and see Reba rising and hear Mistress Wadlow gibbering in her sleep—on her way to Bermuda. She turned, startled, to the man who accompanied her.

"But you have not destroyed the *Mary Constant!*" she exclaimed. "I thought—" She let her voice die away at what she had thought.

"You thought I would have burned her by now and sunk her." He frowned. "But she is a goodly vessel, dear lady—and worth a deal."

"And you think to put a prize crew upon her and sell her in Tortuga to one of the traders who come there to buy captured ships?" she suggested.

The tall Englishman gave the wench beside him a frowning look. It was indeed what had occurred to him—what had in fact deterred him from promptly firing the trim little merchant vessel. But Tortuga was Kells's stamping ground and he feared to show his face there. It was indeed a knotty problem.

"I have not yet decided what to do with her," he said shortly.

Carolina turned her head away to hide her suddenly knowing expression. It was easy for her to guess his predicament!

Definitely on her bad behavior this morning, she now turned to the cabin boy who had served them their breakfast. He was just passing by in tattered shirt and trousers torn off at the knees. "You can throw away your blonde wig and your dress," she told him flippantly, and was amused to see the dark-haired lad start in surprise and turn crimson.

"The lady means that we have found our Silver Wench, Ned," translated his captain. "And she knows us for what we are."

The ship's doctor was leaning on the rail nearby and heard that. He turned and looked Carolina insolently up and down; she felt his gaze tearing right through her muslin gown. "She looks the part," he admitted. "But the real Wench is said to be a lady. How does this one talk?"

"Watch your tongue, Yates," said his captain roughly and the "doctor" subsided. "This lady is under my protection."

With a shrug Yates turned away but Carolina felt a shiver go through her. She was very much alone on this vessel and playing a desperate game—with none to save her if she slipped up.

The tall Englishman had noted Carolina's slight shiver.

"Don't mind Yates," he said quietly as they took up a place at the rail. "We needed a ship's doctor to sail with us and he's a fair barber surgeon in case of accident."

"Keep him away from me," she muttered. "I don't like the way he looks at me."

"No, nor do I—ho, there!" He clutched the rail and reached out to steady Carolina as a sudden list of the ship almost threw both of them off their feet. "I hope that navigator knows what he's doing," he muttered. "He came well recommended, but I had to have a man who was above all else discreet, and God knows he has got us here in one piece, but these are treacherous waters!"

Carolina glanced back at the *Mary Constant,* sailing along briskly behind them, manned by a small prize crew. "You should have kept Captain Dawlish in charge," she remarked. "He is a good sailor. He would have had no difficulty negotiating these waters." ·

Her Englishman gave an expressive shrug. "Ah, but then he would have known too much and I might have had no choice but to kill him—or risk discovery."

The expression she turned on him was one of dismay.

"Ah, dear lady, I was but joking! I never killed anyone in my life," he told her engagingly. "This is all a glorious game to me—and one which may make me rich again!"

But the sheen of the gray eyes watching her seemed to have tarnished now. He was not quite the charming adventurer he had so briefly seemed.

She gave him a shadowed look. "But *I* will know too much," she pointed out.

"Ah, but that is different, dear lady." He flashed her his sunniest smile and leaned lazily against the ship's rail. "Captain Dawlish would have been my captive, *forced* to play his part, and none would doubt that. *You* on the other hand will stand radiant and smiling upon the deck observed by all with your hair shining silver in the sun—a perfect Silver Wench. *You* will be a part of this mad scheme—and as such likely to hang with the rest of us should things go wrong. *You* will not betray me."

"The law is fiercer to women," she murmured. "I would doubtless be burned at the stake. We will never hang together, my captain."

"'Tis death all the same," he said airily. "And I've no desire to land in hell for some time yet."

Hell is here and now, she thought gloomily. *We find our own hell, each of us. I found mine by falling in love with Rye only to lose him.* She did not voice that thought. Men preferred a laughing lass to one who moped.

"Where are we?" she asked. "For I can see land over there."

"We are negotiating the Fayal Channel," he told her. "And that little village off to starboard is Horta."

"Where you have your laundry done?" she guessed.

He laughed and stood with his arm lightly about her waist while she clung to the rail. "You have guessed my secret!"

Carolina suffered him to hold her thus while she contemplated the distant village. Crowned by lacy white clouds, the island seemed banked with bursts of colorful flowers that wandered down the slopes. Terraced patterns of cultivation lay checkerboard fashion among occasional windmills—the rich green testimony to a damp mild climate. Looking tiny in the distance but growing ever larger as the wind whipped their sails, the low white houses were set among banks of blue hydrangeas. Now as they came closer Carolina could see, wending its way down a steep narrow lane between blue hydrangea hedges, an ox cart jolting along.

There was a beach below the village and along that beach were boats which had been hauled up onto the sand. And two of them—!

"Quick," she cried. "Give me your glass!"

He obliged her and she stared through the glass eagerly at the volcanic sand and the beached boats. Yes—they were! There were the boats from the *Mary Constant,* unharmed, and looking quite at home below the low white houses. Which meant—although she could not see them for they were undoubtedly resting or dining in those houses she could see through her glass—that the passengers and crew of the *Mary Constant* were all right; they had made shore safely. Reba and Mistress Wadlow had lost their luggage—but not their lives.

Buoyed by this good news she returned his glass with a brilliant smile. "It's a lovely island," she told him.

His dark brows lifted. "Lovely indeed," he murmured, putting aside the glass. His gaze was not on the island, though, but on the pair of white shoulders before him. Lightly he took those shoulders in two caressing hands. "But alas, dear lady, Horta is not our destination." He sighed. "Our destination is somewhat more bleak, as you will observe."

With his hands on her shoulders he propelled her about so that she might look off to the port side of the vessel. There rising out of the mist was a sight Carolina would always remember—the great bleak cone of a volcanic mountain. Dark and menacing, it came up out of the sea to tower some seven thousand feet—a sleeping giant, seemingly at rest.

"Pico," he said, waving an arm whimsically across the Fayal Channel at the great sea mountain that rose like a black wall before her astonished gaze. "Our destination lies around the point yonder—no, perhaps you cannot see it from here. It is Espartel Point and beyond we will find a black sand beach. It is where we are to rendezvous."

"A strange choice," murmured Carolina, thinking that Rye would surely have chosen Horta or some other pleasant place to await the ransom ship!

"Yes, well"—the Englishman sighed—"the Duchess of Lorca has no great regard for my navigational skills, nor does she trust my navigator. She said—and said it with some asperity"—his wry tone suggested with just how much asperity—"that it was the one place I was likely to be able to find in the vastness of the Atlantic since its peak sticks up taller than the mountains of the rest of the Azores."

"A good choice for her," Carolina muttered caustically, looking up resentfully at the inhospitable landfall the Duchess had chosen for them. "Black—like her heart."

"And her mantilla," he laughed. "But we must not think of her too badly, for it is the Duchess who brings the treasure to us."

Carolina watched the sea scud by and contemplated the great hulk of Pico, looming ever larger to port. She could not know that what she gazed on was—like the tip of an iceberg—the only visible part of a mighty undersea mountain, one of a chain of undersea mountains that rose from cold dark unimaginable depths to break the shining surface of the sea. These were the peaks of the mid-Atlantic Ridge, sea girt islands of fire and brimstone, their shrouded peaks concealing crater lakes, jewellike blue and green calderas where once fire and ash had burst forth to heaven—and would again. From the sides of these sulphurous unforested mountains rising from the sea, hot springs gushed and ran down—on the older islands—through banks of flowers to steep scree-lined shores and black sand beaches, sooty dark against the white surf.

Fascinated, Carolina stared at the black mountain, endlessly tall, rising above her.

Pico—their destination.

A bleak place and drear—chosen by the Duchess for its inaccessibility, no doubt. And because it was a place to hold secrets.

Carolina's lovely face hardened.

She would use it for the same purpose—as a place to guard secrets!

And perhaps to give *one* secret away.

THE ISLAND OF PICO, THE AZORES

1689

Chapter 28

Staring up at that black mountain, Carolina made up her mind. Here on Pico she would throw out the dice—win or lose. With that in mind, as they sailed round Espartel Point, she turned to the tall man at her side.

"I should like a swim," she said regretfully. "It is too bad we cannot have one."

He looked over the ship's side at the blue-green water, clear and tempting. "I do not see why not," he said calmly. "Once we have cast anchor."

"Oh, no, I couldn't!" She looked shocked. "Swim without my clothes here by the ship? Your crew would be watching!"

The thought of her lithe body slicing through the clear blue-green water heated his blood. She would be a mermaid, he thought, miraculous, with her long fair hair trailing, a sight for a man's eyes to feast upon.

"I would order them all to the other side of the ship while we swam!"

She gave him a whimsical look. "And do you think

they would obey you? They would all be finding
something desperately urgent to do, some rigging come
loose, a ratline fraying—anything that would bring
them over to peer over at us!"

He frowned at that. He was eager for the display of
her white body but he wanted that display to be his
alone. "There is a beach yonder. It is of black sand and
rubble but the ship's longboat could take us there—and
pick us up later."

It was by now mid-afternoon.

"We could take along food and have a picnic there on
the sand," she cried. "Alone together without all this
rattle and bang of sails around us. But—no, it would be
too hot, I suppose. We would burn our skin."

"I will have my men erect a lean-to on the beach,"
her captor offered gallantly. "With a sail for a canopy."

"But even then," she objected, "they will be watching us from the ship—they will observe our every
movement through a glass as we run splashing through
the surf!"

The very thought of this elegant silver wench splashing naked through the surf, her slim beautiful legs
sending up a crystal shower of spray to sparkle against
her smooth white thighs was too much for the lean
adventurer.

"I will have the ship withdraw just around the
point," he said. "After the longboat has delivered us
and the lean-to has been constructed. We will take
along food and we can spend the night there, if you
like."

"I would like that," she murmured, gazing up at him.
"For I have something to tell you—something that I
would prefer no one else to hear."

The Englishman had often heard words like that
from feminine lips—and always the "something" meant

for no other ears had been words of love, urging him never to leave them. His heart expanded.

"But would that not upset your rendezvous with the Duchess?" she asked provocatively.

"That rendezvous is not for another week," he said with a chuckle. "For she wanted to allow time for the ransom to arrive from Spain. And besides—she is always late."

A week to woo him then . . . to make *absolutely certain* that he had been won away from the Duchess before he saw her again.

It was done as the captain ordered. In the gray ship's longboat they were rowed to shore—a bleak shoreline of black volcanic sand and rocky debris. Farther back, up the slopes of that frowning mountain that towered dark above them there were signs of life, low scrubby growth taking root here and there. In several places Carolina could see the glossy leaves of pomegranates rising from the thorny shrub. Life was finding a foothold here on the sides of the great volcano. Given time, this dark forbidding island would be as lovely as any of the others in the Azores. . . .

Swiftly the men set up a lean-to. It was merely a sail supported by poles to protect them from the full rays of the sun that beat down wickedly on the black sand of the beach, making it hot underfoot.

Ned, the cabin boy, who had come ashore with them, kept stealing surreptitious wondering glances at Carolina as he spread out a tablecloth and set upon it a large bowl of fruit, tankards, bottles of wine, and, still wrapped in linen napkins, bread and cheese. His admiration of Carolina was so apparent that it was the subject of much gibing among the crew.

At last the longboat was rowed away, leaving Carolina and her captain standing on the sand, shading their eyes with their hands and watching the longboat's progress across the sparkling water.

They strolled on the beach, they ventured a ways up the slope of the black cindery mountain. And then, when ship and longboat had disappeared around the point, they undressed—Carolina behind the lean-to sail—and ran into the water.

In the foaming incoming surf they gamboled like children. A carefree spirit seemed to possess them. Like Adam and Eve, alone in a pristine world, they could cast off whatever they had been and suddenly be innocent again, fresh and uncaring of what life might bring.

Carolina, who was a good swimmer, knifed through the blue-green water and her captor, an excellent swimmer himself, paced her as she swam. He would pull ahead with longer, stronger strokes and look back laughing at his mermaid, her long wet hair streaming behind her, her eyes sparkling like the bright droplets of water that flashed around her.

Tired at last, they struggled out of the white frothing surf and threw themselves down upon the beach. They lay there on their backs, letting the waning sun dry their wet bodies. Carolina's eyes were shut against the slanted rays of that sun, but the Englishman watched her through the slits of his half-closed eyelids. The picture she made, stretched out in gleaming beauty, lit by the last rays of sunlight against the black sand of the beach, was one he could scarce look away from.

He felt desire rising in him as he studied the sweet lines of her young body, her easy feminine gestures as she moved slightly, the better to dry herself.

But she had felt the pressure of that gaze and was watching him now from beneath lowered lashes. And before his rising desire could be expressed, she scrambled up, laughing—for it was no part of her design to let him take her too soon.

"We should dine," she told him merrily, "while there is still some light—because I see the one thing that has been omitted is candles!"

He saw that it was so and muttered a soft curse—for he had been planning both before- and after-dinner delights with this wonderful carefree wench.

"But some clothes first," she said, disappearing behind the shelter of the lean-to sail. She tossed him out his trousers and while he was donning them, put on her light chemise and joined him.

When he gazed at her appreciatively she gave him a chiding look that said as plainly as words, *Dinner first!*

They sat cross-legged on the sand in the gathering dusk and Carolina sliced the bread and cut off slabs of the golden cheese while he poured the wine. They were hungry and the food tasted wonderful. Afterward they leaned back on their elbows and nibbled the fruit.

Carolina paused in taking a bite of a golden orange. The stars were out now. "What do you plan to do with your share of this treasure?" she asked casually. "When the necklace is sold?"

His dark head swung around and he looked down on her with a whimsical smile that did not quite reach those strange empty eyes. "Why, I will save the Hall with it of course!"

"The Hall?"

He was in an expansive mood, out to impress her. "I inherited Basing Hall near Basingstoke along with half a dozen other great manors when my father died. And shortly found I had gambled them all away—all but the Hall. I married an heiress to save me, but her money was soon gone too."

"What does she think of your present scheme?"

Carolina asked curiously, surprised to learn that he was married.

"She would have disapproved," he sighed. "For she loved me dearly. But—she died, alas. . . . And now I am out to save the Hall again."

"I am surprised you did not promptly wed another heiress!"

He shrugged. "I was about to but it seemed she had fallen from her parents' favor—I could not be sure. You understand, a man in my position must be *absolutely certain* of a dowry—it would be fatal to make a mistake!"

Beneath a thin white sliver of moon, Carolina gave him a jaded look. "And so the Duchess of Lorca happened along at exactly the right time with an attractive offer and you took it?"

"Well, it was not exactly a sudden offer," he admitted. "I had been toying with it for some time. I am no seaman and did not really relish pirating as a way of life."

Carolina laughed and tossed away her orange peel. "I never imagined that you did!" *Nor do you do it well,* she could have added. *For you have left your ship and let the longboat go away and leave us here on a deserted shore. Kells would never have done that.*

"No," he said, and moved toward her with a gleam in his eye. "I was ever a lover. . . ."

"Kells," she began, using the only name he had given her a little unsteadily, pushing him away as he would have drawn her down upon the moonlit black sands beside him. "Oh, I do not want to call you Kells when we are alone. What is your real name?"

"That's right." He grinned. "You do not know it." He scrambled up and stood upon the sand, his lean body silvered by moonlight. "Permit me to introduce myself." He made her a courtly bow. "I am Robin Tyrell, Marquess of Saltenham."

Carolina found her eyes starting from her head.

This was Reba's marquess!

This dissolute charming man bowing before her was the man who had married Reba in Fleet Street and deserted her in Hanging Sword Alley! Deserted Reba —even as Kells had deserted *her*—for the fascinating Duchess of Lorca!

He peered into her face, noting her expression with alarm. "Do not let my title frighten you, dear lady."

That snapped Carolina out of it. "Your title *does not* frighten me," she declared. "It is just—just that I think I have heard that name Robin Tyrell mentioned . . . in London."

He laughed. "You will have heard of my excesses, I take it?"

"Perhaps," she murmured. But she must summon her wits. Who he was must make no difference to her—he was still the Duchess of Lorca's lover. The Duchess had taken him from Reba just as she had taken Kells from *her*. Reba, she told herself, would applaud having the Duchess lose out—by any means. Indeed, in a way, she was *avenging* Reba! She went back to the subject of the ransom. "The fifty thousand pieces of eight you can divide, but the necklace . . . do you intend to break it apart, divide the links?"

"It would be a pity, since the main pendant is a ruby of great weight, and the rest are all matched stones."

"So you do not think you will break it up?"

He shook his head. "No."

"Then the Duchess," she pursued, "will endeavor to sell it?" *Only royalty could afford to buy such a piece,* she was thinking.

He shifted his feet on the sand. "She has suggested that."

Carolina shot him an oblique look. "She will cheat you," she said bluntly. "You know that, don't you? A woman who would connive to have her own husband kidnapped is surely not to be trusted!"

He sank down beside her on the sand. "What would you have me do?" he asked whimsically. "Would you have me try to sell the necklace on Tortuga along with the *Mary Constant?*"

He had thought to jest with her, but unknowingly he had given her the opening she wanted. He had brought up Tortuga.

And now—*now* she would spring the trap that would bind him to her!

"You would be well advised not to try to sell *anything* on Tortuga," she warned him. "For you have a man on your ship who has been impersonating Lars Lindstrom and Lars lives in Kells's house on Tortuga. And if *he* did not kill you, Katje, who loves him, would! And if they only *half* killed you, I doubt me Dr. Cotter would bind up your wounds once he discovered that you have such an unattractive fellow masquerading as him on your ship!"

She watched him. *That* should wipe the smile off his face!

"On Tortuga," she continued, "they would recognize the Silver Wench, however. *She* could sail into Cayona Bay and make arrangements for the sale of the *Mary Constant.* Or the necklace. All would believe her if she announced that Captain Kells was ill of a fever that might well be contagious so that it would be best for none of his friends to venture out aboard the *Sea Wolf.* Of course," she added carelessly, "you would have to keep your ship at a good distance offshore for on close inspection she bears little resemblance to the real *Sea Wolf*."

"How could you know—?" he began.

Her voice went on, overriding him relentlessly. Her silver eyes glittered as she spoke. "Nor could anyone who had ever been invited into the *Sea Wolf*'s great cabin ever mistake it for yours. I will have you know that Kells and his lady drink from goblets of gold, jewel-encrusted. The candlesticks upon his table are of gold, his cabin is littered with navigational equipment for"—here she paraphrased one of his remarks in some derision—"regardless of anything you may have heard, dear Robin, Kells is indeed a navigator. The hangings are of a rich red, the bulkheads heavily carved, the stern windows are somewhat larger. Do you want me to describe Kells's house on Tortuga?"

He was staring at her, astounded. "You have actually *been* in Tortuga? You *know* the *Sea Wolf*?"

She nodded and her smile mocked him. "And I have drunk from those jewel-encrusted goblets at Kells's table in Tortuga and sailed away with him in the great cabin of the *Sea Wolf*."

He swore softly. "I should have known. You *are* the Silver Wench!"

"None other," she admitted. "Mistress Christabel Willing, if you please." No need for him to know that she was really Carolina Lightfoot—Tortuga did not, why should he?

He continued to stare at her, swearing under his breath in amazement. Then he rolled back upon the sand and roared with laughter. "No man would dare to dream of such good fortune! To have the Silver Wench fall into my hands just when I need her!"

"Your good fortune stretches only so far as *I* care to

stretch it," she reminded him coolly. Her sheer chemise blew against her body in the sea wind. As if she found her position cramped, she rose and stretched her slim arms above her head the better to allow her lovely breasts to ripple before his enchanted gaze.

Lying on the sand, he dragged his attention away from those winking pink crests half seen beneath the gauzy material, and stared upward into her lovely face. He saw there a sardonic expression. "How so?" he demanded.

"If I risk my life by sailing into Tortuga for you," she said scathingly, "for that is indeed what I risk if it becomes known that I am assisting the man who masquerades as Kells—I will hardly expect to find the Spanish ambassador's wife occupying my bed upon my return."

"Ah, the Duchess." Comprehension flooded him and he lay back looking rather pleased. "Well, she should present no great problem," he said at last, scrambling up.

"Indeed?" Her winglike brows shot up.

He stood before her, smiling down at her. "I would trade a dozen such duchesses for a woman of silver and moonlight," he said in a rich voice, and she felt her heart lurch. She could almost believe him. "And you are Kells's wife. . . ." He still sounded incredulous.

"Not any more," she said moodily. She turned away from him, looked out to sea. "And never unless you count buccaneers' marriages and Fleet Street marriages legal. . . ."

"I don't," he said.

She gave him a narrow look. "I thought you might not."

And when she did not continue, but stooped to scoop up a handful of black sand, and let the words fade away to be drowned in the sound of the surf, he said thoughtfully, "From your tone, I would wonder—is Kells not all they say he is?"

Carolina threw her handful of sand at the sea. "He is *more* than they say!" she said stonily.

"Then if he is such a great man, how does it happen," he asked, puzzled, "that you are not together?"

Now was the time for disclosure if ever such a time would be. She turned and looked him full in the face.

"Because he left me, Robin," she said simply. "For a woman who resembled an old love. He left me for the Duchess of Lorca."

Robin Tyrell could not have been more astonished. A myriad play of emotions passed over his face: anger that his duchess should betray him; astonishment that Kells would ever leave this woman of light; unease at this strange new liaison which could bring him unforeseen dangers.

"It is true," she said. "He has sailed away with her."

His face had lost color beneath his tan. "Then," he said thinly, "you are telling me that I will make this rendezvous *with Kells himself?*"

"With none other," she said, shrugging. "Unless the Duchess has doubly deceived you, and Kells is taking her and the Duke's ransom away to some far island to live on love and the necklace!" Her voice had grown bitter and she could not resist one last jibe—for this man, however damnably attractive he might be, had wrecked her wedding plans back in Virginia. "There is of course another possibility," she suggested grimly. "Kells is well aware of your impersonation of him and he may have persuaded her to bring him to you!"

"She is capable of it," he muttered and began to stride up and down the sand in the moonlight. "I am tempted to upanchor when the ship returns—and sail away."

"And what of the Duke of Lorca? He is aboard your ship. What will you do with him?"

He struck his hand into his palm. "Send word to Spain that I am holding him for ransom!"

She shook her head, for it was not in her plans to let the Duchess escape so easily. She wanted to separate the Duchess from both lover and ransom—yes, and expose her too as a wicked double-dealing woman! Let Kells learn a bit more about this woman who had stolen his heart! "But then the Duchess will find a way to circumvent you, Robin, for this is *her* plan, remember, and she knows all about you."

"It is even her ship," he muttered. "She bought it with gold she filched from the Duke's strongbox. This was easy for her since he kept the keys by his bed. I was given to believe that it was not just love of me"—his lips twisted—"that had prompted her mad scheme but that she had been regularly pilfering his strongbox to pay blackmail to someone who threatened to expose her past affairs to the Duke. She told me she was afraid he would find out and so—this!"

The Duchess had even bought the ship! Carolina's head reeled. "Have you money to pay your crew?" she asked.

He shook his head bitterly. "I had expected to pay them out of the fifty thousand pieces of eight."

"Then, Robin, you dare not sail away and try again to ransom the Duke, for they will surely mutiny. How long can men be asked to sail round the seas while their rations grow thin, waiting for something that may never happen? They will see at once, if the rendezvous is not made, that something is wrong. They will not accept your ready explanations, they will want to know more,

they will wring it from you! And when they learn that
you mistrust the Duchess and that this is *her* plan, they
may well take over the ship, sail you to Tortuga, and
turn both you *and* the Duke over to the buccaneers,
taking their chances that they will be forgiven and will
eventually share in the ransom—for they will say you
duped them, that they thought you to be the real
Captain Kells. No, I do not see much future for you
there, Robin."

"But what am I to do?" He frowned. "Sail back to
England?"

"That door too is closed to you. I doubt your crew
would do it. After all, you have promised them a share
of the ransom, I don't doubt. They won't want to return
without their gold."

"By the lord Harry!" he cried angrily. "I will get me
to London in some fashion or other and expose this
woman who has betrayed me!"

"No, you are not thinking now. You cannot do that
either because to expose the Duchess is to involve
yourself." She sighed. "You have dug a shallow grave
for yourself, Robin, and there is now nothing left for
you but to play the game out."

"But," he exploded, "if Kells himself—"

"There is a good chance he will not have told the
Duchess that he is really Kells," she said. "She may
know him only as 'Ryeland Smythe,' which is the name
he wore in London. It is even possible she plans to trick
him—as she seems to have tricked you. I think the
Duchess plays her own game and all of you are only
pawns."

"Oh, she plans to kill her husband all right," growled
the marquess, and Carolina's eyes widened.

"But if you were to *save* the Duke?" suggested
Carolina. "For I take it the Duchess does not care to do

the deed herself or she would already have done it—in London, she would not need to wait for the Azores! And I can assure you that however much Kells may hate the dons, he would never take the life of a lone defenseless old man! No, I think the Duchess still relies on you, Robin, to rid her of the Duke. And if we take him into our confidence we may yet be able to clear your name. And although you may not have the ransom money, you may still be able to sail this ship to Tortuga where I could sell it for you."

That the death of Kells would clear Robin Tyrell's name as well—and more handily—she had not even considered.

But Robin had, and was toying with the idea. That vial of poison the Duchess had thrust into his unwilling hand was still in his possession. Suppose . . . suppose the Duchess really did not know Kells's true identity, suppose she had seized upon him merely as someone to sail her to this rendezvous, suppose she intended to leave his body upon the sand as well as the Duke's. . . .

That would change things.

But then the treacherous nature of the woman assailed him and he voiced his thoughts. "She could have sold me," he said in a grating tone. "Indeed she may well have done so. She is a trickster, she has had many lovers!"

"I am glad to hear of her many lovers," said Carolina dryly, thinking how pleasant it would be for Kells to learn about those other lovers! "But Kells is a man women love easily and the Duchess may in her voyage have fallen in love with him."

He glowered down at her. "You know this buccaneer," he said at last. "What is Kells likely to do, do you think?"

"I do not know him so well as I thought," she said

bitterly. "But I know that he has ransomed many Spanish captives—and let many go without ransom."

He was startled. "But surely—"

"But Kells is a sentimental man, and who knows what terrible stories she may have told him of the Duke's treatment of her? Indeed he might have enlisted himself in her behalf in this venture because"— her voice blurred because the thought hurt—"because she bears such a startling resemblance to one Doña Rosalia Saavedra whom Kells once loved in Spain."

"Resemblance?" He stared at her in the moonlight. "The Duchess of Lorca *is* Doña Rosalia Saavedra—or was before she married the Duke!"

Chapter 29

"What did you say?" whispered Carolina. Her face had gone ashen.

"I said the Duchess of Lorca was born Doña Rosalia Saavedra."

"Yes, I heard you." Her voice had no strength. She felt as if a great sword had descended from heaven and cleaved her in half. Rosalia—*the real Rosalia,* not a shadow! Rosalia had come back! A dead woman had come back to take Rye from her. "Oh, God," she whispered from a dry throat. For in her heart she now faced the shattering truth: She had hoped that by proving this shadow Rosalia false she could win Rye back—and now that hope was gone. Vanished forever.

She knew Rye very well. He would not desert his wife. Rosalia, romantic bride of yesterday . . .

"You are saying they were lovers once?" The marquess was dumfounded. He leaned forward to peer down into her face.

"Yes. Lovers long ago. Married long ago." She was weeping.

"Married!" The word sprang from him like a bark. "You say the Duchess *married* this buccaneer? Then she is a bigamist, she has deceived the Duke, for surely he could not know of it—he would never have married her if he had!" A low whistle formed between his teeth. "So she has a more pressing reason to wish to rid herself of the Duke! Her first husband has turned up, her great marriage is illegal, her house of cards could come down upon her head!" A frightening new thought occurred to him. "But then she will know that Ryeland Smythe—or Rye Evistock, as gossip has it—is Kells!"

"No," Carolina said dismally. "He wore another name in Spain. She would not know that he was Kells unless he told her."

He would not tell her. Or would he?" The marquess was thinking out loud, muttering to himself. He came at last to the comfortable conclusion that Kells would *not* tell her, and so there was still a rag-tag of hope that they all might get out of this alive.

But on Carolina his words fell like so many raindrops. She had just seen her world dissolve away. For a woman who only *resembled* Rosalia, a woman who could be proved unworthy, would have left a chance for her. But the real Rosalia—never.

She had lost him.

And now she knew that she would never win him back.

In that shattering moment she was conscious only of an overwhelming need to be comforted.

"Oh, Robin," she choked. "Robin, hold me. Don't let me think, don't let me remember. . . ."

And Robin Tyrell, Marquess of Saltenham, lover of

women that he was, heard that desperate plea in her voice and was not averse to answering it.

She went into his arms like a hurt child.

They stood there, pale moonlit figures swaying upon the black sands in the shadow of a black volcanic mountain that had risen up out of the fathomless deep and made itself part of the Azores. Stood there embracing. But there was a change in Carolina since last night and Robin Tyrell felt it.

Last night had been playful. Tonight was real, and as poignant as a cry for help in the dark. Robin could feel her wild appeal throbbing through his veins even as she seemed to melt like hot metal in his arms, no longer a fascinating worldly woman playing languidly at love, but a girl whose lacerated spirit called out to him wordlessly. And the tall Englishman heard that silent wail. It reached him as clear and pure on the night air beneath the great volcano as the far-off plaintive cry of a sea bird calling to its mate, as rhythmic and enveloping as the soft steady roar of the surf racing up the black sand beach toward them.

Together they swayed, locked as one. Together sank to the black sand. He felt her supple body shudder against his, felt the white lacy surf lick at his feet as he lay stretched out with her beneath him. It was an elemental need that he answered and they embraced with a tingling savagery, timeless, the world forgot. There was a low moaning in her throat as he closed with her, and in it grief and surcease seemed blended. The pounding of the sea against rocks born beneath the ocean floor became their heartbeats, throbbing in unison.

And the masquerader, who had taken his women so lightly, was stirred to the depths of his being by the wild freshness of her, the childlike lack of reserve, the shockwaves of her ardor as she gave herself to him without restraint.

The foaming surf surged over them and their wet white bodies on the sand writhed as silvery as ocean creatures. The surf poured over them only to drain away again, leaving around them only the dark wet glitter of the sand.

And Robin Tyrell, Marquess of Saltenham, product of a misspent youth, a man who had gone through two fortunes already and was looking for another, found himself awed by the extent of his own passion for this unpredictable silver wench. Clasping her thus, as the tumult in their breasts coursed and mounted, as they strained in rhythmic passion, he had a sudden over-whelming sense that life was fleeting—and that he might never again know a night like this or a woman like this. His blood sang in his veins and he felt singularly blessed. And over the pounding exhilaration that throbbed through his veins as he took her, he felt in those splendid moments—with her wet silken body pressed against him while the sparkling surf raced over them both—that life for him would never be quite the same again.

His passion drained away at last, he looked down at her tenderly and thought that she was crying—but who could tell? For the last great surge of the surf, sweeping like a curtain of lace across the beach, had washed over their faces and sent them gasping with spray-wet hair.

Carolina sat up. She leaned her head against his chest and he held her so while the incoming tide lapped around their hips.

Curse the ransom, all he needed was the woman! For Robin Tyrell was a man of ardor and passion, and although he had loved many women he knew he had never known a woman like this one. He looked down at her and she seemed to him a wondrous jewel, there in her gleaming nakedness, something risen splendid and shining from the sea.

Tonight he needed no ransom. Tonight she alone was enough for him.

Tomorrow perhaps he would have to leave her. Tomorrow he would have to make plans. He looked down wistfully at the woman he was caressing, seeing dimly in the pale moonlight that tear-streaked lovely face, hearing her intimate sigh against his chest. Tomorrow his plans might or might not include this wonderful woman fate had tossed so surprisingly into his lap.

His arms tightened about her. Life was fleeting. Tomorrow might see Robin Tyrell, Marquess of Saltenham, carted away to the headsman's axe. But this night she was his. This starlit night by the sea. . . .

He carried her to the lean-to shelter, laid her down. . . .

Dawn came eventually though sleep had not. Carolina sat up at last, hugging her knees in her arms. She was a betrayer—she saw that now, bitterly. She had betrayed them all: Rye, Reba—and now Robin. For last night she had made him think that she cared for him and in her heart she did not. It was Rye she loved—and Rye she could not have!

Silently she flayed herself. Oh, she was not to be trusted. Indeed the world would be far better off if she were dead—and who would really care? Who would mourn if she were to walk out into the sea and swim toward America?

So depressed was she that she almost did it. She had risen to her feet and was standing on the sand outside the lean-to when she saw far out a gray ship glide around the point. She looked at it with little interest, for that would be Robin's ship come to pick them up.

A moment later a gray longboat headed their way.

"Wake up," she said wearily, stirring Robin's prostrate figure with her foot. "They're coming to get us."

She went back behind the lean-to sail to dress.

Robin was stretching when she left the shelter of the lean-to and stepped out onto the sand, shaking out her long hair to rid it of sand. He had pulled on his trousers before he came out and now he sat down, shaking sand from his boots before he dragged them on. His back was to the surf and the oncoming longboat, which was beached very neatly by several men who sprang out at just the right moment.

His boots on, Robin was still leaning back staring up at her, enjoying the sight of the blazing sunlight on her hair, watching her blink into the sunlight.

Suddenly her expression changed, grew incredulous.

"Robin," she said hurriedly. "Stand up."

For now the brilliant sun no longer blinded her vision. Now she could see that those grinning men who had leaped over the side of the longboat had familiar faces.

And Rye himself was running the longboat up the beach!

Robin Tyrell had swung around and now he scrambled to his feet. He gave her a wild look. "Is this Kells?" he demanded hoarsely.

"None other!" Rye's voice rang out and at the same time his sword left its scabbard and described a wicked arc as he bounded forward. "Stand away from him, Carolina. Has he hurt you?"

"No, he has not," gasped Carolina. But she did not

494

step back. Instead she pressed forward. "Oh, Rye, do not kill him," she pleaded.

She had never heard his voice so cold as when he next spoke.

"And why should I not? He has like as not put my head in a noose and all of these gentlemen with me as well!" He moved to brush her aside.

In panic she clung to his left arm. "Because it was not *his* plan. He was dragged into it because he needed money!"

Rye shook her off. "I care not whose plan it was! Defend yourself, whoever you are!"

"But you *will* care!" cried Carolina. "Because it was the Duchess of Lorca who lured him into this with the promise of rich rewards—he told me so!"

Robin Tyrell was hastily backing away toward the sword he had yesterday left lying on the sand.

But her words stopped Rye in his tracks. "Rosalia?" he said blankly. And then he turned a hot face toward Robin. "You lie!" he said through clenched teeth. "She would not do such a thing!"

"She could and she did!" panted Carolina, this time flinging herself upon Rye in earnest and refusing to be shaken off. He paused to extricate himself without hurting her, while keeping a wary eye on the marquess, who had by now gained his sword and was looking desperately around him at the circle of steel that surrounded him—for not a man there but had his hand on his cutlass and yearned to chop down this insolent fellow who, just when they thought they had left the buccaneering life behind them, had brought them back into the shadow of the gibbet. "Tell him, Robin, *tell him!*" she screamed. "Tell him *why!*"

"I was the Duchess of Lorca's lover," the marquess

told Kells bluntly. "So it was natural enough she'd turn to me when she wanted to rid herself of her elderly husband. *I* am in this only for the ransom, but Rosalia—"

"Rosalia intends to kill the Duke," interrupted Carolina, afraid there would be murder done here on the black sands of Pico. "And blame it on you. She *recruited* Robin because he fit your description. All the information he has about the men of the *Sea Wolf* he got from her."

This last bit of information did indeed cause a change in the countenance of the tall buccaneer.

"Is this true, Carolina?" he asked softly.

"Yes," was her desperate answer. "Robin has told me all about it."

"He has told you—?" Rye stopped short, considering her narrowly.

"I have the Duke on my ship," explained Robin.

"No, *I* have the Duke of Lorca on *my* ship," Rye corrected him. "For we took *your* ship in the night. First the *Mary Constant* with her sleeping crew—not even a deck watch posted. Then, with my men manning the *Mary Constant,* we sailed up to your ship—collided with her actually and boarded her. The sleepy crew were cursing us for bad sailors before they realized they had been taken." His lip curled. "And you call yourself a buccaneer?"

"He is calling himself a fool at this moment," Carolina said. "But you must not kill him, Rye. I do not want his blood on your hands."

From behind Rye one of his men now spoke up. "It was nice o' the Wench to cut their captain out o' the pack for us," said a voice she recognized as belonging to one Bailes. "But now I think ye might let *us* have him, Captain." He edged forward, his voice persuasive.

The suggestion brought a faint smile to Rye's lips but it sent a shiver down Carolina's back.

"Is that what *you* want?" he asked abruptly, turning to her.

"No, it is not!" She stepped forward to confront Bailes. "We can have Robin write out and sign a full confession, Bailes—one that will exonerate all of you, one that will explain everything."

Bailes laughed nastily. "When have kings ever listened? Or king's governors read papers presented by buccaneers?"

"I know that is true," Carolina agreed desperately. "But this man is Robin Tyrell, Marquess of Saltenham and—"

"Saltenham?" exclaimed Rye, startled. He stared at Robin. "By heaven, it's true! I remember seeing you once at a race in Surrey."

"My horse lost," said Robin with a wry smile. "I don't have to ask which race it was because they always seemed to lose—'tis one of the reasons I find myself in this predicament."

"Title or no," Bailes said heavily, "his blood will run just as red along the sand." He was advancing on the marquess with cutlass drawn as he spoke.

Robin retreated warily a step or two across the sand.

"Oh, Rye, stop him," moaned Carolina. "Don't you know that if you spill such noble blood as Robin's there'll be a furor that will keep you from *ever* being pardoned?"

"Hold, Bailes." Rye threw out his arm and the length of his sword barred Bailes' way. "This needs thinking on." He frowned down on Carolina. "What is your interest in this man that you plead so for his life?"

"'Tis not *his* life I plead for but yours! All your lives! To kill him would be to throw your lives away—or condemn yourselves to live on Tortuga forever. You would never see home again—except at the end of a rope."

If Rye considered this somewhat of an overstatement, he did not say so. Instead he considered Carolina. "I think there is something more," he murmured. "Something you have yet to tell me?"

"There is," admitted Carolina. "This is Reba's marquess—you remember I told you she had been seduced by a marquess in Hampshire while she was still in school? Well, she'd been living with him in London —until the Duchess of Lorca seduced him away from her!"

"But I left Rosalia on Horta with the stranded passengers from the *Mary Constant,*" objected Rye. "I did not speak to Reba but 'twas obvious they did not know each other."

"No, all Reba knew was that Robin had left her for another woman. Actually he had sailed away at Rosalia's insistence."

Rye turned on the marquess. "Is this true, Saltenham?" he asked sternly.

Robin gave a wary nod. "It is true—basically."

"And I beg you to spare his life—oh, I do beg you *all* to spare his life"—Carolina was almost in tears—"so that he can marry my best friend and make of her a marchioness for that is what she has longed to be!"

Rye quirked an eyebrow at her. "You say he has already seduced and abandoned Reba? Faith, there's no good reason to assume he'll marry her now."

"Yes, there is!" Carolina's silver eyes flashed. "With all these cutlasses to prod him, he'll be glad enough to marry her! And Captain Dawlish can perform the ceremony on board the *Mary Constant!*"

Rye's gaze swept around him at his men.

"And it would be a fitting punishment," Carolina insisted. "For death is quick but Robin here will have *years* in which to atone. For I promise you"—her voice rose almost to a wail—"that he will have the world's worst mother-in-law!"

Her words struck just the right note. Bailes, who had been glowering, hooted. There was a general roar of laughter and—Carolina saw with relief—a lessening of tension.

"Then, by heaven, we shall have us a wedding!" cried Rye. "Drop your sword on the ground, Saltenham, unless you want to be chopped to pieces."

Robin hastily dropped his sword and for a moment Carolina caught his eye. A look flashed over that dissolute jaded face that told her he knew why she had saved his life—and that the reason had nothing whatever to do with Reba.

Carolina flushed.

"You say you left Rosalia in Horta?" she puzzled.

Her tall buccaneer nodded. "Aye, there was likely to be bloodshed and I won't have a woman aboard my ship when there's fighting. *You* should remember that."

She smiled on him sadly. He had told her bluntly on Tortuga that he would never take her out with him on a venture—and he had kept his word.

"Come," he said. "I will take you to Horta."

He had not embraced her, he had shown her nothing but a stern face. Nor did his features lighten when they were aboard ship and a sulking Robin stood watching them from far down the ship's rail.

Perhaps it was the shock of finding her alone with Robin, she mused. For all she knew she had been observed through a spyglass when she had come out of the lean-to before she dressed! What was he thinking? she asked herself, stealing a look at him. He had just learned that the lady of his heart—Rosalia—was untrue, had been untrue all along. Was that the reason for his silence?

He stood beside her, lost in thought, watching the coast fly by from the railing of the *Sea Waif*. There was nobody near.

"Carolina," he said—and there was a sigh in his voice. *"Why did you do it?"*

Carolina did not insult him by saying, *"Do what?"* They both knew what he meant. She took a deep breath.

"I did it," she said in a level tone, "because the morning you left London I followed you in a hackney coach, meaning to persuade you to take me along at the last moment. *And I saw you leave with another woman!"* Her voice caught. "A woman whose perfume I had smelled on your shirt the morning after we went to Drury Lane to the play—and I remembered it because it was the perfume worn by the woman whose mask I knocked off. You broke faith with me, Rye. And"—her chin lifted defiantly—"if I had it to do over again *I would do the same thing."*

He studied her, his gray eyes impenetrable. "I still could kill him, you know," he flung at her. "All on board save yourself would applaud."

"Yes, and it would be of a piece with your character!" she flashed. "I wonder that you did not kill him on the beach!"

"I thought to. . . ." he said softly, and there was death in the dark glance that strayed down toward Robin, still lounging sulkily by the rail. "Do you love him?" he demanded.

"What does that have to do with it?" she cried, exasperated. "Robin was the Duchess of Lorca's lover and since *she* had taken *you* away from me, I meant to take Robin from *her!*" *And I have done so!* she almost shouted at him.

He shook his head as if to clear it, turned away from her and went back to his musing. His silence infuriated Carolina.

"And when we reach Horta, you can hand me over to Captain Dawlish and I will continue my journey—you will never have to see me again!"

His head did not even turn.

It was a very dissatisfying confrontation and Carolina flounced away from him and—in a perverse spirit of discontent—wandered down to where the marquess was standing.

"You had best away from me," he warned her. "Yon scowling fellow may throw us both over the side!"

"Then we'll swim to shore, Robin," she said sweetly.

A bleak look was his only comment on that. But it was a wistful look too. Because—rake that he was—he had found himself wishing, even in this extremity, that this woman of light could love him.

And now he had found that her love too was owned by the tall buccaneer whose menacing figure seemed to Robin Tyrell's gaze to fill the prow of the ship.

"Do you think Evistock really intends to force me into this marriage?" he wondered.

"Oh, yes," she said, nodding vigorously. "Reba will be a marchioness before this day is over—if she desires to be one."

He looked startled. "But how? Your buccaneer spoke as if she was among the passengers on the *Mary Constant,* but surely I would have seen her if that had been the case!"

"If you had looked beneath the widow's weeds of one of your captives," she told him tersely, "you would have found Reba. I suppose she missed you too, scurrying into a boat, head down in the dark! She is on Horta now, waiting for us. Robin, you will not—spoil this for her, will you? Reba loves you dearly, you must know that!"

The marquess looked dazed and lapsed into a brooding silence.

To annoy Rye, Carolina stayed by Robin's side all the way to Horta. Once she sighed. "I wonder what Rye sees in Rosalia," she said gloomily.

Robin snorted. "Rosalia? 'Tis *you* he loves—'tis plain to see!"

"Not to me," she sighed. "What makes *you* so sure?"

His dark head swung about to consider the lean buccaneer, out of earshot up the deck. "The way he began toying with his sword hilt the moment you began walking down the deck toward me, the way he has half turned around now so that he can observe us without appearing to, the sound of his voice when he called out to you when he came ashore—all signs of a man in love."

But his face turned ashen when he saw Rosalia, Carolina remembered sadly. "Rye has complicated reasons for what he does," she scoffed. "He is not looking at us, he is studying the shoreline. And as for toying with his sword, I doubt he was even aware of doing so."

The marquess sighed. "I wish I could agree." He continued to watch Rye warily. "Where did you meet him?" he wondered.

"In London—as a schoolgirl."

"And all this time he has been living a double life? An English gentleman and an Irish buccaneer?" He shook his head in wonder.

"Oh, more than a double life," she corrected him.

"You have forgot his days as a Spanish *caballero*."
Those days when he knew Rosalia, loved Rosalia. The
thought hurt.

"A man of many climes," he murmured. "I had not
thought I was taking on so much when I set out to
impersonate him."

"No one can truly impersonate him." She sighed.
"For there is no one like him."

She reached up to push back some tendrils of fair
hair which were flying wildly in the strong wind that
swept down from the heights and made their passage
rough—and through her fingers she studied Rye, still
standing where he had been, down the deck.

Was he really watching them out of the corner of his
eye? she wondered. She could not be sure. He *might* be
studying the shoreline of Fayal coming up ahead. But
just in case he *was* watching, she perversely turned all
her charm upon the marquess, laughing aloud at his
pleasantries, throwing back her head vivaciously and
letting her laughter carry down the deck to Rye.

"You will get me killed," muttered the marquess.
"Your buccaneer would like nothing better than to run
me through at this moment!"

"No, he will not kill you, Robin," said Carolina with
a shrug. "We are past that stage. Indeed," she added
thoughtfully, "from the look he just turned this way, he
is far more likely to kill me!"

THE ISLAND OF FAYAL
THE AZORES

1689

Chapter 30

The little village of Horta with its low white houses, set among flowers, gleamed fresh and immaculate in the morning sun. The *Sea Waif* had rounded Espartel Point, swept north into the Fayal Channel, and was now beating up the blue-green waters of the channel with the lovely island of Fayal to port and the looming black shape of Pico off to starboard. The houses became larger as they approached, the long streaks of blue became hydrangea hedges, the dots in the distance were oxen hauling carts. As they came nearer, the clouds that had obscured the peaks seemed to blow away, and above the pattern of terraces and stone walls and open fields they could see a black cinder cone.

"Pico Gordo," the marquess told her, waving upward at the peak on Fayal which, though formidable, was still dwarfed by the black heights of Pico across the channel. "My navigator had been here before and he told me that it erupted seventeen years ago and covered the mountain with ash—there is a crater lake up there in the caldera. He described the lake as a vivid green—or blue, I cannot remember which. I suppose we will not find out," he added dryly.

Carolina threw him a scathing look. Exploring calderas was not on her program today; she had more important things to do. Her whole life seemed to have funneled her here, led her down disastrous pathways to this great final disaster—this meeting with the woman Rye loved better than he loved her. . . .

As if he could not help himself, Rye now walked down the deck toward her—and found her laughing. Deliberately. To bait him.

"You seem very merry," he observed and gave the marquess so menacingly cold a look that that gentleman stepped nimbly back.

The marquess cleared his throat. "You are caught between two women, Evistock. Faith, I don't envy you!" He shook his head. "It would take the wisdom of a Solomon to know what to do in your position."

"Solomon . . ." mused Rye. Of a sudden his gray eyes lit up. He looked upon Robin almost kindly. "I thank you for that suggestion, Saltenham," he said obscurely. "I will take it to heart."

Carolina, who had been watching this exchange between the two men, frowned.

"What on earth did he mean?" she demanded of Robin, when Rye had hurried on.

"I have no idea," said the marquess, loosening the lace around his throat. "But at least he has left the immediate vicinity." He sounded relieved.

Carolina watched Rye covertly. His tall form was moving about among his men; he seemed to be talking confidentially to each of them. They were giving him astounded looks, she thought—and one or two broke into raucous laughter which was immediately quenched. Then promptly some of them seemed to melt away.

What on earth was going on?

Rye did not come near her again until they had dropped anchor just off the village of Horta. Then he strode down the deck to get her.

"You are coming ashore with me, Carolina," he told her, brusquely taking her arm. "For I will not trust you out of my sight." And when the marquess would have stepped forward as well, Rye turned upon him with blazing eyes. "*You* are *not* coming ashore, Saltenham. And do not try my patience or I may remember what you have cost me!"

Before the warning menace of that tone, the marquess stepped quickly back and watched them go.

As she climbed down the ship's ladder into the longboat, carefully guided by Rye, one thought dinned in Carolina's mind: *Rosalia is here in Horta.*

But it was not Rosalia she found when Rye, having lifted her out of the longboat, set her down to walk beside him over the black sand of the beach to a white house near the shore. It had a low-walled garden with pink and red roses clambering in wild profusion and a big yellow cat sitting in a window. The cat yawned at sight of them and then daintily began washing its paws.

There was an old woman in the courtyard wearing one of the black enveloping *capote e capellos,* but she had merry eyes in her weathered face and she gave Rye a respectful nod as he passed.

"This is her house," Rye told Carolina. "She has been gracious enough to let us use it." Carolina turned to smile at the old woman, and found she was being regarded with lively interest.

A moment later Rye opened the door and Carolina stepped in among the passengers of the *Mary Constant.*

They were gathered about a wooden table in the low-ceilinged room, talking and drinking some kind of wine which was being poured into wooden cups, and the conversation stopped abruptly when Rye and Carolina entered.

"Carolina!" Reba dropped her cup in her excitement, and wine splashed her widow's weeds as she flung her black veil aside and ran to embrace Carolina. "We were afraid you were dead!"

"Yes, indeed," Mistress Wadlow echoed. For her own widow's weeds followed hot on the heels of Reba's, to welcome Carolina back among them. There was a general murmur of greeting.

"You can take those dismal garments off now," Carolina said gaily, almost weak with relief that beautiful deadly Rosalia was not among those present. "For no one is going to steal your clothes. Indeed I am sure that all your possessions will be shortly restored to you. Will they not?"

She turned to Rye, who nodded. "It is pleasant to see you again, Mistress Tarbell," he told Reba, and the other passengers exchanged significant glances. Not Jones—Tarbell. They would have something besides their capture to gossip about this night.

"Why—Rye Evistock!" Reba looked startled. "Where did you come from?"

"He was no doubt too busy to make himself known to you," Carolina said laughingly. "And you were too busy worrying about saving your wardrobe to know who captured you."

"'Twas Captain Kells that captured us," said Mistress Wadlow severely.

"No, Mistress Wadlow, it was not," Carolina said earnestly. "It was a man posing as Captain Kells."

"Well, I hope he has been dealt with most severely!"

507

Mistress Wadlow said with a sniff. "Frightening us all to death like that, setting us into open boats in the middle of the ocean!"

Carolina drew Reba aside.

"Reba, I know you'll find this hard to believe," she said. "But the man who was impersonating Kells was your marquess."

Reba gasped. "Not—not *Robin?*"

Carolina nodded soberly. "The very same."

"Oh, I can't believe it!" Reba was looking around her now. "Where is he?"

Carolina turned back to Rye. "Could Reba be taken aboard the *Sea Waif?* I am sure Robin has something to say to her."

"Presently," he told her. "Just now, if you would all stay together in this room, ladies and gentlemen . . . ? You will shortly be taken back aboard the *Mary Constant* and will continue your voyage to Bermuda. But first we wish to search the pirate ship and find any of your possessions that might have been carried aboard her."

There was a general murmur of approval and even Mistress Hedge, who had been eyeing Carolina and Reba with some disdain, began to look upon them more kindly.

"We have but one more errand," Rye told Carolina, "before we can go back on board. I would speak to Captain Dawlish and his crew. They are in a nearby building." He beckoned her to come with him.

Carolina paused but for one thing. "Reba," she whispered, "Robin wants to marry you. Would you be willing to let Captain Dawlish perform the ceremony on board the *Mary Constant?*"

She left Reba gasping, and could barely keep up with

Rye as he strode out, shutting the door on the eager throng behind him.

The old woman was still in the garden and she watched their progress past massed hydrangeas to the next house, which was a little more impressive and had a small paved terrace. Carolina looked up as they walked through its garden among climbing yellow roses, so at odds with the dark cinder cone frowning above them against a blue sky. The lower slopes of the volcano were a vivid green and laid out in patterns of vegetation—obviously it had not taken long for plant life in this damp warm climate to reclaim its own.

Glad to be bringing the good news of the *Mary Constant*'s restoration to kindly Captain Dawlish, Carolina's step was light as she crossed the small flagged terrace and ducked slightly as she went into the dim interior of the low building.

And there she came to an abrupt halt.

Captain Dawlish was there indeed—and he came to his feet, smiling at sight of her. His crew also looked none the worse for wear.

But it was a figure standing at a small window that faced toward the slope of the volcano that captured Carolina's attention. A figure that turned lazily to regard them as Carolina entered, followed by the tall buccaneer.

The Duchess of Lorca.

She was not dressed as a proper Spanish lady—not in rustling black as Carolina had seen her at Drury Lane. The Duchess had made good use of their stay at Plymouth, and she seemed to have undergone a sea change during her voyage. She was wearing a handsome gown of crimson silk that was cut so low it almost revealed the rosy tips of her breasts. She had drawn herself up haughtily at the sight of Carolina and Rye coming in together. Her chin was lifted, her aquiline features disdainful. But her shining dark curls rested upon a luminous pale olive skin and the dark pools of her eyes were endlessly enticing. . . .

This then was the Duchess for private consumption. That other masked woman, handsome as she had been, could not touch this fiery beauty who gazed at Carolina so contemptuously.

At sight of her Carolina's heart sank—but she held her ground and gazed back just as contemptuously.

"Captain Dawlish," said Rye, ignoring the Duchess except for the barest nod, "I have come to report that your ship is unharmed and will be delivered to you shortly. You will be able to continue your voyage to Bermuda—with my compliments."

The crew members nodded and smiled their approval. They were at the moment seated on long benches around a table, drinking from wineskins. But the little captain was effusive in his thanks. He shook Rye's hand and clapped him merrily on the back. This was to be his last voyage before retiring from the sea, he explained. And to have had it end in capture and disgrace—well, he had been saved from that and would be forever grateful!

If the Duchess was bewildered by that interchange, she did not say so. She maintained an icy silence. Neither she nor Carolina spoke. They were regarding each other narrowly, each measuring the other. Deadly enemies with drawn swords meeting beneath the dueling oaks at dawn would have contemplated each other with more warmth.

And then the unexpected happened.

The heavy door behind them was abruptly kicked inward by a booted foot. Its wooden timbers crashed against the wall. Soldiery in corselets and headpieces with muskets at the ready sprang into the room. Above the hubbub as the lounging sailors leaped to their feet, overturning their chairs, a commanding voice roared in Spanish for them all to stand fast.

Captain Dawlish and his crew, so recently rescued from pirates, stood aghast at this turn of events, staring in horror through the incoming soldiery at something bright outside—the red and gold flag of Spain.

Carolina, in the dim interior, had found herself swept to the back of the room by the Spaniards. She surmised they must have been watching from the windows of one of the other houses, waiting for this moment when Rye was away from his ship to pounce upon the famous buccaneer who had a price on his head of fifty thousand pieces of eight back in Spain.

Carolina's Spanish was very good. She heard the leader of this band cry, "You are all under arrest for you are in the company of a *pirata* wanted dead or alive in Spain!"

Rye had detached himself from Captain Dawlish's company and stood a little apart. Carolina guessed that he was going to make a break for it—and knew that he would never make it. Even master swordsman that he was, he would be cut down by that massed wall of armor before he reached the door.

"I think it is only myself you want, gentlemen," he said in his excellent Castilian Spanish learnt from Don Ignacio of Salamanca. "These gentlemen with me are the captain and crew of an honest merchant ship who have recently escaped the attack of a *pirata*—and the ladies are but passengers."

Carolina struck aside a crew member who was standing uncertainly, barring her way.

"But you must not take this gentleman!" she cried.

511

"He is no *pirata*. He is Diego Viajar and this lady"—
she made a wild gesture toward the Duchess—"is his
wife. They were both my prisoners, but they escaped
and took me with them as a hostage. You will have
heard of me for I am the famous Silver Wench of the
Caribbean, wife to Captain Kells who is, unfortunately,
far away or he would make short work of you!"

She had put her head into a noose and she knew it.
Or perhaps they would burn her for a heretic once they
transported her to Spain. At the moment she did not
care.

She turned toward the Duchess—it was now her
move.

Rosalia had risen with a sinuous gesture and her
contemptuous laugh sounded scornful. "This woman
lies! Our marriage was annulled long ago in Spain!"
She stepped forward with a rustle of crimson silks and
fixed her glittering eyes upon the leader of the Spanish
soldiery. "I tell you I am the Duchess of Lorca and I
have been abducted by this man! As was my husband!"
She indicated Rye who gave her a sardonic look. "He
goes by the name Rye Evistock or Ryeland Smythe but
he is the buccaneer, Captain Kells. Seize him!"

All the joy Carolina might have felt on learning that
Rye's marriage to Rosalia had been annulled was
entirely quenched by the circumstances. She felt a sob
rise in her throat. Her sacrifice had been for nothing.
They would never live together—they would more
likely die together. But that treacherous woman would
go with them! She snatched at the dagger that hung at
the belt of the nearest Spaniard and hurled it at the
Duchess of Lorca.

Her aim was not very good. It went wide of the
Duchess and clattered against the wall—but it brought

the Duchess spitting like an angry cat to her knees as she ducked away.

"Carolina, that will be enough." Rye's authoritative voice rang out and he stepped forward and caught her by the shoulders before she could launch herself at the Duchess. "Miller, Sparks, Waite, all of you—thank you for a job well done. It was most impressive."

And now abruptly the "Spanish" soldiery had relaxed their military bearing. They were laughing and taking off their helmets and talking in English.

"A good show we put on, didn't we, Captain?" cried their leader merrily. "And we fooled the Wench!"

Rye smiled past Carolina's bewildered face and agreed. "Aye, you did. A good show."

"What—what madness is this?" cried the Duchess, scrambling up in her crimson silks, her dark eyes wild black spots in a face gone ashen. *"Who are you?"*

Their leader grinned. "Don't you recognize us? We're men that was taken on in Plymouth to make up the crew of the *Sea Waif* when she put into port there short-handed. We're Cap'n Kells's men." He nodded toward Rye, who was grinning at him. "And we was all picked because this little lady here"—he nodded at Carolina—"wouldn't know our faces since we'd never been on Tortuga."

"On *Tortuga?*" gasped the Duchess. She seemed near fainting.

Carolina gave Rye a dazed look.

"I always carry an assortment of Spanish uniforms on board the *Sea Wolf,*" he explained, "in case I decide to make a raid on the Main. I'd meant to sell these in England, but I sailed away before I'd got rid of them."

"But—why?" she asked dizzily.

He gave her a broad smile. "I wanted to know who

loved me—and who didn't," he said. "And by heaven, I've found out!" He turned to the Duchess. "Your husband is even now being delivered to the shore, Rosalia," he said. "He is an old man and his health has not been improved by incarceration in the cellar of an English inn before he was put to sea. With a little luck and your famous charm, I am sure you will be able to persuade some Portuguese fishing boat to sail you both to Genoa or to Cadiz."

"You—you have not told him that I—?" she choked.

"No, I have not told him," Kells said grimly. "I will leave him to make his own discoveries. That red dress you're wearing will tell him much for he is not a fool, your husband—only apparently preoccupied with other matters that blinded him to your schemes, Rosalia."

She gave him a wild look. "But I—"

His expression grew sardonic. "He knows only that you brought here a substantial ransom with which to free him. And that ransom is now safe upon my ship and will shortly be en route to Tortuga—along with the ship you bought with the Duke's money, which I will take along with a prize crew aboard."

The Duchess was by now collecting herself. "But it cannot end this way, Diego!" she cried. "For if you are Kells, and Kells has flown a black petticoat in memory of a Spanish lady as his standard on the *Sea Wolf* all this time, then you must have flown that petticoat for *me!*"

"No longer," he said briefly. "Now I fly a new petticoat." He glanced meaningfully down at Carolina's yellow petticoat. Perhaps not that one," he added. "But I am sure my Silver Wench has a red one that will do."

"Pirata!" screamed the Duchess. "Spawn of the Devil! Oh, why did my uncle not kill you when he had

the chance?" For it had come to her that she would never wear the necklace now, she would never claim the fifty thousand pieces of eight, she would never be free—indeed she would stay shackled to the elderly Duke of Lorca, and as soon as he saw her in this startlingly low-cut gown, she might as well be under house arrest for all the liberty he would give her!

"Spawn of the Devil I may be, Rosalia," responded Rye coldly. "You are the best judge of that for you are surely the Devil's own. Come, Carolina." He escorted her out into the sunlight and his "Spanish" troops clanked after them, bringing their wineskins with them.

"That is what you meant when you were talking about Solomon," she guessed. "You were thinking about the two women who both claimed the baby and went to King Solomon?"

Kells nodded. "And he offered to cut the child in half and give half to each. One was quite agreeable, but the other cried out no, that she would give the child up—and King Solomon awarded the child to her for he said she was its true mother." He looked at her keenly and with great pride. "It occurred to me that a similar situation would be very instructive. And Rosalia was quite willing to turn me over to certain death, while you, Carolina"—his hard gray eyes softened—"were willing to turn me over to another woman if it would save my life. And to die for me in Spain."

Carolina blushed brick-red. It was, she supposed, exactly what she had done.

"It was—the heat of the moment," she protested angrily, "that made me do it."

"Was it?" he asked skeptically.

"Yes. It was," she said with a toss of her head. For she had not yet forgiven him.

"Take the lady to the *Sea Waif*," Rye instructed his lately "Spanish" followers. "See that she has anything she wants."

"Aye, Cap'n," was the energetic reply. "We'll see to the Silver Wench for you—she'll come to no harm with us!"

"Reba has already been taken aboard," Rye told Carolina. "You'll want to talk to her, I'm sure, before she and Saltenham leave us."

"But where will they go?" cried Carolina, faced with this new problem.

"They will be allowed to follow us in the *Sea Wench*—which is the name I'm giving his ship. And they'll be transferred to the first English ship we pass. One of my men—who used to be a scribe back in Devon—is writing out the confession now for Saltenham to sign."

"But if we don't pass an English ship?" she cried. "What then?" For she foresaw short shrift for Robin if ever he reached Tortuga.

The tall buccaneer beside her shrugged. "Then I'll set them ashore on some convenient island—possibly in the Bahamas, possibly Bermuda—where they can get a ship back to England."

"Without money?" She was scandalized.

"Oh, I'll pay their passage," he said easily. "As a present for the bride who, after all, brought us together."

His voice was caressing and Carolina blushed again. But she turned her head away. Rye might choose cavalierly to dismiss this whole affair but she was not ready to forgive him—not yet.

1689

Chapter 31

On shore in Horta a tearful duchess was trying to explain her shocking décolletage to an angry husband made querulous by long incarceration. On board the *Mary Constant* the jubilant passengers were tallying up their baggage to make sure that nothing had been lost. On board the newly christened *Sea Wench* a buccaneer prize crew was drinking from wineskins and calling taunts down into the hold at the former crew that had manned it.

But in the great cabin of the *Sea Waif*, the buccaneer captain and his lady were having other difficulties.

No sooner had she entered than Carolina had sniffed the air and turned vengefully on Rye. "I can smell her perfume! I will not stay here—set me ashore!" she cried.

"We will air the cabin," said Rye. He moved to open the stern windows. "We will fill it with a new perfume— one that belongs here," he added caressingly.

"If you leave me in this room, I will lock the door

517

against you," Carolina warned, "the moment you go through it!"

"And I will break it down," said Rye amiably. "Will that please you? To be thus besieged?"

"No, it will not please me!" she snapped. "I want to be rid of the sight of you. Why do you think I sailed away from London, leaving no one any idea of where I had gone?"

"I think you were under a misapprehension," he said in a level tone. "You thought yourself abandoned."

"It was no misapprehension." Bitterly. "You took your choice between us and you chose *her*. Admit it!"

"I do not admit it." He sighed. "I was caught in the jaws of a trap with two brides—one of the past and one of the heart. Both had a claim. Can you not see my dilemma?"

"Tell me you did not lie with her!" she demanded.

"No, I will not tell you that." His gaze was stern. "Let there be truth between us, Carolina. In London, I was drawn into the past. But remember, I thought Rosalia still to be my wife, to have a legitimate claim upon me—"

"And my claim was *not* legitimate?"

He winced. "Can you not understand how it was? New risen from the dead, she threw herself into my arms. She swore she had been forced into marriage with the Duke, she sought my protection—and before God, I believed her to have need of it, for to have bigamously married a Spanish grandee would have brought her certain death. And probably torture as well."

Carolina sniffed.

"In the light of events, it is clear I played the fool," he added with a sigh. "*That* I will most readily admit!"

Somehow his bland admission that he had fallen
under Rosalia's spell in London, that she had lain with
him in that very bed at which Carolina was just now
gazing, that they had cozily taken their meals here on
this very table on the top of which Carolina was
leaning—all this maddened her—although she had
been sure of it all along. She sprang back from the table
as if it were contaminated. "I will not have you back in
my life!" she cried. "Set me ashore—I will find my own
way to America!"

"If America is your destination, then I will sail you to
the Tidewater," he said suddenly. "Indeed I will sail
you straight up the York and deposit you at Level
Green—or up the James to Sandy Randolph's door-
step! I will set my course now."

He was striding across the great cabin on his way to
the deck when she stepped in front of him to block his
way.

"You cannot go to the Tidewater and you know it,"
she declared scornfully, eyes flashing. "Both the James
and the York are closed to you—forever. The king's
pardon you hold will not save you there. You could go
there once because none knew you—but now they
know your face. You would be seized and hanged from
the highest gibbet!"

"Nevertheless," he said casually, "if that is your
destination, I will trust none other to take you there."

Lord, how adamant he could be! She wanted to
stamp her foot, to lash out at him.

"I hate you!" she said between her teeth.

"Is that why you saved my life just now?" he asked
coolly.

"I did not save your life—it was all a charade!"

"But you did not know that when you hurled yourself

in front of the Spanish guns," he pointed out. "And consigned yourself to death as a sea rover." He smiled at the thought.

"I was distraught," she muttered. "I was not thinking clearly. I would not do it again!"

"I would hope not," he agreed politely.

"I must have been mad!"

"Undoubtedly."

"And anyway I could not let you die because—because of what you had once meant to me."

"My feeling about Rosalia exactly," he told her evenly. "When she told me her husband had been kidnapped, I felt I must get her out of her predicament —for what she had once meant to me."

Damn him, she could not get the better of him! Her eyes narrowed and she took a deep breath. "I have not been faithful to you, I want you to know that."

"No." He sighed. "Women have never been faithful to me, it seems."

"Do not compare me with Rosalia!" she flashed.

"I will not. Indeed I think you both had reason to desert me—at first. You when you thought I had abandoned you, Rosalia when she thought me dead."

"You believe she thought you dead?" she asked derisively. "More likely she deserted you when she discovered you were a heretic and she did not wish to throw in her lot with you!"

"Very possibly." He acknowledged the thrust gravely. "For now I have come to know the lady somewhat better."

"I–I deserved better than I got from you!" She felt tears sting her eyes.

"You did indeed," he agreed promptly. "But remember in my behalf that I tried to shield you, I tried to leave you in Essex in safety until I could return—"

"You did not intend to return!"

"Carolina." His voice had deepened and now he took hold of her shoulders and held them firmly even though she tried to shake him off. "I know now that I *always* intended to return. But it was my duty to find Rosalia safe harbor—or so I thought." His voice roughened with feeling. "Leaving you in London, Carolina, was the hardest thing I ever did. I ached for you this whole mad voyage. Had I known you were on the high seas, I would have pursued your ship until I found you. To hell, if need be!"

"And what of Rosalia, pray tell?"

"Old flames are hard to rekindle, Carolina. In my case they flickered out entirely. Rosalia is not the woman I knew. Life has hardened her, the world has cheapened her. The Rosalia I knew was very young, untried, greedy for life. I saw in her qualities she no longer possesses. In my heart I had tried to make of her the woman I was looking for—the woman I found in you."

For him it was a very long speech, and it went straight to her heart. It made her feel desperately ashamed of the past two nights—spent in the arms of the Marquess of Saltenham.

"It's all—ruined, Rye." Her voice broke. "We have betrayed each other—you with Rosalia, I with Robin. No matter what our reasons, we can't go back."

"We can if we forget the past, if we leave it behind us here in the Azores where it belongs," he said calmly. "Carolina, I was angry enough at first to kill Saltenham, but I have since had time to think. To realize that it was I who drove you to what you did. And when you had a choice, Carolina—you came back to me. You could have told me that you loved Saltenham, and I would have left you together—but you did not, you

521

came back to me. And tried to throw away your life to save mine. Why did you do all that, Carolina, if you do not love me?"

"I do love you, Rye." She choked out the words. But when his arms would have enfolded her, she held him off. "But I think we have no future together because although now, in the heat of the moment, you say you can forgive me, I do not really think you can."

"Why not?" he asked in a surprisingly reasonable tone. "You did not come to me a virgin, yet still I loved you. Nor does anything that has happened since alter my feelings for you." He sought for words and found them not. For how could he tell her why he loved her? That it was so much more than her winsome beauty. That she was proud and foolish and wonderful. That she tilted at life with such glowing joy. That she was gloriously loyal when loyalty was needed. That she made him feel humble that she would deign to share his life, share his bed. That just holding her in his arms had made him one of life's fortunates. No, he could not tell her all that. "I love you for what you are, Carolina." His voice had grown husky. "To me you are the one woman, the only woman. And I will sail you to Hell, if that is your desire."

Wordless, she collapsed against him, felt the strong beating of his heart through his cambric shirt. For these were words she had thought never to hear him say again.

It was all there in the timbred richness of his voice as he let his lips rove over her face, her hair, and murmured almost roughly, "Carolina, don't you know —haven't you always known—that I love you?"

And in her singing heart perhaps she had. Known it all along, down deep in some secret hidden place, known it even through the darkest times, known it even when she was reacting with spite and fury to what she had wrongly believed was his disavowal of her.

She had tried so desperately to throw herself away. Had indeed done it. But the gods who pity lovers had smiled upon her—not once but twice. They had given Rye back to her.

And now she was back in the right arms—and those arms were beckoning her on to ecstasy.

"If I didn't know," she whispered, just a breath away from tears, "I know it now."

"And now," he said, pushing her away a little and smiling down at her. "Let us marry off my rival and so be rid of him. For I'd prefer to sail with the tide. These are not waters for a buccaneer to linger in."

"Reba will be pleased for I am sure she is eager to have the ceremony held," laughed Carolina. And it was a lighthearted laugh again. Gone was that brittle mirthless sound she had heard so often from herself of late. Gone the anger, gone the hate, gone the terrible burdens that had weighted down her heart.

"And Carolina, once we get Reba safely married to her marquess, will you allow Captain Dawlish to marry us as well?"

Carolina missed a step and turned to look up wonderingly into his face.

"Shipboard marriages," he reminded her, "are legal —and God knows I've been trying to get you before an honest parson long enough!"

Looking up at him, all the shadows blew away and the world was suddenly a glad place, a scene of love and laughter, of winged things taking flight. She might never be a lady of Essex, but she would be back in that big house in Tortuga, back where she now told herself she belonged. Would forever belong.

He took her arm and they left the cool interior of the

great cabin behind them and walked out upon the deck. Above them the sky was a blinding blue and their step was light for they were on sure ground now—once again they had taken each other's measure, once again passed every test.

The tall buccaneer smiled down fondly upon his lady whose hand rested feather-light upon his sinewy arm. And Carolina looked up and gave him a brilliant smile, her luminous eyes flashing silver against her dark lashes as the sunlight caught them. Proudly now she could walk forth into the sun—Rye's woman, once again.

And now there were weddings to consider and they all must go aboard the *Mary Constant.*

When told that his wedding ceremony would begin as soon as the bride was dressed for the occasion, the Marquess of Saltenham had the grace at last to inquire about his men.

"What will happen to them?" he wondered. "I have not seen any of them. Can it be that they are all dead?"

Rye gave him a lazy look. "They are none of them dead, Saltenham. They are chained in the hold of the *Sea Wench* and will remain there until they reach their destination—it will be an unpleasant journey for them and will give them time to meditate on their sins."

"Their destination? Where are you taking them?"

"To Tortuga," said Rye with a sardonic look at the marquess. "They yearned to be buccaneers—faith, they will have their chance! I will set them ashore on Tortuga and they may thereafter fend for themselves, signing on whatever ship will have them."

Robin shuddered.

"It is no more than they deserve," said Carolina.

"And you may count yourself lucky not to be among them, Saltenham," Rye added with a bland smile that made the marquess give him an uneasy look. "You owe that kindness to a lady. Remember that."

"I am well aware of that and I will indeed remember it," the marquess said hoarsely. "I ask only that you give me time to escape into Europe before you use that paper—that confession I have signed."

"Official channels move slowly," Rye said, and there was a glint in his eye as his gaze raked over the marquess. "But you," he added ironically, "doubtless will move somewhat faster."

Carolina felt compelled to speak for Reba, who had just joined them on deck, and was looking alarmed. "You will have time, Robin," she said. "I promise you that."

The marquess flashed her a grateful look—and it was a yearning look too, a look of farewell.

"There will be very little trouble," Reba said abruptly. "For the *Mary Constant* belongs to my father and it has been saved, and one of the other ships Robin took—and sank"—she gave him a reproachful look—"belonged to my father too."

"You will already have won the approval of your father-in-law, Saltenham," Rye murmured humorously.

Reba turned upon him with some heat.

"My father will forgive Robin," she declared. "For after all Robin will be my husband!"

"And will he pay the owners for the other ship that was sunk, the one your father did *not* own?" Rye wondered aloud.

"Yes, I am sure he will," said Reba. But she sounded less certain.

Rye's brows shot up. "Faith, you'll have an indulgent father-in-law, Saltenham!"

"And a harpy for a mother-in-law," Carolina murmured in Rye's ear as Reba spoke to her marquess. "Do you remember what she was like?"

"All too well," Rye said under his breath. "Saltenham may wish I had run him through and got it over with before he is done!"

Carolina gave him a reproving look and he subsided.

Tandem weddings took place aboard the *Mary Constant* that afternoon. Reba's was first and Carolina thought she made a starry-eyed bride, standing beside the tall marquess in her best bronze silk and wearing (borrowed only!) the enormous ruby necklace that was part of the Duke of Lorca's ransom.

Robin and Reba sighed in unison when she reluctantly took it off and handed it over to Rye to clasp about Carolina's neck for their own ceremony.

Carolina had balked at wearing either her ice-green ball gown or her yellow sprigged muslin—for they were both gowns she had worn just before falling into Robin's arms. Rye did not argue with her and if he guessed her reason, he kept it to himself.

"I had bought you a present," he said, "in Plymouth, where we stopped for what seemed to me a lifetime." And he brought out a handsome riding habit of scarlet silk, tailored and elegant.

"You had *this* made up for me while you were in Plymouth?" she marveled—and she was thinking, *How angry that must have made the Duchess if she knew!*

"Not exactly," he admitted. "The riding habit had been made up for a young lady as part of her trousseau. But she ran away with her tutor before it could be delivered and her father refused to pay for it. The tailor was bemoaning his ill fortune in a tavern and I chanced to overhear him. It sounded like something you might like and he had described the eloping young lady as being just about your size. I bought it from him on the off chance you'd care to wear it in Essex." He smiled wistfully. "But now there's little chance you'll wear it there."

"Scarlet silk?" said Carolina. "I am surprised Rosalia did not want it!"

"She did," he admitted. "But I refused to give it to her."

And that would make it doubly precious! Carolina's silver eyes sparkled as Rye brought out the riding habit and let its scarlet silk ripple for her inspection.

"'Tis thin enough to wear in the Caribbean sun," she pronounced with delight. "And so beautiful! 'Twill be my wedding dress!" She ran out to show it to Reba, who was changing into her traveling clothes in a nearby cabin.

Reba looked at it doubtfully. "The color is bad luck for a bride," she warned.

Carolina laughed. She was holding the tailored silk habit up to her shoulders for Reba to see and now she twirled around, letting its skirts fly out.

"Married in red, you'll wish yourself dead!" muttered Reba, quoting a time-honored rhyme.

"Not I!" protested Carolina. "Nor, if I married Rye in black, would I wish myself back! Oh, Reba—I've never been so happy!"

"Nor I," said Reba, smiling in the mirror at Carolina as she carefully applied Spanish paper to her lips. "Do you know, Robin told me that he had been thinking about me all this time? That he had only left without telling me good-by because that terrible Duchess insisted that he leave on the instant—and he was so desperate for money that he did it! He said his thoughts have never strayed from me—not even once!" She breathed a deep blissful sigh.

"How—very nice of Robin," murmured Carolina, trying to keep the irony out of her voice. And then she tossed aside the dress and embraced her friend. "Oh, I do hope you'll be happy, Reba!"

"Why should I not?" Reba shrugged airily. "I shall have my Robin—and I shall go home a marchioness and sweep all before me!"

"Well," Carolina said doubtfully, "there's the matter of his confession and arranging for his pardon and—"

"That will be no trouble." Reba had regained her old jauntiness. "My father will arrange everything."

Looking at her confident friend, Carolina hoped so. She hoped that Robin never told her of a night in the *Sea Wench*'s great cabin . . . or of another night on the black sand beach at Pico. She hoped he would not have to see too much of his mother-in-law. She hoped he would set a straight course at last—and now that Reba would be there to steady him, as a wife this time with rights and responsibilities, she rather thought he would do so.

God grant us all happiness, she thought. *Although perhaps we none of us deserve it!*

She had been thinking that when she saw Reba wed.

Robin had glanced up at Carolina just before he slipped a heavy gold ring (Carolina's gift to the bride) on Reba's finger. And for a split second she saw in his eyes a yearning that spoke louder than words. *I could have loved you,* she read in that glance. *And you could have loved me.*

Carolina's chin had gone up haughtily, warding off that look, and she had moved a step closer to Rye.

The marquess took her meaning. He had sighed—and Reba had taken that sigh as a sigh of love—and slipped the ring on her eager finger.

And afterward everyone had embraced and Carolina

had thrown flower petals at the bride and groom—yellow rose petals from that garden in Horta—and some of the yellow petals had caught in Reba's hair and shone like fireflies in the slanted sunlight. Carolina would always remember her like that, flushed and happy, with her arm locked in Robin Tyrell's and her russet eyes glowing.

And now it was Carolina's turn.

Dressed at last in her scarlet silks, Carolina swished out on deck. It was deepening dusk now; the sun had sunk behind the horizon. But the huge rubies around her neck had the glow of a setting sun themselves. She knew the necklace looked overdone atop her tailored riding habit, but she did not care, she had promised to wear it. The sight of it overwhelmed the female passengers of the *Mary Constant*. They muttered enviously to each other that the necklace was now "really hers," for the buccaneers who had set out from England to clear their names had been so grateful to the Silver Wench for managing to separate the pirate captain from his ship at exactly the right time, and later for keeping them from murdering the marquess—which they now realized would have made them permanent exiles from England—that they had voted to award the necklace to the Wench to wear around her pretty neck when she wed their captain. The rest of the ransom, fifty thousand pieces of eight, was prize enough.

"And will she *keep* the necklace?" murmured Mistress Hedge enviously. Her voice had a trace of a wail in it.

Her husband nodded. "So they say."

"Wild creature that she is—I wonder what she did to earn it!"

"Hush," John Hedge said severely. "The brides are coming out on deck. You can see the necklace now—on the neck of the first bride, the auburn-haired one. But 'tis the blonde who will keep it, so they say."

And keep it she did. Though not to wear riding, of course. Rye, looking at it, said ruefully that it was a pity she could not be presented at Court wearing it. The Queen would envy her.

Carolina thought the Queen might better envy her something else—the tall strong man who stood beside her and took his vows with a ringing voice and a stern look upon his saturnine countenance. Carolina stole a look at him as he promised "with all his worldly goods to her endow" and wondered if stout little Captain Dawlish, who was performing the ceremony, had any idea of the amount of loot the bridegroom had stored in banks in Amsterdam and with goldsmiths in London— poor Captain Dawlish would choke if he knew, she thought in amusement.

For herself, she would take the man and let the treasure go, if it came to that. She knew it—she had always known it. Reba might sigh enviously over the ruby necklace that now blazed on Carolina's throat, but Carolina would promptly have flung the necklace into the sea if God would but grant her an extra year of life to spend with Rye.

For the last time she stood on the deck of the *Mary Constant* as she spoke her vows in starlight—and the glow of the swaying ship's lanterns. Beyond the ship's rail the surf foamed up the black beach toward the low white houses of Horta, and they and their roses and hydrangeas were blurred into pale romantic shapes against the night. Around her now was no clamoring crowd of buccaneers—they waited to drink to their captain's health aboard the *Sea Waif*, for they had already seen the Silver Wench married once to Captain Kells on Tortuga and most of them—lawless men that they were—thought a second marriage, however legal, to be redundant.

And then Reba was embracing her—Robin prudently did not—and everyone was crowding around wishing her well, and she was smiling up at Rye and thinking humorously that the middle of the ocean was a strange place to be wed.

And then Reba and Robin were being hurried onto the *Sea Wench*, which was about to cast off, and the passengers of the *Mary Constant* waved good-by to Rye and Carolina as they in their turn boarded the *Sea Waif*.

Her last memory of the Azores was of standing on deck in her brilliant narrow-waisted red silk riding habit with her wide skirts whipping about her slim legs and the enormous ruby necklace gleaming barbarically about her neck in the starlight. On either side the peaks of those enormous undersea mountains called Fayal and Pico were dark hulks rising from the glittering water as the *Sea Waif*'s great sails took the wind, and the ship soared like a swallow and fled down Fayal Channel, heading across the mid-Atlantic ridge toward the endless wastes of the broad Sargasso Sea.

They had left behind them the world of town, and courtliness, and the leisurely life of English country houses. They had left behind the world that was their heritage.

But for Carolina and her tall lover, leaning against the taffrail in the starlight, that world seemed well lost. With the rakish *Sea Wench* looking like a shadow of the lean gray *Sea Wolf* (for *Sea Waif* would be painted out once they struck open ocean) they were sailing toward their future—a future to be found in the sparkling Caribbean waters of the Spanish Main.

There in the Caribbean a man might seek a pardon—however unjustified the circumstances that had made him need it—from his king. There in the Caribbean, if money changed hands, he was likely to receive that pardon. And even if he did not, he could live out his life in those jewellike islands, owner of all he surveyed. He could raise his children and smile into his wife's eyes and know that life was good—and always would be.

So, Rye promised himself, it *would* be for Carolina—always good. He blamed himself for her straying, but now she would have no need to stray for he would always be at her side, protecting her, loving her. His arm tightened around her and he bent his head and buried his face in the heady lemon scent of her hair, and felt her feminine body quiver a response.

And Carolina pressed closer to him, her every breath an invitation to a silken joining, her body one with his in silent communion in the starlight. She lifted her head and her luminous silver eyes focused lovingly upon that dark sardonic face above her, looking down into her own so intently and with such tenderness. Silently she promised him everything—her heart, her body, her very soul until the last wave had crashed upon the last shore.

They had forgotten the world now, these star-crossed lovers, forgotten the ship with its great timbers creaking, forgotten the winds of chance that had brought them here.

Sighing, lost in each other, they moved in unspoken agreement toward the great cabin for this, their third wedding night—indeed almost their fourth! Moved toward crisp smooth sheets and ardent fiery kisses and dizzy flights of passion—and a homecoming of the soul.

And above them in the crackling shrouds, as they moved together raptly toward that wondrous fulfillment, the wild winds flying down from the heights of Pico seemed to sing their own song that drifted out over the glittering wastes of the Atlantic, those seas that as they swung southward would change into the clean shining aquamarine waters of the world Rye and Carolina had made their own. It was a song of love, that windsong, and it swirled to its own music, endlessly sweet.

In moonlight and in starlight
Their dangerous nights were bathed.
And now at last, by grace of God
They're through it all—unscathed!

EPILOGUE

Naught but love to guide them now,
They who've broken every vow,
The winds of chance have blown and brought them here.
But the love they once had known
And the courage they have shown
Have won them through to all they once held dear!

In Williamsburg on a crisp fall day Aunt Pet received a package. It was delivered in mid-afternoon by a laconic sea captain who said he had promised Captain Dawlish faithfully to deliver it. Eager to get back to the Raleigh where a certain pretty tavern wench had brushed him twice with her ample breasts (and not by accident, he hoped!) as she squeezed by him through the crowd, the captain merely rapped the knocker of the checkerboard brick two-story house and thrust the package in without comment, other than that he was Captain Wentworth of the *Philadelphia*. It was received by a white-aproned serving girl who answered the door.

All the serving girl had caught of the captain's mumbled words was "Philadelphia" and so, when she carried the package in to her mistress—who was in the midst of serving tea to a group of ladies who included Carolina's mother, Letitia Lightfoot—she announced

534

prettily that it was a "package just come from Philadelphia."

"Oh, I wonder what my friends have sent me!" cried Aunt Pet, naturally assuming it was from the friends she had visited earlier in the year.

Everyone watched brightly as she unwrapped it among the tea things—and there it was, her cherished silver chamber pot!

One of the elegant ladies dropped her cup and another gasped, but Aunt Pet clutched her treasure to her and beamed.

"He has returned it!" she cried joyfully. "Can you believe it? That pirate has *returned* my chamber pot!"

Among the ladies, Letitia Lightfoot restrained the bubbling laughter that rose to her lips at the sight of a chamber pot being clutched to her hostess's ample silken bosom, and reached forward a violet-gloved hand to indicate something that had fallen to Aunt Pet's lap.

"There's a note, Petula," she pointed out.

"Why, yes, there is!" Aunt Pet set down the chamber pot and picked up the note.

"It seems hastily penned," remarked a pink satin-clad lady, looking curiously over Aunt Pet's shoulder.

"And full of blots," added her lace-trimmed daughter, craning her thin neck.

"It says 'Aboard the *Sea Wolf.*'" Aunt Pet looked up with a shiver.

"Well, read it, Petula," said Letitia in a bored tone. "We're all dying to know what's in it."

"*Dear Aunt Pet,*" read that lady in a trembling voice. "Why, it's from Carolina, Letty!"

Letitia sat up straighter. "What does she say, Petula?" she asked sharply.

"She says: *Rye has retrieved this for you from the real*

culprit about whom you will soon hear, I've no doubt. Captain Dawlish must sail with the tide so there's no time to write, but I wanted to tell you he has married us aboard the Mary Constant—*I am Carolina Evistock now, and I hope you will wish Rye and me happiness. Ever your loving, Carolina.* And wait, there's a postscript: *Tell Mother she was wrong about Rye—he'll make a wonderful son-in-law!*"

There was a general gasp and a rattle of teacups, but Letitia leaned over and snatched the note from Aunt Pet and studied it. She was not sure how she felt about this marriage. Her daughter had found a husband who could drape her in emeralds—but one who might also get her killed. She pondered the matter and decided that, overall, Carolina had done no less than she would have done in her place.

Fielding Lightfoot took another view—one of relief. He doubted that tempestuous Carolina—that daughter he had felt forced to claim even though the shoe rubbed—would ever see the Tidewater again. No, she would be off somewhere else, making endless trouble beyond a doubt!

But it was Sandy Randolph who, hearing of the returned chamber pot and reading the note, shook his head and sighed.

"I misjudged young Evistock," he said. "I see that he was every inch a buccaneer. . . ."

And in a way that was a benediction, coming as it did from the real father of the bride.

Circuitously Carolina received a letter from Virginia who was still in Essex. It was mostly about the glories of the Essex countryside and the books she and Andrew were poring over together, but there was one passage she would never forget.

I have been wearing your clothes, Carolina—as you

told me I might, the letter said. *And I hope you will not mind that I have had them let out because I fear that since eating my meals with Andrew—who eats heartily for all that he remains thin as a rail—I have burst my bodice and strained my stays! Still Andrew beams on me and says I am fast becoming the best-looking woman in Essex (I think it is the glory of your gorgeous gowns that blinds him!).*

Carolina read that over and over, with laughter—and with tears. For there had been a time when she had thought that Virgie would starve herself to death. Now it seemed she was to be a plump and happy Essex bride—for Carolina had no doubt that if thoughts of marriage had not already occurred to Andrew and to Virgie, lost in their own little literary world, they would soon. And before long they would be bringing up a raft of bookish children in the glorious Essex countryside.

As for Reba and her Robin, Rye's prediction proved correct. The marquess and his bride made it back to England well in advance of any nasty rumors and promptly sped by hired coach (they arrived with the bill still owing) to Essex to confront Reba's family. As they passed the gates of Broadleigh and pounded in style down the long winding drive that led to the great house, Robin muttered feelingly that he hoped Reba's merchant father would be home for it would be the Devil's own luck if he were to be hurled into debtors' prison before a king's pardon could be had.

But it was Reba's mother who rose as if jabbed by a hatpin at the news that waiting downstairs to be received were the Marquess and Marchioness of Saltenham.

With her most elegant gown—one adorned with jet, seed pearls, spun gold lace—only half hooked, so impatient was she to greet this exalted couple whom she had never met, she dashed downstairs at some danger of falling half a flight—to be confronted in her drawing room by a somewhat travel-stained pair, one of whom was her own daughter.

Nan Tarbell checked her advance so quickly that she almost tripped.

"Reba!" she exclaimed. "But I thought"—she looked around her in bewilderment—"where are the marquess and the marchioness?"

"We are here, Mother." Reba made her mother a dignified curtsy. It was a triumphant moment and her russet eyes were sparkling. "Allow me to present my husband—of whom the world has heard if you have not—the Marquess of Saltenham."

It was the nearest Nan Tarbell had ever come to fainting.

Robin Tyrell had approached this meeting with foreboding. Now he fixed his new mother-in-law with those interesting empty eyes and his heart sank. A termagant this—in fact, a harpy—for Reba had been telling him the unvarnished truth about her mother all the way from London. But—his effervescent spirits rose—perhaps a termagant to be turned to some account. He made the lady such a deep bow as she had seldom received.

"Dear lady." His voice grew deep and resonant. "I must repent me that fate did not allow me the opportunity to meet you sooner—and to ask in proper fashion for your lovely daughter's hand, for now I see where Reba inherits her beauty!"

Beside him, Reba suppressed a derisive gasp, for whatever else her mother might be, at the moment, with that dumfounded look overspreading her hard features, she was certainly far from beautiful.

"Oh, Mother, we would have sought your permission

—we would!" she cried sweetly, backing Robin up. "But we are in the most terrible trouble. And we do need your help—in fact we need it now, to pay the coachman!"

At that moment Nan Tarbell, who was overwhelmed by having her hand kissed by the highest-titled gentleman she had ever met—and whose breath had just been taken away by the news that he was her son-in-law— would have granted them anything.

As indeed she later did.

Of the enormous ruby necklace which Carolina had worn at her wedding on board the *Mary Constant,* Carolina often laughed and said that she had traded emeralds for rubies—that Virgie was wearing her emerald necklace in Essex while she wore the ruby necklace in Tortuga.

Which was not entirely true for even Carolina had underestimated the cunning and perfidy of Reba's mother.

On hearing of the marquess's involvement in the affair of the kidnapping of the Spanish ambassador and acts of piracy on the high seas, Nan Tarbell had counseled her new son-in-law—and indeed had taken high-handed action on her own. The "confession" was promptly disavowed as false and written under duress, and "witnesses" hired by Nan Tarbell testified that the Marquess of Saltenham had never left England during the entire period in question—they had dined with him, gamed with him, etc. The matter was heard before a bored admiralty court that promptly ruled in favor of the marquess; Rye was not present, of course. And the result was that a search to discover buccaneer loot was ordered of Rye's father's house in Essex—and only circumvented by quick (and illegal) action by Andrew, who got wind that the authorities were coming and promptly rode for London to deposit with the gold-smiths the jewels Carolina had left behind.

Usually Carolina's ruby necklace was locked in the strong room. But sometimes she wore it at dinner in the great rambling house in Tortuga which she had thought never to see again—and found she had missed. She and Rye would sometimes sit in the "English" dining room of that house dressed as if they were to dine with royalty and would imagine themselves in Essex . . . or London. And on those rather wistful occasions they toasted other times and other faces that they might never see again.

But on the whole life for them was joyous on Tortuga. Wealthy enough that Rye had no need to go a'roving as he waited for a pardon which seemed slow in coming, the dazzling young couple flashed on horse-back up into the hills—she in her brilliant red silk riding habit, he in carelessly open white shirt and leathern trousers for, as he said with a shrug, he had no need to impress the people of this island with his sobriety. Here, for better or worse, they knew him as he was.

Carolina would have told you they scarcely knew him at all. Only she *really* knew him, only she *really* understood the sinister but chivalrous "Petticoat Buc-caneer" whose heart she held in keeping. It was a red petticoat he would fly now, should the need arise—one of hers which she had presented to him with great ceremony one night, at a dinner for two in the inner courtyard. He had accepted her proffered "flag" with an elegant bow, thrown a long leg across one of the stone benches and lifted his wineglass to toast her eyebrows.

Half a life, some might call it, the way they lived on

tropical Tortuga, but for them it was whole. And wonderful. And beautiful. And lasting.

The buccaneer and his lady had found each other again. All was right with their world.

And looking deep into each other's eyes, they knew it always would be.

The lady and her buccaneer, a driven pair, you say?
Who fought their way across a world not meant for
*   such as they?*
Ah, yes, perhaps, but also note, nights when the
*   wind is fair,*
Twinkling in starlight, see that sail?
They're making love out there!
And wafted on the gentlest winds that e'er caressed a
*   maid,*
Repeating vows upon the wind never to be gainsaid!

From the Bestselling Author of LOVESONG

Valerie Sherwood

The excitement lives on as Valerie Sherwood brings you a breathless love story in her new tantalizing trilogy. Sherwood first captured the hearts of millions with LOVESONG a sweeping tale of love and betrayal.

And the saga continues in WINDSONG as you are swept into exotic locations full of intrigue, danger, treachery and reckless desire.

_____ **LOVESONG** 49837/$3.95
_____ **WINDSONG** 49838/$3.95

COMING IN SEPTEMBER
NIGHTSONG

POCKET BOOKS, Department VSA
1230 Avenue of the Americas, New York, N.Y. 10020

Please send me the books I have checked above. I am enclosing $_____ (please add 75¢ to cover postage and handling for each order. N.Y.S. and N.Y.C. residents please add appropriate sales tax). Send check or money order—no cash or C.O.D.'s please. Allow up to six weeks for delivery. For purchases over $10.00, you may use VISA: card number, expiration date and customer signature must be included.

NAME _____

ADDRESS _____

CITY _____ STATE/ZIP _____